In each and every one of us there is…

The
Illuminated Forest

An
Illustrated
Novel

EDWIN FONTÁNEZ

for
Scott and the motley crew

In loving memory of
Juanita Fontánez and
Emiliano Fontánez

ARLINGTON, VA

TABLE OF CONTENTS

FROM MATEO'S JOURNAL

First Entry

My heart skips a beat every time I think of her, and there's nothing I can do to stop the hopelessness that begins to creep in. I live with the conflict and guilt that I was not there when she needed me the most but I try to take comfort in believing she knew that I loved her, deeply. I smile every time I look at the young tree. A beautiful pink dogwood that stands gracefully next to the cluster of black-eyed Susans that crowd the bright flower garden with the butterfly bush shading the busy bird bath where the blue jays cleanse themselves, splattering water with the vigorous flapping of their wings. And then it hits me as I remember it is also the same flower bed that marks her final resting place.

I want to believe she loves the sunny spot and that she is grateful for my decision. I can't stop the rush of memories the thought of her brings me. I tell myself I want to tell the story, her story, as I want to remember her, before the color of my memories begin to fade, before I get older and my mind challenges every bit of my existence. I want to remember how I survived the blow and how she helped me. It's been so many years since her passing and I still wonder, was it really her? And yet I still choose to believe. The coincidence was too great and the timing too mysterious.

I'm relieved the dreams are no longer sad. I have to confess I no longer laugh when people say "love comes in every shape and from unexpected places." I no longer feel embarrassed to admit that an animal, a stray one at that, helped me heal the deep wound left by her absence. I never want to forget the story because if I do, I will forget her too. I choose to think it was her final act of love. I have to believe too that, yes, there is indeed a heaven.

I know a bank where the wild thyme blows,
Where oxlips and the nodding violet grows,
Quite over-canopied with luscious woodbine,
With sweet musk-roses and with eglantine.

—William Shakespeare, *A Midsummer Night's Dream* (Act V, Scene I)

Hurt, Rage, Rebellion, Redemption, Forgiveness, and Love.

PROLOGUE

The Illuminated Forest

There are tales that rise like the early sun, breathe, and take on a life of their own. There are ones that flow quietly and effortlessly until time forsakes them, but there are others that fight until they find their way to the edge of reality, as if coming straight out of a dream.

With every sip of water from the stream, the stray cat swallowed the moon and a handful of stars. Weary with exhaustion and not knowing how it ended up there, it lay alone, surrounded by darkness and the agitated sounds of other animals. Luckily, it had found safety in a secluded spot deep in the forest beneath the branches of an orange tree. The stray finally settled in for the night behind a soft, tall fortress of grass that ensured temporary privacy. It now felt protected by a canopy of shrubs entangled with vines and wild flowers. But still the cat could not find warmth, even on the improvised bed of dry leaves and brush. As the creature lay quietly, tired from wandering, it tried to ignore the hunger gnawing at its guts. Soon, the night's symphony of frogs, crickets, and sleepless birds soothed him to sleep.

A sudden far away rumble shook the dew off the jasmine and interrupted the cat's fitful sleep. As it lifted its sleepy eyes to the sky, it discovered the burning tail of a beautiful falling star whose brilliance transformed the tranquility of an otherwise ordinary night. The stray watched as a thin flash of lighting cracked the sky open to a dazzling rush of shooting stars. Among them, the brightest of them all fell from space at an overwhelming speed, making its fiery way past other stars and planets, following the invisible curvature of space as it began to penetrate the Earth's atmosphere...

FROM MATEO'S JOURNAL

It's been a long time but I still remember the dream vividly. The chaos, the sound of rushing wind, the horse's whinnies, the sparks of blinding sun, the disembodied scolding words, and the faint warning voices. I can't see the horse but I can sense the formidable energy of its muscles, churning, turning, and twisting beneath its lustrous chestnut coat. Its musculature glistens with sweat in the morning light. I'm riding the horse between her lap and the cantle of the saddle. I can feel its warm, aged softness as she holds me and maneuvers the reins. Amid the chaos, she manages to make me feel safe, secure. I look up but only see a halo behind her obscured face. Her hair, the horse's mane, and her dress all flow around her as if caught in a vortex. I'm blinded by the strong sunlight then the day fades into darkness.

Then I hear her laugh, her reckless laughter, as she spurs the stallion's ribs with her bare heels. I can't see much beyond the back of the horse's crest but its black mane brushes against my face and makes me giggle. I'm two years old and I giggle because I'm terrified. But she holds on to me tightly as the magnificent purebred barrels and rumbles through the field. I can sense how the horse makes the earth tremble with its potent hooves, disintegrating it into clouds of red dust as its perfectly chiseled legs hit the ground. The spirited horse takes a leap when it reaches the river bank and suddenly I find myself airborne, flying off the saddle as she loses her hold on me. I can only see the upside down sky and myself rushing up higher and higher into the air.

I'm a little boy but I know I'm about to hit the ground, hard. I flap my arms as if trying to fly. I'm headed downwards now. I feel the terror lodged in my throat but I can't scream. I'm so close to the ground I can almost smell the moist grass and taste the small clumps of red soil dug out by the hooves of the magnificent beast. And then it happens! Suddenly, I feel a hand wrap around my tiny wrist and pull me back. "I got you little one!" To this day, I still can remember her laugh, clear as a chime…

PART ONE

A Different World Altogether

Mateo leapt up the steps to the front door of his house. He dropped his backpack and searched for his keys inside the front pocket of his jeans. Even before the key had unbolted the door, he heard the muffled sound of tiny, hurried steps racing down the carpeted staircase. He flung open the door and watched the thin, graceful cat jump from the last step and rush towards him, warbling excitedly in greeting. As Mateo stood on the rush mat, the cat dropped at his feet and happily arched its back. This was their daily routine. Kneeling before the animal, he vigorously ran his fingers along its arched back, making it rock back and forth with pleasure.

"Hey, you, have you had a good day?" he asked as he scratched the purring cat's tummy.

Without missing a beat, the cat jumped to its feet and, as if leading a town parade, guided him with bouncy steps to the plush couch in the cozy living room. As soon as Mateo had settled in, the cat claimed its place on his lap. On that crisp early spring morning, the young cat stretched to twice its length over his legs in a relaxed purring trance and watched the day through the glass panes framed with deep green ivy. The boy and his cat kept their eyes on the garden that was buzzing with early morning activity. Mateo was now fifteen. Three years had gone by and like many times since then, the memory of Palo Verde made him relive the story of a stray the color of *a silver cloud filled with rain…*

THREE YEARS EARLIER...
PALO VERDE 1977

The poet's eye, in a fine frenzy rolling,
Doth glance from heaven to earth, from earth to heaven;
And as imagination bodies forth
The forms of things unknown, the poet's pen
Turns them to shapes, and gives to airy nothing
A local habitation and a name.

—William Shakespeare, *A Midsummer Night's Dream* (Act V, Scene I)

As the faint light of the dying sun silhouetted the spine of the nearby mountains, the balmy August afternoon transformed into evening and illuminated the spine of the mountains. The town's hectic life came to a halt and the quiet stream at the edge of town began to carry the stars' reflection into the heart of the forest. The dense gathering of trees stood still, as if in vigil, and the night breeze shuddered with the metallic cries of the old bell in the town's only chapel. Its mournful toll signaled the passing of the young seamstress of the small village. The forest fell still as it watched her spirit ascend into the perfect infinite dome of the universe. The young woman, whose life had been extinguished quietly and too soon, began her spiritual journey into eternity.

To a boy of 12, rage was easier than love, so his anger became a numbing cocoon where his true feelings could hide before they were acknowledged and dealt with. The news had left him breathless. He felt his pain slowly transform from disbelief to hopelessness. "Why?" he kept asking, sobbing, his throat raw.

"Why didn't you tell me before?"

But Maria had no answers that could ease his pain. "She's in a better place now."

He heard the words but he knew better. "That's a lie!" he screamed back. Mateo felt the veins in his head about to burst. He couldn't put it into words but he knew that a pat on the back and a white lie was not enough comfort for such a loss. "She's in a better place." He kept hearing the meaningless words and he resented her for it. Empty words hurt the most when they came from a loved one. His body trembled with fury and deep sadness. "I'm not a little child! Stop lying to me! I hate you!" He knew better. She should have too. Sadness and hopelessness were replaced with anger and he did not have the strength to fight it. The time for answers was over, he decided. He began to build his cocoon.

Hopelessness, pain, and emptiness were powerful emotions for a boy of 12. But the feeling of betrayal was more than he could stand. He resisted Maria's embrace like a wild animal fighting at the sight of a cage. "Everything could have been different! You lied to me!" he screamed at her.

Rage is also debilitating. Mateo cried himself to sleep. His black mane of tousled hair stuck to his temples as sweat and tears stained his white pillow. His body became feverish and vulnerable, and his eyes, red and burning from crying, finally closed. Yes, rage is easier than love. For Mateo Detente, a boy of 12, who feels his world is brutally shaken by cruelty and distrust, a cocoon built upon rage, it's the safest place to be.

Rage is easier than love. But how does rage begin? Some people are marked, damaged for life. Even as children, you can see the cold, unflinching scowl on their small faces. A child's face reflects his purity of soul, the face of a benign new person filled with promise. But a child with a broken soul will show its rage even in its tiny hands. It is a sad thing to see a child like that but it happens. There was one of those children in the tiny mountain town of Palo Verde. No amount of love could heal him. His soul was broken from the beginning.

Rage feeds on itself, and it moves effortlessly back and forth in time. Many years before, another boy of 12 had faced this lesson. His fury was so intense he could feel it rise from the arches of his feet, boil through the cavity of his chest and up into his throat, leaving a taste of copper and venom. Sadly too, rage is a one-way journey to nowhere. The child with the broken soul learned about its roots but chose to ignore its consequences for the rest of his life. It was a family tradition: one started neither by his father nor his grandfather but by their fathers and grandfathers, long before he became a bundle of inconvenience many generations after. It was programmed into every cell of his body. He grew up to be the latest link in a long chain of men with a misplaced sense of right and wrong. His was the unfortunate kind of childhood shaped by a skewed sense of reward and punishment.

Maria felt powerless. She watched the boy's body coiled up into a tight knot. To hear him wail like a hurt animal made her forget her own pain. Her heart was broken knowing her only sister was gone. But to watch him, her dear boy, rocking back and forth in anger left her speechless, hopeless, and beaten. *"What can I do?"* she thought. *"Not much,"* she realized. So she embraced him, against his resistance, against his will. He had banged his fists against her arms but she did not mind, not at all. She let him vent and rant. *"Maybe. Maybe I can help him through his first life lesson. Maybe time will indeed heal. Maybe someday I'll deserve his forgiveness."* Maybe.

Maria pressed her head tightly against his so he would know she was there for him. "You'll get through this," she promised, and tried to push her own feelings down. She would take him through the hardest, most disorienting life lesson of them all—coping with death. Minerva's untimely death had thrown him into a spiral of pain and confusion. Maria feared this devastating loss would add to a life of regrets. Nothing had prepared her for this precise moment in their lives but deep inside her mind she had anticipated it was up to her, somehow, to weather the incoming storm. So she endured his rage.

"You lied to me! I hate you!" His words still made her soul crumble.

"Yes, it's not fair," she cried softly with him. With a heavy heart, she agreed with him. A boy of 12, who hadn't even begun to question the meaning of his own life, suddenly had to understand—in a shockingly brief period of time—life's random flow. Ashamed, Maria remembered her own empty words, "It will pass." But she knew she was lying again; pain never passes. It just goes to sleep under the skin, latent, until it hears its name called out. Then it rises once again to the surface, like a crazed beast who suddenly remembers its prey.

Maria felt the heat of his burning forehead against hers, "there, there..." and it felt good. His cries began to subside into a soothing, dull hum. She closed her eyes and breathed in his tangled hair soaked with moisture and the comforting smell of youth. *"When was it?"* She tried to remember the last time he had fallen asleep in her arms.

Gently, so as not to wake him from his peaceful sleep, she opened his grip and removed the piece of smooth glass hanging on rough twine—*"His magic crystal,"* she remembered with a smile—and placed it in his pocket. With her thumb, she traced the deep, red circle it had left in the palm of the boy's hand. Maria knelt in the middle of the small room and held his head against hers, listening to his heartbeat. Calm at last.

Heart-beat... heart-beat... heart-beat.

* * *

Time seems to travel in circles. A life that began twenty-seven years ago
flashes back and forth and up to this day, as if it was only
a single breath in time. Where does time go?

What seems like only yesterday has in fact been twenty years. A little girl of seven plays by herself in a gathering of trees and clears away the tangles from an orange sapling. With careful, delicate hands she brushes away the mulch of rotten wet leaves, breaks the black, moist ground by the river bank into clumps, and digs a hole. The little girl settles the fresh seedling in its new cradle of dirt. The seedling has a desire to grow so tall it could see over the nearby hills, tall enough to watch the radiant white clouds migrate across the sky. *Right by the young coffee trees,* the orange tree still remembers. But most of all it remembers the little girl's warm, loving touch like it was yesterday. The touch of her small hands clumsily patting the dirt around its frail stem made it feel cozy and safe. Even now it can hear her small voice, *So you can be beautiful!* The thought made the orange tree rattle its leaves with happiness. *Kind. Yes, that is what she was!*

The orange tree had seen many wonderful acts of kindness and it never forgot the little girl who first discovered it choking under the grip of wild vines, hidden from the sun. The little barefoot girl had cleaned and nurtured it. How could it forget her? She who folded broad yautía leaves to bring a drink of sweet water from the nearby stream, the very same one that rolls by after all these years. In fact, the tree could trace the length of her whole life. But how could it not? They had grown older together. In later times, when its arms were covered with perfumed white blossoms, it watched as the girl gathered them for her hair. Through the years, the tree had listened to her songs many times as she sat on its moss covered lap. Every creature around fell quiet so as not to disrupt the sound of her voice. The tree listened to the small girl singing her made-up, silly songs. Later on, as a grownup girl, she sang quiet songs, as if her heart belonged to someone. But the tree still remembers the little girl of seven singing her made-up songs, just being a child…

* * *

Mateo pushed the phone closer against his ear. The heavy interference made it difficult to make out Minerva's broken words.

"He--o Mat-o, c-n you hea- me?"

"Meva, are you there? I can't hear you!" He paced across the room.

"Yes, I can he-r you. The reception h--e is not very g--d. I will ha-- to climb a t-ller mountain!"

Mateo covered his ear, pleased to hear her laugh again. In spite of her cheery tone, he could sense her weakness. "Meva, do you feel OK?"

"Better th-n ever! You kn-w, I will beat th-s th--g," he heard Minerva joke.

"I'll be seeing you soon," he promised.

"Ye-, I know. I c-n't w--t to s-- yo- too! Let's…" The line went dead.

The soul is the essence of the body. A lost soul is the essence of a body in transition. A soul in Limbo is caught between death and a higher plane of spiritual transformation. Much like a broken tower unable to dispatch and interpret signals, a ghost's journey can be interrupted by the slightest interference.

A soul that smoothly navigates the magnetic powers of the universe breaks free of its past life and takes spiritual form. But a soul that struggles to rid itself of earthly bonds cannot lift into the next dimension until it finds its peace. It becomes a ghost until it can break its earthly chains.

The lost soul did not remember when or how it had gotten there. It found itself floating in the infinite, open universe, surrounded by total darkness in an unknown galaxy, stranded in a sea of absolute silence. *"Where am I?"* It felt overwhelmed by the perfect peace.

"Perfect peace. Is this—?"

The perfect darkness and silence were at first frightening. Then, a sudden, blinding light. It was the biggest of stars, quite possibly. The lost soul felt lifted by its warmth.

"Weightless as a feather? No, lighter! Yes! Much lighter!"

The lost soul welcomed the warm light. It sensed ripples in the perfect atmosphere.

"Not yet."

It heard the living light's voice and it couldn't move forward.

"Not yet!"

The soul heard it repeat *not yet*. Then came the soft cries. *"Who is that?"* The pulsating white light became more intense, burning splendidly. Holding a sword above its head, the angel stepped out of a burst of light, and the rush of millions of stars was reflected in the folds of its robe. *"Many like you too are trying to find their way. You'll have to go back,"* the angel warned. *"You'll have to go back!"* it repeated. From far away, the soul heard the sad cries again.

Interference.

Twinkling bright spots burned in the distance. As they approached and gained speed, they soon became a dizzying shower of stars, zooming by, faster than light itself.

"Transparent fireflies?"
"Lost souls," the angel answered.

The lost soul felt closer to the white light of the angel.

"You'll have to go back. You'll only have one single moment!
Only then will you be able to ascend."

Surrounded by the white, warm light, the lost soul heard the angel's voice once more. *"You'll forget everything."* Such intensity made it forget its place. The lost soul saw itself traveling through levels of consciousness at a speed only possible in a dream.

"You won't remember." The lost soul sensed the warning. But it wanted the cries to stop. It knew it wouldn't be able to go on. *"You'll have to undo your path."*

"I won't know how," answered the lost soul.

"Find your way," were the last words the lost soul heard, when it found itself hovering over the forest, burning like a supernova. A lost soul. Earthly bonds. Earthly interference. Before the angel disappeared, the lost soul saw the burning fires of a thousand suns rage around the angel's head.

THE HEART OF THE FOREST

Nestled high among the mountains of Palo Verde lies an ancient forest...

A forest never forgets. Through the years—hundreds of years in fact—it had witnessed its share of savage acts of destruction, as it had also observed quiet miracles, miracles of life that went back centuries to the time before Palo Verde was even a glint in someone's imagination. Hundreds of years ago, the Taínos, aborigines of the island of Borikén, fled from the coastal villages to save their race from the merciless pillaging of their homes and the depredation of their women by heartless conquerors. In the heart of the forest, *El Bosque*, they began to thrive once again. Here they found safe refuge from the greedy colonizers who enslaved their children and forced them into hard labor in their unstoppable quest for gold, and when an early death was often the only liberation from their oppressors. Now there was new life near the river, the lively artery that crossed the heart of the forest surrounded by mountains. Once there, they gathered to adore the moon, the sun, and the harvest; their long nights were filled with chants, music, and endless dancing.

The forest kept vigil during their rites to appease the thunderous, impending arrival of Huracán, the merciless god of wrath and destruction. Even the forest marveled at their prayers for mercy, prayers for better crops, uttered in a Cohoba-induced delirium. The beating of drums, tum... tum... tum... tum..., dull, uniform, steady, hypnotizing, conjured up spirits to come out and dance. Tum... tum... tum... tum..., the sound of a hundred drums traveling at night over mountains, down to valleys, and over the waters.

Tum... tum... tum... tum.

The Great Cacique Guacabó sat on his throne carved from caoba wood inlaid with gold. Parrot feathers crowned his forehead. Shells and glass beads hung around his neck and ears, sending sparks of light through the dark into every corner of the living forest. A golden guanín hung from his chest, ablaze with the light of the bonfire. He looked up to the starry night under the dense canopy of beautiful, regal tabonuco and maga trees. Shells rattled and the deep-throated sound of the fotuto, the biggest of the sea shells, shook the trees to their roots. The soul of the forest stirred. If a tree could cry, the big ceiba would have fallen to its knees at the sight of the men and women dancing around its massive trunk, in respectful adoration. Man, woman, and child danced and breathed with the trees as one.

Tum... tum... tum... tum...

Areyto of life! Stories of hardship, injustice, and oppression, but also success and life, were wrapped within clouds of red clay dust. And they danced and danced, until the light of a new sun leaked through the leaves and broke the sky into morning. The forest still remembers those nights, hundreds of years ago. It listened, watched, and hummed. As their bonfires burned in its heart, the forest came alive and sensed their honor. "Sacred!" It heard the rising chants of the Indians. And their music, the beating of drums, thunderous voices of drums that roared along with the shaman's incantations, invoking the spirits within the tree and stirring its ancient soul. The shaman's voice rose above their prayers. "No ill shall find peace or shelter in this sacred garden and no punishment is too great to be rendered against a transgressor." And with his cohoba induced warning he empowered them, the peaceful Taínos, an enlightened people who understood the power of that promise.

It was then, in return, the forest made its silent oath to protect whatever miracle happened in its embrace. The Taínos danced and celebrated. "A sacred place!" The surrounding mountains, still healing from their spiritual wounds, agreed. The forest, for hundreds of years, had witnessed, endured, and thrived. It had always known how to protect those seeking refuge from the storm.

In that forest, there was also a river that crossed its heart. And there was a new vibrancy around its banks; the lively artery that bonded the heart of the forest with the soul of the mountains. A river so ancient, the mountains had watched its birth as it sprouted from the womb of the earth and made its way down the sides of hills, carefree and fearless as a new life. This river witnessed great beauty along its banks, and when the gold began to run low along with the invader's patience, it carried the blood of the gentle Taínos into the open arms of the ocean. Legend has it that ever since, the Cebuco river purged the evil from the forest along its current, out into the open ocean, purifying its spirit and healing the natives' broken existence.

In the beginning, there was no rage in the forest. It came later, quietly simmering as low as the Taínos' pepper pots. Rage came into the forest as the Taínos watched their land, their sacred land, invaded and their women and children killed by new and strange diseases. A wrath so corrosive, even the gods turned a deaf ear to their prayers. Ever since, rage too, lived on in the forest, beneath fallen limbs, a secret, necessary force to protect itself and one of its own...

Just like a child's, the life of an animal is fragile. Unlike toddlers and kittens, humans can be cruel. Some may even say, "Animals have no souls. They have no feelings. They don't have the capacity to understand..." So in the blink of an eye, the life of a cat changed for the worse. Once surrounded by love and affection, it found itself alone, hungry, and confused.

Sadness is not reserved only for humans. It is not limited to boys of 12. Sadness arrives unannounced and snatches its prey by surprise, taking over where love used to be.

Kittens and toddlers are alike in many ways. They both look out at the world with a sense of wonder. A baby grabs the finger of his father, happily puts it in his mouth and instinctively bites it. When his mother lifts him up, the baby chuckles with a sparkle in his eye, and instantly forgets his lonely crib. He squirms contentedly and flaps his short chubby arms like a young bird attempting to take flight. The baby makes happy, gurgling sounds and thrusts his little, short legs as if pushing the pedals of the bicycle he'll ride in years to come. And he wrinkles his nose at the familiar scent of his mother.

Much like a toddler, a kitten is full of energy and races around its home without a clear focus. In calmer times, it waddles around with short, unsteady steps. Its eyes capture every corner of the home. Quiet times never last long. Suddenly, a big chair becomes an obstacle course to claw up and down at unimaginable speeds. The kitten does back flips, climbs up walls, and hides under the furniture until it's time for a much needed nap. A subtle movement wakes it up. Next, it sits on its hind legs, and pulls and juggles the laces on a shoe. An empty paper bag instantly transforms into a fortress, a secret place from which it will pounce on an unsuspecting passerby. Then suddenly, without explanation, the happy life of a young cat takes an unexpected turn. After a few weeks, the adorable kitten has become a young cat, and its guardians suddenly lose interest. If it's lucky, it might be rescued from a cruel fate by some caring being saying, "Don't be afraid, little one, I'll take care of you!" or "I'll find you a good home!"

But circumstances might change for that loving being and, without any choice, the kitten is passed from loving hands to indifferent ones. That is how a young cat can find itself without a home. Once it chased playful shadows in the middle of a warm room, now it is chased by threatening shadows in the middle of nowhere.

"*Why?*" wonders the kitten.

Sadness travels in circles. Meanwhile, thousands of miles away, an unhappy boy was dreading the day ahead, not wanting to return to the place he had left behind. Palo Verde now seemed remote to him. The disconnect he felt was greater than he could bear. "I don't want to go back! I will not go back." He had drawn a line and was not ready to face a new sad day.

Palo Verde, the town of his grandparents, was so small it hardly made a visible mark on his wall map. Going back would force him to relive earlier memories of his childhood in the tiny rural town in *el campo*. "I don't want to go back!" He had made his mind up. Palo Verde had lost its meaning for him; the claustrophobic place up in the mountains where he first bonded with his dearest Meva now seemed far away in so many ways, even more so since her death.

Conflicted even in his rage, he could not help but wrap his thoughts around the shy little town where the evening light covered the rooftops with a mellow haze. And the thought of the sun, the burning disk of energy bathing the nearby mountains with the opulent colors of molten gold and honey, stirred something in him. Even though he was too young to grasp the cruel irony of the island's exuberant beauty and the misery of its inhabitants, Mateo sensed Palo Verde's dark side.

"*She's not there anymore.*" The thought went through him like a cold knife. Clearing his eyes of tears, his breathing almost stopped. The fleeting afterimage made him blink, but as soon as it appeared, the flash of light was gone. "*What was that standing by the window?*" He felt his heart race.

To the young stray, the open world became an enormous, puzzling labyrinth. "*I miss home,*" it lamented, trying to find its way down a dirt road. The newly stray cat walked through heaps of dirt and garbage in search of food, its fur stained by the muddy water. "*Where to go?*" it wondered over and over. Sitting on its hind legs, it stretched its neck above the tall blades of grass and lifted its nose in the air, trying to catch a familiar scent. *"Home?"* But there was nothing, not even a familiar sound along the solitary road. Hopelessly lost, the young cat walked aimlessly, not realizing how far it had wandered. As hunger, thirst, and exhaustion overpowered its body, the stray slowed down its steps, hanging its head. If the stray could have put its thoughts into words, it would have said, *"Do not trust Biganimals."* Yes, those would be the words that described its feelings best. *"Home, so far away!"*

"Home, so far away!" Mateo had to look out the small window to convince himself the jet was moving forward. Outside, a bumpy white quilt blocked his view of the ocean below. Through a break in the clouds, he caught a glimpse of intense ripples pushed by the wind through the water. He pressed his forehead against the plastic window and scanned the horizon for something interesting—*nothing but sky and water*—and he took a deep breath. The glare of the sun off the plane's wing made him squint but he was still able to make out the crests of the rising waves. *"Way cool!"* he thought, in awe of the living sea. Some 40,000 feet below, big and small ships left behind foamy fish tails as they broke the green surface of the water.

Mateo squirmed uncomfortably in his seat. *"Is this really happening?"* He could not stop the thought from popping into his head over and over but managed to push down the anger that occasionally reared its head. He tried to read his book but could not concentrate. *"What if I jump out and leap from cloud to cloud?"* His gaze bounced over the extended blanket of white on the other side of his window. *"Those clouds seem solid enough to step on—"*

"Are you doing okay?" Maria's voice pulled him out of his flight of fancy.

His impulse was to turn to her and say, "Thank you for being here with me" but a boy of 12 is proud and instead his answer was a curt "Fine." He plugged in the small headphones of his transistor radio and sank into the seat. He wished she would leave him alone.

"We'll be there soon," she said but Maria's words fell on deaf ears. He stared blankly out the window, his gaze lost in the horizon…

The musical *ding-dong* over the sound system made him lift his eyes up to the lighted seatbelt symbol above his head. The jet penetrated a thick curtain of smoky gray clouds. As it came out the other side, the small island finally materialized on the horizon. Mateo's gaze glided over the heads in the seats before him, up to the cockpit. He noticed the jet tilt to one side, smoothly, much like a silver eagle gliding across the sky. There was a loud, sudden thud of the landing train. *"The tires are coming out."* He watched as the aluminum spoiler and flaps in the wings began to lift gently, one after the other, as if they were made of thin rice paper. As the jet decompressed, he was pushed back against his seat and felt a slight turn in his stomach. He closed his eyes and tried to relax, *just for a minute.*

At that precise moment everything went wrong! Mateo noticed a plume of gray smoke and sparks coming from one of the engines. He sank into his seat, overcome with terror. As the jet jerked violently, he heard the screams of frightened passengers. From the cockpit, one of the flight attendants came out pleading desperately, "We need help!" But in the chaos, no one could hear her. People began to jump out of their seats. Some cried out loud, some prayed on their knees, but most held on to each other for comfort, as if their closeness could make the jet correct its path.

"Can somebody help? Please!" The voice of the flight attendant was almost drowned out by the noise and loud cries. There was no other choice; Mateo jumped out of his seat and ran past her towards the cockpit. What he saw made him stop cold: The captain was slumped over the plane's flight deck, unconscious. Worse yet, the co-pilot was out cold too, still belted to his chair, arms akimbo, a little bit of foam on the corner of his lips. At that moment Mateo's hopes for a positive outcome diminished considerably. "HOLY CRAP!"

Mateo knew he had to act fast. Overwhelmed by the bizarre situation, he stared at the confusing array of flashing buttons and needles bouncing back and forth out of control. Every instrument in the plane was going berserk, flickering warning lights, in every color and shape, much like a Christmas tree gone haywire! Mateo's attention was drawn to an even more troubling sign: the stick, basically the control column of the plane was shaking vigorously. A cold sweat covered his forehead then, "We're going down!" A quick look at the vertical speed meter showed the plane was losing altitude at an alarming velocity. Mateo did not know much about flying technology, but a look at the horizontal situation indicator showed the aircraft was veering into a weird angle. "IT'S NOSE DIVING!" He decided the first thing to do was to stabilize the plane so it could reach the tarmac safely. He pushed the captain gently to one side and grabbed the radio to place an emergency call to the control tower. Through people's frantic screams, Mateo heard the voice of the flight attendant over the sound system: "Dear passengers, thank you for flying with us on such beautiful day! We'll be dining this evening on delicious fried chicken.

But we'll have to give you a voucher for the mashed potatoes…"

"WHAT?—*did I just*…" He couldn't quite process the bizarre announcement. He had to tend to the bigger crisis at hand.

"Hello, Control?" He could not believe the sound of his own voice. "I'm a boy at the controls of a big aircraft above your airport. I need help to land this thing. Please help! Copy."

After what seemed like a long time, the control tower finally answered his S.O.S.

"Heeeelllooooo there, young man! Is this your first time flying with us? Just kidding!"

Mateo could not believe his ears. *What is this?* "Sir, please, we need help! The plane is in trouble! Copy." He held his breath as he waited for a response.

"Oh, it's okay, you don't have to say 'copy.'"

"PLEASE SIR! I haven't got much time!" Mateo nervously adjusted his glasses.

"By the by, is that your plane, the one with the ball of fire on the wing? I must tell you, count your blessings. It could be worse; the other one could be on… whoops! And there it goes. Never mind! WAIT! Did she say there's fried chicken? Well! Some people have all the luck…"

"ENOUGH WITH THE FRIED CHICKEN! I HAVEN'T GOT MUCH TIME, SIR!" he yelled exhausted, his throat now dry with terror. The jumps and rattles of the plane unsettled him. Mateo felt like he was riding a wild bull in midair.

"Okay, okay, look for the gizmo in the whatchamacallit, close to where that other thingy is and jiggle it. You know the one that goes like this? But not the one that looks like that? You know what I'm talking about."

"NO, I DO NOT! WHAT ARE YOU TALKING ABOUT!!!" Dizzy with fright, he held on to the joystick until his knuckles turned white.

"Well my friend, patience and politeness are the key to… Whooops! Time for a break. Union rules! Well, it was nice chatting with you."

"WAIT!! WAIT!! DON'T GO NOW, WE ARE NOT FINISHED! HELLO… ANYBODY THERE?" Exhausted, he gave up and collapsed against the co-pilot's chair. But just when he had lost all faith, he realized the captain had regained consciousness.

"Did I miss anything?" said the captain, adjusting his cap and taking control of the plane. "Young man, you're a true hero! You can go back to your seat now. And remember to keep your tray in the upright position." He said to Mateo with a wink.

Once safely on the ground, the plane was immediately surrounded by fire trucks and ambulances, their engines blaring at deafening decibels. Mateo's heart beat a little faster when he spotted a long, black limousine with the presidential emblem making its way through the crowd and the congestion of noisy vehicles. As an officer in full regalia opened the door of the black limousine, a tall man with gray hair dressed impeccably in black got out and made his way towards the plane. Mateo stood at the top of the movable stairs and waited for permission to come down. As the tall gentleman with gray hair got closer, he opened the black velvet box he was holding. Inside was a sparkling gold medal attached to a beautiful purple ribbon.

Suddenly, Mateo noticed a gorgeous woman wearing a bright red sash across her bosom. Standing on a service cart, she tossed her long brown hair in the wind, as her crown sparkled with the red lights of the fire trucks. With a flourish she announced to the crowd, "I, Miss Universal Global Warming, with all the powers bestowed upon me by the powers that be on this glorious evening, welcome home this hero. This man, who endangered his own life rescuing helpless seals from the frozen tundra…"

"Honey, honey, get off the cart. This is not the guy. We have to go," an invisible voice called out to her.

"What do you mean? Who's this guy then? Does he have a debilitating disease?" the beauty queen hissed under her breath.

"Nope," answered the voice.

"Is he poor, missing a limb?"

"Nope."

"Is his only friend in life a goat? Because if not…"

"Nope. He's some guy who saved a plane, no one really important."

"You know, I'm going to sue this flipping pageant's board and their corporation for Global Warming Universal. First these bastards send me on the road to open damned supermarkets just because *mizz* first runner-up has the runs, and now they bring me to this hell-hole. I've had it up to here!" she screeched as the service cart brusquely took off.

Suddenly Mateo realized the tall man with gray hair was none other than the President of the United States, Mr. Clint Eastwood! As the President got closer, the captain of the plane cut in, "I'll take that, Mr. President. You shouldn't have!"

"Nice try, apple pie. Move over," the President coolly replied.

Mateo could not contain his excitement when the President extended his hand holding the black velvet box and asked him, "Would you like a bag of pretzels?" Startled, he heard the voice again. "Young man, would you like a bag of pretzels?" He rubbed his eyes and saw it was the flight attendant offering him a small shiny bag of snacks. Would you like a bag of pretzels?

"Mateo, wake-up. We've arrived," he heard Maria say.

It had become an open secret all over Palo Verde: animals were disappearing from porches, windows, and balconies, and patios. Typical of a small town, Palo Verde's citizens had suspicions but no one dared say a word for fear of retaliation. In the crosshairs were their two likely culprits: the first was a boy who dragged his dark moods around the neighborhood more than he dragged his feet. His surly stare was enough to make anyone cross the street and he knew it. Once a shy boy, his demeanor had changed the moment his mother left their house. The boy was crushed and convinced he was the cause of his mother's defection. After her departure, he removed all color from his limited wardrobe and black became his preferred shade of gloom. The absence of color: an accurate reflection of how he saw the world around him.

The second suspect was the cruelest man in town, and the boy's father. After all, the rotten apple hadn't fallen far from the rotten tree, the townspeople gossiped. But there was one difference: the boy's dark moods sometimes softened at a kind word, showing a glimpse into his deep hurt. But his father, the cruel man, was impenetrable. Like an unstoppable boulder rolling down a hill, he left a path of destruction and never looked back. Yes, the small town of Palo Verde knew this, and they steered clear of the cruel man. And this was how they dealt with the disappearance of their animals. As long as the cruel man was around, there was nothing anyone could do.

For a young cat kept from danger in the safety of a loving home, the outside world is a big and scary place. Thoughts crossed its mind all at once. *"Where to go? How to get there?"* And then it sat—or rather slumped—by the side of the solitary road, looking all around, wondering for the hundredth time, *"Why?"* The road was such a cold, unfriendly place. *"What did I do?"* And nothing could mend its heart.

The young cat, now a stray, took a few tentative steps in every possible direction, only to end up in unfamiliar places. Its heart pounded when it first noticed a pair of bright eyes in the distance. *"Biganimal!"* The eyes became bigger as they got closer. The cat's whiskers bristled and its back hair stood on end. There was no doubt, *Biganimal* was about to pounce. There was a sharp, grunting noise and the cat prepared for the beast's attack with an arched back. But instead, a splash of dirty water covered the stray from head to tail. As the glowing eyes grew faint in the distance, the cat ran back to safety behind a heap of trash and concentrated on cleaning itself.

> *Lick paw, lick paw, rub face.*
> *Lick paw, lick paw, rub face.*
> *Lick paw, lick paw, rub face.*

The cleansing routine helped the young stray cat relax. Suddenly, another pair of bright eyes appeared down the road. By then the stray knew better as the car rumbled by. *"No Biganimal, good!"* The young cat lifted its nose up and examined the air, *"Home?"* If anyone could have seen the young stray crying from hunger and loneliness, their heart would have broken into tiny pieces. They would have understood the fear behind its eyes. The cat was used to hearing, "I looove yoouu,"

and having its fur caressed by the tips of loving fingers. Today—*or was it yesterday, or weeks ago?*—it heard, "Scoot!" And with that one word, the young cat was left behind on the side of a road. *"Why?"* it wondered, *"What did I do?"* Its body shivered in the night's chill.

The jet banked as it began to circle the sky for the final landing. Mateo gasped at the sudden view below, thousands of rooftops squeezed together. *"Wow, it's like a graveyard down there! Where are the trees?"* Yet another view took his breath away. Beyond the stale gray image of overcrowded living was the comforting sight of placid mountains spanning the island. The majestic *cordillera* mountains, with their soft peaks and dramatic drops lying against the horizon, so tall they seemed to hold the weight of the sky on their backs. Even more dazzling was how the afternoon haze made them glow. *"Somewhere among those mountains is Palo Verde."* He was not very pleased to recognize his destination, but it was also hard to ignore the hard and claustrophobic slabs of cement rooftops down below. *"How depressing, it looks like a cemetery!"* Mateo took another deep breath and instead kept his eyes set on the impressive chain of blue mountains that merged with the horizon as the jet jerked its way down to the tarmac.

Sergio jumped off his bike and dropped it by the side of the road. In one swift leap, he was over the barbed wire fence meant to keep the cattle secure in the pasture. He ran to find his usual hangout under the guava berry trees, across the tangled field of grass. Running against the dry, hot wind, the curls of his long brown hair bounced over his forehead. "Hurry up, Stumpy!" he called out to the dog trailing him. As he ran past the cows grazing by the watering hole, Sergio felt the sweat glue his shirt tightly to his bronzed skin. Sergio and Stumpy thrived in wide open spaces, *felices en el campo;* happy in the open fields.

The light, the breeze, the sun all around: this was Sergio's home. "Never!" had been his response when friends teasingly raised the possibility of him living outside the island. "Never!" He was certain. It would be like a fish taken from the ocean and left gasping for air. Sergio had a pretty good idea how that fish would feel. "There's no place like this on the whole planet!" he declared with conviction, despite having never set foot outside the island. But he had a pretty good idea of the remote chance of him ever leaving his land.

"Is it Nueva Yor that's always covered in snow?" He had seen the blazing white

images on his television, snow burying whole towns, swallowing them whole. The image of people wearing so much clothing, hardly able to move, made him shiver. Sergio could not bear to think of carrying anything heavier on his back than his loose T-shirt. "Cold!" Yes, he was sure. If he wanted to see snow, all he had to do was open the door to his mother's Frigidaire. That was his answer to one and all who teased him. "My thing is the sun! The beach! Open spaces!"

Sergio watched the jets above him trace their way across the sky beyond the mountains, so low he could identify the stripes of each particular airline. He could almost make out the heads of travelers looking down, anxiously counting the minutes before touchdown.

"Maybe he's in that one!" Sergio was certain he saw his friend's face through the tiny window. He could hardly wait to see his old pal again. Sergio let his body collapse in the middle of the grass field. Above him, the guava berry tree spread open like a wide umbrella. He looked up to the bright sky through the leaves and folded his arms behind his head, his palms cradling it comfortably. "Is he in that one?" He went on with his game. Another gray metallic bird left behind the thunderous roar of its powerful engine.

Whaaarf! Whaaarf Whaaarf!

The deafening rumble of jets made Stumpy bark excitedly. "Yes, Stumpy, I think he might be in that one!" Sergio smiled in anticipation. His good friend from first-grade was on his way. "My brother!"

* * *

The essence of a person is contained within their name. It had been recounted through ancient poems, legends and myths: a name can be whimsical and highlight a beautiful spirit, but it can also serve as a warning. Athena, Minerva, Greek goddess, daughter of Zeus and Hera, was an unconventional creation. Fiercely independent and resolute, she was born in shining armor, sprouting full grown from her father's head. In 1951 Minerva was born a soldier ready to battle at the slightest provocation. A personality so strong that even the resolve of her powerful parents could not contain it…

Minerva: warrior and troublemaker. She was the true essence of a free spirit; one terrible little girl and a most difficult child. "Minerva, *tú eres tremenda;* you're a handful." The little girl was puzzled by her mother's words. She did not understand the stern look in her mother's eyes either. *¿Una tremenda qué?* "Handful of what?" she had asked innocently. Her mother walked away in frustration. Minerva's mother, Doña Sol, mistakenly thought her youngest daughter took pride in being difficult.

"She's a free spirit!" Minerva heard her father say in her defense, without a hint of judgment. Don Genaro held a purer picture of his daughter from the time she was a little girl. He had remained optimistic, despite the news coming from the schoolyard. By her ninth birthday, Minerva had been branded a hell raiser.

"Who's gonna stop me now?" she challenged her schoolmates. Minerva was a tight bundle of kinetic energy and her classmates, in awe of her determination, were careful not to stand in her way. Once her books were stashed in a disorderly pile, she tossed her black shoes aside and ran across the school yard like a wild goat heading up the hills. Minerva never missed an opportunity to show off her athletic superiority, especially during the school's field day competitions when her popularity soared. "Go, Minerva, go!" She was energized by her classmates' cheers. Minerva: the wild goat, the barefoot wonder.

But Minerva was also vulnerable about her failures. She knew her teachers wished she had half as much interest in school. "I'm a free spirit," she defended herself, repeating her father's words. Minerva also took great pleasure in provoking horrified looks from her teachers by taking her shoes off during class while her amused classmates giggled uncontrollably. Minerva was indeed a free spirit. She could not channel her nervous energy even if she tried. Anyone who knew her could not help but feel sorry for her. When the other girls started to take an interest in boys and their own appearance, she began to isolate herself and create a protective cocoon. When Minerva looked in the mirror, she was not pleased with the plain-looking girl staring back. *"No one will ever love me!"*

* * *

"What is THAT!?" Mateo could not believe his eyes.

"Keep your mouth shut!" Maria warned him through gritted teeth as they began walking towards the short, balding man who, from a distance, seemed to

have a small dead animal resting atop his head and was now beckoning them. The smiling man standing by the side of his car was dwarfed by the sheer immensity of his vehicle.

"Is that a cruise ship?" Mateo wondered aghast.

"Mateo, I'm warning you!" Maria's jaws clinched.

"Well, hello there! Are you Maria? I'm Agripino. I'm a friend of the family and I'm here to pick you up. I'm deeply sorry for your loss." The short man greeted them, extending his arm to Maria. Maria in turn, was momentarily aghast at the sight of the stocky, short man wearing a fashionable but inappropriate ensemble that was obviously meant for a much younger fellow. With a discreet cough she tried to conceal the effect of the aroma assaulting her nostrils that was probably sufficient enough to perfume a small village.

"Agripino? What kind of stupid name is that?" Mateo was astounded by the multitude and variety of gold chains hanging from the round man's neck. He stared at the rings, too big in proportion to the short, stubby fingers.

"Yes, they're the real thing!" The man mistook the boy's curiosity for admiration. "Please come on in and make yourselves comfortable," he offered, opening the back door to the ostentatious car. Mateo was embarrassed by the farting sounds the supple leather made against his bare skin.

"I didn't—"

"What?" Maria asked.

"Nothing," he answered annoyed.

"We'll make it to the church as soon as I possibly can. In the meantime we're going to have ourselves a wonderful drive!" the short man said from behind the wheel.

"How can he see?" From the back seat Mateo could only see the top part of the man's bald head and suddenly was scared for his safety. He ducked at the sudden sound above only to realize Agripino had begun to lower the car's top.

"It's a convertible!" he clarified, just in case his guests hadn't figured it out.

"How is he going to drive this mammoth thing through the street?" Mateo whispered to Maria, who glared at him in response.

"Mateo, I'm warning you..."

"This is a '63 Eldorado Cadillac and it's a beauty. It has a heater and defroster, and cruises smooth as butter!" Agripino boasted. "I dreamed about this car for a long time."

Mateo could see tears forming in the corners of the man's eyes as he turned the ignition key. "I guess some dreams come true!" he added, raising his voice over the car's engine that was grumbling as if it had woken up annoyed from a comfortable sleep.

Mateo had serious doubts. "How is it going to fit in the street without pushing other cars into the gutter?" he whispered to Maria.

"I will not repeat myself. Shut. Up. Now!" Maria warned with a stern look.

Mateo could not hold back a sneeze.

"Are you getting sick? It's probably just the change of climate," Maria said, as Mateo discreetly pointed to Agripino, who wore his Paco Rabanne cologne with a layer of sweat and desperation as if it was going out of style.

It became clear to her that the man would use every possible opportunity to show off this over-the-top contraption he called his vehicle. Mateo in the meantime, amused himself watching the back of Agripino's head dip, bob, and weave as the man maneuvered the massive car along the main freeway.

"I've been blessed!" the chatty man went on, "After all I only lost three fingers, but check out where I am now!" And for the next few minutes, Maria and Mateo came to learn how an affable man, without an intelligent thought or common sense, had managed to acquire such an impractical, ostentatious, and definitely expensive driving machine.

"Mariposa was in no mood!" Agripino continued as if he was reading Maria's mind. "That morning I brought the daily slop and was feeding my boss's hogs down in the slaughter house. I told him, 'There's something wrong with Mariposa.'" Agripino's face acquired a somber shadow of concern.

"'Don't get too close to her, she's pregnant, and jumpy and moody,' my boss warned me."

It became clear to Maria that he was referring to the biggest sow in the sty.

Agripino shared in detail how he had taken a look at the huge, pink sow Mariposa who, unlike the graceful, light insect that inspired its name, weighed over three hundred pounds and was always covered in mud. Like many times before, Agripino had approached her with a bucket of the week's leftovers he had gathered from the neighborhood. He had called out to her but Mariposa had kept her head down, snorting into the mud as if she had lost something. Agripino had cared for her since she was a chubby piglet, so it had been a shocking surprise when she had chomped down on the offering of an apple and took his ring and pinky fingers as well. Still, despite causing such a tragedy, Mariposa's life (which was valued by the pound) was spared until the next round of Christmas festivities. Sadly, Agripino was permanently left with a deformed hand. Ironically, his tragic mishap only seemed to boost his image in the community, since every time he waved goodbye, people mistook his gesture as the thoughtful, universal sign for peace.

"Thank God the lawsuit money came at the perfect time, and suddenly I find myself at the top of the world!"

Mateo marveled at how the poor man with short, stumpy fingers managed to delude himself with such a positive spin. He had to stifle a chuckle when Maria, from the front seat of the car, turned her head back towards him with pleading eyes and mouthed, *"HELP ME!"* She could see Mateo was as red-faced as a beet, with tears in his eyes and a heartbeat away from bursting into laughter. Maria bit her lip.

Sinking comfortably into the leather back seat, Mateo closed his eyes. The rush of passing cars, blaring horns, and other machine-created noises soon became an abstract soundtrack. Without bothering to look out his window, he even enjoyed their raging velocity. There was something strangely soothing about the steady noise of haphazard drivers as they sped by. Divorced from the hectic visual scene, he found it quite entertaining. Just minutes after leaving the airport area, Mateo felt lifted by the smell of salty ocean water as it filled and expanded his lungs while the hefty car suddenly and effortlessly cruised along the edge of the road and just a few feet away from the water. He leaned his head out the window and let the humid breeze play havoc with his hair. Only a few short feet away and behind the sea-grape trees lay the luminosity of a turquoise ocean. Waves crashed noisily against the white sand as the foamy residue lapped and fizzed invitingly. Suddenly a flock of squawking seagulls crossed the sky and nosedived into the water, maybe eyeing some kind of tasty fish. A row of palm trees swayed sensuously as the wind twirled and lifted their crowns. Mateo wished he could jump out of the car and let the warm waves swallow him. He closed his eyes again. No one, not even Agripino, said a word as they cruised along the edge of the ocean and listened to the soft lapping of the waves against the shore.

Mateo felt his head buzz. *"I'm exhausted."* Resigned to the fact there was still a long stretch to go before they reached Palo Verde, he absorbed the scenery as Agripino navigated his enormous vessel through the countryside's narrow, winding roads. Palo Verde, the tiny town that sat in the lap of mountains, still seemed far away. With a turn off the main avenue, the largest artery of traffic was left behind. There was a gradual change in the atmosphere and the air felt fresher without the fumes and noise of so many cars. He stuck his head out the window feeling the breeze rush over his face. He opened his eyes as the car cruised down a long corridor of *flamboyant* trees that edged the road with flaming crimson blossoms.

"*Flamboyanes!*" The ancient line of trees, brought to the island from exotic Madagascar by colonizers, had thrived for centuries in the merciless heat, making the island their own. The simmering August heat intensified the color of their vermillion bouquets. Hypnotized by the lush greenery he suddenly realized how the inroads to Palo Verde were transforming into an exotic and alien jungle. "*I'm in the Amazon now!*"

Meanwhile, Agripino, knowing the way by heart, forged ahead with his car, as if a road map had been inserted into his brain. It was clear he could find his destination along the treacherous roads even if blind folded. "We'll be there soon," Agripino said, clutching the steering wheel as if it was trying to get away from him.

Even through half-closed eyes, Mateo could see the patterns of light and shadow glide over his face as the warm breeze blew his hair into a tangled mess. As the car turned onto the poorly paved road, the wheels groaned and spat loose stones. The vehicle maneuvered its sinewy way up the hill, jumping and twitching, like a wild colt resenting the load on its back.

The young stray foraged for food without rest, roaming aimlessly around the neighborhood for days. "*Hungry. Thirsty. Where to go?*" Its eyes searched desperately for a clue. Hopefully the new day would bring the chance for a meal of leftovers, if only scraps from discarded containers. Even some old, spoiled food could help it get through another day. Maybe its luck would begin to change. "*Finally, maybe.*"

"*Biganimals!*" The sight of people in the distance was a positive sign of a new food supply. The stray sat on its hind legs and slowly lifted its nose, trying to pick up the scent of food. It was encouraged by the activity not too far away.

The cat had been walking for many long days. "*Home?*" it wondered, exhausted and panting from thirst. "*Where to go?*" Its long journey seemed without end. It remembered the days when all it had to do to eat was run to the dish that was always filled with food. How long had it been since it had taken little sips of water from the bowl right next to it? Or gone back to the warm place by the open window for long, placid naps in the sun?

The stray wondered what exactly its mistake had been. What had it done to upset the *Kindanimals* that had cared so much for it before? But the young stray found no answers. *"Where I go now? No home, no home!"* It was hopeless. But finally it seemed the long, treacherous journey through brush, grass, and wilderness might pay off. Encouraged by the cluster of houses down the road, the cat picked up the pace and tried its luck in the first heap of trash it encountered. *"Hungry!"* Its heart leapt excitedly. *"Food!"* And with a determined, hopeful strut, the young stray—for the very first time—set its small paws into the cruel man's junk yard.

The cruel man abruptly stopped filing his machete. "What the—?" Something was moving in his yard. Cautiously, he brushed the metal shavings piled in his lap onto the floor. He squinted but still could not identify the invader. "Is that a squirrel? … A small dog? … A big rat?" He looked around, assessing his arsenal of potential weapons. He got up from his chair, knocking it on its side with a thud. He watched as the animal lifted its head; its ears were now pointed in his direction. *"Damn, be quiet!"* He tried not to lose control. The best plan of attack was always surprise. "Animals are so damn quick!" he reminded himself.

The cruel man cranked his neck above the veranda to get a better look. "A filthy cat!" All he had to do now was figure out the quickest way to tread through the heaps of discarded car parts. He knew from experience that a stray animal can be very skittish, so he lowered his machete slowly to the floor. Since he had just finished grinding it, he deemed the animal unworthy of his precious weapon. The cruel man took another quick look around. A broom suddenly seemed as good a weapon as any and *"if used correctly,"* he thought, *"a fatal one, too."* Taking his hat off, he wiped the sweat from his forehead with his shirt sleeve and, with measured, quiet steps, set foot into the car cemetery that was his front yard.

"Steady… steady…" he reminded himself, as he decided to ambush the animal from behind. *"That filthy cat won't stand a chance,"* he thought.

Keeping the broom hidden behind his back so as not to alarm the animal, he inched closer. He could tell that the cat, now halfway inside the overturned trashcan, did not suspect what was coming. The cruel man wrapped both hands around the handle of the broom so tightly his knuckles turned white. Holding his breath, he lifted the broom as high as he could. The cruel man had no compassion at all, as the clueless cat was about to discover.

Excited at the sight of the overturned trash can, the stray paused for a moment and sniffed the contents. *"Finally!"* It dug in, examining opened cans, bottles, papers that had been wrapped around cheese, meats, even a half-eaten sandwich. Its nose followed every lead.

"Where to look…
Here?
Yes! Yes! Inside."
Scrape, dig, and scratch.
"Smell something!"
Scrape, dig, and scratch.
"Maybe… Ughh! No good, no good…"

Unfortunately, the animal's hunger was so desperate, it was not aware of the presence that had snuck up behind it. The cat did not see the tall figure lifting a broom as far as it could go and swinging it with brutal force.

"GOOTCHHAA!!" By the time the stray heard the cruel man's booming voice, it was too late.

MEEEEEEAAAAEEEEUUU!!

Disoriented by the excruciating blow, the stray found itself flying across the yard. Pain burned the side of its ribs. It landed with a thud on the side of its face, still not realizing what had happened. Humiliated and hurt, the cat spat out a mouthful of dirt and snorted out the dust that was lodged inside its nostrils.

"GEEETOUUUT OOOF HEEERE YOOOY FIIILTHYYY CAAAT!!"

The cat heard angry sounds but it took a moment for it to gather its strength. *"What happened?"* Suddenly the stray was overwhelmed by the throbbing pain in its ribs. Confused and not knowing what to do next, the cat began to groom itself.

Lick paw, lick paw, clean face
Lick paw, lick paw, clean face

"Where to look … Here? Yes! Yes! Inside."

Scrape, dig, and scratch.

"Smell something!"

Scrape, dig, and scratch.

"Maybe… Ughh! No good, no good…"

"GOOOAAAWAAAY!"

The cat heard the loud noise again, triggering the crest along its back to stand on end. Its pupils became dilated and its ears pointed stiffly upwards, in anticipation of what was about to happen next. "*Why? What did I do?*" Still panting and confused, the young stray felt the hunger turn its stomach into painful knots. "*Try again.*" The cat mustered its strength but the night was fast approaching. Still exhausted and hungry, he gave up and lifted its nose to the breeze and found the answer: "*The forest.*" The tall canopy of trees nearby seemed inviting. A good night's rest in a safe quiet place was what it needed.

The wandering cat had learned another brutal life lesson in the open world: "*Mean, Biganimal!*" But now the young stray was eager to find out whether the woods could be a new source for a different kind of meal. "*Lizards, bugs, even birds—*" anything would be better than its present options. "*Have to move on.*" After making up its mind, the cat stretched its back and legs and cautiously began to cross the road, heading for the safety of the gathering of trees.

"Home?"

Ghosts are made of bits of memory from past lives, residual energies, recordings of the environment that are manifested in places that once were familiar. A ghost has no discernible powers. They are not shape shifters, ghouls, or vengeful forces. They cannot turn night into day and they do not haunt the living. A lost ghost has no powers of persuasion and does not possess a talent for incantations. They have no knowledge of magic potions that can sway the mind and the will.

A ghost is not made of matter. It is kept alive by the memories of loved ones. But love—or the memory of it—can be a trap for a ghost. A bond of love is also a chain that can hold it to the living. Even a glimpse into its past can disrupt its journey. The quiet sound of a sob can jolt a ghost from its trance. "Who is calling my name?" it will ask. And though it holds no memory, it must find the source of the sadness.

To a living person, the sound of crying might be human but to a ghost, a sob can shake it to its core. Ghosts have a single power that only works when a person opens up and allows himself to believe, to surrender to blind faith. When sorrow and hopelessness bring down the wall of disbelief, when the pain of loss is so debilitating that any resolution is accepted— even if it comes from the other side of consciousness—only then will the ghost be able to address the interference and move on. But before that is possible, it must find the source of sadness. A lost ghost possesses no past memories.

Sadness travels in circles

"Go to sleep, Goaway," the stray thought it heard the orange tree whisper. When a young cat feels betrayed and begins to distrust everyone, the forest is its safest hiding place and an orange tree is its best ally. The tree welcomed the stray with the same happiness it had felt as it watched, a long time ago, a little girl make up games under its young, strong branches. A tree, unlike a ghost, has a long memory. But even when surrounded by the strong maga, the mighty ceiba, and the resilient tabonuco trees, it can still feel lonely.

"Stay with me," the stray heard the tree say with a slight rustle of leaves. For a lonely young cat that had been wandering for a long time, those three sweet words made it feel at home again. It was indeed, a welcome change of pace. So many times had it been told before to leave, to the point that the stray thought its name was Goaway.

The tree watched with joy as the cat dug its small claws into its trunk, like a child playing with the folds of his mother's dress. "Stay with me," it repeated.

Luckily for the stray the tree not only provided shelter, but it also was a great source of entertainment for the cat. Hoping the young stray would stay, the forest mustered its simple but powerful ways of persuasion. The air, drenched with the sweet perfume of flowering honey suckle, carried its message, attracting every neighboring hummingbird. With wide eyes, the stray watched them bob, dip, and zigzag, all over the forest from one blossoming stem to another, as the tiny iridescent birds buried their long delicate beaks into the heart of the flowers and drank their sweet nectar before disappearing in just a matter of seconds.

"Beautiful!" The stray admired the little creatures that glimmered like emeralds in the light of the sun and chased after them, rolling over dry leaves with its tail inflated, its fur bristling with excitement. To its delight there were insects, bugs, lizards, dragonflies, and butterflies too! Beautiful butterflies, hundreds of them, big and small, yellow and orange and white. Exotic ones that had, for hundreds of years, found their way here from far away territories, flying over the waves of the Atlantic and down the coast of the Mexican gulf. The forest was a welcoming host to malachites, gulf fritillaries, monarchs, harlequins, little yellows, and swallowtails that feasted on the red and white milkweed. The tiny sulfurs bobbed in yellow clouds over open fields of wild grass. The stray had met them all, chasing after them, leaping with abandon, swatting at the air as they floated by. *"Beautiful!"*

Filled with wonder, the young stray watched with intense curiosity as the slivers of broken clouds bounced in the stream. But as the stray was about to discover the beauty and peacefulness of such place, was very fragile too, when a new and unfamiliar noise made it lift its head. Now cautiously searching in the direction of leaves crunching, hid behind the coleus. his eyes scanned the distance, wondering, *Biganimal?"* The cat then considered for a moment, *"What should I do?"* The cat was not about to let its guard down now, not after it had been chased down and beaten for no reason, so it crouched, hoping that whatever danger was fast approaching, it would soon go away. *"What do I do?"* it still wondered.

A subtle shaking of leaves gave the cat an idea, so it climbed up a branch of the orange tree, when it discovered the shape of another animal that grazed nearby. Unaware, the strange animal with an unusual marking on its tummy was digging its hooves into the wet mulch, munching on bits of crisp grass, its short tail constantly swatting away pesky flies and gnats. The cat was startled as the creature, hearing noises nearby too, stopped chewing and lifted its head to look up into the tree, straight into the cat's eyes. The cat froze with fear and its fur stood on end. It expected the strange animal to come charging. *"Dangerous?"* the stray wondered. Its eyes were now focused on the small stubs on top of the animal's head. *"Ugly ears!"* Recovering from its initial shock, the cat finally ventured to ask, *"What they call you?"* And the creature, lifting its eyes once more to the cat, answered, *"Zeta, the goat."*

Feeling safe once more, the strange animal with the round tummy soon resumed its meal and ignored the small curious cat hanging from the branch. So it went back to pulling chunks of young grass from the ground, and chewing mouthfuls for what seemed like a very long time. The goat kept its head held upright and a distant look in its eyes with its gaze lost on the horizon as if it was expecting a relative to show up at any minute.

Once the novelty of impending danger wore off, with a brisk jump the cat was again grounded, taking little sips of cold water from the singing river. Life in the forest agreed with the stray cat.

"I was loved." It was hard for the cat to remember that, not too long ago, *"maybe hours?... Days?... Months?,"* it had known happiness. Yes, happiness! Sitting on a warm lap, its fur being stroked gently, a head against its belly listening to its contented purr. *"I was loved."* Yes, it was hard to remember how good it felt, how

good its life was before learning what it was to be hated, before being chased away, before knowing how it felt to be unwelcome. The young stray cat did not forget. "*I was loved.*"

The stifling hot breeze of August made the forest stretch out its limbs. The stray rested under the shade of the orange tree's branches, when it heard it say again, "Stay with me."

And at that happy moment, maybe the happiest in a very long while, the young cat replied, "*Yes, I stay with you.*"

It did not take long for the cat to become familiar with the life of the forest and it sounds. From its new home under the tree, it began to explore its surroundings. On one side of the forest there were the squeaking sounds of egrets perched on the backs of grazing cows, and on the other, the gurgling river and the pond full of singing frogs. From its comfortable place, the stray captured every sound by simply rotating its ears, listening to the call of faraway doves and the hundred steps of a caterpillar making its way up a hibiscus stem. It had also learned to watch the life of the forest through half-closed eyes, its brain snapping to full attention when some unfortunate creature crossed its path. Such was the bad luck and early end of many a lizard and scurrying bug. Without moving a muscle, every complex sound and subtle movement was captured and recorded. The cat was keenly aware of all the activity in its surroundings even when seemingly resting its head on its paws. "*Happy.*" It was then the whole forest heard it purring for the first time as the young stray slept on a bed of straw and dried leaves underneath the orange tree,

Prrrr... prrrr... prrrrrrrr

Nighttime in the forest is a sensuous experience, a magical moment for passion fruit and madreselva vines to wrap themselves around young trees with their sweet smelling bouquets. When dusk descends upon the forest, insects, birds, and animals have a song to sing and a melody to hum. It is hard to imagine danger within its pastoral beauty, but the forest has its own rules for survival—hierarchies to be acknowledged, and rules to live by. Even for a young cat, at the drop of a leaf, the forest could become a very dangerous place, a fertile ground for mischief.

Exhausted from yet another day of wandering, the cat returned to the forest and settled on its bed of dry leaves under the watch of the orange tree. A gathering of trees is a most democratic living enclave for any animal. The forest passes no judgment. Anything and anyone is welcome, whatever their intentions. There are some that come to hide and heal, others to conceal their mischief from prying eyes, but there are also creatures who stake their territorial claims over those who come after; intruders. Respect for the hierarchy had to be preserved at all costs.

Unbeknownst to the stray, there was another long-time guest of the forest who had been watching its every step, whipping its tail angrily as it kept its one good yellow eye fiercely focused on the intruder. The black cat was taken aback when it first discovered that the young stray had set foot into its turf. It did not like it. "*Not a bit. Not at all.*" From a discrete distance, the black cat watched with puzzlement as the stray cried itself to sleep at night. "*Hunger? Loneliness?*" Its great yellow eye glazed over with hatred and its tail puffed up to twice its size, twitching nervously. It was terribly unhappy with the idea of sharing its home and scarce resources. "*Something must be done.*"

The black cat hissed angrily when it realized the new invader had taken up residency between the cozy roots of the orange tree. There were mornings when its long hair stood on end watching the young stray dash out of control from one side of the forest to the other for no apparent reason. The restless black cat held its breath as the intruder made a fool of itself. It could not believe its one good eye as it watched the gray cat dive head first into a heap of dry leaves as if chasing an invisible enemy. "*A mouse, maybe?* The black cat was not amused. "*Fool.*" The black cat had forgotten that it too had once behaved like a silly kitten, when everything seemed new with the possibility of adventure.

Still, it was intrigued by the stray's insistence on climbing over the moss-covered boulders with shaky legs to look at itself in the river's current. The puzzled black cat could hear it hiss and growl at the passing water down below.

For many years the black cat had fended for itself; it was not willing to start sharing the scarce food supply. "*Not now. Never.*" The last thing it needed was a helpless, hapless runt to distract it from its own responsibilities. "*This is my territory!*" This was the precise message the black cat intended to deliver to the young invader. As an experienced warrior, it knew in order to get its message across, timing, not method, was the best strategy. So it waited for the right opportunity. Of all the many traits it possessed, patience was the hardest one for it to manage. "*Your time is coming,*" the black thought frustrated, whipping its tail furiously...

From the back seat, Mateo watched Agripino's shoulders struggling over the steering wheel, as if the man was using every bit of his bodily strength. He gasped with fright as the car whooshed along, blurring the flowering trees alongside the curvy road with its sheer velocity. But still he could not help but to feel entranced by the splendor of the mountains and trees, and how, once small and insignificant on the horizon, their awe-inspiring colors became real and vibrant up close. *"Everything is getting greener,"* he thought. To his dismay the road ahead to Palo Verde seemed endless.

As the car made its way through the rows of trees bowing towards each other to create a green tunnel, the air became crisp and easier to breathe. Still the drive up to Palo Verde was not an easy one. "Maria, I feel dizzy," Mateo complained after what seemed like hours of traveling along narrow, twisting roads darkened by trees. He felt his stomach drop every time an aggressive driver materialized out of nowhere along the dangerously narrow curves.

Mateo held his breath and grabbed on to his seat as, to his horror, the car veered dangerously towards a steep precipice without a barricade or protection of any kind. He was convinced that the overgrown thickets and the feeble blades of grass along the margins of the road would *never in a million years* prevent a moving car as massive as the one he happened to be riding in from plunging over the edge and tumbling into the abyss. With sweaty hands he held on for dear life.

"When are we going to get there?" Tired of being bored, he straightened up in his seat and let his gaze travel over the vast greenery of the open fields and the multi-colored rooftops down in the valley that looked like tiny doll houses. A long warehouse almost as big as the top of the mountain it sat on loomed

ahead. "Is that a ranch?" he asked Agripino.

"That's a porqueriza where they slaughter pigs." Agripino's answer made Mateo cringe with a new wave of disgust.

The comment served as a reminder that the island was just that kind of mix of old and new, crazy and sane, logical and senseless, that he found so perplexing. And just when he thought he'd seen everything, he leaned over the door as young kids cantered their horses alongside. To his amazement, some of them were even younger than himself. Noisily flanking the car, the young bareback riders spurred their horses on with surprising skill. Mateo covered his face as the young horsemen left a dense, dusty cloud in their wake. *"Yessir! This is the country all right."* The unexpected and colorful scene was yet another unequivocal sign that they had left the city behind and were finally getting closer to their destination. Slumped in his seat, Mateo followed the continuous blur of the landscape rushing by. The music from the radio began to fade as sputtering static interrupted the already intermittent reception. It gave him a clear idea of just how isolated the place they were going to was. Interference.

Sergio sat on his bike, nervously fidgeting with the hand brakes, when at last he spotted Agripino's huge vessel making its way up the hill. "He's here!" His eyes were fixed on the distant road, watching as the car weaved in and out of view among the tall thick rows of roble oaks. Sergio jerked the handle of his bike excitedly; his old friend was back in town. In the small, remote little town of Palo Verde, good friends were hard to find. But his feelings for Mateo went beyond friendship, "Hermano!" That is how Sergio felt about his old friend. Brother.

Whwaaarf! Whwaaarf!

Sergio looked down at his dog. "Yeah, Stumpy, he's here!" he said, giving the dog a pat. Deciding to get a head start, he jumped on his bike and sped off for the town chapel.

As the car finally reached its destination along the narrow dirt road, Agripino let it idle in front of the small and crowded chapel. From the glow on his face, it was clear he enjoyed the sudden gasps his vessel elicited among the parishioners. Mateo, followed by Maria emerged out of the car as if stepping into a surreal dream.

"Where am I?" To him, Palo Verde seemed strange and unfamiliar this time, even more so without Minerva waiting for him. Gone forever. He felt his body shrinking in this unsettling frame of mind. Distraught by the memories lurking everywhere, he relived the pain of days past and, once again, went deeper inside his cocoon, forcing everyone around him to keep their distance with his warning glances. His protective shell made him immune even to his grandparents' warm touch. His eyes were lost in the distance, above the mountain ridge that encircled the diminutive town. Even the priest's prayers seemed alien and abstract.

"You didn't know her!" He resented the bland, generic eulogy. *"You didn't know anything about her,"* he kept thinking. Mateo avoided looking at the gold plated urn resting on top of the altar, as if his detachment could prevent the moment from becoming real. A sudden heavy drift of hot and humid air pushed through the claustrophobic chapel overcrowded with its plaster saints and fresh flowers. The thinly veiled impatience of the meek parishioners, with a prayer on their lips and their eyes on the exit, made him feel even more alienated from the scene. *"What am I doing here in this place?"* As the ritual proceedings got underway, with every passing minute the event felt increasingly uncomfortable and overpowering. Only the gentle sobs of Maria brought him back; only then did the moment become very real indeed.

He felt the burn of tears in his eyes, and he bit his lip until he tasted blood. But he was not about to show any signs of weakness. *"Not now, not in front of these people. Who are they? I don't even know anymore."* Mateo almost choked as the surge of anger closed up his throat.

Amid the rites and the oppressive mood, at least one familiar face in the crowd lifted his spirits: Sergio, his friend from first grade, had made a point of connecting with him as soon as he heard the news of his arrival. But even Sergio seemed unfamiliar. *"How long has it been?"* Mateo tried to reconcile his memories of his short and pudgy friend with this guy's wiry frame and unkempt auburn ringlets cascading over a tanned forehead. He was struck by the change; Sergio was now almost a man.

"Hey, Mateo. You okay, man?" Sergio whispered in his ear during the service.

"Yes, I am," he lied. Feeling Sergio's hand on his shoulder made him grateful for the presence of his only friend on the island.

"This dying stuff, it freaks me out, man. It's preposterous!"

"Preposterous!?" The unexpected word made Mateo smile. "I know what you

mean," he answered truthfully.

"Do you ever think about what happens after you die?"

"I don't want to think about it!" The blunt question made him uneasy.

Sergio brushed the curls off his forehead with the tip of his fingers like a little boy, adding, "I'm not sure, either."

"I have to get out of here. Now," Mateo took a deep breath and anxiously looked around the crowded room for his family.

Wharf, wharf, wharf, wharf

The insistent barking of Stumpy bounced off the walls of the small chapel, breaking up the monotony of the occasion. Sergio turned his eye towards the chapel's doors. "That darn dog is going to drive me nuts!" he told Mateo under his breath, holding back a chuckle. "Hey, you wanna get together later?" Sergio asked before heading out.

"Don't know. Maybe."

"Cool, I'll catch ya' later then."

Mateo watched his friend sprint for the door and jump on his bike. Stumpy, who had been waiting anxiously, raced after the bike, yapping happily. Mateo smiled as they disappeared in the distance.

Overwhelmed by the emotions of the long day, Mateo was relieved when the funeral was finally over. *"I can't deal with this."*

Once at his grandparent's house, the family's attention shifted towards him. Mateo noticed his grandfather's eyes glaze over with tears. "The Angel will forgive me!" he heard him say softly to himself, heartbroken. Mateo watched him walk away sobbing quietly, his shoulders slumped by the weight of his grief.

"Where should we keep her ashes?" Doña Sol asked her grandson, hoping for some positive sign from him. But Mateo gave her a menacing glare and, without an answer, plugged in his earphones. He did not appreciate her patronizing attitude and the sudden weight of the responsibility she was now laying on his shoulders.

"Are yo okay?" Maria asked him.

"I said I'm fine!" he snapped at her when she had tried to intervene.

"I'm not a baby!" His rage rose to the surface of his skin again. "You are all liars!" he screamed. He could not breathe; he needed fresh air.

He ran out of the house looking desperately for a place to get away. "I can't breathe!" Mateo grabbed his chest, feeling his heart leap furiously under his T-shirt. His face was now covered with a mixture of sweat and tears. The pulsing music inside his ears became unbearable and with a yank, he pulled out the small earphones. He sat at the bottom of the stairs, feeling out of place. *"What am I doing here?"*

Mateo stared at the empty hammock hanging across the open-air room, beyond the double tin basins where his grandmother washed the daily laundry. Breathing easier, his focus became clearer as his eyes traveled along the mishmash of potted flowering plants lining the driveway all the way to the pasture behind the house. At that moment, Mateo discovered the dirt path that snaked down the hill and into the forest was barely visible, but the sight of it refreshed his memory. *"I remember now... The river, the forest..."*

But he was not fully prepared when his eyes finally settled on a rustic red door; Minerva's room, where she had lived the last year of her life. He swallowed hard as his eyes lingered on the lock. *"What's in there?"* But he did not dare to even consider to cross its threshold.

Mateo turned his head away towards the garden where he noticed a pigeon pea bush by the chain-link fence, the small bed of pink impatiens his grandmother had planted, along the bed of purple ruellia and feathery potted ferns.

His frantic state of mind finally calmed down as he took in the familiar setting. When suddenly, and out of nowhere, a small, gray cat appeared in his grandmother's garden. Mateo watched it run behind the begonias, sitting half-hidden between the ferns. From its hiding place, the cat looked straight at Mateo from across the garden. But before Mateo could figure out where had it had come from, the cat had disappeared. *"What was that about?"* Something in the cat's stare greatly unsettled him...

FROM MATEO'S JOURNAL

I will never forget that moment. To this day it is etched in my memory and forever will be. It was just a cat, and God knows I've seen a lot of them in my life. Still there was something about it that stopped me in my tracks; it was the saddest cat I've ever seen. Suddenly I could see myself reflected in its eyes, and there I saw someone scared, lost, and at the end of his rope: a true reflection of myself at that moment. It made me think about the heavy dark cloud of foreboding that had been hanging above my head long before my arrival. In the years after, I tried to rationalize this chance encounter that, at the time, seemed to carry no significance. It was a simple, unassuming moment. I didn't suspect it then but that precise moment was the beginning of something big. Was it fate, coincidental timing, or a more significant message? It simply blew my mind; the cat looked at me as if he had been waiting for my arrival all its life!

WHERE AM I?

"Wake up, Mateo!"

The town of Palo Verde stirred as the morning fog turned transparent and the nearby mountains began to soak up the sun light. The first drizzle of the day momentarily polished the town's only beaten down road. Gusts of cold wind swept over the sleepy town and shook the moisture from the trees. Soft sounds of rain hammered the uneven quilt of tin and cement roofs. Mateo was awakened by the murmur and chatter of early-rising children and the spirited call of roosters. *"Am I dreaming?"* The frogs abruptly stopped croaking as the early sun began to unfurl ribbons of warm, golden light, dissolving what was left of the night. In brushstrokes of pink and soft lavender, a layer of thick clouds rushed by. *"Where am I?"* His thoughts were entangled in a web of confusion. Soon the darkness of the room softened as slivers of light began to squeeze through the window slats of the *persiana*. A sudden chill filled the room and made him snuggle deeper under his blanket.

"Wake up Mateo, time to get up!" he heard his grandmother say. But the call only made him pull the covers closer. "It's just too early," he mumbled and turned over, ignoring his grandmother's wake up call. As long as he stayed in bed he didn't have to face the day. But when the strong, pungent aroma of freshly made coffee rolled across the living room, down the narrow hall, and filled his bedroom. *"Am I still asleep?"* He could hear his grandmother in the small kitchen—stirring, venting, and lifting with her spoon the dark column of liquid that folded into a bed of its own foam. *"It's just another day, the same as yesterday."* Finally Mateo resigned himself to getting up; the persistent call of birds made it hard for him to stay in bed.

"Wake up, Mateo!"

Alone, and surrounded by shadows, his mind tried to distinguish the blurry line between dream and reality. *"Where am I?"* It took a few seconds before his memory brought him up to date. Suddenly, his stomach quivered with uneasiness. *"She's not here anymore."* The thought raced around his head as he realized the nightmare was very real. The sun began to filter between the white metal shutters and he resented it, but he knew it was time to get going. He put on his glasses and as the bedroom emerged from the shadows, Mateo's gaze landed on the wooden dresser where Minerva's photograph was perched in a corner. The image of a girl with short, wind-swept hair made his eyes fill with tears.

Every object around him began to come to life. He resisted thinking about them. It was as if he had suddenly walked into a field of land mines. Something as simple as an ordinary picture, an object with no apparent presence, was a powerful trigger capable of unleashing a torrent of memories, memories of Minerva. *"She's gone,"* Mateo shook his head.

Even more dangerous were the smells in the room: the sweet perfume she favored, the musty scent of dried flowers, the smells of forgotten books, of trees drenched in early rain, and the moisture of raw earth carried by the breeze. *"There's only one way out."* He bolted from the bed and looked around for his shirt. *"The sooner I get out of this room, the better!"* Hurriedly, he grabbed his pants from a pile on the floor and jumped in them. From his pocket he pulled out an object carefully wrapped in paper. *"I almost forgot about this!"*

He stared for a long time at the small piece of glass nestled in the palm of his hand; an object that had seemed so big to him as a child. Mateo twirled the glass around and held it up to the light. Carefully placing the twine over his head, he was finally ready to face the day ahead. In the light of a new morning, he questioned his clarity of thought when he had asked Maria a few days before, "Can I stay here a little bit longer?"

Mateo never knew his father, but by now it didn't matter to him. Not anymore. He had been surrounded with so much love, he didn't have time to stop and think about it. At an early age he had learned to create a world of his own populated by animals—sometimes cats, sometimes dogs, other times toads, and turtles, but usually all of them at once! He had more than enough chores and distractions to ever wonder what was missing from his life. He could not even remember exactly when he had become aware of Maria's presence; it seemed to him she and Minerva were one entity, intertwined. Maria started where Minerva ended. It was undeniable Minerva had been his rock even as she struggled to keep her life together, but it was Maria who had gone out of her way and beyond the call of duty to smooth out the rocky road ahead of him during difficult times.

"I'm not so sure about that," Maria had replied skeptically but secretly pleased by his unexpected change of heart.

"Tell me why not," he cornered her. To his surprise, he heard her say, "Okay, you can stay in Palo Verde."

But it didn't take him long to realize he had made a mistake. *"There's nothing to do here!"* The sparkling sounds of the new day drew his eyes across the room and out the window slats. Yes, the Palo Verde outside his window was beautiful, but he suspected there was a price to be paid for his return. Mateo sat motionless on the side of the bed, listening wistfully at the wind shredding the wide banana leaves into ribbons. And as the mamey apple tree began to drop its fruit to the ground like improvised bombs, he could hear the alarmed ruckus of grazing hens and roosters scattering noisily, horrified by the startling and unwarranted attack. *"Bombs."* A thought so accurate, it made him smile. Yes, there were some similarities, him sitting in his room listening to falling bombs. *"Emotional land mines."* Mateo was taken by surprise at the free association. *Palo Verde: land of emotional land mines.*

As the fair morning faded away, the strong gusts of wind came to a sudden stop. In the absence of clouds, the light of the sun beat down mercilessly on the backs of the mountains and turned the asphalt of the town's only road into a boiling steamy pot of black tar. The inhabitants of Palo Verde retreated to cooler corners, under trees and balconies. Even the animals weathered the heat wave under the green, shady retreat of the nearby forest.

Thankfully, the tropical heat is always in perfect sync with *siesta* time in the forest. Under the protective canopy of the trees, the young stray dug itself out from underneath the pile of fallen leaves, disappointed to find nothing interesting hiding there after all. Covered from head to tail in wet mulch, the cat began to clean itself methodically.

> *Lick paw, lick paw,*
> *Wipe face, wipe face.*
> *Lick paw, lick paw,*
> *Wipe face, wipe face.*

But even deep into a rigorous cleaning routine, a young cat could still pick up the slightest of noises. It was then something made it prick up its ears. The cat had a sudden realization, "*Someone's watching.*" One yellow beacon burned brightly in the darkness of the forest. The young cat jumped at the unfamiliar growls. The warning sounds made its back arch and its fur stand on end, but the bright yellow light soon was swallowed by the thick shadows. With measured, cautious steps, the young cat inspected its surroundings, tail held high, nose busily capturing any new scent.

"*Biganimal gone!*" The stray looked from side to side before it sat on the leafy ground, its heart still racing. A thought then crossed its mind, "*Not alone.*" The cat knew it had to watch its step very carefully.

Lick paw, lick paw,
Wipe face, wipe face.
Lick paw, lick paw,
Wipe face, wipe face.

All life activity in the forest came to a lull. The withering afternoon heat went on beating down on the surrounding foliage. The young stray settled down comfortably and rested on his bed of dry leaves and concentrated once more on the soothing sound of the river.

* * *

Doña Sol and Don Genaro rushed to the school after hearing the news. The principal ushered them into the privacy of his office, away from prying eyes. He felt sorry at the sight of the two diminutive parents sitting shyly side by side in front of him. He could see the slight tremble in Doña Sol's hand as she nervously wrung a small handkerchief between her fingers. Don Genaro's face was set in a frozen expression; only the tiny beads of sweat across his forehead betrayed his innermost fury. Minerva had crossed the last line of decency. This time around she had left him no choice.

"Don Genaro, Doña Sol, I don't want to take much of your time." Mr. Amador did not want to extend the difficult moment more than absolutely necessary; still he could not help noticing Minerva's parents squirming uncomfortably in the hardwood seats. "We've tried very hard to help Minerva, but at this point, we've run out of ideas. This is it," he said, getting up from his seat in time to prevent Don

Genaro's appeal. "She has to go; at this point she's a bad example for the school and the other children."

Mr. Amador swallowed hard. Even with all his experience in handling difficult situations, he was not immune to Doña Sol's pleas. "I'm sorry Doña Sol, she has to go. Today."

Disheartened and hopeless, they were both dismissed as Mr. Amador turned his back and walked to the window. "Have a good day," they heard him mutter, as they closed the door with the small glass pane behind them. And just like that, Minerva's education abruptly ended at fourteen.

Don Genaro's sympathy for his daughter soon turned into rage. "She'll pay for this," he said under his breath, gritting his teeth.

"Please, Genaro. This is not the moment," Doña Sol begged, her eyes now blinded by tears. "What are we going to do now?"

* * *

"What am I going to do now?" Mateo polished his glasses as if the lack of activity around the neighborhood could be remedied with clearer vision. Still in the early hours of the morning, there was no sign of anything interesting happening; even the road seemed strangely deserted.

Finally a welcome sound broke the monotony: the ringing of a bell, the wheezing of bicycle wheels and the insistent ring of a bell. Barking sounds drew him to the window. He watched as Sergio sped up the empty road followed by his dog. The small, yellow mutt raced alongside him, determined to keep up. With a broad sweep, Sergio steered his bike towards the chain link fence, jumping off in such a hurry he let it crash against the fence. Simultaneously, the small dog following him threw itself onto the grass, panting but happily exhausted.

Mateo was relieved to see his friend again. The sight of the exhausted yellow dog with the hanging tongue made him smile. "Hey, Serge!" he greeted him, noticing the cuts and bruises on Sergio's bare legs. *"True biker dude!"* he thought, happy to see the familiar face. Sergio would certainly be the cure for the Palo Verde doldrums.

"Hey, Mateo! Whass' up?" Sergio grabbed at the wobbly wall of metal links of the fence, pushing his face against the fence.

"You wanna come in?" Mateo asked, "You look like you're in a cage!" Mateo had a vision of his friend in a prison.

"No, I'm good. How you holding out, man? That really blows." Sergio tried to show his sympathy. Without waiting for a response, he asked, "What're you doing to keep busy around here?"

Mateo had to think. "Not sure," he answered truthfully.

"Family okay?' Sergio pressed.

"Yes…well, it's bad, you know…" He was at a loss for words. "Hey, is Billy still around?" he said, changing the subject.

"Yeah, he's around all right. But, you know, he always has some crazy beef. Can't deal with him no more. He's always at war with his father, besides…" Sergio caught Mateo's glance.

"What?" Mateo pushed.

"People are talking shit, man! Nothing new in this place." He tried to shake Mateo off.

"C'mon, what do you mean?"

Sergio's eyes darted nervously over to Billy's house. "People say he's stealing their animals… they disappear for good," he whispered.

"You mean killing them?" Mateo blurted out, alarmed, "Has anybody caught him?"

Distractedly, Sergio brushed aside the locks of hair in his eyes. "Well, nobody's been able to prove anything. Guess you have to catch him in the act," he said, picking up his bike. Trying to ignore Mateo's intense stare, Sergio dismissed the harsh news with a question, "So, what you doing later?"

"Don't know," Mateo answered, still staring at Billy's house.

"Mateo!" Sergio snapped.

"What?" answered Mateo, caught off guard.

"You listening to me?" Sergio laughed.

Mateo was not listening. His eyes were now glued to the junk yard that was Billy's house across the street.

"MATEO! You listening to me?" Sergio repeated.

"Yes, I am," he lied. "Is that your dog?" He tried to pick up the thread of the conversation. "He's loving it, that's for sure!" He was amused by the dog's antics, rocking around on its back, coughing and making happy sounds, clearly enjoying the feel of the wet grass against its fur.

"Oh, yeah! That's Stumpy. He's my *sato*." Sergio referred affectionately to the mutt. With its very short legs and tail, its given name made sense.

"What happened to his tail?"

"It's his real tail all right," Sergio answered. "Not sure if he was born that way—" He toyed with the dog's long floppy ears.

"Where'd you find him?"

"He was abandoned. I found him wandering. He's such a hound. He could be a great detective!"

Both boys laughed, watching the short-legged dog snort loudly and wallow in the grass.

"Hey, you feel like hanging out later? A bunch of us are going to the beach. You game?"

"Don't think so," Mateo replied, avoiding the look of disappointment on Sergio's face.

"Well, catch you later then!" Sergio jumped on his bike. "C'mon Stumpy! Let's hit the road!" At the sound of his name, the dog jumped to his feet, ready for another race.

Wharf, wharf, wharf!

Mateo watched his friend's open shirt flapping in the wind as he disappeared down the road with Stumpy racing close behind. Even before Sergio and his dog vanished from view, Mateo began to regret his decision not to join him. But boredom is fertile ground for the unoccupied mind and Sergio's visit had planted a seed. *"Hmmm. Billy."* Something needed to be done about him. *"I'll think of something."* Mateo's imagination began to brew as he stared at the house behind the leftover skeletons of cars across the street.

"What's his problem?"

Billy did not like it a bit. From his front steps, he could clearly see the other boy across the street staring him down. Billy did not like it, and in return he shot a hard, cold glare of his own. *"What have I ever done to you?"*

Billy did not take kindly to provocation. God knows his head was turned inside out just dealing with his father's craziness. Without taking his eyes off the boy standing in Doña Sol's garden, Billy crossed his arms defiantly. He had never backed off from a fight before and was not about to start now. But it became clear to him that the boy across the street would not back away either. Billy stretched his

❖ 75 ❖

right arm towards him and slowly raised his middle finger.

"He's gone far enough!" The black cat's patience had reached its limit. Something needed to be done about this new intruder. It was about time it sent the clueless stray an unmistakable message of the serious consequences that were in store. For a cat used to having its own domain where it could move freely about without territorial worries, where there was always a delicious supply of treats like succulent mice, yummy lizards, and fresh water from the nearby stream, sharing was a very unwelcome idea.

The black cat finally decided the time had come to make its move. With its bright yellow eye flickering in anger, the black cat searched every corner of the forest to track down the young stray. *"This place is not big enough for the both of us!"* it thought after watching the young stray chew on blades of grass, blissfully unaware. *"There is no backing down now."* As an experienced fighter, it knew a successful attack was only possible after detecting the opponent's weakness. *"It will be easy,"* the cat thought without taking its big yellow eye off the unsuspecting intruder even for a moment.

One afternoon, just as expected, the black cat discovered the young stray sunning near the moss-covered boulders. It was the moment it had been waiting for. Without missing a beat, it jumped in front of the stray with an arched back, its tail fluffed up and all its claws out. Looking straight at the frightened young cat, it spread its jaws open in an intimidating hiss, displaying its sharp dagger-like fangs. Uttering the most blood-curdling, guttural warning it could, the black cat swatted the young stray across the face.

Taken completely by surprise, the cornered stray hissed and arched its back too, but it soon became clear it was no match for its opponent.

With another precise swat and a heart-stopping howl, the black cat smacked the small face of the stray again with its powerful paw and little red beads of blood glistened above the young stray's nose. But the black cat did not count on the young stray standing tall on its four legs, as if walking on stilts. The black cat began to feel it had miscalculated the situation.

Although unprepared, the young stray was putting up a surprisingly good fight. Not expecting such a challenge, the black cat began to growl and spit. Its menacing breath made the small cat tremble as if faced with an oncoming storm. With fangs in full view and its good eye on fire, the black cat struck the young stray once more. "*Sssssss! Stay away!*" it warned with a deep, menacing growl. "*A lesson for you!*"

Still, to its surprise, the young cat did not give up and stood its ground. The black cat then abruptly turned and walked away. It had made its point. "*Stay away! Sssssss!*" it warned one last time before vanishing among the trees again.

Still standing on all fours, back arched, and pupils dilated with excitement, the young stray watched as the black cat licked its lips in anger and walked away slowly, as if being careful not to give the impression of a defeated exit.

But in fact, the stray had nothing to feel bad about; the experience had been a good one, after all. For the first time in its life, the stray had learned how to defend itself and its turf. Survival in the wild. So it moistened the back of its forepaw, and methodically began to clean the beads of blood from its nose.

> *Lick paw, lick paw, clean face. Lick paw,*
> *lick paw, clean face. Lick paw,*
> *lick paw, clean face.*

PART TWO

The Greenest Prison on Earth

Mateo held the skateboard under his arm as he faced the road. His shoulders slumped with disappointment as he watched cars dangerously speeding by as if the narrow, tattered road was a race track. He recognized the pointlessness of his idea. The skateboard suddenly seemed ridiculous. He was left to wander around his grandmother's garden almost all day, like a solitary animal trapped in a cage. His eyes had searched for any stimulating sign of life beyond the chain link fence. Even at the height of the brightest afternoon in Palo Verde, the day was almost indistinguishable from the one before. Mountains, rain, and sun, and still it felt like the greenest prison on the planet.

Wishing Sergio had stuck around, Mateo retreated to his room with nothing to do. Trying to escape the suffocatingly humid heat, he leafed distractedly through the pages of his book. Unable to concentrate, he even lost interest in his music. *"Another wasted day."* He glanced over at the calendar that hung on his wall.

Nearly bored to death, he was gazing out of the window for what seemed like the hundredth time when a soft rustle from the towering mango tree brightened up his face with a new idea…

Doña Sol watched him run out of the house, fly down the stairs, and come to a stop underneath the leafy tree with its ripe bouquet of low hanging fruit. *"What is he up to now?"* she wondered with dread. She waited to find out what crazy thought was boiling inside his head. Puzzled, she watched as he walked slowly around the massive trunk, looking up at the branches.

"What in heaven's…?" She stopped her washing when she saw Sergio come rattling through the front gate on his bicycle along with his dog. Judging from their body language, she could tell the boys were planning something of great importance. Her curiosity grew as they continued walking around the tree, as if searching for something among its branches. Mateo walked towards her with a serious look on his face and she braced herself.

"I wanna build a tree house!" Mateo announced, watching his grandmother's jaw drop slightly. "Do you have any wood around here we can use?"

Doña Sol said nothing.

"It doesn't have to be big. Just so Sergio and I can hang out," he added, to justify his enterprise.

Recovering from the outrageousness of her grandson's request, Doña Sol replied, "I don't think that's a good idea. I don't want you to hurt that tree!"

"Why not? I know what I'm doing!" Mateo protested.

"Mateo…!" She admonished him with a pointed look, then resumed her washing.

"What am I supposed to do in this stinking place? THERE'S NOTHING TO DO HERE!" Sergio knew Mateo was pressing his luck, so he watched from a safe distance. "If I had known it was gonna be like this…" he continued, avoiding his grandmother's stern expression.

"You can give me a hand around here if you're so bored," Doña Sol replied, to put an end to the argument. From the corner of her eye she could sense Mateo's bruising stare and arms crossed like a shield. She knew it was far from over. She hated to admit it but his steely defiance reminded her of Minerva. She had to think fast: she could dig in her heels but the result would unequivocally be a sullen, unhappy almost-teenager turning the house into a pressure cooker. It was enough to make her break into a cold sweat.

Mateo waited expectantly for his grandmother's answer. By now he had reacquainted himself with that familiar stance—*Minerva's unflinching stubbornness*—in the way Doña Sol slightly cocked her head to one side and made her lips disappear in a horizontal line.

"Well, maybe on one condition…" she said, watching him perk up.

"*What* condition?"

She had to come up with something fast. "That you'll be careful with the tree, and… that you have to obey when I…" She trailed off as Mateo ran to celebrate with Sergio and Stumpy. Ultimately, she was relieved to have him out of her hair for a few hours. From the kitchen window, she could hear the boys planning their project, hammering and running back and forth in their search for building materials, with Stumpy barking at every step.

Attracted by the commotion, Don Genaro walked to a corner of the balcony and was amazed by the raw energy the kids were investing in their venture, hovering around the tree trunk, measuring, cutting, banging. He gazed with amusement

at their purposeful comings and goings, improvising building materials, the little dog barking loudly as if it was dispensing directions.

After a busy afternoon, the boys dropped with exhaustion onto Doña Sol's sofa. Stumpy panted heavily at their feet.

"Are you two finished?" she asked, intrigued to see the final outcome. Meanwhile Don Genaro, sitting quietly at a corner of the breakfast table stared at them, enjoying the moment as if he too was part of the action.

"It's fantastic!" Mateo announced happily.

Doña Sol watched them wolf down their food then sprint out the door. She looked out her window and saw for the first time the haphazard contraption they called their tree house. She could hear their laughter behind the curtain of leaves, and saw the dim glow of a flashlight that escaped now and then through the branches. *"This boy is something else!"* she thought with a sigh.

Mateo retired for the evening filled with a renewed sense of purpose. Building the tree house with Sergio had been, without a doubt, not only the highlight of the day but a stroke of genius. He then busied his mind considering the possibilities for his newly built fort. Suddenly the quiet monotony of his room was disturbed by a brief but rather spectacular rain shower. He looked at his watch—*6:13*—and walked over to the window. Pressing his face against it, he closed his eyes and took a deep breath. Still he had to admit, *"Such a beautiful place!"*

The unexpected shower and the ensuing quiet served as an overture to the end of the day. The faint light of the setting sun made the neighboring rain-soaked field sparkle as if covered with broken diamonds. Thankfully too, the simple spectacle had helped settle his anxiety.

Turning away from the window, he examined the room filled with his grandmother's personal belongings: the small closet with folding metal doors that contained her dresses, most of which, he suspected, never saw the light of day. The small teak chest of drawers, dressed up with a dainty white lace runner, was topped by a mirror that reflected the endless loop of daily life outside the window slats. Her prayer book, weathered from constant use, sat next to a small stack of old letters. Mateo ran his fingers along the top of the brown wooden jewelry box adorned with gold inlaid. The rustic rectangular box contained an assortment of coins, hair pins, medals, and a forgotten empty perfume bottle. *"Nothing of value,"* he noted.

Inevitably his thoughts drifted to Minerva. He still could not come to grips with the event that had brought him back to his grandparent's home. Mateo gazed at the simple drawing, yellowed by time, that hung on the back of the door and recognized the childish, sloppy handwriting. *"I forgot about that drawing!"*

"Mateo, finish your breakfast.
"Why?"
"Because we need to get going to the shop."
"Why?"
"I need to finish a dress, so the person can wear it."
"Why?"
"Mateo! I will not repeat myself."
"Can Canela come with us?"
"Doesn't she always?"
"Titi Meva, how the machine goes?"
"It goes BROOOM, BROOOM!"
"Hee, hee, hee!"
"Mateo, get your crayons and your drawing pad."

Finally, the signs of a fading day began to shade the town. From his corner in the bedroom, Mateo heard the absent-minded humming of Doña Sol as she washed and put away the dinner dishes. Like white noise, the muffled conversation between her and Don Genaro in the living room served as a relaxing tonic. He tried to concentrate on his book once again as the songs of the diminutive coquí frogs, chirping crickets, and roosting birds pervaded the evening as it turned into night.

For the first time in its life, the young stray heard the river's voice—a clear song, soft and secretive—sliding among the boulders. "*What is it?*" it wondered, gingerly taking small steps towards the singing water. Its short legs waddled through the dry mulch and fallen branches. Its little paws clumsily but firmly climbed up the tall, slippery stones. The young cat needed to find out. "*What is it?*"

The moment it saw another face staring straight at it, the young stray froze in its steps; its entire coat stood on end as if it had swallowed a bolt of lightning. With wide, frightened eyes, the cat fixed its gaze on the face staring back. The young cat then crouched slowly, struggling to get a closer look at this new intruder. The other cat dared to do the same. Remembering its last encounter, the young stray realized it had a responsibility to claim its territory, so it arched its back, growled, and hissed as convincingly as it could. With a series of low and high moans the

young cat sent its clear warning, "*Stay away! Sssssss.*" A cat, even a young one, has to learn not to walk away from a territorial challenge. With decisive aim, it swatted at the other cat's face only to see it break into ripples, dissolving like a liquid puzzle pulled away by the current. Feeling confused, the young cat retreated to its bed of dry leaves under the orange tree.

Lick paw, wipe face, lick paw.
Lick paw, wipe face, lick paw.
Lick paw, wipe face, lick paw.

As it groomed itself diligently, the young cat heard the amused laughter of the river…

One of life's underappreciated lessons is that sometimes conflict is the best way to make new friends. No longer resentful of the smaller competitor, the black cat claimed its fair share of the forest. Now it felt free to walk in front of the stray with a swagger, growling, its tail fully fluffed, expecting the little thing to shake with fear. The black cat hissed and carried on so as to leave no doubt who was boss. But sometimes it confronted the stray with its fiery eye and flattened ears only to be challenged right back!

The black cat was taken aback by the stray's aggressive hissing and spitting. To its amazement, the other cat matched it growl for growl and never backed down from the bigger menace. Suddenly, the black cat had a revelation: with its naive yet intimidating display, the little one revealed its fighting spirit. It made the black cat remember its own early life. "*Fighter.*" It had to concede, "*He's determined.*" Yes, the little young stray had finally earned the older cat's respect. The law of the jungle, the survival of the fittest, and respect for the hierarchy had been set in motion.

The young stray, like a child who does not understand why his parents are angry at him, crouched and watched with big, attentive eyes as the black cat jumped out of the blue and circled him menacingly. It did not take long for it to make sense of the dangerous situation. Thankfully it had learned its lesson early on. It understood now that survival was not about showing force but rather respecting and allowing every other creature their space. It clearly understood that a cat, even though hungry and thirsty, might want to be left alone. So the young stray walked away and found its place under the orange tree.

A quick snack of insects and a few sips of fresh water from the river was enough for the time being. Resting on its bed of leaves, the stray tried to decipher the wonders of its surroundings. Its eyes followed the flock of egrets keeping company with the grazing cows nearby. *"Respect for all."* An older cat knows more about survival. *"Not easy."* So the stray learned when to step back and acknowledge the value of experience. Respect had been a very hard lesson and one it could not forget if it wanted to survive in the wild. Respect is the first rule of the wilderness.

The stray remembered the first time it was attacked by the one-eyed black cat. It shuddered at the thought of the fat paw swatting at its face. It had been effective enough to put the stray in its place; it had been a very humbling moment indeed. The sting of tears blurred its sight as rejection and loneliness overwhelmed it all over again.

But the stray's pain was replaced by surprise when, not long after, the big black cat placed a lifeless bird at its feet. "Here. Eat," the young stray heard it say. As it watched the black cat walk slowly away, the young stray feasted on the much needed meal. The black cat settled comfortably in its part of the forest, resting its head on its paws while ignoring the growls of hunger in its stomach.

"Thanks, One-eye!" the black cat heard through the purrs of the young stray.

The sun quietly disappeared behind the mountains, dissolving what little was left of the day. A far away rumble shook the dew off the jasmine vines and a flash of lighting cracked the sky open to the dazzling rush of shooting stars. The sudden nocturnal display interrupted the cat's fitful sleep. Lifting its tired face to the sky, the stray discovered the burning tail of the falling star. The animal let its stare linger in awe as the fiery mass made its way past other bright stars. Its brilliance transformed the tranquility of an otherwise ordinary night, and the forest, once flush with the chatter of animals, became eerily silent. Even mourning doves stopped their cooing and became quiet.

Suddenly, suspense spread over the forest. The warm evening breeze that had flowed freely suddenly turned heavy and dense. The entire community of trees trembled as if a hurricane was about to strike with unforgiving force. From one side to the other, trees talked amongst themselves in their secret language. "She's here!" The sour sop shook its leaves in a welcoming gesture. "She's here!" hummed the coffee and the guava tree . But it was the ceiba who said it best, "We've been waiting!" Every living animal in the forest heard the call. All creatures, big and small, stirred excitedly and came out from nests, branches, and burrows.

By the stream, the young stray took long sips of water and lifted its head up to the chatter of the forest animals. *"What is happening?"* it wondered, as the astral beauty tore a path through the sky with its radiance, penetrating the Earth's atmosphere. *"Beautiful star!"* The young cat could not take its eyes off the streak of energy descending from the clouds into the forest, and it felt its heart leap inside its chest as it followed the star's broken reflection in the stream. *"Sky on fire!"*

Once so far away, the falling star finally melted the forest's impenetrable shadows, prompting a baffled, solitary rooster to flutter its wings and call the day. Meanwhile, all life in the forest retreated as the fiery mass got closer. The trees reached out to each other like frightened children. As the star hovered above, it began to release soft beams of white and blue light. The forest watched in fascination as the star began to transform. Insects, bugs, and mice peeked out from under leaves, astounded as the light hung suspended in midair. Brimming with energy, the star's brightness became more intense then suddenly, a fantastic explosion of warm light flooded the valley and lit up the crowns of the mountains. For a magical instant, even the river seemed to have caught fire as fragments of vivid light splattered through the forest in a kaleidoscope of colors. The stray was paralyzed in awe of the star's beauty and, before it knew it, was completely engulfed in its warm light. It was impossible for the cat to escape now and with great apprehension, it eyed the transparent shape floating before it.

As the star's intense glow faded, the only remnants of its magnificent rebirth were the scent of wilted wild flowers and deafening silence. The ghostly light then spoke to the stray in a whisper so soft that the animal mistook it for the murmur of the water. As the ghost approached, the crest along the cat's arched back stood on end. "There's no need to be frightened little one, there's no need," the ghost whispered...

The walls in the room gradually acquired the soothing, mellow tone of aged amber from the setting sun and the song of crickets intensified as the night began to envelop the town. A flash of bright light illuminated the window frame and Mateo lifted his eyes from his book. *"What was that?"* He looked out his window at the nearby mountains and sensed an unusual charge in the atmosphere. He scanned the sparsely clouded sky and felt the air crackling with energy.

"Have I been asleep?" Puzzled, he studied the starry night. *"Doesn't look like*

rain." He adjusted his glasses.

Suddenly, the sky lit up as an extraordinary light made its way across the sky, down into the nearby woods, disappearing behind the trees as if the forest had swallowed it up.

"*A shooting star, maybe? Did I just—?*" He rubbed his eyes, unsure of the flood of brightness emanating from the trees as if they were on fire.

"*What was that?*"

The splendor of the moon bathed the ghost as it knelt on the ground, glimmering in the night as if made of fireflies. The translucent shape scanned the dense canopy of trees as if in a trance. The penetrating light of the silver disk in the sky scurried through the leaves creating bright silvery patches in the humid shadows. The ghost was startled by a sudden gust of wind that shook the ferns feeding off the nearby river. Its eyes followed the water's course as the river turned around the bend and disappeared behind a thicket of angel's trumpet.

"Who am I?" the restless ghost asked the stray, who was staring with a great deal of curiosity.

"*Fallingstar,*" the stray answered, without saying a word. The cat understood the ghost's words in the same way it had learned to interpret the messages of the forest.

"Where am I?" the ghost asked again.

"*Home,*" answered the young cat.

"Where do I come from?"

"*Up sky.*" The cat lifted its nose and sat upright with its ears cocked at full attention.

"What happened to me?"

The stray had no answer.

The ghost spoke again. "Who are you?"

The stray had to think before it answered. It had been a long time since anyone had called it by its proper name. And then it remembered. "*Goaway. Yes, Goaway everybody calls out to me.*"

The cat's crest finally receded and it began to feel more relaxed. The transparent being did not seem so threatening now. The ghost's voice was as sweet as the song of the crickets. As the high moon followed her own path across the arch of the sky, the ghost watched the cat circle around before settling down on its bed of dry leaves under the orange tree. Even in the velvety darkness, the ghost could still see a pair of green eyes peeking out from behind the coil of the cat's lithe body.

"Can you help me?" The ghost seemed lost. "I need to find..."

"*Who?*" the cat asked intrigued, licking its paws once more before bedtime.

"I don't know," the ghost answered, hopelessly lost.

The young stray did not dare move as it watched the sad ghost walk away and dissolve into the forest's dense cloak of shadows.

Yanked out of a heavy sleep, Mateo opened his eyes and looked around the room. By now he was accustomed to the inconvenient wake up call of constant bird chatter in the mamey and the urgent rustling of banana leaves. It surprised him how a small town could produce so much noise—early, sharp noise. He could identify all the activity outside without even opening the window: a neighbor's calls to unresponsive children, somebody pushing a phlegmatic lawn mower, cars speeding—more like flying—down the narrow road, the alarmed clucking of hens for no apparent reason. "*What kind of place is this?*" Between the closed window slats he could already see slivers of daylight flooding the backyard. Like the white gardenias in his grandmother's garden that opened up to the early sun, the morning began to breathe too.

Mateo joined his grandfather at the breakfast table.

"Good morning, Buelo. Did you sleep okay?" Mateo saw Don Genaro smile and lift the cup's rim to his lips.

"Yes, but not for too long," Don Genaro answered.

Mateo was perplexed when his grandfather extended his arm and politely asked, "And who do I have the pleasure of talking with on this beautiful day?"

"It's me, Buelo. Remember me? I'm your grandson," he answered reassuringly. It saddened him to see his grandfather still smiling as if Mateo was the nicest stranger he had ever met.

"Do birds ever sleep in this town?" Mateo asked rhetorically, taking a bite of the pastry his grandmother had laid out for him. Strangely though, he realized there was indeed something missing from the morning scene, *"There's no sound of dogs."*

"It seems someone rounded up every animal in the middle of the night!" he added half-jokingly. Taking another big bite of the crusty pastry he felt the warm, gooey stuffing filled his tongue.

Don Genaro chuckled and almost spit out his coffee. "That's funny!"

Mateo looked at his grandfather in silence.

"She is coming, you know," he heard his grandfather say softly.

"Who?" Mateo asked, caught off guard.

"I know she'll be back. She promised me!"

Mateo realized his grandfather's moment of lucidity had been too brief to be true. Don Genaro's delusion alarmed him. *"What would it be like to be lost like that?"* His grandfather's mind seemed to wander through a dark, unknown galaxy.

He watched his grandfather and felt pity for him. The frail, sun-aged, shrinking old man sat against the frame of the window, silhouetted by the morning sun like a shadow puppet. Tiny specks of light filtered through the brim of his white straw hat and danced around his body with every slight movement of his head. Under the hat's crown, Don Genaro hid more than a shaded face. More than a protective accessory, the hat was now a wall from the rest of reality. Grief had softened his once lucid mind, along with his taste for life. Since then he took to dressing in gray from head to toe, that way removing all color from his existence, as if to create a neutral slate for a new beginning that never came. With every button and cuff of his shirt tightly fastened, Don Genaro attempted to shut down any external influence or incoming thought that would spark painful memories of what he had lost. Only the benign shadow of the hat softened the deep furrows on his face, conveniently hiding the deep shame of his tortured life. For a man who believed that his final departure from this world would not, should not, be preceded by that of his offspring, Minerva's death dealt him a blow from which he could not find the strength to recover. From that moment on, his reality began to retreat into the nebulous lagoons inside his mind.

Mateo studied with sadness the frame of this man, his grandfather. The same man who once had stood up against anything obstructing his determined path was now a shrunken ghost. He could not get used to the man's tired gaze searching the distance in vain, waiting but not knowing for whom, let alone why.

"Where's Buela?" Mateo called into the kitchen but got no response. Don Genaro was once again lost in thought. Before heading outside, Mateo took notice of his grandparent's house. His grandmother cleaned and polished it like it was a doll's house, with everything is in its proper place. Spread around the shelves throughout the room were a mix of colorful displays: a plaster figure of a female saint with attire and make up better suited for a Hollywood starlet than a martyr; the 3-D backlit portrait of a blinking Sacred Heart that never failed to make him jump a little every time he passed it; a clock framed in resin fairies and cherubs; plastic frogs; and ceramic yellow rose candlesticks. To the untrained eye, the display was a dysfunctional collection of objects, but Mateo knew firsthand that every single object on display was tended to and accounted for and, most of all, lovingly preserved by Doña Sol. Mateo could not avoid thinking *"this is so psychotic!"* but he still had to admit that, even in this disparate display, there was a certain sense of warmth, comfort, and continuity.

Mateo followed the busy sounds to find his grandmother in the backyard.

"Have you had your breakfast yet?" she asked. "I left it on the stove. Your favorite, guava turnovers."

"I just had some, thanks," he answered, still remembering the fragrant cloud of sweet-smelling, fresh-brewed coffee that had pulled him out of his sleep. Doña Sol seemed pleased with his answer and continued hanging the wet laundry, securing each piece with the wooden pins she pulled from the pockets of her apron.

Mateo examined the line of colorful garments extending along the wash-line from the side of the house across the small backyard. He watched as she picked up a soaking sheet from the foamy water of the tin washtub. For a brief moment, he was entranced by the water splashing against the floor and disappearing into widening circles. The contact of cold water against his bare legs made him jump.

Casting a glance around, he took a moment to admire the array of pots in his grandmother's garden: a broken terracotta pot filled with purple orchids, a rusted tin overflowing with thick ferns, a small plastic tub housing a healthy looking bougainvillea vine covered in the reddest flowers he'd ever seen. Red, pink, and white periwinkle and impatiens spilled out of a square cookie tin to the edge of the garden, creating a fanciful barricade. And then there were the sweet smelling geranium and roses, so colorful they brightened the whole garden. Undeniably, his grandmother possessed the greenest thumb in all Palo Verde!

"Can I help you?" he asked. Without waiting for her answer, he submerged his hands in the sudsy water and pulled out another sheet, gushing bubbling water onto the cement floor. The water splashed noisily onto the ground, creating transparent ripples that overflowed into the nearby patch of turf.

Still, Mateo's thoughts were somewhere else.

"Would you like to go to Minerva's workshop?" He was taken aback by Doña Sol's sudden invitation.

"How could you even ask that!" he thought but instead heard himself answer, "I don't think so. Not yet."

Without another word, he climbed into his tree house, to hide from everyone while ha waited for Sergio to show up. In the meantime, he entertained himself by spying on the neighbors, watching them go about their business secretly hoping to catch them in some crazy behavior. The woman down the road just kept sweeping her front steps for a long time, failing to do anything remotely mysterious. The man fixing his car never pulled out a hidden hi-tech communication device from under the hood, nor did a single engine plane drop a bag of stolen money. Boring! Mateo's patience was being tested. Without discovering a single adventure-worthy event, he resigned himself to watch his grandmother sweep the patio.

He had discovered the hardest part of being in Palo Verde was finding things to do. Finally venturing out of the tree house, he opened the chain-link gate that faced the desolate road, and stepped onto the bank of short grass that bordered the front fence. "There's nobody around!" he observed, looking to both ends of the road.

On impulse, he raced along the fence and up a small hill covered with grass. A shoelace from his sneaker came undone, entangled his foot, and sent him flying face-first down the hill where he landed with a heavy thud and a mouthful of grass. He was feeling around for his glasses when, out of nowhere, a shadow fell over him. Lifting his head, he discovered a pair of black, mud-covered boots standing inches away from his face. His eyes traveled up the sharp edge of the blade next to them, up to the face obscured by the wings of a straw hat. As he retracted his gaze back down the machete, he noticed its tip stuck in the ground. It was so close he could smell the clippings of fresh grass that stuck to its sharp blade. Surprisingly, he could even smell the long metallic dagger. The hunched-over man holding the knife did not say a word but just his presence made Mateo shudder.

Mortified and embarrassed, Mateo looked up but could not think of a single word of self-defense. But as it happened, he didn't even have the opportunity. Before he could regain his composure, Mateo heard the man's warning. "I've seen your friend with that little filthy dog and I will repeat to you what he already knows—I see that mutt around my property again and I will show him what I'm capable of."

Mateo was speechless. *"Trouble. This man is trouble,"* he thought, seeing nothingness in the man's eyes. Still lying on the ground, he watched the man walk away, slowly grinding his teeth and looking back like a resentful dog.

Mateo kept still, unsettled by the encounter. *"What is it about that man?"* he wondered, puzzled by his rudeness. It wasn't until later that it became clear to him. *"His eyes don't reflect the light!"* The observation made him shudder. From then on, he could not shake the memory of the man with eyes like deep puddles of dead water. The surprising encounter left him feeling numb. He looked across the street at the strange man's yard littered with rusty car parts and garbage. A sure sign of his contempt for not only the community but for himself. Still, Mateo could not keep his eyes off the man filing his machete on his front steps.

The unfortunate encounter with The Cruel Man left Mateo shaken to the core. This was without a doubt the man the whole town was afraid to let their animals near. *"He's stealing their animals... they disappear for good. Was it him? Or was it his son?"* Mateo understood then, The Cruel Man was the character everyone in town both feared and secretly despised.

"That's Severo. Stay away from him. That man has no heart!" His grandmother's warning still rang in his ears.

"Severo!" Even his name, *severe,* hinted at the depth of his damaged soul.

> Watch the falling raindrops, singing as they fall,
> and like ballerinas spinning on their tippy toes,
> falling over the flowers and the oleander,
> and like ballerinas spinning, start to dance again.

Mateo could not believe his eyes the first time he noticed the unusual black bird. He had followed it to a raucous gathering of grackles and watched how, with a coordinated flourish, the flock cawed and screamed along the power lines, claiming their positions with energized musical shouts. Among them, the one that

caught his attention was a magnificent specimen.

"Is that a raven?" Mateo wondered out loud.

"No, that's a *garrapatero*," Doña Sol offered, noticing Mateo's intense stare. Unlike the rest of its chatty companions, the bird held its own, plumping up its feathers and calling out—almost singing—with a deliberate casualness, as if thoroughly aware of its beauty.

Ah-nee, Ah-nee, Ah-nee...

There was something else of extraordinary rarity in the bird. As the black beauty slid across the swinging power line, the light of the sun sparked iridescent tones of blue in its plumage. Its most amazing feature was its curved beak that made it look like a parrot covered in lustrous tar. Mateo was not quite sure whether he had seen one before but was quite convinced that if he had, it would have been almost impossible to forget the unusually long three feathers in its tail. Of the three, one stood out for its singular beauty. Unlike the perfect symmetry and regal elegance of a peacock's tail, this single boisterous feather shimmered under the glare of the sun like a rainbow over Iguazú Falls. The three feathers were so extraordinary that an image struck him, *"Like a black quetzal!"* He was now convinced the dazzling bird was staring right at him. Even at a distance, he could detect the intelligent sparkle in its smart, darting eyes.

Through a frame of tall banana trees that flanked the edge of the house, Mateo marveled at the sky's gray hues—much like the cast of aged silver—and was surprised at how quickly the day changed colors. A sudden wave of hot air intensified the humidity in the atmosphere as a mass of storm clouds swept across the sky. The pungent petrichor—the warm, comforting smell of the earth just before rain begins to fall—penetrated his nostrils.

As the wind cleared a small opening in the foliage, Mateo watched the rain clouds hanging low over the canopy of the slim yagrumo trees. The wind, charged with humidity, furiously beat their leaves into an agitated dance, showing off their contrasting green and silver faces. A sudden whip of lightning created a filigree of energy that lashed out into the atmosphere and rushed downwards, seeking host in the ground. The day abruptly changed colors and, without warning, claps of thunder pushed open the gates of the sky. Within seconds, rain poured over every tree, rooftop, and road, sopping up every inch of the red soil.

The sun shied away as the rain drummed on plantain, orange, and banana trees. The splash of raindrops mixed with loud flapping leaves, creating an elaborate, organic symphony. As huge thunderclouds unleashed the inevitable deluge, the neighborhood ran for cover.

Life in Palo Verde came to a screeching halt. Even animals looked helpless as they sought shelter under steps and porches. Mateo enjoyed the sound of the falling rain over the open field and observed with curiosity and humor how people glared from behind their windows as if the rain had unleashed a cruel and personal attack.

"It rains like this all the time, without much warning. Comes out of nowhere!" Doña Sol held a handful of clothespins, resigned to the forced delay of drying her laundry, now hanging from the clothesline like soggy, empty balloons.

For a suspended moment, the beautiful spectacle of wet and sparkling greenery renewed the day. The sharp sound of falling rain brought a welcome respite from the constant flow of noise and hustle. Mateo watched the rain coming down as if he had been given a new chance to rethink the day ahead. *A new beginning, maybe,* he wished.

Sadly, even the rain carried memories. He had learned to love rainy days after he began spending his summer vacations at his grandparent's home. Where the frequent summer showers bounced off the red tin roof, converting the modest house, into a music box on stilts. The rain also made him remember how, when he was just three years old, Minerva's games helped him forget the frightening blasts of thunder...

"Boom, Titi, boom!"
"What's the matter Mateo, are you afraid of thunder?"
"Boom!"
"Don't be. That's the sky's way of crying."
"Don't like it, scary."
"C'mon on, let's play a game." Minerva tried to soothe the three-year-old boy.
"Yes, yes, a game!"
"Let's hide here under the table. Let's pretend this is a cave and we are bears!"
"Bears!"
"Yes, and we are inside the cave and it's raining. But we are sad bears. You know why?"
"No, why?"
"We are sad bears because we can't go out to play. So we'll hide here and wait for

the clouds to go by! You like that?"
"Yes!"
"Let's sing the rain song now.
'Watch the falling raindrops, singing as they fall,
and like ballerinas spinning on their tippy toes,
falling over the flowers and the oleander,
and like ballerinas spinning, start to dance again.'"

* * *

"Why can't I go to school anymore?" Even at the fragile age of fourteen, Minerva's world began to crumble. She could not bear the anger and disappointment reflected in her father's eyes.

Her mother, on the other hand, stood silently, leaning against the wall looking hopeless, as if someone had told her the end of the world had arrived. "How could you?" Minerva heard her say lifelessly.

Minerva went back to the only place where she could think clearly: through the thick wall of trees, down the dirt path, across the grass field to the hidden place in the forest where she could get away from everything and find serenity. She gathered her dress around her as she stepped into the current. The cold water and the smooth stones under her feet made her forget her troubles. Following the water's flow, she listened to the songs of the mockingbirds and bananaquits hidden among the branches. Not too far away, a goose and gander emerged from the river and flapped their wings vigorously like feathered angels, contented and refreshed after their intimate cleansing ritual. Minerva watched with delight as the gander, fresh out of the water, followed its mate dispensing guttural honks accompanied by a menacing flapping of wings—a clear warning to potential rivals to stay away.

Minerva waded down the river and let the current guide her. Her eyes followed the interlaced awning of trees: guava berry, pomarrosa, yagrumo, coffee. In the folds of her skirt, she gathered handfuls of the red wild berries and coleus that bordered the river's edge. She paused by a clearing where the sunlight descended in slanted, unfiltered columns and illuminated the flat stones sitting at the bottom of the water. A fallen tree trunk upholstered in velvety moss bridged the river's banks; the very same hollow trunk over which she had tread gingerly many times before. Her eyes took in the narrow waterway and the pale fragments of light that shifted and danced over its current: this was Minerva's secret place, the forest, the river, where she felt everything was right with the world. At the age of 14, the forest was Minerva's intimate retreat, where everything was forgotten, where she always found her center. Now she had come to the same spot to nurture yet another worry, *"What will happen to me?"*

* * *

There's nothing like the aftermath of a furious downpour to stir up the island and make it come to life. The sweltering heat melted away the morning. Mateo felt he needed to get away, to escape. Clouds had scurried off but he still could hear the confused crickets chirping their song. Soon, all that remained was the soaked earth and the sweet smell of blossoms stirred by the rain. Translucent beads of water wobbled down huge elephant ear leaves and disappeared into the grass. A thin shroud of fog drifted casually among the trees and waves of humid air made the pitirres sing with relief. The late morning air was filled again with the sounds of blaring radios. A speeding pickup truck with giant loudspeakers advertised a chaotic mismatch of local supermarket specials and social events to take place in the town's square. But its messages were distorted beyond recognition by the deafening beat of salsa music. Like a sudden flash, Mateo remembered the bright light in the forest the night before and decided to make his way through the brush and tall grass down to the river. *"I wonder if it's still there?"*

Mateo's eyes followed the narrow lane down the hill. It had been partially erased by a thicket of shrubs but he could still make out the red dirt footpath, the same path he and Minerva had created with their constant outings to the forest. "The forest with the yellow butterflies!" as she loved to say. He remembered running after her. "C'mon, Mateo, we haven't got all day!" He still could hear her laughter as she ran barefoot, carrying a small net and her drawing pad. With the other hand, she held his arm tightly as he struggled to keep up with her...

The little dirt path, now forgotten, had been invaded by milkweed bushes and lantana. Still, he could see it faintly snaking its way down the grassy hill. He stopped for a moment and took in the beautiful greenery of the forest ahead. *"The illuminated forest!"* he remembered and from his pocket pulled out a small circular crystal hanging from twine and lifted it up to the sky. A fleeting ray of light hit its surface and the crystal glimmered like the sun. *Mateo's Magic Crystal.* As he took in the magnificent view of the forest and the surrounding hills, something suddenly made him change his mind. *"This is not a good idea."*

Retracing his steps, Mateo ran back up the hill, without taking a breath. Dangerous memories were like emotional land mines. "This is not a good idea," he kept repeating.

Deep in the farthest corner of the forest, the ghost was restless. From behind the coffee trees it searched the distance, looking for a clue. "I haven't got much time." But there was only so much the ghost could do.

Soon enough it had discovered it could only travel in shadows. A ghost cannot travel in the plain light of day at will. But it was of no comfort to learn that shadows, even the ones that grew large at the feet of the mighty ceiba, only went so far. So the ghost walked around the forest helplessly. "I haven't got much time."

In a voice only birds, animals, and a ghost could understand, the trees asked, "How can we help?" But the ghost had no answer. It wandered aimlessly, hoping to find its way by chance. "But to where?" Adding to its confusion, it could not remember how or why it had found itself in the middle of this unfamiliar place.

"Don't you remember?" the orange tree asked but the ghost just looked off into the distance, unsure of its purpose, not knowing what to do. There was something the ghost remembered, a clue even, "I hear the cries," and the memory made the ghost sad. There is nothing more unsettling for a ghost than to be able to roam the world again but not know it anymore. "Is it a boy? An old man?" but the ghost was not sure.

A sudden spark of light rushed through the leaves across the forest among the guava trees and angel's trumpet and bounced off the back of the river. *"Lightning?"* The ghost looked up to the clouds. *"What was that?"* But no, there was something else. Once again the blast of light penetrated the thickness of the treetops. Climbing on top of the boulder, the ghost searched in the distance. "Something familiar!" And just then it saw the figure of a boy holding a crystal up to the sun.

The shining light in the distance made the ghost tremble. There was definitely something familiar about the boy. Sitting on the moss covered boulder by the river, it could not take its gaze off of him, the boy holding a crystal up to the sun, the boy with fire in his hands.

The orange tree sensed the ghost's sadness, so it tried to soothe its hopelessness. "You'll find the way." It watched the ghost sit on a big stone and stare beyond the river's bank. "If I could only—" the ghost wished. But it was impossible; ghosts cannot walk over water. And with that, it retreated within the shadows of the majestic ceiba.

Try as he might, Mateo wasn't able to resist visiting the place where many of his early memories still lived. The bigger his reservations, the stronger his desire to run down the hill and into the forest. There was no way of avoiding it; he felt as if the tight cluster of trees were calling out to him. *"The illuminated forest!"* With tentative steps, he began to widen the path, following sleeping memories down the same narrow way that neglect and forgetfulness had turned into unfamiliar territory.

Overwhelmed by the strong smell of rotting leaves, he was not happy to discover his shoes were already soiled by wet mulch. Even with careful steps, he became aware of the magnified crunch of rotten leaves and dry twigs that snapped under his weight. He wandered around, trying to adjust to the sudden loss of sunlight. The eerie darkness and chilly air made him shiver. The thought of the magical star shower from the night before crossed his mind. Its bright glare still burned vividly in his memory. He scanned the ground where he was certain it had landed, searching for any remaining signs, *"But where?"*

Mateo found a corner where he could sit and sort out his thoughts. In the safety of the woods, he could breathe easier. Looking around, he realized he recognized this quiet spot. Minerva's playground, her temple of inspiration, was now overtaken by brambles, weeds, and wild vines.

The forest was the secret place where she had impressed him with her improvised picnics, *"White rice cooked in a can over a small fire!"* Mateo fondly remembered the bland, undercooked rice, *"The best rice I've ever tasted!"* Minerva had offered him ripe yellow guavas and perfumed pomarrosas for dessert. "Everything seemed so big back then," he mourned. He looked around, as if trying to bring her back with his thoughts. Only the old trees stirred and hummed. He felt secure there in the same old forest, the place where crickets sang in the middle of the day and the only loud sounds came from the mockingbirds and the flowing river.

Without another thought, he stepped barefoot into the gentle creek and curled his toes as the cold, crisp water squeezed through them. The river, that many years before seemed so powerful, now felt gentle. Looking down at his feet through the water, he could see the trees gazing at themselves in the current. The sunlight filtered through the branches and landed on the moving water, making it sparkle and dance. The river was the singing heart of the forest.

"There it is!" To his surprise, he discovered the same moss covered boulder that had overlooked the passing river where Minerva used to sit and sketch for hours. Like opening a scrapbook, he marveled at the familiar view. This gem in the river's crown, the biggest rock, the majestic boulder that jutted from the riverbed like a launching pad. The place where she bent her knees, stretched her arms behind her back, and jumped into the air in a graceful arc, as if she had been shot out of a cannon. He remembered how with the tips of her fingers she shattered the plate of water into big rings and after a resounding sssspppppllllaaaaaaaasssssshhhhhhhhh! disappeared under the current. Mateo held his breath until he saw her emerge laughing on the other side of the river.

Like rummaging through a forgotten trunk, everything around him was becoming familiar again. *"The orange tree!"* Mateo touched its bark, now covered with white fungus. The tree Minerva had been proud of saving from certain extinction. The cozy place where he had been entertained listening to her tall tales of constant run-ins with anyone who attempted to curb her impulses. Mateo pulled a folded piece of paper out of his pocket. *"She's so funny,"* he thought. He ran his fingers around Minerva's image. The stern look on her face, her short wind-swept hair, and her dress flying wildly around her, brought back memories of the stories that had made him roll on the floor with laughter...

"...When they pulled me out of school I was so furious, I snuck my mother's sewing scissors into my room and chopped all my hair off!" Mateo watched her spin her tale, amused by her defiant swagger.

"What did Grandma do?" the boy asked, hoping for a dramatic twist.

"Well, she said, 'You demon child! What have you done now?' And she ran after me, but luckily I was faster. I hid at Doña Victoria's house until she forgot about it," Minerva answered with a sparkle in her eye.

"Did she forget about it?" Mateo asked.

"No, she ran after me with her broom. For three days, I was too afraid to get close to her!"

Mateo laughed until his stomach hurt.

"Aunt Meva, why did grandpa take you out of school?" he asked unexpectedly. He regretted the question the moment he saw Minerva hide her face away from his gaze, as if she was suddenly ashamed. He could see the glimmer of tears in her eyes. Pulling herself together, Minerva took pleasure in Mateo's laughter and regaled him with her most bizarre story yet...

"The way I remember it, it was 1963 and I was 13 years old. I was not allowed to go to the movies to see *Cleopatra* because Mother said Eleesabet Tailer was a slut and a hussy with pretty eyes. But I got it inside my head I was going to find a way. All I could think of was how beautiful she looked on the poster in Maruca's house of cinema.

"So one Saturday afternoon, Arcadio, Maruca's son, was in charge of selling the tickets and I knew he was not going to let me go through the front door, so I figured out a way to sneak in. I told him his mother had been mugged in front of the panaderia and he screamed, 'Oh my God!' and before he ran to the bakery, I said to him, 'You better hurry up because she was banged up pretty good,' and I told him not to worry, I would gather the tickets, and be responsible for everything and he was so grateful. I watched him run up the street and turn the corner, then I went in and served me a big heap of popcorn and went to find a seat.

"But there was this little girl there, Margarita, who was so dirt poor, her single mother could hardly ever afford to feed her family, let alone take them to the movies. And Margarita was staring at my popcorn like she had never seen popcorn before, so I offered her a handful and I said, 'Go get your brothers and sisters; the movies are free today, so hurry!' And I swear, that was the happiest I've seen Margarita, and in a matter of minutes she got her sisters and brothers, nine in all. But then she begged me that even though she was grateful for my kindness, she would feel very guilty leaving behind her cousins and friends. So right behind them, before I had a chance to respond, a throng of cantankerous, happy children invaded the theatre while I could only step aside and watch them race down the aisles like wild ponies! So we all watched a really big chunk of the movie before Arcadio and Maruca came through the doors screaming bloody murder! So me and Margarita and her brothers and sisters ran out screaming in the street like rats in the light of day, and Arcadio was egging Toño to arrest us, like he was the town's policeman, when in reality Toño was only the watchman at the elementary school. The ruckus was so big that to this day many people who never saw *Cleopatra* thought it was a horror movie."

Minerva went on, "Well, the real story is, when I saw Eleesabet Tailer come onto the screen, I almost fell off my seat. OH, MY GOD! I couldn't believe the color of her eyes, I was beside myself. I remember when I told my friends at school, Martina, the classroom know-it-all and official bitch, said to me just to get under my skin, 'Oh, I thought you were in jail. Tell me, is it true that you had no toilet in your cell?' So I screamed back at her, 'I WAS NEVER IN JAIL!' So she said,

'Whatever! Anyway, that color is named *violet* and if you want to have eyes that color, it's very simple, you just put mashed-up grape compresses over your eyes for two or three days. The longer you keep them, the more intense the color will be. And then the acidity will turn the color of your eyes into violet.'

" 'How do you know that?' I asked her with suspicion.

" 'I take super-advanced chemistry!' she smirked at me. 'If you would come to classes more often, you would know that. That's public knowledge!'

"I was so excited to discover the secret to violet eyes that I forgave her smart crack and I almost forgot to ask her if this color change was so easy, how come I had never heard of it before? And she answered before walking away, 'Privileged information.'

"So I begged my mother to please, please, please, get me two pounds of grapes; the more purple, the better, which totally befuddled her because she knew I hated grapes.

"So it happened that after two days of compresses, my eyes got a nasty infection but I told mother that Martina had said it was part of the process. So they took me to the emergency room and Dr. Arias was so horrified. He said it was the grossest thing he'd ever seen. I was so scared, I asked him when the color of my eyes would change to violet. And he answered, 'Maybe when you're seventy and they are covered in cataracts; that is, if you don't become blind first.'

"I cried so hard, I couldn't even hear my father and mother laughing their heads off. After that, when I went back to school, everybody called me Eleesabet Toilet.

"And for more than a month, Martina, that bitch, was hiding from me when my friends told her I was carrying a razor in my socks, and when I caught her, the least I would do to her was to stuff that ratty messed-up wig of hers in her mouth. And the only good thing that would come out of this was when they finally found her begging for change on the side of the road with the word 'bitch' spray painted on her forehead! But lucky for her, the only thing I did when I finally cornered her in the lunch room was to yank her hair so hard I ended up with a handful and she ended up with a bald spot that I think she still has to this day!"

Mateo fell to the ground roaring with laughter so hard he felt something warm wet the front of his pants…

Maruca's Curse

What Minerva never disclosed, and Mateo did not find out until much later, was that Maruca's house of cinema was just an elegant euphemism for a place of cheap school supplies and low brow movies which, due to her stringent budget, were only pirated copies of questionable quality. The cinema was not just the only place of its kind in town but for many miles around. If the patrons were not too hung up about outdated showings and willing to share the sticky floor with the rats that nested inside the speakers, then they were sure to have a good time.

Maruca's enthusiasm was greater than her resources, so in the spirit of good customer service, she occasionally inquired among her clientele which movies they would like for her to bring. Once she got an interesting suggestion, she would make a note of it on her Wish List for future reference.

"Doña Maruca, can you bring Bonnie and Clyde?"

"I'll see what I can do," she would reply.

"Maruca, can you bring something with songs in it? I would be much obliged."

"I'll make a note of it and put it on my list right now."

"Hey, Maruca, what about the Lawrence of Arabia one?"

"Absolutely, that one's top on my list!" she exclaimed with shared enthusiasm.

"Maruca, would it kill you to bring something lively... something, let's say, for the men's delightment? You know, something sexy."

"Umm, eeep, huuummm—" Maruca tried to disguise her secret disgust at the offending request. "That's something I'll have to discuss in counsel." Which simply meant she would never, ever dare cross the line that would put her in the crosshairs of the town's real authority: Father Emeterio, the ancient and nearly blind priest.

It didn't take long for the townspeople to catch on to her. Her establishment soon became the butt of a running joke once they figured out she had no plausible means of getting the movies they wanted to watch. "If there's a movie in the world you wanna see, it won't be showing in Maruca's movie house of rats!"

Of all the movies requested, the one that scared the bejesus out of her the most was Rosemary's Baby, due to the highly sacrilegious and blasphemous nature of the film and her irreconcilably strict Catholic upbringing. The thought of featuring the incarnation of Satan (even as a baby) in her respectable place gave her nightmarish chills. Besides, she did not look forward to having to defend such a questionable choice to Father Emeterio, whose chapel was right across the street. She could predict with certainty that he would insist on a novena beforehand and an exorcism afterwards to clean out the place, if not try to shut her down completely.

As accommodating as Maruca was willing to be, being excommunicated and sentenced to eternal damnation for corrupting the town's morality and decency was not worth the risk. After all, she had to consider her prestigious standing in the congregation as a member of the Hijas de Maria sorority.

Still, to most of the town's population, Maruca's legendary entrepreneurial audacity was itself a rich source of entertainment. More than a few times, her well-intended choices had backfired. Among them was the time she promised her fans more wholesome movie choices that would enrich the town's cultural side. So it was that, without seeing the feature in advance, she sang the praises of a movie that would carry a positive message to the local children about the blessings of good education. It was a win-win formula to show a feature film with a strong civic mission. In her words, it was 'a worthy movie that would inspire the town's children to excel and achieve the high school diploma they so desperately need to succeed in life!' She was so convincing, the town turned out in droves to experience this uplifting film, *The Graduate*.

Unfortunately, and way too late to correct the situation, she had learned to her dismay that due to her ignorance of English, she missed the message in the discarded letter specifically containing a stern warning about the movie...

Dear Mrs. Maruca Montes,

WHAT PARENTS NEED TO KNOW is that this unique picture charts the affair between a young man and a much older, alcoholic, married woman who is a friend of his parents. Much time is spent on the boy's initial seduction and the subsequent clandestine sexual meetings in hotel rooms. There are brief shots of female nudity during the seduction and later, in a cabaret, a dancer strips down to her panties and pasties. Although the language is fairly restrained, it contains the words "ass" and "damn." Many of the adults are shown drinking alcohol and smoking cigarettes very casually and with an air of decadence. Please include in all marketing materials that this movie is not appropriate for children.

Sincerely,
The Management at MetroPlex Entertainment Imports

For the next few days after the showing, Maruca laid low in her house atop her school supply store/cinema, ignoring the loud banging at her door from outraged parents asking for her head. Once again, Maruca was accused of arousing the secret passions of highly hormonal adolescent boys. She refused to acknowledge that her "educational" film was nothing more than a flimsy excuse for the blatant seduction of a young man by a sexually crazed middle-aged woman, filmed in beautiful Technicolor.

But Maruca was not about to be kept down by the town's harsh critics, and so she tried to rehabilitate her image. To her credit, she managed to swallow her prejudices for the sake of entertaining her small but devoted audience and got her hands on a worn-out copy of Cleopatra. She was a fan of all things Egyptian, especially the beguiling history of its crafty queen, but she realized too late that yet again she was responsible for arousing the male population with the ravishing beauty and magnetism of the movie's star.

It wasn't long before Father Emeterio, tired of Maruca's irresponsible movie choices, used his pulpit to condemn such sinful displays of unnecessary sexuality. "Bosoms are for nurturing," he proclaimed red-faced in his impassioned Sunday sermon. "They are not to be gawked at, lusted after, or held as the object of unbridled desire despite their girth and size," he continued to scold, only to witness their adverse reaction, and watch half his congregation get up from their pews and stampede across the street to Maruca's cinema where ticket sales soon reached an historic high.

Maruca could barely conceal her glee but played down her success so as not to ruffle any feathers. Secretly, she was more than grateful for Father Emeterio's unintended but ringing endorsement of the movie. After a profitable trip to the town's only bank, she thought it prudent to veil her true feelings, so quite disingenuously she issued a mea culpa for single-handedly unleashing onto the town's consciousness that she-devil, husband-stealer, pointy-titted hussy in elaborate wigs, mzzz Elizabeth Taylor.

After that, without any logical reason, Maruca was perceived as the town's cultural pervert. For a woman of devotion who was dedicated to educating and bettering the lives of others, it was quite ironic that he she was painted to be a sort of ignorant sex peddler. It became a thorn in her side to learn that, behind her back, some townspeople referred to her as "that sex-crazed old woman" who got cheap thrills at the expense of their religious community.

But even a spotty history of misses and backfires could not stop Maruca's fate. Things changed in her favor the moment she decided to bring a pop singer to town whose star had begun to rise. Booking Miss Lucinda was quite a feat. Her fee was on the cheap side due to her fresh notoriety, but Maruca also knew the young singer would bring to town the throngs of new adoring fans who had catapulted her from a grainy midday TV show to heavy rotation on the most listened-to radio station on the island. A huge star in the making, Lucinda was not only building up her reputation as a difficult diva, but was also quite clearly destined to sing her way up the charts that her male counterparts had dominated for decades. So bright was her star that she even managed to obscure from the island's musical panorama (although only briefly) a new sensation: a British act of four young faces that the town referred to as "those long-haired sissies and hippies!" but who were better known throughout the world as The Beatles.

"Lucinda is coming to Maruca's! Can you believe it?" The news spread so fast that Maruca didn't even have to invest in any paid publicity.

With this uncharacteristically smart move, she managed to clean up her sordid reputation as the town's pervert to the more respectable and less corrosive image of a promoter. The town's enthusiasm for the young singer was so intense that it became the single most memorable event in its history, causing a legendary traffic jam that paralyzed the only street in and out of Palo Verde and extended into the next town. From that day, most of the community agreed that Maruca had single-handedly dragged Palo Verde into the 20th century.

The local press lapped it up, giving Maruca a surge in popularity that could have catapulted her into super-agent status, but she lost her resolve the moment the young singer, crippled by stage fright, refused to set foot on stage, instead requesting an extra dinner and entertaining herself by throwing spitballs at unsuspecting passersby from the balcony of her second-floor suite.

"I'm too old for this shit!" Maruca recounted later on. The day Maruca stopped traffic was, nevertheless, the single event in the town's history that woke it up from its complacency and put it on the map. Soon after, Maruca resumed her duties selling school supplies and bringing movies nobody wanted to see. Maruca's House of Movies: where the movies are dated and the rats eat like family...

Mateo wallowed in the warmth of the memory. For a brief moment, he felt the burden of the present lift off his shoulders. He took solace in the thought, *"What matters is she'll always be with me, here or anywhere I go."*

But sadly, not all the memories pleased him and he felt as if a knife had gone through his chest. *"How could they lie to me?"* His sense of betrayal was even more painful. Mateo wished he could do it all over again, sit here soaking his feet in the river's waters, listening to her tall tales, laughing and eating guavas and pomarrosas. He let his mind wander with the rhythmic, soothing sounds around him. Good dreams always come to an end.

"Mateo!"

He was pulled out of his trance by a voice in the distance. *Or was it the trees?*

"Mateo!" He heard the call again. He lifted the green crystal out of his shirt pocket and rubbed its smooth surface with his thumb. After staring at it for a moment, he watched as the sun filtered through the leaves and made the crystal scatter bright, colorful rays of light that pierced the sleepy darkness of the forest.

The flying sparks of the crystal woke the ghost up from its dream. "Who is it?" Walking among the shadows, it discovered the boy standing on the boulder. *"Something about him…The fire in his hands!"* Peeking from behind the angel's trumpet, the ghost watched as the boy waded into the water. From its shadowy place, the ghost followed the boy's steps as he wandered among the trees and into the river as if he too was looking for something. It watched with curiosity as the boy jumped into the water, splashing and diving to the bottom of the river and back.

"Who is he?" the ghost asked no one in particular.

Not far away, the young stray was also watching this new tall figure approaching in the distance. *"Biganimal?"* it considered. It was clear to the cat that it had to be careful not to become the target of another possible attack. *"Don't like it."* The cat stretched its neck, and watched with concern as *Biganimal* got too close to its bed. The stray whipped its tail around and tried to decide if the tall figure was safe. But the cat sensed something about the moving figure, something familiar, very familiar indeed. *"Biganimal, sad."*

So the young stray crouched in its nook and quietly watched the sad tall figure turn back and make its way slowly along the narrow red dirt path as if carrying a heavy load on its shoulders, up the hill overtaken by tall grass, milkweed, and lantana.

If the forest could talk it would have told the boy that under the same tree a hungry stray in great need had carved out a spot to sleep and feel safe; that as he mourned the death of his beloved Minerva, somewhere in its beating heart there was a young stray—a kitten really—that mourned the loss of its family too. Right under the orange tree's branches, it shivered and whimpered from loneliness. If only the trees could talk, they would have told him to go find it at once. "He's heartbroken too."

They would have told him that there was a lost ghost—searching, not knowing how to find its way—that needed to say its piece and move on. The trees would have told the boy about the ghost that sat every night staring at the moon, reassuring the young stray, "You'll be loved again." But trees can only bear witness, offer comfort and intimacy with its shade, and listen.

As the day dwindled slowly into thick pools of shadows, the young stray couldn't forget the tall figure sitting by the river, the same tall figure that had wandered around the forest as if it was looking for a place to hide too. The stray understood very well. It knew the world beyond the walls of the forest was a very sad place. Still, it could not help but be curious.

"*Sad, Biganimal!*" The cat remembered the quiet figure, sitting under the ceiba. It was then the stray heard the ghost's words of warning, "Careful, little one!"

But the stray did not want to listen anymore and made its way up the narrow foot path hidden by the brush. It spotted the bright light at the top of the hill. Sitting on its hind legs and stretching its neck in the direction of the house, the cat followed the tall figure's trail. Finding its way through the garden, the cat's green eyes shone like two emeralds in the dark. It could hear soft voices coming from the house. Taking up a spot under a bed of begonias, the cat looked up at the house where warm light poured from between the window slats into the garden. The welcoming glow of the house made the cat feel more alone than ever.

Once again it mourned its lost family. "*Are you there?*" the stray called into the house, as loud as it could. Lifting its nose to the night air, it tried to find the smell of the tall figure, "*Are you there?*" the cat called out again, remembering the young girl, the one that had loved it for a short time. "*Kindanimal,*" as it used to know her. "*Where are you?*" the cat repeated. It cried for the love and the life that now was gone.

From his bedroom, Mateo heard the sad meows of a cat. "*Must be a stray,*" he thought, adjusting his glasses. He went back to his book, trying to ignore the pain in the cat's cries.

Like a regal queen, the full moon sat among the stars and looked down upon the crown of trees stretching their arms across the landscape. Velvety shadows flew alongside birds retiring for the night, as a sharp wave of cricket and cicada song

washed over the darkened fields.

Sitting by the orange tree, the ghost and the young stray looked up to the moon, too big to fit in their eyes. The young cat yawned and stretched and flexed its paws before settling on its bed of leaves. The ghost sat nearby. "I haven't got much time," it said wistfully. As the moon navigated among the branches above, the stray and ghost remained still, watching fireflies bob around, weaving their threads of light in the darkness. There was only one thought in the ghost's memory. Looking beyond the dark curtain of shrubs, it wondered about the burning light in the boy's hands. There was something familiar about the sparkle that made the ghost tremble. "But I can't remember." And the uncertainty made it sad. Once again the ghost's eyes got lost in the starry sky, "where I came from." Still, it could not forget the glare of the stone. "The fire in the boy's hand! What does it mean?"

Like a warm breeze, the ghost's voice woke up the cat.

"How did you end up here?" The ghost wondered about the cat's journey.

The stray sighed and batted its eyes. "*I was loved,*" began the stray, its head nestled on its paws, "*then, all alone.*"

The ghost sensed the young stray's heartbreak. "But you're here now!" it said reassuringly. "You'll be happy again, I promise. You still remember good times, don't you?"

"*I do,*" answered the stray, now sitting up on its hind legs, scratching the side of its head. "*Yes, I do.*"

The ghost and the cat fell silent. As the purring cat settled back down on its bed of leaves, the ghost let it be. It watched the stray's tummy sink with every breath. "*Poor little thing!*" It broke the ghost's heart to see how, in its fitful sleep, the young cat opened and tightened its claws, kneading for its mother's milk. Its round pink nose wiggled as it made soft, suckling sounds. In its dream, the warmth of its mother was all around, making the young cat feel secure, loved again.

"It is safe here! Away from cruelty. Safe in this forest." The ghost then sang to the stray so it could dream and be as happy as it used to be. The cat's purr made the ghost smile.

Above them, the orange tree listened just as it had many years before to the made-up songs of a little barefoot girl dressing her hair with its white blossoms. As it remembered her quiet songs, the tree shimmered as if made of glass, luminous under the light of the queen moon. Illuminated.

Rock-a-bye, rock-a-bye,
Rock-a-bye matted in cobwebs,
I can see, there it goes
Early light over the mountains.

Go to sleep, go to dream
Let yourself fly over palm trees,
Sing a song, laugh out loud
Let the music heal your heartache.

Rock-a-bye, rock-a-bye
Rock-a-bye matted in cobwebs,
Night is long, go to dream
Let the moon shine on
Your heartache.

* * *

It didn't take long for Minerva's father to make up his mind. In his haste to protect his child from the storm that was about to come, he called his older daughter Maria. In a desperate move, Minerva's fate was decided for her, then and there. Before she had the opportunity to protest, she found herself in an unfamiliar, cold land. Feeling hopeless and confused, thousands of miles away from home, Minerva wondered, *"What am I going to do now?"*

In 1964, at age fourteen—with just a phone call from her father to her sister—Minerva found herself far away from the place she loved, away from home. Consumed with rage but powerless to fight back, she was banished from Palo Verde and transplanted to an unfamiliar land. "Where is the green of the mountains? The wind that shakes the trees and slides off the river's back? This place is not home," she complained.

Maria, in turn, looked through the smoky windowpanes of her apartment, out at the decades-old row of scruffy looking buildings ingrained with soot and neglect. She stared blankly at the patches of grass by the sidewalk partially covered in the remnants of a previous snow. But Maria had no answers. She ignored Minerva and concentrated on the pile of dishes resting under the soapy water. She looked over at the crib where Mateo had fallen asleep listening to the melodic rattle of the heater.

"You know why you are here, Minerva," she said, without cruelty. Meanwhile outside the window, the powdery snow began to fall again, gathering in sparkling mounds over the grass. Maria watched dispassionately as the thickening flakes diffused the light of the lamppost, as if it was enveloped with a gossamer veil. She felt the chill of the cold night wash over her body.

* * *

As the new morning began to rise, the stray was awakened by the sharp squawks of the egrets riding on the backs of cows. "*A new day!*" it thought as it stretched and arched, digging its claws deep in the orange tree's trunk. It decided to give the neighborhood another try. With bouncing steps, it followed the narrow dirt path up the hill to the house where the "*Sad Biganimal*" was hiding.

As it neared the road, the cat recognized the other house nearly hidden behind heaps of garbage. With a shudder it remembered its attacker but hunger left the stray no choice. It had to take the risk even if it meant another encounter. For a brief moment, as it calculated a new strategy, the cat sat by the edge of the empty lot across the road and swayed its tail from side to side. Lifting its nose and wriggling its whiskers, it sought the scent of food. "*Hungry.*" The stray felt the rumble in its tummy but before it decided to cross the road, it licked its paws one more time in preparation for another adventure.

Lick paw, lick paw, lick paw.
Lick paw, lick paw, lick paw.
Lick paw, lick paw, lick paw.

This time around, Severo was waiting. From his seat on the porch, he spotted the cat. Without taking his eyes off it, he put down the file and machete as quietly as possible. Severo held his breath; he was determined to teach the hapless cat a lesson. This time he was going to make sure it would never set its filthy paws in his yard again. "*Once and for all!*" he thought. Afraid that even his breathing would tip the cat off to his presence, he slowly turned around and got hold of the broom. As he watched the cat waiting to cross the street, Severo walked around the back of

the house. "I'll surprise him!" He was about to make good on his promise.

Meanwhile, Severo's son Billy had been watching through the window slats, wondering what his father was up to. Billy could not see the cat; he did not need to. Just by watching his father's body language he knew exactly what was about to happen. Billy felt his heart sink deep inside his stomach. "I can't watch this!" he thought with disgust and hurriedly shut the window.

Severo could see the cat in plain view as it hurriedly dug halfway inside the metal trash barrel. *"Damn stray!"* He bit his lip and grasped the broom handle with both hands. After deciding where and how to apply the blow most effectively, he lifted the broom high in the air just as he had done before. Once again the cat's cries of pain could be heard all over the neighborhood.

Even under a partly cloudy sky, the bright sunlight made Mateo squint. He tried to diffuse the glare bouncing off the pages of his book. A thin row of sweat began to moisten his brow. Even the shield of his hand over his forehead proved futile. The intense light made him lose focus as his pupils contracted. Still struggling against the glare with half-opened eyes, he could see white and red dots dancing inside his eyelids. He closed his book and decided to find a shady nook. His back was covered with sweat which made his loose T-shirt cling to his body.

"Grandpa, I need to find a cool spot." He excused himself and headed downstairs for the hammock.

"What a hot and muggy day!" Mateo surprised his grandmother as she pulled handfuls of weeds from the fringes of her garden.

"I think it's going to be like yesterday, a sunny morning and then a downpour." She was happy to see him out of his room. "Sudden showers are never a surprise here, especially in August when it's so hot," Doña Sol added. Mateo watched as his grandmother blotted the sweat from her forehead with her sleeve.

"What are you—?" But he didn't finish his thought, the question trailing off into space as he was suddenly interrupted by the distressing sounds of an animal in pain.

MEEEEEAAAAAOOO!!!

The stray animal trembled when it recognized the abuser who had beaten him before. *"It smells!"* The stench of alcohol lingered on the tip of the cat's nose and almost made it choke. The pungent odor of sweat traveled through the air. "*Stinkanimal!*" The one mean, scary creature who always chased it away with threats and screams.

"GOO AAWAAY! Yooou fiiillthyyy caaat!"

Before the stray realized it, the blow to its rib cage had whipped the breath from its lungs. Without even trying to defend itself, the stray ran away in a panic.

"*Stinkanimal, long stick. It hurt, it hurt!*" seemed to be the only thought that rushed through the cat's mind.

"Shooo, Goo awayyy!"

Still feeling the sting of the hit, the cat ran for its life away from the angry calls. It could still see, within the periphery of its vision, *Stinkanimal* waving a long stick.

"*What it means? What I did?*" the small stray wondered as it ventured, still confused, out into the road. Unfortunately, it was not out of harm's way yet. In its haste to escape, the cat failed to see the heavy car speeding its way. With a menacing roar and a smoking tail, the powerful creature suddenly appeared in the middle of the road, hurtling towards the cat.

SCREEEEECH! HOOOOONK!

The deafening shriek of brakes and the unnerving loud hooting of a horn made its skin crawl and its fur stand on end. Feeling ambushed, the stray had no time to think. Terrified, it took a huge leap across the street and landed in a muddy ditch.

MEEEEEAAAAAOOO!!!

"*Where I go, what I do? What happen?*" Clawing its way out of the muck, the cat ran to the safety of the empty lot nearby. Hunger and thirst still turned its stomach in painful knots. Panting from exhaustion, its only concern was finding a quiet place to stay away from trouble. "*No Stinkanimal now. Grass. Safe now.*"

Lick paw, lick paw, rub face.
Lick paw, lick paw, rub face.
Lick paw, lick paw, rub face.

"Dirty!" The cat bit between its claws and desperately tried to remove the red mud on its face with the circular motions of its paw. The repetitive, soothing routine helped calm it some. Tilting its head upwards, the cat sniffed the air. *"Stinkanimal gone,"* it finally sighed with relief.

Mateo froze in mid-sentence when he heard the cat's distressed meows from across the street. He was alarmed by the sound of agonizing screams mixed with loud curses and threats coming from the neighboring house.

"Shooo! Get away, daaamn yooouuu!"

Just then he saw the man clumsily swing a broomstick in the air as if dueling with an invisible knight. "Severo!" By the time Mateo's eyes located the man's target, all he could see was the end of a tail flashing across the street. He watched as the animal jumped into a ditch, barely escaping a screeching, swiveling car.

Speechless, he watched the frightened creature run into the empty lot next to his grandmother's house and sit on the red clay to catch its breath. He noticed the animal panting as if trying to regain its bearings. Mateo studied the cat as it groomed itself, desperately trying to restore what was left of its shredded dignity. From just a glimpse of the terrified animal, he suspected this was not an isolated event. He could tell the poor thing was exhausted and nearly starving.

His grandmother's voice pulled him out of his thoughts. "There goes Severo again, chasing away defenseless animals!" Doña Sol was unable to mask her disgust. It was not the first time she had been appalled by the neighbor's constant attacks. "No strays—dog or cat—are safe in his presence."

He could tell how upset his grandmother was by the way she smoothed the hair over her temples. "When is he going to learn to have some respect?" Her face became red with indignation.

"Buela, why is that man so mean?"

Doña Sol shook her head in disbelief. "Next time he comes around here, I'm gonna let him have it! For the life of me, I can't understand how he can be so cruel," she fumed. Mateo knew she was dead serious. Severo was running the inescapable risk of being caught in one of her withering tongue lashings.

"How can you be so vicious?!" Billy hated his father so much it made him bite the inside of his cheek. Even though his back was still burning with pain from the swelling, Billy resented his father's verbal abuse more than the lashes of his belt.

"You're worthless," his father had yelled at him with alcohol-soaked words.

"Who treats their own kid like this?" Billy screamed back in protest, only to set off a new round of beating. "Why did you hit that cat? What did it ever do to you?" Billy's eyes burned with fury.

"You're a failure!" his father answered back while still keeping at him.

Deep down, Billy wondered whether his father was right. He had nothing going for him, nothing at all. He was a failure at school. He was a failure at home. At 12, he had no idea what to do with himself. He thought hard and tried to pinpoint exactly when his life had began to unravel. "What have I done to deserve such treatment?" The only thing he ever wanted was to have his family back again. Billy had loved his mother but he understood why she couldn't stay in the poisonous air at home. More than his father's blows, his mother's sudden disappearance had hurt him the most.

All she left him was a message, a brief note to account for her abrupt but not surprising disappearance, "I'll come for you, I promise." Billy's eyes read the words over and over but as time passed with no news of her whereabouts, he felt betrayed. Billy had cried himself to sleep many nights. "She was supposed to care for me!"

When a neighbor had offered him a puppy out of compassion, Billy decided it was the best way to comfort his loneliness. He knew he was risking his father's rage but for once he was willing to assert himself. Surprisingly, Severo showed no emotion at the sight of the small animal and Billy for the first time in his life, felt relieved. *"Finally!"*

But the following morning the animal had vanished from the house, never to be seen again. Now Billy was afraid his father had found another victim, the unlucky animal that had set foot on his property. *"Poor cat!"* Billy could taste the venom inside his mouth. "You're an abuser! Why did you have to hit that cat?" His words had caused Severo to unleash his wrath unmercifully. But even his father's punishment could not erase the cat's cries of pain from his memory.

Across the street Mateo and Doña Sol heard an argument break out between Severo and his son.

"What has Billy done now?" Doña Sol wondered out loud.

Mateo could not get the image of the starving animal out of his head. He feared for its safety but as suddenly as the incident had occurred, the cat disappeared from view.

He tried to ignore the sudden flush of anger that made his face burn. *"Easy, Mateo,"* he thought, struggling to keep his rage in check and resumed his conversation with his grandmother, thinking the poor animal had at lest escaped its sad fate and gone on its way. Mateo tried to push the unsettling episode out of his mind but could not help feeling a shiver. There was no way to explain this feeling of a black cloud hanging over his head.

As much as he tried to ignore it, his anger finally boiled over. Before he could stop himself, he walked up to the chain link gate.

"HEY, YOU SHITHEAD!" Mateo screamed across the street, taking Severo by surprise. "Why don't you pick on somebody your own size? You loser!" His face burned with rage. Billy stood by his father, speechless.

"If I ever catch you—!" he threatened, just as Doña Sol came running after him.

"Mateo!" she called out. Alarmed, she saw the stones in the boy's hands.

"STOP RIGHT NOW!" She pulled him by his sleeve. "You're going to stop this nonsense right now, you hear me?"

"GET OFF ME!" Mateo snapped, fuming.

Even her warning could not stop him from hurling a rock at Severo's head, missing it by just inches. He was not ready to back down, even as Doña Sol struggled to defuse his menacing stance.

"Please, Mateo, come with me. You don't act like that with an adult." Doña Sol was puzzled by the boy's unusual behavior. *Perhaps my angry rant had set him off.* She promised herself to be more careful around him; his emotions were still running very high.

"You saw him! Why are you taking his side?' he snapped angrily at her. Doña Sol was shaken by the intense hatred in the boy's eyes.

The morning's incident sent Severo off on another abusive rant against Billy.

"What did I do?" Billy complained.

But Billy was not only his immediate outlet to quench his frustration, but he was also the easiest target for Severo's disciplinary techniques. "When I was growing up, my father would wrap a telephone cable around his hand to show me who was boss," he threatened his son, wearing his old scars as badges of honor. "That's how

I became a man! So it will help you to remember this!"

Severo knew a thing or two about rage; its proof stretched along the length of his back. He had embraced the legacy of his father, and his father's father before him. Rage plus Manhood equals Respect. Severo had tried his brand of hostility with humans, even on his own wife and son. Soon, he discovered that animals were an easier, more accessible target.

He grew up in Palo Verde and had never set foot outside the small town. His misery and alienation were evident to anyone that crossed his path. His face had become a tangible, visual symbol of his broken soul. It had happened one day during a game of craps. Severo watched his gambling buddy with increasing suspicion when, with one swipe of his hand, he lifted the dice and a handful of red clay dust. Blowing into his fist, he shook and rattled the dice before letting them hit the dirt and calling out his bet.

What happened next was the subject of legendary gossip. Brimming with the arrogance of youth and the artificial self-confidence only alcohol can create, Severo was consumed by greed. Offended by the other man's cheating ways, he took the opportunity to make his point. To Severo's misfortune, he miscalculated the resolve of his opponent.

"You are not a man of honor!" he challenged, and pushed his chest forward, his arms spread like the tail of a sad rooster. With that, a very fine line was crossed and improvised weapons were drawn. Before Severo could implement his strategy, his intended prey, with incredible precision, traced a bloody path down his face with the broken neck of a beer bottle.

Since then, his new face offered a clear glimpse into his dark side. He was fully aware of the town's callous comments, uttered contemptuously behind his back. But to the whole neighborhood, the awful nickname was a justified moniker of justice well served. From that fateful moment on, Severo's divided face served as a telling metaphor for his psychological makeup. One side reflected the wrathful disciplinarian and small town bully. The other side—though rarely visible—represented a serviceable, meek worker, socially invisible as long as alcohol wasn't running through his veins.

But alcohol was his lifeline. "I drink to forget!" Sadly, this wasn't a lie. The jagged scar that divided his face began around his hairline, ran down the middle of his left eye, through the lips, and curved around the jaw. A badly healed wound had defined him for life. Drunk in a corner of the small pub, his fingers followed the map carved on his face. The humiliating scar had hardened, frozen his face permanently in a misshapen mask. Since then, Severo carried a machete accessibly fastened to his belt. It was his weapon of choice for future targets, both real and imagined.

News of the young man's life-changing experience blew through Palo Verde faster than the wind over the sides of the mountains. Severo—hardly after the blood of the scarlet furrows down his face had coagulated on his lips—had been baptized as El Rajao, Broken-Face. To a man of lesser grit, the blow would have served as a wake-up call, a firm deterrent to future mischief. But Severo, far from learning a life lesson, unleashed his appetite for self-indulgence and recklessness, bearing his jagged, broken face as a warning. Soon enough he found a new target for his frustration and anger: defenseless animals, preferably strays. It was perfect, *"They won't fight back."*

The people of Palo Verde were soon onto him and kept their animals close by, as far away as possible from El Rajao. He noticed how the neighbors pulled their dogs closer at the sight of him. Others got nervous if they caught him staring for too long at their cats. "Keep your pets away from him," they warned each other. No animal was safe, not a single one. El Rajao seemed to read their thoughts...

Mateo bristled at the thought of the man across the street. Neither did he appreciate his grandmother's reprimand. "He had no right to hit an animal!" he repeated to her over and over, trying to make his point. He could not believe his grandmother's inaction, *her weakness,* when she too was visibly offended by Severo's act of cowardice.

"Mateo, you know better than to talk to an adult like that. Even if he's wrong, you have to conduct yourself with dignity."

Her comment made him feel even more enraged. "He does not deserve respect!" But he did not want to go on trying to explain himself to her anymore. "Fine!" he shot back, "What do you know about pain anyway?" The cruel comment left his lips, but much like unable to rein in horses escaping out of a gate, he could not take his words back. Frustrated, he climbed the ladder's steps up to the tree house, sulking and hoping he would never have to climb down, ever again!

Doña Sol watched him run off and hide away in his tree house. She was deeply hurt by her grandson's coldness but remembered the boy's painful path. *"If he only knew."* She not only knew about pain, hardship and loss but was familiar with dreams that were broken one by one as her life progressed. She'd had two beautiful girls, one as responsible as an old soul and the other as wild as the weeds that inhabited the fringes of her garden. She had worked shoulder to shoulder with her husband in the hard sun-beaten fields, harvesting yams, yucca, plantains, and tobacco.

There was never a chore too small, a job too hard. Sol learned early on to obey her husband's mandate. She had put aside the vanity of her young years and learned to rise early before the moon slid off the sky. God only knew how many mornings, with fingers numbed by the early cold, she had lit the wick of the kerosene lamp over her head and waited for its timid flame to wake-up (much like herself) and steady its nervous dance so she could tend to her babies before leaving for the field. What did Mateo know about the countless mornings when she had exhaled small clouds of condensed air in the stinging cold of the pre-dawn fog walking through solitary fields? What about the long days of back breaking work she endured under the scorching sun, working side by side with the rest of the pickers? Meanwhile nearby, her babies giggled, nestled in straw baskets normally used for storing the fresh-picked tobacco leaves when coffee was out of season.

As time passed, she watched her precious daughters grow up, but one of them took an unexpected path. Mateo was wrong, Doña Sol knew about pain. She had valiantly weathered misery and adversity thoughout her life, but there was only one thing that made her crumble and she had to admit: the first time she saw him cry for Minerva. There was nothing but forgiveness in her heart for the boy. In the grand scheme of things, even her pain could not compare to his loss.

But in spite of her stern words, Doña Sol had to admit that Mateo's perception of her neighbor was not far-fetched. Not by a long stretch. In fact the encounter between her grandson and Severo made her shiver when a memory, long tucked away in her subconscious, reared its evil head through the tangled cobwebs inside her mind. She had to agree, Severo was indeed a deeper shade of evil.

Even after Mateo made his peace with his grandmother, the annoying thought bounced around inside his head, *"Severo... Severo. Now, where have I've heard that name before... Hmmm?"*

Doña Sol turned around and took a look at Mateo holding his chin, frowning and gazing far beyond the window's frame. She faced the stove again still hearing the sound of her grandson's fingertips drumming distractedly on the breakfast table...

The Sign of the Beast

The sweltering heat and humidity pressed against the sides of the wooden house, making them crackle. The pressure of the asphyxiating atmosphere forced the corrugated tin roof to expand noisily, groaning like an old man carrying a heavy burden. Under the ceiling, the stale air steamed the insides of the dwelling, until finally the end of the day gave way to a lukewarm, evening breeze that flowed in and out of windows like a free spirit out of purgatory. While the bundled mass of golden and purple clouds diffused the brightness of the setting sun, the day seemingly, resisted its impending demise If it wasn't because the mockingbirds, like clockwork, began to populate the power lines with their melancholic calls, and the faint beginning of the distant song of frogs filled the rural town, nobody would have believed the night was upon them already. But eager fireflies had already begun to spun faint abstract scribbles of light in the air.

"It's going to be a beautiful night," Maria said.

"Should we go to Nicomedes' for a visit?" Minerva asked her mother, as she pulled the milk bottle from Mateo's lips. "I wouldn't mind watching a bit of TV," she suggested, given the lack of entertainment at home. Nicomedes, an old friend of the family, had the rare privilege of owning a second hand black and white console, putting her home way ahead of the neighborhood and most folks around.

Doña Sol packed a brown paper bag with cookies and a loaf of freshly baked bread as her offering to her dear friend. Even the mile-long walk was a welcome change of pace and an opportunity to breathe in the fresh night air.

As they made their way, the evening began to turn into night. Doña Sol grabbed the hand of the two-year-old toddler and encouraged him to walk over the uneven surface of the dirt road. Minerva grabbed his other wrist and watched him navigate the dusty terrain with decisive, optimistic small steps. Maria walked behind and watched them, smiling.

"Look at the sky, Mateo. What do you see up there?" Doña Sol pointed at the dark space above pierced with winking stars.

"Uuumph!" the toddler answered with a sense of wonder.

"Yes, bright stars!" his grandmother said proudly.

As the night tightened its dark grip, Maria, Doña Sol, Minerva, and Mateo negotiated their way with careful steps. Guided only by the faint splendor of the sky above their heads, they broke into bursts of laughter when any of them missed a step and almost took an embarrassing fall. Finally from out of the darkness, a bright speck of light on Nicomedes' porch signaled their proximity to her humble house.

Soon the threshold was alive with greetings, kisses, gifts, and the simple joy of seeing old, familiar friends. A lively chatter began to fill up the room and aromatic cups of sweetened coffee were distributed among the guests. Nicomedes then turned to the console and clicked the dial. After a few minutes, grainy interference became moving graphic patterns that, as the set warmed up, coalesced into moving images to everyone's delight.

It couldn't have been more than a few minutes when Adela, Nicomedes' older daughter, came out of the kitchen looking slightly pale, though hardly anyone noticed now that they were all glued to the hypnotic moving images. Only Maria saw the woman's change of disposition but soon was pulled back to the flickering box where the story was unfolding. She was mesmerized by the sight of Mothra carrying the two diminutive Polynesian songbirds on its wings back to their native island of Infant, but not before the miffed moth created a national incident wreaking havoc in the city of Tokyo leaving a massive mess on its wake. And not to mention what the vengeful radioactive moth did to the cities of Rolisika and Newkirk, which ironically weren't booked for any shows yet. Predictably, it was a reasonable price to pay after Nelson the ruthless impresario illegally kidnapped the lovely synchronized-talking twins from their enchanted forest just so they could do their thing in front of a paying audience...

Maria lifted the cup of coffee to her lips and blew into the cloud of steam to cool off its sweet contents. From the corner of her eye, she saw Adela disappear outside the house into the pitch black night. She heard muffled sounds of voices outside as she took another sip from her cup.

"Who is she arguing with?" Minerva asked Maria under her breath. Minerva thought she sensed a truce had been reached when Adela emerged from the other side of the house through the kitchen and casually began to shut the windows around the house one by one, securing them with wooden pegs.

"What are you doing, Adela?" Nicomedes finally asked her, intrigued.

"Oh, nothing. It's just starting to get a bit cold," she answered matter-of-factly. As soon as Adela had locked and secured the very last window, a scream—more like a howl—broke the peaceful night, and a flow of insults, curses, and threats invaded the living room like a diabolical monster suddenly let loose. When the first blow of the

machete struck the window, Doña Sol dropped her cup which shattered into small shards all over the floor boards. Meanwhile Minerva and Maria's sharp screams of panic fused with Mateo's cries as they held him tightly, enveloping him like a shield. With every blow, the walls trembled and threatened to collapse on top of them.

"YOU ALL ARE GOING TO DIE TONIGHT!" The yells and grunting came through the walls and with every blast of the blade against the window, splinters of wood flew around the small living room at a terrifying speed. It had become painfully clear to Nicomedes and her guests that it would only be a matter of moments before the devil himself set foot into the humble house, before their lives would be unmercifully extinguished. Whatever the creature outside was, it was hellbent on carrying out its deadly promise.

"OPEN THE DAMN DOOR, YOU COWARDS! YOU ALL ARE GOING TO DIE TONIGHT!" the terrifying beast outside yelled again. The screams and cries of the women inside only served to fuel his determination. As his frustration grew with each passing second, his deadly fury increased tenfold and the loud blows of the machete became even more forceful.

"I SWEAR TO GOD, YOU ARE ALL GOING TO DIE TONIGHT, OPEN THE GODDAMN DOOR NOW!" As the hinges of the window began to come undone with each new assault, the beast hacked away relentlessly, like a mad logger determined to chop down the biggest tree in the forest. The prisoners' panicked screams and prayers increased along with the certainty of a violent and untimely death.

Giving up on his machete, the beast outside pounded the walls with his bare fists, and the amplified tremors sent bigger waves of new terror among the women. Only an act of divine intervention could save them now.

"YOU ALL ARE GOING TO DIE TONIGHT GODDAMIT!" the beast howled. Finally Nicomedes recognized the heavily intoxicated voice. Jumping out of her seat, she walked over the shards of broken china, swiftly turned off the set, and pleaded, "SEVERO, FOR THE LOVE OF GOD WHAT ARE YOU DOING?"

"YOU ARE GOING TO DIE!! LET ME IN!!" Severo persisted, crazed with uncontrollable rage. "I'LL SPARE YOU IF YOU OPEN THE DOOR NOW," he slurred in a demented attempt to negotiate. But even the collective desperate cries of the women were not enough of a deterrent for a madman, and Severo was not about to waste a golden opportunity. Not now. Not ever.

As the women and children gathered and held each other, Severo continued his litany of blasphemy, curses, and deadly threats. In real time, it had only lasted minutes but to the house's inhabitants, it seemed to stretch into an eternal night.

Outside, muffled, anxious voices approached the front door. The sounds of a new struggle, with loud voices and bodies slamming against the hardened red dirt, filled the night air. Whatever forces had intervened outside, they were apparently successful in subduing the offending beast. The moment Nicomedes opened the front door, they all witnessed the bloodied face of Severo as he was hauled away, his clothing shred to ribbons and his body caked with blood and mud. As Severo continued to throw his terrifying threats to the wind, Nicomedes crossed herself and muttered, "God forgive that poor soul!"

Nicomedes and her guests, still shaken, tried to recover from Severo's outburst of lunacy. By then, the partial magic of the moving pictures had lost all appeal. Soon enough, Minerva, Doña Sol, and Mateo ventured back into the cold night. Minerva held the sleepy child against her shoulder as a crisp layer of dew began to cover the silhouetted foliage. Maria steadied herself, deeply breathing the night air. Minerva and Doña Sol walked arm in arm slowly and in silence, letting the half-moon illuminate their careful steps while the stars above pinned the dark fabric of the sky. A thick wall of cricket calls expanded over the open field and enveloped them, as comforting and secure as a cozy blanket. Suddenly the darkness made them feel safer. Doña Sol then had a terrifying thought. "Genaro! God help us all, when he finds out."

With the passing of time, the frightful experience fused into legend, its sharp edge dulled like an over-used knife, but it was never to be forgotten by the townsfolk, even as both parties were forced to cohabit. It took a great deal of social grace for Don Genaro and Severo to keep their distance from one another. Sol's willingness to forget was the only attempt at superficial cordiality. If not for Doña Sol's sense of propriety, pity, and her idealistic concept of atonement, an encounter between the two men would inevitably have stained the pavement with their blood. Don Genaro bit his tongue, which Doña Sol mistakenly interpreted as forgiveness.

As Severo went on with his petty life, the assault, in his mind, simply became yesterday's news. Don Genaro made a promise to himself. The important thing now was to bide his time. Rage, much like pain, never goes away. It just hides under the skin, dormant, until a new beast calls its name. As far as personality traits go, it would only be a matter of time before Severo would stumble again, so Genaro willed himself to hold his temper while waiting for Severo to lose his, and then...

Mateo had had enough. It was high time he admitted, "I've made a mistake." No one could blame him for making questionable choices in times of turmoil, but his decision to stay behind in Palo Verde was his and his alone. Sitting in the middle of his tree house for hours with his book spread open over his lap, he still managed to ignore every single word in it. Every time he willed himself to read, he ended up going over the same lines again and again, until every single sentence lost its meaning. Nothing made sense. He might as well be reading the letters in his alphabet soup. Every time he took a deep breath in frustration, the cycle started over. He stared out the window slats, looking at nothing. Nothing. His eyes lost focus after a while.

At last a new idea popped into his head, something so original, it snapped him out of his inertia. "I'll make a list." He had already misjudged the whole outcome of his trip when he had insisted on staying behind. His disastrous impulse to stand up to Severo had incurred his grandmother's wrath. *"There's still time,"* Mateo though hopefully. He could not take back his bad behavior but he could certainly make sure no more unexpected events occurred that could put him at a disadvantage. Not on his watch. Not anymore. Mateo dropped his book and set out to make a "reminder list" he could file in the back of his head for future reference.

He stared at the last line he had scribbled on the paper. He felt a chill as he read Severo's name again. But with that last line, he was putting the cruel man in his crosshairs.

"Not bad. Not bad at all!" He examined the list carefully. At last he had created a map to help him navigate the unpredictable flow of Palo Verde's life events; a code of preventive conduct. All he had to do now was stick to it and, for once, he would honor his last name, Detente, *stop*. He would show nothing but restraint. The less he did to unsettle the sleepy waters of Palo Verde, the better off he would be. From now on, nothing would go wrong. Absolutely nothing.

~~MATEO~~
"MY ACTION POINTS"
by MATEO DETENTE
1. don't STICK my nose in NOTHING that is NOT my bisness.
2. Do not get TOO ATACHED to NOTHING and anyone
3. Dont' bRing Home anything i did NOT TAKE with me (IN THE FIRST PLACE)
4. STAY AWAY FROM ~~Cevero~~. He eat SHIT (big TIME !!!!)
mateo Detente

PART THREE

What Have I Done?

"**W**HAT DO YOU THINK YOU'RE DOING?" *The memory of Minerva's angry voice as she rushed towards him still made him shiver.*

"Don't you ever do that again!" she snapped, snatching the small animal, dripping wet, from his hands. By the time he realized what he had done, he had received a vigorous spanking.

He still recalled how betrayed he felt by Minerva. "I was just playing," the four-year-old pleaded in self-defense.

But Minerva was relentless. "You will never treat an animal like that again, you hear me?"

He remembered he had cried his eyes out. With the passing of time, he forgot the spanking but he never forgot the hurt in her eyes. For him, that had been the most painful punishment. Respect the life of an animal—a lesson never forgotten.

Mateo finally ventured out of the house and kept his eyes on the spot in the empty lot where the cat had been earlier. The neighbor's attack on the stray had left him shaken and unsettled. *"That poor animal. What's going to happen to it?"* He could not understand such cruelty. He could tell the animal was tired of running. His eyes scanned the lot looking for signs of the stray. *"It's gone!"*

He thought of his contract, the one he specifically designed for an occasion like this. He took a deep breath, *"Clause Number One: Don't stick my nose in anything that is not my business."* He was pleased to put the wisdom of his own words into action. *Don't stick my nose in anything that is not my business.*

Doña Sol was relieved to see a more relaxed Mateo. She was determined to keep him distracted and handed him a plastic basket.

"Would you please take the clean laundry upstairs?" she asked and watched as he began to work. One by one, he pulled down each sun-dried sheet from the clothesline. In the meantime, he watched his grandmother walk up to the leafy bush by the fence and start to pull off the small, green pods, filling the pockets of her apron. He could hear her humming a tune as she reached out for the branches and was relieved to see her finally calm.

There was no doubt that the man across the street was a despicable being but Mateo still hated himself for embarrassing his grandmother. *"I was out of line,"* he thought with regret, pulling the laundry off the clothesline and into the basket. He was so focused on his task that he failed to notice a pair of almond-shaped eyes in the bushes by the chain-link fence examining his every move. The cat popped its small, triangular head from behind the flower bed and took inventory of the scene with great curiosity.

Just the thought of that unruly child made Severo seethe. There was something about the boy he did not like. He could not pinpoint what it was, but the boy's judgmental stare unsettled him. He knew he was just a kid, but that made no difference. Billy, his own son, was proof of that. He would not put up with his childish outbursts. As a parent, it was his responsibility to keep him in his place, so he expected no less from an unruly neighbor. Severo continued filing his machete. He did not have to lift his eyes to feel the boy's stare from across the street. "I'm keeping my eye on you, too."

Severo did not take kindly to the boy's verbal attack. *"That little punk!"* Most of all, he could not forgive the humiliation he had endured in front of his son and the nosy neighbors. Severo knew he could take his revenge at any time. He possessed a great ability for remembering offenses and holding grudges. "The beauty of revenge," Severo considered, "is that it can be inflicted when the prey least expects it. I'm going to teach you a lesson," he promised. "I'll make you regret the moment you set foot on my turf." The thought made the veins in Severo's temples pulse with intensity as if they were about to explode.

Severo had learned the invigorating power of rage early on. Unafraid of its consequences, he had never learned its limits either. He grew up believing the ultimate proof of manhood and virility was to unleash his anger onto anyone who crossed his path. The effectiveness of discipline and control through unwarranted aggression had served him well. Even though discipline and control were missing from his own life, Severo grew up proud of his skills as executioner of the weak.

Years of insecurities had shaped his body into an arch, a bent tree carrying the wind on its back. He had become a sad slump of a man, a walking contradiction to his favorite advice, "You have to stand tall in life!" Severo's twisted sense of righteousness was not meant for human beings. Unsure whether to lift his head up to the sun in defiance or lower it in shame to hide his ever present scowl, Severo was always ready to prove he wasn't as feeble as everyone thought. "I demand respect," he would say and he would go to any lengths to prove it. "Let them see how justice should be served!"

In the heat of the early afternoon, the stray found a cool hideout under the bushes. A safe hideout where it could observe the *Biganimal* across the yard.

"*Who is it?*" the cat wondered as it watched the boy move around. To a starving creature, the presence of bigger animals indicated a food supply. The painful turn in its stomach reminded the cat of its hunger, as it folded its legs under its body.

"*Food?*" But the stray had not forgotten the previous attack either. "*Stinkanimal!*" Its fur bristled with fear.

"*Should I?*" From a safe distance, the stray considered the possible risks of another encounter with these new animals. Exhausted, hungry, and thirsty, the cat weighed its next move carefully. "*No, I wait.*" A cat that has been attacked repeatedly keeps the memory.

From across the street, a familiar voice made the stray's fur bristle with terror. "*Stinkanimal!*" But it kept its eyes fiercely focused on the boy in front of it. "*Safe here,*" it thought.

The clean and infinite expanse of the blue sky seemed naked without clouds. The heat of the afternoon sun punished the earth mercilessly, but down in the forest by the river, existence was bearable. A forest has a big heart, a living, breathing heart. And it has powers, powers that only Mother Nature can dispense. A forest can capture a tenuous breeze and push it through the branches, up the crown of royal palm trees, under ferns, and shake the coleus down by the riverside. In no time, the breeze that was just a whisper becomes a *vendaval,* a blustery draft that can throw ocean waters off their course and uproot the strongest of trees. But the forest only summons such powers on unique occasions.

The forest's big heart broke for a lost ghost wandering among the shadows, not knowing where it came from, not knowing what it was searching for. The time was now, the forest decided, to come to the aid of a lost, helpless spirit. The forest had watched the ghost at night, sighing by the light of the moon. It had traced the ghost's steps at daybreak as it wandered among the trees, behind the angel's trumpet and the tall ferns. It would be heartbreaking for any living being to watch the ghost, transparent as a cloud of morning mist, stand on the boulder and look down at the current as if the river held a clue. The forest understood then that the ghost traveling in its shadows was not only lost but trapped. "I haven't got much time," it had heard it lament throughout the night, sitting on the mossy boulder. When the thought of the spark in the boy's hand made the ghost wonder, "I need to find him." The forest understood. Now, there was no time left to waste.

It was time to come up with a solution and help the ghost cross the river. So when a random leaf fell floating in the air gracefully and effortlessly, the coffee trees took notice. As the soursop and the yagrumos watched it dance from side to side in the breeze before spiraling down to the back of the river, they began to shimmy. By the time the leaf landed in the river's lap, their crowns had begun to shake. Then it just took a faint movement from the ferns drinking by the river bend to call all the trees to stir up the wind. A gentle whimper that began within the wild petunias soon became a fierce gust. It rattled the leaves of the orange tree, frantically shaking its branches, and traveled across the river—the breeze was now a powerful gust—and up through the guava berry trees and shook the passion fruit vines. The wind then began to turn around in columns, making the banana trees dance furiously and shredding their fronds into ribbons. In no time, the whole forest bowed before the force of the mighty whirlwind that lifted dry leaves, frogs, and grasshoppers into the air.

"What is happening—?" but the ghost had no time to find out.

"Goaway, where are you?" the ghost called out as the dark cloud of revolving wind lifted it into the air. The whirlwind gained more strength and carried the ghost across the river, pulling prawns from underneath their rocks. The gray cone of wind traveled through the bushes and up the hill covered in wild vines and lantana, bending and twisting the tall grass in its path. A forest has a big, breathing heart and the power to aid one of its own. As if remembering an ancient grievance, the forest has mustered its rage, the rage that lived hidden beneath fallen limbs like a dark secret. It had employed the necessary force to protect one of its own...

The invisible, revolving cone of air pushed its way through high tree tops and the open field of grass, finally sweeping down past the pigeon pea bush and through the dusty backyard. Before the ghost realized, it had landed in the middle of the garden on the back of the vortex. The ghost looked around. "Goaway, where are you?" asked the ghost softly without hearing an answer from the cat.

"Goaway, where am I?" The ghost knew the cat was ignoring its call and felt terribly lost.

"Goaway?"

"Heeere," the cat finally answered from the bed of begonias where it was busy removing dirt from its claws, biting into them with a great deal of concentration.

"Dirty." The cat paused for a moment and lifted its nose to try and pick up the ghost's scent.

"Where are we now?" the ghost asked again, taking in the new surroundings from the gray shadows of the pigeon pea bush. Uninterested, the cat continued biting its toenails.

"How can we go back to the forest?"

"Do not know." The stray answered without abandoning its cleansing routine.

"Who's that?" The ghost was intrigued by the boy standing under the sun.

Annoyed, the cat settled in its shady spot to rest from the heat and ignored the ghost. The grumble in its stomach served as a reminder of a more pressing matter, *"Hungry."* Ready for a quick nap it blinked lazily and rested its head on its paws.

Meanwhile, the ghost tried to remember this unfamiliar place. "We need to find our way back, Goaway," it pleaded. "I don't have much time."

The stray looked up at the ghost with pity.

As the sun came out from behind a cloud, a flash of light caught the ghost's attention, the same spark it had seen days before in the forest. The familiar glare was coming from across the garden. The dazzling object was dangling from the neck of the boy. Then, as if the gates of a dam had opened, memories rushed through the ghost and its past life appeared before its eyes. Jolted by the impact, it stood motionless as if the slightest movement would cause the boy to disappear from sight.

"This place is familiar to me!" It watched the boy standing in the garden. *"I remember now."*

"Goaway! The boy with the fire in his hand!" It made the ghost happy to recognize the green, shiny object around the boy's neck. *The Magic Crystal!*

Looking across the yard, the ghost said to the cat, *"Who is he? The boy who had cried himself to sleep?"* It could see the sadness in the boy's eyes, but the ghost still found no answers. There was something intriguing about him; The boy with the fire in his hand had made the spirit awaken from its dream. Interference.

"The boy!" A boy, a great boy, with a broken heart that deserved healing. The ghost remembered him well now, the sad being that days before had wandered around the forest, lost and carrying a great burden. And then there was the stray,

a young cat that missed its family and deserved a loving home. Like a bright light making shadows scurry away, the answer was suddenly clear. It was sitting right by the ghost's side. "Goaway, this is your new home!"

Mateo heard the rattling shower of dry leaves rushing across the yard. A sudden draft of hot air combed the bare ground and forced him to shield his eyes. The

whirlwind displaced dust and leaves all over the backyard and made the bushes dance maniacally. Mateo turned to Doña Sol, who was also caught in the dusty upheaval. "Buela, cover your eyes!" he warned his grandmother as the nearby bushes went on rattling and swaying from the powerful whirlwind. He squinted into the dust where for a brief moment he thought he saw someone under the tree.

The unexpected sight of Minerva standing in the garden shook him up. *"How could it be?"* he wondered, convinced it had been a trick of light. Mateo wiped the thin layer of dust from his face. *"Did I see her—?"* But his eyes had betrayed him. He glanced over at the place where the gust of wind had swirled around, and realized it had just been an illusion. Without giving it another thought, he tried to remember what he was doing before the sudden arrival of the whirlwind.

A subtle rustle in the bushes led his eyes to the flower bed. *"There's nothing there,"* he thought, but another movement under the shrubs by the chain link fence revealed a small pair of almond-shaped eyes staring out from the safety of a cluster of plants.

"Oh, no! There's that cat again!" He recognized the stray that had stared at him from across the garden on the day of his arrival. Sadly too, he realized it was the same animal that Severo had attacked the day before! Mateo froze in his tracks as if trapped in mud. *"The same stray! What's it doing here now?"* Caught in the cat's stare he thought, *"This is not good."*

"This is not good at all," he muttered. His throat became dry and the inside of his mouth tasted like copper, as if he had sucked on a penny. "This is not good. Not good at all," he kept repeating to himself, as if he had been handed an unwelcome and unexpected burden.

He kept his attention fixed on the stray. *"Is it checking me out? That poor animal, it's starving! It probably thinks there's food here."* He studied the cat's body language. He sensed hesitation in the animal's movements, as if it was calculating the distance between the fence and the house. He imagined the stray saw him as a bigger threatening animal. What he could not explain was the sudden feeling of butterflies fluttering wildly around the walls of his stomach. *"It's looking at me as if it knows me!"* Even from a distance, he could see a special light in the animal's eyes, like an old friend that unexpectedly shows up on the doorstep. Inexplicably, he could not help feeling that a responsibility had been placed on his shoulders. *"This is no good. No good at all."* He remembered his own promise: *don't get too attached to anyone or anything.* He must not forget one of the most, if not THE most, important clause in his contract.

Mateo jumped when he heard the rattling of the chain-link gate. He turned his head in time to see Sergio opening the gate as Stumpy charged through the yard ahead of him. For a moment, he forgot all about the cat hiding in the begonias.

"Hi Serge! What's up?"

"Wanna come for a ride?" Sergio asked, brushing the sweat off his brow.

"Maybe," he answered.

Whaaarf! Whaaarf! Whaaarf!

Both boys looked towards the dog that was busy sticking its nose into the bushes.

Mateo was alarmed at the dog's insistence. "Stumpy, stop!" He feared for the cat.

"What is it?" asked Sergio.

"There's a stray hiding in the bushes. He might hurt it!" Mateo ran after the dog.

"Don't worry, he's harmless. He's just finding out what's under the bushes. C'mon, Stumpy, enough!" At the sound of his name, Stumpy stopped his barking and ran back with his short tail upright, forgetting all about the cat.

"Have you given it any food?" asked Sergio.

"No. I think that's a bad idea."

"Maybe you're right. Then it may stick around." Sergio jumped on his bike. "Are you coming?" he asked again.

"I'll catch up with you later." Mateo still had no clear idea what to do.

Stumpy looked straight at the cat hiding behind the shrubs.

"Who are you? Do I know you?"

The cat answered, *"I need my rest. Go away! Don't bother me!"*

* * *

Four years after being exiled from her beloved island, Minerva's fighting spirit suddenly tore through her skin like a flower bursting through the ground at the touch of the spring sun. She was determined to prove to herself and others that she could be responsible, *respectable,* to use the hurtful term she heard from her parents.

"Soon enough, I can begin work as an apprentice seamstress!" she promised Maria. So it had been indeed a very proud day for her when she purchased a second-hand sewing machine. Minerva the seamstress was finally ready to take on the world. This time around she was going to show everyone what she was made of. At school, she had come to agree with her teachers that she was "slow," but she also knew that with somebody's help, "I could take the words out of my head and put them down the way they are supposed to be. Even the numbers running around inside my head were not the ones I scribbled down! It makes me mad. I can be somebody."

But nobody seemed to appreciate her struggle. Instead, the other students had taunted her for their own amusement. "You are a retard." But Minerva was determined. "I can still be somebody, someday." She kept her hope alive.

At nineteen years of age, Minerva took a hard look at her life. "I want to go back!" she pleaded with her father. "I have to go back," she repeated, growing increasingly defiant. She knew that going back home had a price, but Minerva was willing to risk it. "It's my time!" she declared. She dreamt of being able to see the island's horizon, far beyond the mountains, where the sea merged with the sky. To be standing once again beneath a limitless sky, surrounded by unspoiled mountains and the familiarity of a small town.

But Minerva also knew that in order to achieve her goal, she had to accept the other reality that in the harsh light of day was not so romantic: Palo Verde was a small-minded town where a free spirit could feel suffocated. She heard the accusation in her father's voice, "What would you do in a place like this?" She accepted her father's concern but was determined. This time around, there was nothing that could stop her.

"I can make a good living as a seamstress," she said, trying more to convince herself than her father.

"It might be good for her," Doña Sol finally agreed.

"But you cannot bring Mateo."

Minerva shook as if a bolt of electricity had run down her spine. Deep inside she knew this was the price she had to pay for her independence. "Mateo!" she repeated his name as if to find her strength and direction.

"You can't take him back with you! You know you can't take care of him properly, Minerva. Don't be selfish, think of his future!" Maria was startled at her own words. The same words she had hated hearing her father say were now pouring freely from her mouth, without a trace of guilt or irony.

"You are right. He'll be better off and have a better life." Minerva began to accept her destiny.

Holding the boy in her arms, Maria promised him, "Mateo, we'll go back and see her soon!"

"I promise you we'll be together again!" Minerva said but she was not sure how she could ever keep her promise to the four year boy.

Saying goodbye to the child proved to be harder than she anticipated. Minerva struggled with her words. She knelt on the floor so Mateo could see her eye-to-eye. She cupped her hands around the boy's face. With trembling fingers, she brushed the bangs off his forehead.

"You'll come and visit, right?" Minerva clenched her teeth, fighting back tears for the boy's sake. Saying goodbye to him was the hardest part of her plan. And Mateo's sweet face did not make it any easier.

* * *

Mateo could not quite explain the feeling the sight of the stray had given him and he deliberately tried to ignore it, busying himself with the laundry basket. Before heading upstairs, he looked for his grandmother. She was still busy picking ripe pods from the leafy pigeon pea bush. A subtle movement in the flower bed drew his eyes back to the site where the cat had peeked out before. He was not pleased by what he saw. *"Oh no, the cat is still here!"* He set the laundry basket down and once again locked eyes with the stray.

The cat, in turn, studied him as if it was trying to predict his next move. *"If I ignore it, it will go away,"* Mateo hoped but it was clear the stray, having taken up residence under the bush, had no intention of going anywhere. *"What should I do?"* he wondered. *"This will not end well."* He wished someone would tell him what to do. But Doña Sol, absorbed in gathering the small green pods, was unaware of the exchange between the boy and the stray. Mateo decided he must do something.

"Grandma, do you see the cat by the fence?" he asked Doña Sol. "I think it's the same one Severo was chasing away!"

Doña Sol turned her gaze towards the small gap in the fence where the attentive cat was resting in her flower bed. "Whatever you do, do not feed it," was her warning.

"It looks like it's starving!"

"Mateo, listen to me. If you feed it, it will hang around waiting for more." Doña Sol turned and continued filling her hands with the ripe shells of pigeon peas.

"What to do now?" He could not help it but felt sorry for the hungry animal.

Across the garden, the stray and the ghost carefully examined the scene. They watched as the boy hurriedly moved around as if searching for something. As the hungry cat watched the boy intently, it searched for more clues with its nose up in the air.

"Goaway, look!" The ghost pointed across the garden. Encouraged, the cat lifted its head once again and focused on the activity in the distance.

"Biganimal! It looks me now?" the cat wondered at the sight of the boy.

"Yes, it does!" the ghost answered reassuringly.

"Biganimal. No angry. Yesss?" asked the cat, remembering an earlier attack.

"Yes," replied the ghost. "Go now!"

Still the young stray hesitated, *"No yet. I sit. I wait…"* But it could barely resist anymore.

Trrrrring, ting, ting, ting

The sharp noise of dry food hitting the bottom of the dish made the cat's ears prick up. Its hunger pains intensified but still it did not move. Its tongue began to circle its lips in anticipation. *"Biganimal good?"*

"Go on, now," the cat heard the ghost say. "Go now, he's waiting for you!"

"Meesu, Meesu." The cat heard the call from across the garden.

"What it mean? What it mean?"

"It's calling you. Go on, little one. There's no danger."

The young stray considered the ghost's advice but instead sat down and watched the boy fill up another dish with water.

"Eaaats, yeees!" Its tongue started to circle its lips again and wondered how safe it would be to approach. It carefully examined the tall figures standing nearby. It couldn't wait to dig its face into the bowl of food. *"Hungry!"* The intense grumble in its stomach reminded it of the urgency. But first, it had to make itself presentable to its hosts.

Lick paw, lick paw, rub face.

Lick paw, lick paw, rub face.
Lick paw, lick paw, rub face.
Lick, lick, lick tummy.
Lick, lick, lick tummy.
Lick, lick, lick tummy.

Ignoring his grandmother's warning, Mateo had filled a small bowl with a handful of dry dog food he managed to find another one with fresh, cool water from the garden hose. He saw the small cat's ears prick up at the prospect of a meal, but it struck him as odd that the starving animal hesitated and remained crouched under the bush.

"It's afraid I'm going to hurt it!" He was sure the memories of Severo's attacks were still fresh in its mind.

"A stray animal doesn't trust people," Doña Sol pointed out.

Retreating to watch from his hammock, Mateo observed the creature pause and swivel its head from side to side as if it weighing the possible consequences of its new venture. Bemused, he saw the stray sniff the air once the food's scent had tickled its nose, and throw an interested look from across the yard. The cat began to flex its legs.

"What is it trying to do now?" Mateo wondered. *"Hmmm, it looks like it's thinking!"* Soon enough, the cat's pressing hunger began to break down its caution.

Once it regained its confidence, the cat was ready for another adventure. It shot another cautious glance before venturing across the garden, making its way to the waiting bowl of food.

As it took its first steps into the yard, Mateo realized this was no ordinary cat. For a cat that has been hungry, homeless, and vulnerable, behavior that was skittish, even distrustful, would be a reasonable expectation. Instead, the stray strutted towards the bowl displaying a curious air of abandon and detachment, a very rare trait in a stray.

"Buela, look how it walks!" Mateo was already smiling, entertained by the cat's self-assured strut. It became clear to him that for once, the stray felt out of harm's way. He saw his grandmother was smiling too.

"It walks with its tail up like a guajana!" He pointed out the cat's upright tail, swaying in the wind like the silk of a sugarcane stalk. With graceful bouncing steps, the small gray cat made its way towards the bowl of food, completely ignoring the two *Biganimals* standing by.

"*Safe!*" The cat finally felt comfortable with the two *Biganimals* and, without a hint of shyness, desperately dug its face into the small dish, alternating mouthfuls of dog food with long sips of water.

As the stray bit noisily into the hard morsels of dog food, Mateo noticed a very peculiar feature in its appearance. "Buela, check him out. He has a mohawk!" He admired the crest of dark hair that extended from the top of the cat's head to the end of its back.

"I've never seen such a thing!"

Doña Sol smiled at the sight of the singular looking cat. "He certainly is something else," she said, choosing her words very carefully.

"Poor thing, it really is hungry!" His pity for the stray only increased when he noticed the knots of mud in its fur. He watched it eat, relieved that the improvised meal had appeased its many days of hunger. Listening to the soft sound of its purring, he could tell the stray was showing its contentment.

"I don't think it has a home," he pointed out. Taking a closer look, he examined the stray's sunken stomach and protruding rib cage.

"Pobrecito, it looks like it hasn't eaten in days!" Doña Sol answered, staring at the cat. "This poor thing is all skin and bones! It looks like it's seen some trouble in its young life."

Mateo waited until the stray finished eating. He noticed it glancing at him and his grandmother between mouthfuls of food. "Well, hopefully it feels better now." He was confident he had done something good. "Even if it's only a handful of dog food, at least that will help it survive until its next meal."

But he suddenly was weighed down by a premonition, he realized too late the possible consequences of his impulsive act and hurriedly tried to distance himself from the stray. He had to admit that underneath its sad and disheveled appearance, this was a very special animal. He felt his heart sink when the cat looked up at him with what seemed like gratitude.

"He's beautiful!" Mateo said almost absentmindedly. He couldn't ignore the striking contrast between the stray cat's unhealthy physical condition and its gentle personality. "I think this cat must belong to somebody. It's too tame to be a stray." Looking into the cat's big, green eyes, he was amazed by the unusual scalloped markings on the sides of its belly. "*Like a miniature leopard!*" he thought. Still he was careful not to allow himself to become too invested. Somehow he had to find the strength to fight his impulses. *"Quick! Which clause applies to this situation? Remember! Pledge number two: don't get too attached to anyone or anything. I have to go back home soon."*

But now it was too late. He was not pleased with this new and disquieting sensation. *"No, this is not good."* The feeling was eating at the insides of his stomach, turning into twisted knots that pulled and poked. Worry. Yes, that was the new feeling for today as he studied the tenacious cat sitting in front of him, waving its tail as if it already had a plan. Mateo had good reason to worry. *"Something's about to go wrong. Very wrong!"* He felt it in his gut.

"It's a stray, they're a dime a dozen," Mateo heard Doña Sol say as she pushed her broom from side to side, lifting clouds of red dust off the cement floor. "They come out of the woods looking for food and water but nobody wants them."

"That's sad." Unfortunately he had just witnessed the truth of his grandmother's words firsthand. As his thoughts traveled up to the clouds, he watched the cat sitting on the floor, softly batting its eyes and shifting its gaze from him to his grandmother as if following their conversation.

Prrr, Prrrr, Prrrrrr

Mateo heard its purrs of contentment. Worry. Mateo had a very good reason to worry now.

"Heeesss beeaautifulll."

The cat heard one of the *Tall Biganimals* talking but the sounds had no meaning. It was too busy taking sips of cold water from the small bowl to be concerned. *"Hmmm! Drink. Good."*

"Heeesss sssstrraee"

"What it means?" Puzzled by the sounds of their voices, the cat lifted its head but stayed put. Noticing the *Biganimal's* stare, it wondered, *"Animalfriend?"*

Once its hunger was satisfied, the stray yawned, relieved, while it examined its surroundings, trying to decide whether to stick around. Feeling relaxed, it began its grooming routine anew.

Lick paw, lick paw, rub face.
Lick paw, lick paw, rub face.
Lick paw, lick paw, rub face.

"Animalfriend?" The stray looked up again at the boy without feeling threatened. But then a sudden move by one of the *Biganimals* made the cat's body stiffen with fear. *"BIGANIMAL BIG PAW! BIG PAW!"* Overcome by fright, it lowered its body to the ground. The fur along its back stood on end. It looked up with fear at the *Biganimal* reaching towards it, and holding its breath, the cat waited for the blow. But it never came. Instead, the stray felt a gentle touch on the back of its head.

"Oooh! Scratch, scratch. Good."

Meanwhile not too far away, under the shadows of the pigeon pea bush, the ghost smiled. *"Good!"* it said. *"This is very good, indeed!"*

"Poor animal." Mateo had watched in disbelief as the skinny gray cat ate the dog food as if it was the most scrumptious of meals. Still, he could not shake the sinking feeling. *"What have I done?"* He was surprised at his own lack of judgment. What on earth made him ignore his grandmother's warning?

"Soon it'll disappear back into the wild," he hoped.

But he could not ignore the cat's sad destiny. "It'll probably have to find its next meal in the garbage," he shuddered, pitying the animal. Nevertheless, he suspected that he was about to pay a price for his act of kindness.

His grandmother's words broke the silence. "Nobody wants them. They look for food and more often than not they get killed by speeding cars." These were harsh words to hear but he had to agree his grandmother was probably right.

He was pulled back from his racing thoughts by the cat's soft purring. To his dismay, it was now rubbing against his legs and walking around him as if roping him within invisible circles. "I hope you have a home. I have no place for you," Mateo muttered.

However the cat showed no intention of leaving, at least not in the near future. It licked its paw, licked its paw over, rubbed its face, and then did it all again with almost military precision. But Mateo knew that, although it might be hurtful, he had to bring the situation to a swift end. He had hoped the cat would go on its way after the meal. Instead, it sat looking directly at him without batting an eye. The cat's deliberate body language was not lost on him.

"Strays are nomads. If it came from the wild, then it belongs in the wild." He struggled with the facts of cold, precise logic. *"Why am I trying to convince myself?"* He tried to make sense of his muddled mind.

"Stray animals can't be household pets." Doña Sol said. He felt as if his grandmother was reading his thoughts.

"Are you kidding? I'm not taking in a stray that just showed up out of nowhere!" He surprised himself with his own outburst, and was confused even further by what his grandmother said next.

"A cat like that would never survive confined inside a home."

Suddenly becoming defensive, he shot back, "What do you mean? I am not taking it home!" But he couldn't miss how the small cat looked at him as if it knew it was the cause of this heated debate that somehow involved its future.

"I can't do this!" Overwhelmed, he picked up the blue plastic basket and headed for the stairs. He needed to get away from the cat as quickly as possible. He couldn't risk any further chance for bonding. Mateo then made a serious mistake: he looked back over his shoulder and saw the gray cat still sitting there on its hind legs, licking its right paw and grooming its face and stomach. Sadly, his grandmother's words seemed to apply to the present situation: *"The world is full of abandoned animals. It's impossible to save them all."* He hated the thought but there was nothing he could do. *"I hope it'll survive."* With a heavy heart, and wishing the cat better luck, he climbed the stairs as fast as he could. *"I won't think about it anymore, I won't think about it, I won't—"*

"Goodbye, little cat," Mateo whispered to himself. He was sure the stray would finally go on to its rightful owner, to its home.

"What have I done?" Mateo realized he had to face up to the consequences of his good will. The slight turn in his stomach when he first spotted the cat had been an early warning, but he had chosen to ignore it. And now it was too late. *"Walk away, fast!"* he decided, heading for the staircase. *"Ignore it! Ignore it! There's only so much I can do."*

Mateo counted the steps up to the front door. One step for every worry that he imagined: *"Step One, Will it go away? Step Two, Does it have a home? Step Three, Who would let a gentle cat roam around starving and thirsty? Step Four, How long has it been homeless? Step Five, He could get killed in the road. Step Six, What if he doesn't have a home? Step Seven, What am I going to do now? Step Eight, what am I going to do now? Step Nine, what am I going to do now? Step Ten, what am I going to do now?!"*

To his dismay, he saw the cat effortlessly pick up the pace and strut up the steps by his side. In spite of his decision to leave it alone, it was hard to dismiss the determined stray that marched ahead without a care. It sat at the top the stairs waiting for him, as if Mateo was the one lagging behind. The stray acted as if it had lived here all its life; and it became increasingly clear that it was feeling very much at home. Mateo had hoped once the stray had eaten, it would go on its way. How was it possible he had miscalculated so badly?

He stared in disbelief at the cat that greeted him undeterred with pleading eyes. It looked at him as if he were an old friend dropping by for a visit. The cat paced impatiently, never taking its big eyes off of him. *"Hurry up!"* it said with loud meows.

Mateo remained calm as the small cat stared intently into his eyes. *"This cat needs help."* He resented that a stray had suddenly made him feel responsible. "This is not going to end well." He was baffled and had no idea what to do next. He felt hopelessly lost.

"See?" Doña Sol said to him from the bottom of the stairs. "You fed it and now you'll have to take it home." She could tell her grandson did not appreciate her teasing. "I warned you not to feed it!" she said, swinging her broom and shaking her head. Doña Sol had to bit her lip to contain a knowing smile. She watched Mateo standing at the top of the steps still as a statue in a wax museum. Holding the laundry basket, and looking down at the stray with a worried look on his face.

An amused "hmmm" summarized Doña Sol's take on the situation.

The ghost watched the scene unfold from the shade of the pigeon pea bush. It studied the boy's every move with interest. "Come on, dear child!" it pleaded, puzzled by the boy's behavior. "Come on, Goaway!" It watched as the cat waited patiently, afraid of being rejected once more. Like a child begging to be loved, the stray looked up to the boy for a sign of affection.

"Come on." And then the ghost saw a glimmer of hope, a flicker of light in the boy's eyes as he offered a fistful of food to the hungry animal. It could sense his reservation but it also knew there was more behind the gesture. The ghost was very

pleased as it watched the boy feed the stray. "Could this be a new beginning?" it hoped. A moment later, it whispered in the cat's ear, "A new friend, Goaway?"

"*Animalfriend!*" the cat had answered. And without wasting a moment, it leapt to its feet and ran after the friendly figure heading towards the stairs, racing with such speed that the boy did not see it pass by.

* * *

In 1968 Minerva arrived in Palo Verde the same way she had left four years before, as quietly as a leaf dropping from a tree. She clearly remembered somebody once saying, "*El coquí no puede sobrevivir fuera de la isla.*" The tiny frog cannot survive outside the island. She knew exactly what that felt like. She had returned to Palo Verde willingly but now in the smallness of the town, she was suffocating. It was time to fight for her own life. A new life away from her parents. And with that thought, she finally left behind Palo Verde's intimacy, for the adventure of city life.

"Good afternoon!" Minerva called out through the white wrought-iron gate, mindful to wait until given permission to enter. The sweltering humidity made her uncomfortable and she fanned the afternoon heat off her face with her drawing pad. She became self-conscious about the sweat marks on her new dress.

"How I hate this heat, dear God!" Minerva shook her head, annoyed. Suddenly she had a greater appreciation for the mountains and Palo Verde's agreeable year-round climate. She wondered how her hair was holding up and whether she had time for a last check. She patted her neck with the already saturated handkerchief. She felt had been traveling for days on a steamboat. "I feel a mess!"

The trip from Palo Verde had started long before the sun had lit up the morning sky. Quivering from the bone chilling early cold, she had waited under the umbrella of the flamboyant tree by the side of the road in total darkness. Finally, the headlights of the public shuttle penetrated the dense fog. Minerva watched the long beams of lights turn slowly around the curve until the dilapidated van came into full view. Minerva was determined to catch the very first trip of the morning into the next town, even if it meant sharing the ride with a gaggle of factory workers, an uncharacteristically rowdy bunch of women who managed to embarrass and humiliate the driver with their saucy banter.

Once in town, Minerva boarded the next car going to the big city. Thankfully the second leg of her trip was less cumbersome. The prospect of a job helped keep her spirits up. *"I have to do this!"* The thought of little Mateo, so far away, made her eyes moist with tears.

"Buenos días, Doña Luz!" Minerva called from the sidewalk.

"She can't hear you." Minerva turned at the voice of a woman next door. "Hi, I'm Benny. She's probably in her sewing shop." Minerva watched the woman hang some glass chimes from her balcony.

Yaaack! Yaaack! Yaaack!

"Bonita, shut up already!" the woman admonished her yapping dog as she began to sing along to her hi-fi and dance around the living room. Minerva bit her lip, hiding a smile.

"Good morning, Meezz!" Minerva shouted. Suddenly an iguana scampered over her foot. She yelped as the spotted reptile wiggled across the sandy ground and disappeared under the flowery mounds of blue plumbago by the gate. Once more, she tugged at the sides of her dress and felt embarrassed at her shoes covered in dust. *"If I could just—"* Her thought was cut short by the disembodied voice coming from inside the pink house.

"Ya voy! I'm coming."

A short, round woman finally came to the front gate, jangling a noisy handful of keys on a long chain. "I'm sorry!" she apologized for her tardiness. "I work in the back and it's hard to hear when people come to the door!"

With a discreet glance, she checked out the young woman—really a young girl—carrying a child's brown suitcase, wearing two-sizes-too-small shoes, and sporting a homemade dress.

"Please, come in!" the woman invited. "May I offer you something to eat, dear?"

"No, thank you, meez. I just had lunch." The woman knew the self-conscious girl was lying.

"Let's just have something to drink then. This heat makes me crazy!" Doña Luz returned from her kitchen with a plate of cookies and glasses of chilled lemonade. Immediately, she felt maternal towards the small-town girl and watched her down the glass of fresh-squeezed lemonade in a single gulp. "So you want to become a seamstress," the woman tried to reassure the ill-at-ease girl.

"Yes, I do!" Minerva answered eagerly.

"How's Maria? Is she still in the States?" the woman asked, noticing the sudden pale expression on Minerva's face. "How's the baby?" the woman continued.

"Mateo… His name is Mateo. He's fine." Minerva tried desperately to hold back tears.

"So you taught yourself to sew?" the woman asked, changing the subject.

"Yes ma'am," Minerva answered, regaining her composure.

"What do you have there?" Doña Luz asked her after noticing the small drawing pad.

"This is where I come up with my designs," Minerva answered, animatedly.

It pleased Doña Luz to see a shine in the girl's eyes. "Well, I think you'll do very well here. You can help me with the cleaning in the mornings and we'll work together in my shop in the afternoons." Doña Luz had a great feeling about the new girl. There was just one more question she needed answered.

"Will you have visitors?" She tried to read the girl's body language.

"No one. Not for a long time," Minerva answered wistfully. Her thoughts were with Mateo, so far away.

* * *

Mateo realized too late that Palo Verde had nothing fun going on. He had complained about the lack of things to do but he certainly wasn't prepared for the sudden appearance of a stray. Much to his frustration, the cat showed no signs of moving on. He tried to ignore its charms without much success. The cat's pleading meows outside his bedroom door were very persistent. That could only mean one thing: the cat was setting up shop. "I give up!" He had no choice but to finally let it in his room and watch it sniff around. It was surprising how the cat, that only hours before was holding on to its life by a thread, was now walking around his room with its tail held high, like a cheerleader holding up a pennant in a homecoming game.

Aware of his grandmother, Mateo was very careful not to show any signs of weakness in her presence. The last thing he needed was for her to catch him worrying about the animal. He headed quickly for his bedroom before his grandmother could chide him with an *I told you so!*

"Where do you think you're going?" he admonished the cat trailing behind him. He could not understand why the cat's presence made him feel uneasy.

Sitting on the corner of his bed, he watched the animated cat jump up and perch on the dresser. Like a fuzzy gargoyle, it swung its tail as it examined the boy's every move. Without warning, the cat jumped to the floor, suddenly possessed by the spirit of a two-year-old. Mateo noticed the cat's crest rise. "There it is again!" The cat suddenly jumped and landed square in the middle of his book as if it had found its long lost sleeping mat.

He could hardly believe the cat's brazen self-entitlement. Nevertheless, he let it nap on the book until a new surge of energy overtook it and made the cat chase the moving shadows reflected on the walls. With its hind legs and pink toes, the cat defended itself from the menacing cascade of fringes that hung from the bedspread, hissing as if its life was in mortal danger. Mateo was exhausted just watching the cat bounce around out of control. Finally the stray jumped on top of his red suitcase and settled in. Within seconds, Mateo heard its loud purrs. The ball of gray fur and energy was already deep asleep.

Exhaling a deep sigh of frustration, Mateo watched the cat as it slept, vulnerable and at peace. He hated himself for what he was about to do. It was certainly against his better judgment. With quiet steps, he approached the sleeping creature. He lowered his head and felt the cat's soft fur as it brushed against his ear. Mateo rested his head against the cat's belly.

Heart-beat, heart-beat, heart-beat.

Mateo pulled the crystal out of his pocket and held it up to the fading glare of the day. The moving specks of light that sprinkled the room sent the cat into a hopping frenzy. With its pupils dilated to big, bright circles, the cat lowered its head and vigorously wiggled its tail, before attacking the reflections that inexplicably got away. With every pounce, the young cat tried to keep up with the moving bright spots.

"Buela, you have to get this cat out of here!"

"What are you going to name it?"

He was in no mood for Doña Sol's teasing.

"I'm not keeping it!" He could barely hide his irritation. "I will not bring home a stray!" he snapped but still he kept an eye on the cat sunbathing on the balcony. As much as he tried to ignore it, he could hear the cat's happy chirps as it rocked back and forth, taking in the afternoon heat off the floor tiles.

"It's not going anywhere any time soon. What are you going to do about it?"

Doña Sol said, trying to suppress her amusement.

"It's not funny!" He did not appreciate her ribbing. "The last thing I need is to worry about a stray!" He had made up his mind.

Mateo looked around for the stray but it had disappeared as unexpectedly as it had shown up. *"Thank God!"* he thought; the cat finally had gone on its way. *"I knew it. It got something to eat and went back to where it came from. Nothing to worry about anymore!"* In the stillness of his room, he could hear his grandmother fussing about in the kitchen with her complicated dinner ritual. A beautiful melody poured from her small radio and drifted into his bedroom.

> *"I've wandered through my life*
> *Not knowing where to find*
> *The love you've given me.*
> *I was lost, there is no doubt..."*

Even through heavy static, Mateo recognized Minerva's favorite song and was instantly transported back to her small sewing shop. The place where as a four-year-old he sat on the floor with a notebook spread over his lap, keeping her company. Mateo remembered Canela, Minerva's old dog the color of cinnamon, squatting by his side and occasionally lifting her sleepy head to check on the progress of his drawings. Canela peered at him with her big warm eyes, then lowering her head on her paws, resumed her nap.

"What're you doing?" Minerva asked him, taking a break from her sewing.

"A pretty picture," he answered, totally immersed in his creativity.

"A picture of what?" she asked again, pushing up her gold-rimmed glasses.

"A pretty, pretty bride with long, long hair and black shoes," he answered, flattered by her attention.

"She's beautiful! Who's the groom?" Minerva asked as she pinned the homemade pattern over a flat piece of fabric.

"Canela," he answered matter-of-factly and without hesitation.

"Where are they going to live?" Minerva began to snip around the paper pattern with her scissors.

"In Mama's car, so they can go for rides around the town. Because the bride works at the supermarket and she can get Canela's food real cheap and they go for walks around the square. Canela drinks water from the toilet and she smells her own butt!"

Mateo beamed, offering all the necessary details. He looked at Canela, whose eyes followed the sound of his voice. He patted her head and the dog snapped her ears in recognition and gently swayed her tail without moving from her comfortable spot by his side. "I love you, Canela!" he said squeezing her head against his.

"But now dark clouds are gone.
I dream and here you are.
Thank you for saving me.
I knew you were the one…"

Another long day had come to an end, and the music on the radio gradually fused with the subdued flapping sounds of the banana leaves. Almost like clockwork, the fruit of the old mamey behind the house began to hit the ground. Mateo still could not get used to being bolted from his sleep by the incredibly loud noise of falling ripe fruit. Outside in his grandmother's backyard, he could tell night was approaching as the tree branches bowed under the weight of roosting hens.

The evening light slowly acquired a mellow, soothing hue of warm colors that made him feel, for once, serene. Beyond the spread of pastures and hills, the burning disk of the sun was already setting, in its descent covering the nearby hills with warm ochre, pink, and orange. As night began to fall, Palo Verde too, began to slow down.

But contrary to Mateo's belief, the day's surprises were far from over. As he turned away from the window, relaxed and relieved, he realized the missing gray cat had not in fact gone on its way as he had hoped; it was napping inside his suitcase in a cozy nest of his white cotton shirts. In the quiet of the room, he watched the sleeping cat purr in harmony with the rise and fall of its stomach. He resisted waking it up, instead marveling at the small creature that twitched in its dreams, its chest expanding and contracting rhythmically as its lungs filled with air. *"What's going to happen to you?"* he wondered. Conflicted by its presence, he could not help but feel the needy young cat had appeared at the most inconvenient of times.

The morning got off to a scorching start. Even the lizards, their mouths agape from the heat, rested against the cool shade of cement walls. The sun, its path unchallenged by protective clouds, beat steadily down on the town. Don Genaro, sitting at Doña Sol's side on the sunny end of the balcony, removed his hat and wiped the sweat off his brow. He looked up at the warning call of a defiant mockingbird perched in the young avocado tree. His eyes followed the small gray bird aggressively guarding its brood from intruders. Don Genaro watched the belligerent bird fly nervously to and from the branches, creating an intimidating barricade. "It has chicks!" He nudged Doña Sol.

In the meantime, outside in the yard, a noisy royal procession emerged from underneath the shrubs led by a colorful rooster. In search of the best places to scavenge for food, the rest of the loyal entourage of black and red hens strutted behind from one side of the garden to the other, scratching the ground for nourishment. The rooster's clucks kept the party together but, soon frustrated with the slim pickings, the entourage ventured across the street in an orderly but noisy caravan in search of greener pastures.

Doña Sol grabbed a green pea pod and ripped open its spine, filling the crystal bowl in her lap with the small shiny beans.

"Did you have your coffee yet, Genaro?" she asked.

"Black as the devil and sweet as love itself," he answered, cradling the cup of steamy liquid.

Doña Sol smiled at his uncharacteristically poetic response. "Want to give me a hand with these? Where's Mateo?" she asked. Without lifting her eyes from the half-full bowl, she handed him a handful of pods.

"On the hammock, reading," he answered, placing the empty shells into a paper bag.

"Have you noticed something about him?"

"What do you mean?" Don Genaro took a sip of his coffee, and looked at her from under the brim of his straw hat.

"You know the little stray that showed up a couple of days back? For some reason, he wants nothing to do with it."

"He's never turned his back on an animal before," Don Genaro answered, keeping his eye on the agitated mockingbird.

"The funny thing is that it follows him everywhere he goes. It walks ahead of him as if it doesn't trust him to find his way!"

"Hee, hee, hee! *Tanto está la gotera, hasta que hace un hoyo en la piedra.* It will keep poking at him until it finally breaks him down!" Don Genaro chuckled as he tossed a handful of pigeon peas into the glass bowl.

"I still don't quite understand why he is behaving like that!" Doña Sol was puzzled by her grandson's inexplicable resistance.

"To make matters worse, the cat goes crazy when he's not around! No matter how hungry, it will not come out from wherever it's hiding until he comes back! And then, it throws itself at his feet and stretches and carries on, happy as a clam!" she said, combing her fingers through the contents of the bowl.

"I'd say that cat has plans for that boy!" Don Genaro concluded.

While Doña Sol and Don Genaro continued shelling the pigeon peas, the gray cat sat in the middle of the garden, studying every thread of activity around it. Lifting its head, it followed the path of a bird taking flight, watched a family of ducks waddle by the side of the road, and it even stared at Billy who was riding around in circles on his bicycle. All while managing to keep track of the insects and lizards scurrying by.

"Look at it!" Doña Sol pointed as the cat lifted its nose to the wind.

"What does Mateo think?" Don Genaro grabbed another handful of the green pods.

"I'm not sure," she answered.

"He likes animals, doesn't he?" Don Genaro was puzzled too.

In search of a clue, Doña Sol reflected on her past conversations with her grandson. She was afraid her words concerning the stray had been unkind. Even she had to admit the gray cat had stolen part of her heart...

"Sorry, Mateo, I just can't," she had answered when he pleaded for her to keep it. "It would be almost impossible. I can tell you, once you leave, it will vanish. That cat is attached to you! Even if I keep it, it is going to get killed on this road." She was well aware of the constant danger right in front of her house.

"How am I going to restrain an animal that has such an active curiosity?" It pained Doña Sol to be honest about her decision, but she knew it would be torture for an animal to be kept against its will. "I've already lost many pets to the road and this cat would be no exception. Of that, I am certain," she tried to explain to him. "I'm very sorry." It saddened her to know she couldn't relieve her grandson's burden.

Nevertheless, the baffling question remained, "Why is he so conflicted and distant towards the poor stray?"

"But there's something else..." Doña Sol continued, softening her voice.

Don Genaro looked at her. "What do you mean?"

"His behavior. I just don't know what to do."

Finally, Don Genaro offered Doña Sol a valuable clue. "Well, maybe it has to do with Minerva." Caught off guard, Doña Sol thought for a moment. She couldn't hold back the tears that streamed down her face into the glass bowl filled with peas. *"I should have known better!"*

Doña Sol watched Mateo run across the garden as if he was under siege.

"BUELA!" he cried out, covering the top of his head as a black bird whipped him with a tip of its wing.

Ah-nee, Ah-nee, Ah-nee...

The black bird called from its perch high on the wires.

Mateo looked straight at the black bird looking back at him with a mischievous spark in its smart round eyes. The beautiful bird exuded a dignified self-awareness, unlike the chatty grackles balancing on the high wires.

"What's the matter with that bird?" There was something strangely disquieting about the bird's behavior. *"Why is it attacking me?"* he wondered, checking for a nest of chicks that maybe he hadn't noticed. Mateo watched as the bellicose black bird cleaned its beak on both sides of the wire and ruffled its feathers into a black puffy cloud. Brushing off the inexplicable attack, he walked away feeling the bird's stare upon his back.

Ah-nee, Ah-nee, Ah-nee

Judging from the way it stared, Mateo had the uncanny feeling the bird was mocking him.

"Are you okay?" Doña Sol asked, rushing towards him.

"Yes, I am," he answered, still befuddled, when he suddenly realized, *"That's the same bird from the other morning!"*

Looking up at the wires once more, he watched the lustrous black bird sing and spread its wings from its perch, as if feeling proud of the ruckus it had caused moments before. But Mateo still wondered, *"Why did it attack me?"*

Ever since their first encounter, Severo had kept an eye out for the stray. A couple of days later, it had the nerve to show up again. At the sight of it, Severo settled his hoe into the mound of red dirt and felt the taste of bile rising in his throat. He watched the cat make its way along the length of the chain link fence as if nothing had ever happened. "There's that damn cat again!" He chewed on the words as he followed its path with a cold stare. Severo did not take his eyes off the stray as it jumped from the fence down into the empty lot, landing on all fours, its tail held perfectly upright.

"Here it comes again." This time around, Severo was ready. He stood motionless; he did not want to frighten the animal away. It was time to teach the cat a lesson it apparently did not want to learn. "Your time is about to come!"

But to his frustration the cat was not the only creature invading his territory. While waiting for the stubborn stray to get closer, Severo witnessed the arrival of another wandering animal. He shifted his gaze to the small yellow dog sniffing around his yard.

"So you're here too! It's about time I rid this place of useless animals." He knew he had to do something about the dog too.

* * *

Minerva's long wait was finally coming to an end. "I'm bringing Mateo to the island," she heard her sister say at the other end of the line.

The joyous arrival of little Mateo brought a shining light back into Minerva's life. "Let's go, Mateo!" Minerva said to the four-year-old, grabbing his chubby arm. The boy giggled happily, trying to keep up with her long stride. "Let's go out to the field and catch us some butterflies." Minerva shaded her eyes from the sun with her small drawing pad while the toddler held onto the folds of her dress. "Mateo, we don't have much time!" she prodded him as they both made their way down the dirt path.

"Run, Mateo, run! It went that way," Minerva giggled, running barefoot through the waving sea of waist-high grass. She was happy to see the small boy following her, trampling through the field with awkward steps. She loved to hear the boy laugh out loud. "C'mon, Mateo, it's getting away!" Minerva whipped the improvised net around. She jumped with ease through the field, not minding the small cuts and nicks on her bare legs. Her dress billowed furiously around her like a flowery flag.

"Got one! Got one!" the boy screamed, his voice breaking with joy.

Minerva laughed, "Good! Let's go this way now. I know where they hide!" She secured the small drawing pad in her skirt pocket. Grabbing the toddler's chubby hand, she tugged him against her waist as they both made their way down the path, searching for more elusive butterflies. "Let's visit our secret place." Minerva's outings were never complete without a dip in the nearby river. Holding him tightly, she followed the sound of running water.

"There!" Minerva saw the boy's little hand extend towards the river.

"Yes, Mateo, there!" She smiled, watching him take small, tentative steps into the water's soft flow. She looked at his hand holding hers with all his trust. *"Such beautiful little hands,"* she thought as they both waded through the clear, running water, watching as little prawns and tadpoles scurried underneath the stones. They stepped on the slippery, soft algae that covered the rocks, feeling it under the arches of their feet, and wiggled their toes in the sandy bottom.

"Good!" Minerva understood Mateo's delighted expression. "Yes, the water feels good!" She watched him as he lifted pebbles and sand from the bottom of the river.

A faint twinkle in the water caught her attention. "Look, Mateo, a Magic Crystal!"

"Magical!" Mateo's eyes got bigger at the discovery. He put both hands together to receive the piece of broken glass Minerva handed to him, a fragment of a bottle polished smooth by the continuous rubbing of sand and water.

"This is your Magic Crystal, Mateo. Always keep it close and it will attract the good spirits!" Minerva was pleased with her little white lie that put such a sparkle in the boy's eyes.

"Crystal!" he repeated in awe.

Back from their adventure, Minerva breathed a sigh of relief, as if an insurmountable weight had been lifted from her shoulders. *"Mateo is finally home!"* she thought, looking out her window, beyond the belt of the nearby mountains, at the sun being swallowed whole by the horizon. Minerva felt complete. *"Everything is finally falling into its proper place!"* Her thoughts dissolved slowly as she watched the boy lie sleeping, happily exhausted.

The golden light of the remaining day settled upon his small face, flushed and luminous with the island's heat, like a cherub in a Raphael painting. Minerva listened to the child's steady, and at times labored, breathing in his deep sleep. She decided to create a gift for him as a reminder of their time together, a talisman that would bind them in good times and bad. "Wherever you are, I'll be with you." Minerva threaded the rustic twine through a hole in the thin disk of glass and carefully tied it around the sleeping child's neck.

PART FOUR

An Unexpected Turn

"*O h, brother!*" Mateo resisted waking the stray up from its nap inside his suitcase. That night, he decided to allow the cat to hang around his room but took precautions to leave the door ajar, "just in case it wants to go home." He was certain this time around the cat would get bored and simply go back to where it came from. Hopefully back to the loving, nurturing family and teary-eyed children that were missing it. Still one question nagged at him. "How come no one's looking for it?"

The following morning he woke up surrounded by an eerie silence. Adjusting his eyes to the early light streaming through the window, he looked for signs of the cat. "He's gone," he finally realized. "*I don't need to worry about it anymore.*" He wanted to believe it. "*It's better this way.*"

But he found he had to get used to the stray's abrupt disappearance. He couldn't ignore the empty spot the cat had left behind. "There was nothing I could do. I knew it would leave." What Mateo didn't anticipate was the sudden guilt that overcame him as his mind struggled with another issue at hand: the day he had to leave the island was fast approaching.

"*Where has all the time gone?*" As much as the island's slow ways irritated him, he preferred it to the city's cold, noise, and constant hustle. "At least here I can see the sun. I don't miss the tall buildings."

As he walked around the room, Mateo contemplated the red suitcase the stray had used as its nesting place. He had promised his mother, "I'll pack ahead of time." But it was the kind of promise he knew was not going to keep. He had intentionally put it off, as if wishful thinking could stop the progress of time. As a result, the suitcase sat wide open like a hungry red monster, forgotten in a corner of the room. "*I have to make an effort, just so I won't forget.*" Once again, he folded the top down on the suitcase and ran the zipper around it. "*I still have a few days.*" He was amazed at how fast the days had flown by as his return home grew closer.

"I'll get around to it." Having made the first and most important decision of the day, he spent the rest of it trying to ignore it.

Still not ready to face the world, he put on his glasses and tried to read his book, but he could not concentrate. Somehow, he felt guilty staying in his room when the morning was spreading under the bright sky. Outside there were already busy sounds of people washing cars, mowing their lawns, and warning their children to stay away from the busy road. The same hectic, small town early morning, much like the ones before, caught in an endless loop of activity.

Walking to the door, Mateo lost his footing and tumbled forward. He checked under his shoe and discovered the red ball the cat had chased around the room just hours before. He did not want to worry anymore about the stray's whereabouts. *"It's gone, and that's it."* But he could not shake off his anxiety. He tried to convince himself it was the right ending to a difficult situation.

An animal that lives by its instincts, knows when it's wanted and when it's not.

A young stray cat will accept a handout but it also knows that no matter how comfortable a new setting becomes, it has to move on. A kind gesture or a warm touch might delay its departure, but a stray keeps its memories of past misfortune. Sooner or later, it will find itself walking on the side of another lonely road. *"Was loved,"* it remembers, knowing that even love is no guarantee of security.

For days, the gray stray had followed the boy's every step. *"May I stay?"* it had pleaded but the *Animalfriend's* heart seemed locked. The stray knew then it would be best to move on, so it decided to go back to the forest where, no matter what, it would always feel secure. *"Home. Fallingstar!"* The cat thought about the ghost and knew it was waiting for its return.

Well rested after a good night's sleep, the young stray jumped down from its nest of shirts before the day began to rise. Once it had stretched its legs and wiped its face clean, the cat snuck out of the room just in time to hear the final hoots of the owl in the breadfruit tree.

"Goodbye, Animalfriend!" And with that, the cat headed back to the river where the frogs sang, back to its bed of dry leaves under the branches of the orange tree, back to Fallingstar.

Doña Sol stopped her sweeping and watched Mateo wander around the garden aimlessly. She felt lost too, not knowing exactly what to do to ease his dark mood. She trod very carefully around him.

"Did you have your breakfast yet?" she asked, trying to break his silence. She only got an unintelligible, muffled response. She watched him hang on to the chain link fence like a hopeless recluse. His body language was sending mixed signals of loneliness and defiance. She knew one more word from her would spark an argument, so she resumed sweeping the coat of thin red dust and dried leaves off the floor.

"You can go for a walk if you want," she suggested, only to be ignored.

Mateo looked across the street. Severo was seated on his porch, filing his machete for what seemed like the umpteenth time. Mateo's only choice for a walk was along the narrow stretch of grass in front of the fence. He took another look at Severo and decided to avoid him at all costs. "*What a big turd you are!*" was his only thought.

The sight of Severo reminded him of the poor stray. He couldn't help but feel pity for the animal that now had obviously moved on. "*I hope it will be safe this time around,*" he wished, uncertain of the animal's fate. He needed to do something soon to get the cat out of his thoughts.

Right on cue, he heard a loud rattling, as if something was falling apart, and with great relief watched as the familiar Jeep came down the road. Stumpy stuck his head out the passenger window, ears and tongue flapping wildly in the wind. The Jeep took a sharp turn and charged its way up to the front gates of the house, sending gravel and dirt flying in all directions.

Mateo lifted his arm up to protect his face from the spray of pebbles.

"Hey, wanna go to the river?" Sergio yelled out the window. "We're going fishing for prawns!" He waved a homemade net around. Sergio's father revved the Jeep's engine as if to help him make up his mind.

"*Fishing for prawns? That's something I don't hear every day!*" He exchanged glances with his grandmother and she waved him on. The instant Mateo jumped in the back, Sergio's father sped the rattling Jeep up the road, leaving behind a dense cloud of fumes.

* * *

"Mateo, what are you doing?" Minerva watched the six-year-old boy sitting on the front steps. Canela sat by his side and made him hold her paw. Canela could be very insistent; the dog just didn't know when to quit. If she got tired, she switched paws. So the boy sat patiently, holding her paw in his small hand. Beads of sweat

rolled down his temples, still he would not let go.

"Hi, Mateo. Are you sitting with your girlfriend again?" Benny the neighbor teased him.

"She is not my girlfriend. She is a dog!" the toddler giggled happily.

"If you keep holding her paw, you'll have to take her to the movies and buy her popcorn!"

The toddler giggled wildly again. "I made her a paper hat," he announced with pride.

"You didn't, did you?" Benny egged him on.

"Yes, and I painted it myself," he answered, never letting go of Canela's paw.

"You are so talented, Mateo. I'm so proud of you," answered Benny.

Clan-clan-keety-clan-clan…

Mateo looked up at the red wind chimes dancing underneath the candy-striped awnings of Benny's balcony. The constant tinkle of the glass panels against each other amused him. He loved to watch their delicate little tinkly song and dance.

"I like them," he said, pointing up to the little rectangular glass plates.

"I know you do. You always sit in the same place with Canela," Minerva reminded him, while threading a needle to fix the hem of a skirt. A gust of wind pushed the chimes into another noisy dance.

Clan-clan-keety-clan-clan…
Tinkle, tinkle, tinkle
Clan-clan-keety-clan-clan…
Tinkle, tinkle, tinkle
Clan-clan-keety-clan-clan…
Tinkle, tinkle, tinkle

* * *

Fishing for prawns proved to be a rather fun expedition for Mateo. He had followed Sergio and his father and Stumpy down along the river's current. To everyone's amusement, the dog showed extraordinary skill navigating the shallow waters, paddling with his short legs. Meanwhile, Sergio and his father stuck the net under the rocks.

"Ready?" Mateo asked Sergio, before lifting a rock and watching the prawns rush out of their caves towards the net.

"We got another one!" Sergio screamed.

The long afternoon finally turned into evening and Mateo returned home sunburned and shiny, carrying a paper bag holding a handful of scrawny prawns.

"Here, Buela, you can make soup." He announced to Doña Sol handing her the paper bag. He was pleased to hear his grandmother's hearty laugh. Discreetly he checked the small, green dish he had filled with dog food that morning but was disappointed to discover it was untouched, a sure sign the cat was gone, probably for good.

"Well, it was a stray after all. It just moved on." He clenched his jaws as he felt a burning in his eyes but he was determined not to show any signs of weakness. Mateo shut the door of his room behind him.

* * *

Keeping her eye on Mateo, Minerva lowered her sewing glasses from her forehead, where they were resting like a bespectacled tiara. She took her place at the stool behind the counter and revved up the sewing machine with a single push of her foot on the pedal. The loud sound shook the walls of the small shop with the blast of a car engine, as if suddenly the room had become a racing track. She knew this was Mateo's favorite part. She enjoyed the curiosity reflected on the boy's face as she pushed the fabric folds under the fast-moving needle that permanently united them.

Over at her working table, she cut out the shapes with the speed and precision of a skillful surgeon. The fabric pieces were then carefully piled up. Once she had all the necessary parts, she sat behind her machine and started sewing them one against the other. From the moment she snapped the presser foot into place and turned the small hand metal wheel, fabric came down in cascades of abstract folds, colors, and prints. In no time, the awkward cuts, loose ends, and hanging threads started to take on defined shapes. Soon enough, a formless piece of fabric became a sleeve, a pocket, a flowing skirt, a beautiful dress.

Mateo watched in amazement and filled with wonder as Minerva performed the complicated routine of draping the unfinished piece over the beaten up, headless mannequin that had stood for years in a corner of the shop. With her yellow measuring tape draped over her shoulders, she placed a pin here, trimmed a bit there, and a finished garment materialized right before his eyes.

He listened amused as Minerva and her customer exchanged family updates along with sprinkles of mild gossip. As the women said their good-byes, he watched Minerva place the garment inside a bag and saw as the customer walked happily out of the shop, disappearing into the busy street.

Once the sewing session was over, it was time to relax. He was entertained as Minerva let herself be carried away by the familiar songs streaming out of the radio. He paid close attention as she sang along to every melody backed up by a noisy chorus of roosters from the neighbor's breeding pen. Early on, Mateo had learned that Minerva was not good at carrying a tune. Oddly enough though, she was good at making Canela and the other dogs in the neighborhood sing along with her, much like a pack of wolves howling at the sight of a full moon. Still, Mateo loved to hear her singing...

* * *

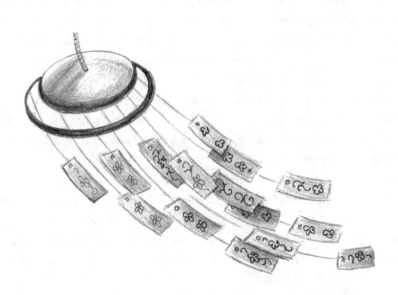

AND REMEMBER, DEAR HOMEMAKER, GIVE YOUR FAMILY THE BEST! AND IF IT'S GOYA, IT HAS TO BE GOOD!... ATTENTION! ATTENTION! HAVING TROUBLE MAKING PAYMENTS ON YOUR NEW CAR? NO PROBLEM, THE SACRED FAMILY UNION COOPERATIVE HAS YOUR BACK!... BEEN ROBBED, SCAMMED, OR HURT IN AN ACCIDENT? MIRANDA, GOMEZ, AND SANCHEZ WILL NOT REST UNTIL YOU GET WHAT'S COMING TO YOU! WE PROMISE, OR OUR NAME IS NOT MIRANDA, GOMEZ, AND SANCHEZ!... FEELING UNLUCKY IN LOVE? CALL SISTER RUMAKI, SHE'LL FIND IN THE STARS THE MAN THAT IS WAITING FOR YOU JUST AROUND THE CORNER!

The sudden impact from the loudspeakers boomed through every window of the house and made the walls tremble. The loud cacophony of noises assaulting his senses pulled Mateo out of his early morning grogginess. "There it goes again!" It was not difficult to identify the source of the disturbance that had left the walls shaking in its wake. "The dysfunctional advertising agency on wheels," Mateo had named it. He adjusted his glasses to catch a glance and could not hold back a chuckle when he identified the culprit: *Agripino!* The disco-loving, middle-aged-young-at-heart, big-car loving man. He could not hold back a chuckle as the pickup truck disappeared down the road, leaving behind a mumbled trail of music and unintelligible announcements. As soon as the racket faded, he could hear horses clacking their hooves over the asphalt like castanets as they galloped alongside speeding cars. *"This is some serious crazy town!"*

Mateo got dressed and went to look for his grandmother. "She's in the garden," Don Genaro said. As he came down the stairs he noticed a rustling inside a tall potted fern in a corner of the garden. A second brisk movement from behind the plant made him more cautious.

Suddenly, whatever creature was hiding there took a huge, aggressive leap towards his face. Not knowing what it was, he had no time to prepare for the impact. With a loud, anxious yelp, he lost his balance and fell backwards. Feeling slightly disoriented, he checked his face for cuts or bleeding then picked himself up, still feeling his heart beating in his throat and eardrums. His temples throbbed from the sudden rush of blood.

The book he had held against his chest like a protective shield lay on the ground with its pages in disarray. His glasses had flown off his face and landed on the rough concrete floor. Placing them over his eyes again, he searched for the ferocious animal. But the shock of the sudden attack did not compare to the bigger surprise right in front of him.

The loud scream and subsequent thud stopped Doña Sol in her tracks. *"What was that?"* She did not know what to make of Mateo sitting on the hard cement, looking disheveled and confused. *"Is he hurt?"* she thought alarmed, loosening her grip on the water hose. She walked towards the boy still sitting on the floor like a rag doll. But everything made sense when she saw the cat rolling on the ground in front of him.

Doña Sol turned away and hid her mouth behind her hand, unable to control her laughter. To avoid embarrassing the boy any further, she masked her chuckles with the sound of water spurting noisily from the hose. Luckily, he didn't see the tears streaming from the corners of her eyes. It had been a while since she had laughed so hard.

"It's back! The cat is back!" he called out to his grandmother while staring in disbelief at the animal lying at his feet, rolling on its back and making its peculiar chirping sounds. It was clear the cat was very pleased with itself.

"Where have you been? You little monster!" Once he got over his embarrassment, Mateo marveled at the cat's mischievous streak, "I should've known!" But with its return, the stray also stirred up his concern. *"What am I going to do now?"*

"What are you going to name him?" his grandmother teased, still holding back chuckles.

"I don't want it. I already told you!" he snapped.

Unconvinced, Doña Sol could see beyond the boy's stubbornness. *"He can't deny it!"* she thought as she watched him kneel on the ground and softly rub his knuckles against the cat's back. He ran his hands up and down its spotted stomach and with the tips of his fingers, carved soft furrows in its silky fur. Leaping to its feet, the cat fluttered its tail and rubbed its face against the boy's legs as if secretly marking him as its personal property. There was no more reassuring sound than a cat's happy purrs.

Doña Sol realized the moment of levity had opened a window, maybe even a way for her to reach him. *"Maybe he'll understand."*

Mateo heard his grandmother's voice. "Here, Mateo," she said, handing him a beautiful red, ripe mango from her tree. The boy lifted his gaze from the purring cat.

"Thanks, grandma... I'm sorry."

"Don't worry," she answered, patting his head and sitting on the old plastic chair by the hammock.

"Do you remember that time when you helped Minerva rescue a family of puppies off the street?"

Doña Sol did not hear his answer, but she noticed as his cheeks blushed and a string of small tears lined his eyelids.

"She was very proud of you. She used to tell me, 'Mateo is very special and he'll grow up to be a good man.'"

Mateo did not dare answer or lift his eyes. From the salty taste of his mango, he realized he was crying.

"We all miss her and we always will. You are young but now you realize how life changes without warning. We are on this earth only for a short while. Even though she is gone, you don't have to stop loving her."

"I didn't get to say goodbye." The words came out softly.

Doña Sol was at a loss as to what to say but she understood he needed her strength.

"You have to understand we all have to move on, each in our way. Death, unfortunately, is a part of life. Sometimes a deep hurt can be healed by a simple act of love. Think about it."

"What do you mean?" he asked with a broken voice.

"It's standing next to you!" She ran her fingers through Mateo's crown of shiny black hair and watched as the cat jumped on his lap, gently rubbing his chin with its head.

"He slept by your door all night, you know," Doña Sol informed him.

From the impressive canopy of a flamboyant trees covered with flaming red blossoms, a band of noisy swallows sprang upward into the cloudless sky and soared above their heads. "Minerva is gone, but her spirit will be with you forever." Secretly, he was comforted by his grandmother's words. "I do hope you find it in your heart to someday understand why your grandfather did what he did. We were naive. You know we did love her and that she loved you more than anything, don't you?"

FROM MATEO'S JOURNAL

"Yes, I know she loved me," I remember thinking then. But I did not need to hear it from her. No matter what, I still held her responsible; accomplice to Minerva's spiritual demise. A mother and father had allowed their self-righteous rage to hide under the guise of love. What did she know about love? As far as I was concerned, the fact my grandmother didn't try to stop her husband from exiling his own daughter out of their lives made her even weaker in my eyes.

How could she talk about love, when she didn't even acknowledge her daughter's bout of deep depression. I do not remember the fight for her life back then, but I still hear her bellowing to the moon like a caged wild animal, her hopeless cries begging to be allowed to return home. She had agreed to leave behind all traces of her life. She just wanted to feel protected once again by everything familiar to her. The threat of being shamed by her neighbors was nothing next to her desire to breathe the air that fed the mountains once more.

Unbearable darkness. I can still see it in her eyes. It was only much later that I realized it was me—her source of joy, her accomplice chasing butterflies—that was a reminder of her darker hour. But it was me too, who had stolen the light just by coming into her life. I could see it everywhere around me. I sensed it in Maria even when she held me close and kissed the top of my head. I saw it in my grandparents' caution around me, as if a sudden movement would shatter the fragile membrane protecting their secret.

I remember her looking at me, her red eyes swollen with tears. "I'm sorry Mateo, I'm really sorry." And she would wrap her warm arms around my head, releasing a torrent of tears down the back of my neck. To this day, I don't understand why Maria chose to divulge the big secret along with the news of Minerva's death, but I can't really blame her. The weight of her burden surely had been greater than mine. So I let my anger sink in. It was the only way for me to move forward. Sometimes I think that love, in many instances, has nothing to do with love...

PEBBLES, TWIGS, AND BUTTERFLIES

From his hammock, Mateo spied the cat entertaining itself in the sunny garden. It pawed excitedly at a twig, sending it flying off into the air, only to catch it and bat it around some more. In the blink of an eye, it turned its attention to a small pile of white pebbles, scattering them around then running after them as if they were trying to get away. Soon, the sight of a lizard interrupted its pebble game, sending it off on another spirited pursuit. Luckily the lizard saved itself from certain death by escaping hastily up a tree. It was only a matter of seconds before the cat found another diversion: chasing butterflies. The butterfly in question was a small and delicate yellow sulpher bobbing around the garden.

Like a heat-seeking missile, the cat's dilated pupils locked in on the small yellow butterfly and traced the direction of its flight pattern. As the pretty insect bobbed overhead, the cat swatted as if to catch it, but it became apparent this was only an excuse to bounce happily all over the garden. With its tail curved into a fuzzy question mark, the relentless cat chased after the butterfly until it finally floated out of reach and off into the open field. Frustrated, the young cat sat silently, swaying its tail softly from side to side.

Mateo saw the cat's apparent disappointment as the butterfly disappeared into the field dotted with white and orange wild flowers. He had to smile though when the cat, once again bored, began to rub its face gently against the orchids in his grandmother's garden. "*He owns them now too,*" he thought.

There was still something bothering him. "*I only have a few days left!*" He decided the only solution was to find the cat a safe shelter before he departed. He feared, with good reason, that the stray would finally meet its fate in the busy street or endure a short life of abuse and starvation. His grandmother's words had not made it any easier. "Strays are a dime a dozen... a lot of them come from the woods looking for food and water but nobody wants them. Even if you give them a home, they can't be household pets." To make matters worse, the memory of Severo's attack a few days earlier was still freshly burned in his mind.

"*I have to save it from this place.*" Just then, he became aware of the stray staring at him as if it could read his thoughts. What worried him the most was the cat had begun to wear down his resistance. For the first time, he seriously considered what seemed like the only alternative left. *"If I'm going to do something for him, I have to do it now!"*

He watched the cat run across the yard and hide under the poinsettias. Sitting in the shadows, the cat watched the road ahead and the traffic running through it. Placidly, it swung its tail from one side to the other. A loud meow made Mateo jump out of his seat. To his horror, he watched as the cat, running across the yard, dodged the prick of the bird's beak on its back.

"That damn bird again!"

But Mateo was not prepared for what he witnessed next. *"What the heck is going on now?"*

Ah-nee, Ah-nee, Ah-nee

He heard the familiar cry, and watched the bird repeat its attack. The cat threw itself onto the ground on its back with claws drawn and managed to grab one of the bird's long black feathers.

Ah-nee, Ah-nee, Ah-nee

Feeling outsmarted, the bird turned and dived for the cat's back again as it tried to get away.

Ah-nee, Ah-nee, Ah-nee

Mateo gasped in terror as the bird took a nosedive and pecked the cat's belly. Finding its chance, the cat swatted at the black bird's head. Mateo was having a hard time witnessing these attacks, until he realized... *"Oh my God... They're playing!"*

Once alone in his room, he hoped the silence would help settle his mind. His grandmother's unexpected words about Minerva had hardly set his mind at ease; instead, they had refreshed his anger. Her words had fanned his sense of betrayal and his struggle to overcome it. And now, to complicate matters even further, there was the impending decision as to what, if anything, could be done to spare the life of the stray. He smiled at the thought of the young cat chasing butterflies

out in the garden.

He shot a glance across the room, as the softening light of dusk silhouetted his suitcase. *"Still not packed,"* he thought frustrated, as the calendar on the wall reminded him the day for his departure was getting closer. Without any clear options or ideas, Mateo felt pushed into a corner.

"What was that!?" A sudden blood-curdling sound catapulted him off his bed and out of the house. Frantic, he followed the cat's desperate cry. *"Where is it coming from?"* He searched outside and discovered the young stray trembling on the ledge, cornered by a yellow feral cat. He noticed the red line under the stray's eye. The yellow cat had left its mark: a bloody gash across the young stray's face. The scary episode convinced Mateo he had to find a way to save the helpless animal. This frightening attack was only one of the many dangers awaiting it. *"I can't leave him behind now."*

"What time is it?" Mateo woke up so early he heard the hoot of a lone screech owl announcing the end of its nocturnal shift. Thin clouds steered away from the moon as it faded into the sky. He checked the pile of clothing where the cat had made its bed. *"Where is it now?"* Searching around the dark room, Mateo felt a gust of cold air rush through, making him shiver. A soft rain began to sprinkle the backyard. *"He's not here!"* He looked out his window over to the flower bed, but the cat was nowhere to be seen. *"Where has it gone now?"*

This time he was not about to sit around and wait. He walked out of the house into the cold dawn. His eyes tried to adjust to the darkness that was just breaking into daylight. *"Why am I out in the cold this early? This cat is insane,"* he thought, pulling the blanket tighter around his shoulders. Mateo searched all the cat's favorite places: under the mango tree, across the garden, by the potted ferns, but it was nowhere to be found.

"Meesu, where are you?" he called out into the ferns.

"Meesu, Meesu," he called again, walking through the wet grass with bare feet. The cold wind was whistling among the tree tops and already he could see light filtering between the clouds and realized there was only moments before sunrise.

"Meeesuuu, Meeesuuu! Meeesuuu!"

"Meeesuu, Meeesuu, where are you?"

A rustling in the poinsettias made him lower his hand cautiously into the leafy bush. He stumbled back as the cat jumped out at him without warning. Mateo was embarrassed at being outsmarted yet again. Yet, he couldn't help but to be amused by the cat's insistence in playing hide-and-seek, when he least expected it. Thankfully, this time there were no witnesses around. From the expression on the cat's face, he could tell it was feeling very proud of itself.

"Ha, ha, ha. You silly cat. Come inside!" Mateo swept the cat up in his arms and headed upstairs, out of the morning cold. "You little savage!"

Prrrrrrr... Prrrrrrr... Prrrrrr...

Mateo felt the cat purring against his chest and knew it felt safe. *"Travieso,"* mischievous cat!

He too understood early on that he was no match for this intelligent and astute cat. It scared him that the stray could easily outsmart him in the blink of its green eyes. Mateo got the strangest feeling that he was digging a deeper hole every time he thought about the cat's future. *A cat that has been abandoned finds it hard to settle down.* He tried to get used to its unnerving habit of disappearing. *"This cat is going to drive me up the wall, I can see it now."* What he did not yet realize was he had been craftily and unwittingly conditioned into a daily ritual.

Once again, Mateo woke up before daybreak to find the cat's bed empty. *"Where is it now?"* he wondered, just as he heard the frightful sound of a car screeching to a halt. He jumped out of bed without bothering to dress and ran outside expecting the worst. "Meesu!!" he screamed in the dark. The car sped away and disappeared down the road. "Meesu!!" he called again.

He opened the gate and ran out into the dark, deserted road but could not see the cat. For a brief instant he was relieved, but he knew his search would not be over anytime soon. A sudden stream of cold air made him shiver. The early sun hidden below the horizon began to streak light across the dark sky still covered with fast moving clouds. The whole neighborhood was still enveloped in an eerie, dream-like glow.

"Where is it hiding now?" Mateo walked the empty yard, his steps slowed by the pain of prickly stones underfoot. His thin pajamas gave no protection from the morning chill, as he walked up to the fence where the young stray had appeared just

a few days before. "Meesu!" As a last resort, he thoroughly inspected the empty lot beyond the fence, calling again and again, "Meesu!" It was clear the cat was simply not ready to give up its independence. He hated the cat's unpredictable habits. In spite of all the attacks it had endured, the cat moved around the neighborhood as if it didn't have a care in the world.

Just as he was about to give up, he spotted the cat curled up into a small, furry ball, asleep on the rain-soaked clay. As it heard Mateo's calls, it lifted its head slowly and threw the boy a sad glance. Mouthing a soft "meow," it acknowledged his presence. The cat then jumped to its feet and ran towards Mateo with loud chirping sounds, coiling its tail around his legs before being led back to safety.

"Let's go home little cat, let's go home."

In an instant, the cat had forgotten the night out on the bare, cold soil and happily ran to the bowl of food which it downed in a hurry.

"You little savage! This is the last time you'll get away from me, you hear me?" But he knew it was hopeless. He watched the cat take eager bites of food from the bowl and gulp down a saucer of warm milk. As the cat groomed itself in a corner of the big chair, it finally it dawned on him, *"This cat doesn't have a name!"* But he was fully aware that it was hardly an accident. As a matter of fact, it had simply been his deliberate attempt to keep the stray at bay. Giving a name to an animal was not to be taken lightly. Once the cat had a name, it would without a doubt change the rules of the game forever. *If you name it, it will own you!*

PART FIVE

You Name It, It Owns You!

"What's in a name?"

—William Shakespeare, *Romeo and Juliet*, (Act II, Scene II)

By now it was clear to him. "This cat has no home, Buela," Mateo said, finding himself at a crossroads.

Doña Sol watched as the cat jumped up on the boy's lap. "You know, if you change your mind... I'm sure he will have a better life with you." But even she doubted her own advice. After all, she had witnessed first-hand the animal's incurable independence.

Absentmindedly, Mateo caressed the back of the purring cat with his fingertips. His biggest preoccupation now was, *"How do I take this cat away from the island? Away from the place where it has roamed freely all his life? Will it survive away from the open space?"* His mind raced as he considered an even greater obstacle to overcome. He had to plan his next move very carefully before he broke the news to Maria...

'Another animal? Forget it! I don't think that's a good idea at all!' he feared his mother would surely protest. To his credit, Mateo's prediction had not been far off.

"Please."

"That's definitely out of the question. I cannot handle another animal."

He was disheartened by Maria's harsh reaction. *"This is not good. Not good at all."* He hung up the phone and wiped away the sweat from his forehead. Suddenly the heavy load on his shoulders had become heavier. "What am I going to do now? I can't leave him, Buela!"

Doña Sol was mindful not to contradict the child's mother. "I'm sorry. I don't know what to tell you. If that was her reaction then you have no choice. I'm sure eventually somebody will come along and like him enough to give him a good home."

Mateo did not like her answer. "Who's going to care for it until then?" he replied, his voice heavy with doubt. But far from giving up, he began to plan his strategy. He realized there was a big job to do if he was going to bring the cat home. A glance at the calendar reminded him there was not much time left. He knew he had to act fast.

"What am I doing?" He was not looking forward to the intense negotiations that would follow. "*Think fast!*" he pushed himself. His eyes lit up when a thought flashed through his head.

"Muddy!" he blurted out.

"What?" Doña Sol was taken aback.

"Muddy Mohawk! That's his name," Mateo declared triumphantly.

"Muddy Mohawk! Why would you name a kitten after dirt?" She was incredulous.

"Because he was covered in mud when he first showed up, remember?"

"What about the Mohawk part?"

"Don't you see the crest on his head?"

She had to admit the boy had a sense of humor. "And how is giving the cat a name going to help you resolve your problem?"

"It's very clear," he was confident.

"What on earth are you talking about?" Doña Sol felt lost.

"Can't you see? If I name him, he's not a stray anymore. That means he has an owner! Can't you see? It makes sense!"

From the look of disbelief on his grandmother's face, it was as if he had suggested he was going to shave her head. He tried to contain a sudden urge to burst out laughing.

"That's the craziest thing I've ever heard!" she answered. Then, like little children, they both began to laugh uncontrollably. As Doña Sol left the room, Mateo's laughter lifted a heavy weight off her heart.

The early quiet of the day was shattered by agitated screams. Mateo rushed downstairs to find out what was going on and discovered Sergio shouting at Severo at the top of his lungs.

"Why did you do that to him?" Sergio yelled.

"Keep that damn dog off of my property, I'm warning you!" Severo hissed.

"You're a nasty turd!" Sergio could not let it go. "Take this, you jackass!" he shouted and flung a stone that landed on the porch, missing Severo's head by inches.

"I'll take care of you later," Severo threatened once more.

"Yeah! You'll have to eat my shit! You nasty, gutless old turd!"

"Keep that dirty flea bag away from me!" Severo screamed.

"Seems to me YOU ARE THE ONE THAT CAN GIVE FLEAS TO HIM!" Sergio flung another stone in Severo's direction. This one managed to zip closely by Severo's head and hit the window with a loud crash.

"What's the matter, Serge?" Mateo got his friend to finally calm down.

"That nasty sunnavabitch! He kicked Stumpy, that's what!" Sergio snapped, his face flushed with the rush of blood.

"Never mind him!" Mateo felt sorry for his friend and the dog. He had not forgotten his own encounter with Severo. In fact it was still fresh in his mind like a recurring bad dream. Thankfully, the dog had already forgotten the attack and was rolling on the fresh grass in front of the chain link gate. "C'mon, let's get out of here." They hopped on their bikes and soon were gliding down the road, followed by Stumpy, who welcomed the challenge.

As they sped away, from the corner of his eye Mateo saw Severo twitching with anger. He felt his stomach turn. *"He's going to get even,"* he feared. It was just a matter of time now.

"He's going to get even," Billy predicted. He watched from his window as Stumpy wandered into the front yard, sniff, sniff, sniffing. *"Hope it'll get out of here before father shows up,"* he thought. Sadly, Billy saw the small dog come into Severo's crosshairs exactly as he had foreseen.

"There it is again, that tick-ridden mutt," Severo muttered as he clenched his teeth and walked towards the dog that was now wagging its tail in greeting.

The dog's screams of pain soon were heard around the whole neighborhood, causing people to stop what they were doing and stick their heads out of their windows. They felt sorry for the animal, but they were thankful that none of their pets had been Severo's target this morning. At least for now.

Severo did not see the boy just steps behind him. Billy cringed as he watched Sergio charge towards Severo from behind with his bicycle. Luckily, Severo managed to dodge the bike but nevertheless lunged back with a steady stream of curses and threats.

Billy felt his stomach turn. He walked away from the window just as a stone hit the frame with an explosive sound.

"You shit head! I'm going to teach you a lesson!" Sergio screamed, searching the ground for more ammunition.

"I warned you before to keep that mutt off of my property!" Severo shot back.

From their furious exchange, Billy suspected Sergio wasn't backing off anytime soon, making Severo run for cover. But he also knew his father would retaliate, "*as sure as there is a sun in the sky.*" No doubt about it.

"I'LL GET YOU FOR THIS, YOU DISRESPECTFUL PUNK!" Severo screamed back. As Billy knew too well, Severo was good at keeping his promises.

It is widely known a stray cat can never stay in the same place for long, especially when there is an orange tree waiting by the river, where it could sleep listening to the crickets and cicadas at night. Even toys and red balls lose their attraction eventually. Although its time with the *Kindanimals* had been enjoyable, the cat had only one thought going around its head, "*Fallingstar, friend!*"

So it headed back to the place it called home, back to the forest where it felt safe. "*Old tree, friend!*" It pranced happily down the familiar red dirt path through the field of grass, beyond the brush and lantana, and into the forest. After quick sips of fresh water from the stream, the cat lay on its bed by the orange tree. With a heavy sigh, it got ready for a nap, swatting away bugs with sharp flips of its ears.

For days, the ghost had been waiting for the cat's return, sitting on the mossy boulder by the side of the river. The crisp, late summer breeze had gradually transformed into stifling afternoon heat, and the parched lips of the earth began breathing out steam. The sheer density of the humidity dampened all activity in the forest. Only the gentle rustle of leaves and the gushing of the river broke the midday silence. As the sun finally settled, the ghost emerged from the shadows of the crimson stalks of canna.

"Goaway, where are you?" the ghost whispered, "Are you back?"

"*Yeeesss, wassss sleeepiiing,*" answered the cat slightly annoyed.

"Where were you this morning?" The ghost sat by the dozing cat.

"*Do not know,*" the cat answered, its patience beginning to wear thin.

"Yes, you do!" insisted the ghost. "*Animalfriend* was looking for you!"

Prrr prrr prrr! The cat jumped to its feet and stretched its legs.

"Good!" the ghost giggled.

"*Yeees.*" The cat snapped its ears.

"Will you leave this place?" The ghost looked for an answer in the cat's body language.

"*Don't know.*" The tip of the cat's tail twitched nervously from side to side.

"Maybe there's a better life for you somewhere else. Away from *Stinkanimal.*" The ghost watched as the cat's body stiffened.

"*Maybe.*"

"Do you trust *Animalfriend*?"

"*Yeees,*" answered the cat.

"I think you already know what you need to do." The ghost was pleased by the cat's purrs.

* * *

The heavy black clouds outside Minerva's window weighed heavily on her psyche. All of a sudden, the day had turned sad and melancholic.

"I don't know how to stop this!" She cried herself to sleep, careful not to allow Mateo to see her in such a state. But it was inevitable, the day she feared the most had finally arrived. "*I can't bear to think he'll be so far away!*" Still she had to admit that the island would one day be too small a world for the child.

Maria had given her the bad news: she was returning to the States with Mateo, now nine years old. Minerva had been dreading the inevitable moment for so long, it was forged into her subconscious. Although she had managed to avoid thinking about this day for a long time, the plausibility of it happening had loomed menacingly. Minerva resented her sister. "*How could she?*" And yet she understood Maria's need to spread her wings and forge her own path. "*But what's to become of Mateo?*" she worried. Yes, the boy deserved a better life. She could barely breathe just thinking about it, but she knew it would be hard enough for him to deal with someone else deciding what was best for him. She felt his pain. Nobody knew the feeling like she did. Nobody.

Within days, Minerva had made peace with Maria's decision to take Mateo away. "A new beginning for everyone," Maria had assured her, to soothe her pain. She could only imagine Minerva's devastation. "Just until you are better again!" she promised.

The boy shrugged in answer.

"You should be excited." Minerva pulled gently at his ear.

"I don't want to go back," he whimpered.

"Your mother wants a better life for you," Minerva said unconvincingly,
as she fought back tears. She did not want to fan the flames
of an already delicate situation.

Mateo stared wistfully at the blue frosted cake set in the middle of the table.

"Go on. Cut the cake before Canela takes another chunk of it!" Minerva said,
making him laugh.

"Now, blow out the candles and make a wish. You're nine years old today! You're
almost a man!" Minerva did not let him see her tears.

"I'm going to miss her." He patted Canela softly on her head.

"You'll be back. Canela will be here and I'll always be here waiting for you too.
I promise you. Now, where's your magic crystal?"

"In my pocket," he answered.

"Well, let's put it on for luck!" Minerva fastened the crystal around his neck.

"Mateo, hurry up!" Sergio called out.

"I'm there!" he shouted back, throwing a pair of cutoff jeans into his backpack. "See ya later!" he shouted to his grandmother, flying down the steps and jumping into the waiting Jeep before she had a chance to ask any questions. The car disappeared down the road, zigzagging in and out of view in between the line of trees.

"You guys be safe now, you hear? I'll pick you up tomorrow." With those words of advice, Sergio's father stepped on the gas and revved his Jeep up through the dunes, leaving the boys under a dense cloud of sand and fumes.

"This is perfect!" Sergio stretched and breathed in the ocean's salty breeze.

Mateo gasped at the sight of the perfect horseshoe shape of the turquoise ocean before him. Sergio stretched his arms up to the sky. "This is the perfect spot for the tent!"

"Don't you think it's too close to the water?"

"That shows how little you know about the ocean, my friend!" Sergio responded with an inflated ego. "It will take a long time before the tide reaches the shore."

"Should we try another spot just in case?" insisted Mateo.

"No way! This place is perfect! See how beautiful it is!" Sergio extended his arms like a proud preacher in front of an admiring congregation, his eyes lost in the distance where a flock of small parrots flew to their social gathering atop the palm trees. "Besides, we better grab it before somebody else does."

Mateo looked around 360 degrees. *"There's not a soul in this place."*

"It's still early," answered Sergio, reading his friend's thoughts. "In no time you'll see how the place fills up. You'll be glad we got here in time."

"Maybe he's right," Mateo thought.

A strange smell hit Mateo's nose. He frowned and sniffed a loaf of bread meant for their sandwiches.

"SERGIO!" He adjusted his glasses with restrained anger, "What are we going to eat now? The gas spilled over the groceries!"

"Relax! Tonight we'll have barbecued chicken."

"And how do you suppose we are going to make a fire?"

"We, the people of this island, are resourceful, my friend! We'll make fire the same way our ancestors did," Sergio bragged, sinking his feet on the hot sand.

"Our ancestors didn't go camping on the beach!" Mateo was starting to lose what little patience he had left. Without an ounce of humor, he shot back, "This is going to be the longest night of my life!"

"You worry too much. Tonight will be a night you'll never forget. So no, please, don't thank me yet!"

Sergio adjusted his sunglasses over his nose. "Food is not important!" He was determined to have a great time. "Hey, what do you think happens here at night when nobody's around?" Sergio's test of Mateo's courage was met with a blank stare.

"You know, Mateo, it's good we're doing this on our own. Being here all by ourselves, testing our will against the wilderness!" Sergio declared with self-importance.

"Excuse me?" Mateo had heard enough.

"There's a time in your life when you have to say to yourself, are we big enough, strong enough, to make life our personal adventure?"

"Well, Sergio... the way I see it is we're not saving people from an earthquake in Guatemala. But if you mean are we camping overnight on a solitary beach and looking forward to eating sandwiches soaked in gas, and hopeful that we are still here in the morning, then I say yes, we are in for an exciting night," Mateo said blandly.

"You know something, Mateo? Sometimes you can be preposterous!"

"There's that little word again!" Mateo rolled his eyes.

Taking off his dark glasses, Sergio squinted at Mateo. "You know, Mateo, that's where you and I are different: you always look for the easy way out. Me, I rough it out. I'm not afraid—" Before he could finish his sentence, Sergio was spitting out the handful of sand Mateo had thrown at him.

Sergio lunged at Mateo. As they rough-housed in the warm sand, rolling into the waves gently lapping at the shore, a flock of small parrots crossed the sky above their heads and disappeared noisily into the foliage nearby.

The afternoon softened as big puffs of pink, cotton candy clouds began to gather around the slowly sinking sun that was now languishing on the horizon. The wind that at the peak of the afternoon had rolled over the waves so forcefully was now just a soft lull. The last faint remnants of light sprinkled the top of gentle waves as night began to fall. Venus, as if announcing its arrival, set itself above the feathery crowns of the palm trees and sea grape shrubs among the little points of light that began to pierce the dark sky.

Sergio and Mateo sat silently around the fire in front of their tent, mesmerized and relaxed by the warm roar and crackle of the burning wood.

"I think this beach is haunted," Sergio broke the silence, looking intently at the bonfire.

"Shut up! That makes no sense at all," Mateo dismissed him but soon was willing to take up the challenge.

"You're so naive. You're telling me NOTHING happens here?" Sergio was not giving up. "You see those woods, way behind the palm trees? Once there was a small town over there where a bunch of angry witches lived. And they put a spell on this beach to keep people away. My father once told me he saw a woman's ghost on this very same beach!" he said dramatically.

Mateo looked at him for a moment, trying unsuccessfully to smother giggles. "I'm sure he did!"

"No, it's worse than you think!" Sergio insisted. "My father told me there was a man that liked to gamble and play craps all the time, so his wife once told him, 'You're an idiot. Why are you always playing craps when the baby doesn't have any milk? And you never have money to take me to the movies'. So he said, 'Shut up, woman, I can make more money and you can buy all the milk you want! What the heck, I'll buy you the goat!'

"And the woman said, 'Fine with me but let me tell you, tonight you'll be eating rice with a side dish of shit if you don't bring home the money' and she ran inside the house because the man was hot tempered and everybody knew it. And he said, 'You'll be singing another tune when you see me with all the money I'm going to make and then you'll wish you weren't so mean to me. But I'll be saying I told you so, so there.'

"So the man went back to his game of craps. When he realized he was running out of money, he said 'What am I going to do now?' He came to that forest behind the palm trees and sat on a big stone right there and started whining, 'Please, I'll give anything to get some money.' But nothing happened. And then he was getting desperate and he said, 'Please, please, I'll give anything if I can get some money!'

"Suddenly somebody appeared. He looked like a man but he was painted red with a long tail and goat legs and long nails and he said, 'Did you say you'll give anything?' The man jumped up from behind the bushes and said, 'Where did you come from?' and the Red Man answered, 'Never you mind, do you want money?'

And the stupid man answered 'Yes.'

"The red man then said, 'I can give you some money but I'll need something in return' so the man said 'Make me an offer.' The red man said, 'OK, I want your soul.' The man thought for a moment, *Is he kidding me?* The Red Man answered, 'No, I'm not.' And the man said, 'Hey how did you—' and the man answered, 'Do you want to make a deal or not?'

"So the man, who never went to church, said, 'Sure.' *I'll be gone before he realizes it!* he thought. So the Red Man said, 'You got your wish so now I own your soul!' The other man answered, 'What?' but when he checked his pockets, they were full of $100 bills. So he said, 'Sure' and rushed back up the hill to go back to his crap game.

"But he did not listen when the Red Man said, 'Be here tonight at midnight.' In no time, he gambled all the money away and when midnight came he decided to go back and ask for more. So when he got there, the Red Man said, 'The jig is up. We need to go now!' The man said, 'Not so fast! I haven't finished my game.' But the Red Man stared at him with fire shooting out of his eyes and said, 'You're toast!' and grabbed him by the scruff of the neck.

"A big sink hole opened up right there and both men started to go down. The man was screaming, 'No, please, I'm too young to die. I'll pay you back! I promise I'll get a job at the post office, they hire all the time,' and the Red Man said, 'Tough, you should've thought about that before. Now it's too late. We made a deal.' The man begged, 'My wife and son are waiting for me!' But the Red Man said, 'They'll get over it.' And both men disappeared into the sky, while the stupid man screamed his ass off, PLEASE SOMEBODY SAVE ME, HE'S GOING TO TAKE MY SOUL!'"

Mateo stared at Sergio in disbelief. "I thought you said they fell into the burning sink hole in the ground!" He then laughed so hard, he could barely speak. After taking a breather, he asked, "So what's the moral of your story?"

"A story doesn't need a moral if it's true!" Sergio shot back.

"So what's the point of it, then?" Mateo howled with laughter so hard he had to grab his stomach as he rolled around in the sand. He stopped long enough to ask, "Is the message NOT to deal with men with horns?"

"NO!" Sergio retorted. "The message is that you have to keep your promises!"

Don Genaro woke up in the middle of the night and walked to the window. *"Am I dreaming?"* He adjusted his eyes to the darkness. *"Did somebody call my name?"*

Putting on his glasses, he looked across the field at the bright light hovering over the trees by the river. He gazed at the bright face of the moon looking down at him. *"I'm coming!"*

He dressed as quietly as possible, put on his white straw hat, and, without hesitation, walked out of the house with such ease and determination that anyone would have thought that, instead of the thick of night, it was the middle of the day.

That night Don Genaro made a wish, a wish so strong and heartfelt that it woke the ghost up out of the shadows.

"Someone is calling me!" The ghost sensed the urgency, the heartfelt desire, the longing, so it rose among the shadows of the forest. "Who is it?" it wondered, as it soaked up the moonlight that made it glimmer. "Someone is in need!" The ghost looked across the dark river, over the tops of the trees, and up to the small house that sat on the hill, the house with warm light pouring out of its windows.

"Who's calling my name?" The ghost felt his sadness, but a lost ghost has no powers. So it wished to the moon, pleading, "Please let the one who needs me find the peace of mind he seeks. Let him move on once again with the flow of life. Please, let the one who is lost find his way to me!" The ghost took its place on top of the mossy boulder, and waited.

A powerful crack of thunder lit up the inside of the tent as if it had caught on fire, jolting the boys out of their sleep.

"Sergio, wake up!" Mateo yelled in the darkness.

"I'm up," he heard Sergio answer. "What time is it?"

The rain hammered the flimsy tent and made it wobble under its weight. The roll of the waves was no longer gentle as the roaring ocean began to claim its space. "Get out, invaders!" it seemed to yell out to the boys.

"Sergio, let's get out of here!" Mateo raised his voice against the deafening sound of the rain.

"No, we better stay inside until the rain passes," answered Sergio, wiping the wet sand off his feet.

"Can you hear the ocean?" Mateo asked alarmed, aware that their tent was about to collapse.

"Yes, I can," answered Sergio, trying to ignore the weaving and bobbing of the flimsy tent.

"Rain is starting to pour in!" As Mateo tried to hold the tent up, water began to cascade down his arms and into their sleeping bags, groceries, and supplies.

"Is this tent cured?" It became clear what the problem was.

"What's that?" answered Sergio, wondering what the question had to do with anything.

"*We are screwed!*" Soon the poles inside the tent collapsed, trapping the boys like cats in a bag.

"Hurry up, Sergio! Get outside and check the stakes! Make sure they are in deep." As Mateo tried to hold up the tent, water continued to pour in, creating messy sandy pools.

"Go out in the dark? While it's raining? Close to a dark ocean?" Sergio stopped for a second. "No! Let's wait until the rain stops!" he yelled as the collapsed tent began to drift from side to side. "*Strange!*" he thought.

"SERGIO, WE HAVE TO GET OUT OF HERE NOW!" Sergio heard the panic in Mateo's voice.

Struggling with the tent's zipper, Mateo screamed, "It's caught!" As the flow of infiltrating water became heavier, puddles of water began to form on the tent floor.

"Wow, what a flood!" Mateo leapt outside, sinking knee deep into the water. When a rolling wave almost knocked him down, he finally figured it out.

"Dear God! SERGIO, GET OUT GET OUT NOW!!" He could not see the waves bearing down on him but of one thing he was certain. "SERGIO, GET OUT! THE TENT IS GOING INTO THE OCEAN!"

Mateo urgently pressed on, "GET OUT NOW!" The strength of the wind and the rain almost knocked him over. As he tried to escape the crash of waves, his feet sank deeper in the wet sand that, with each step, instantly tightened around his ankles as if to hold him firmly in place.

"SERGIO! THIS IS SERIOUS!" he yelled one more time before a thunderous wave yanked the tent away from the shore in one single surge. The roar and fury of the black ocean made him shiver.

In the light of day, the power and beauty of the sea is magnificent but in total darkness the sound of its fury is more terrifying than any horror creature. Mateo could not see the ocean, but as the riptide retreated, the undertow swallowed every wave until it became a roaring menace. It wasn't until a brief flash of lightning illuminated the crown of the rising tide against the darkness, that Mateo realized the true size of the monster wave that surely within seconds was about to smash them against the sandbar, or even worse, pull them into the infinite depths of the raging ocean.

He only had time to scream "SERGIO!!!" before the blast of the crashing wave smashed against the sandbar, sending him and Sergio—who was barely out of the deflated tent—flying headfirst onto the shore. Sergio swallowed a few mouthfuls of salty water and felt the burn in his eyes. With every step, he prayed for deliverance from an untimely death in the ocean. Meanwhile, Mateo was having ominous visions of being dragged from the water, dead and bloated like a jellyfish, only to be left out on the sand for the seagulls to feast on.

Shhhh WHAAAAAMM! *"Get out!"*

Another huge wave slammed both boys against the sand, making them roll over and over, out of control like wet rag dolls. Weighed down by their wet clothes, dripping water and sand, the boys plopped down exhausted, away from the shore. Their throats and nostrils still burned from the salty water.

"Are you OK?" Mateo asked, out of breath and coughing.

"Yes, I am," answered Sergio, panting and wiping his face with the back of his hand. "Are you?"

"What just happened?" Sergio gasped for air while Mateo sat shivering on the cold, wet sand, his teeth chattering like castanets. Their bodies were shaking uncontrollably, not so much from the cold rain but from reliving the frightening experience. As they gathered their strength, a bolt of lightning lit up the dark sky briefly enough for them to see their tent drifting away into the darkest of nights. Mateo and Sergio fell silent as the ocean battered the rocks mercilessly.

"What time is it?" Sergio wondered.

"3:13 in the morning," Mateo answered, spitting sand out of his mouth.

The rain suddenly stopped. Mateo dropped to the wet sand and folded into himself, forming a shield against the cold wind. He pulled his T-shirt around him. The cold made him cough. Sergio crossed his arms around himself and sat down beside Mateo, pulling his knees close to his chest as the wind whistled through the palm trees.

In the faint light of dawn, they watched the tent bob and weave as it was pulled further away into the ocean like a deflated balloon. Only the sounds of the sea and the chatter of their teeth broke the early morning silence.

"What were we thinking?" Mateo asked, still out of breath from the unexpected attack by the ocean.

"The beach looked empty and beautiful when we arrived. Nobody else was camping here," Sergio said in defense of his choice.

"Well, now we know why!" Mateo joked.

Like two orphans out of luck, Sergio and Mateo sat under the palm trees still in a daze, listening to the roar of the darkened sea. As the falling rain again started to needle their backs, the morning light began to streak through dark clouds. The moon began to fade, the boys fell into silence. As if they were reading each other's thoughts, they suddenly burst into hysterical laughter. Thankfully, the moon had been the only witness. Mateo looked up at the sky and wished he was in his comfortable, dry bed.

UNDER THE LUNAR SPELL

"What angel wakes me from my flowery bed?

—William Shakespeare, *A Midsummer Night's Dream* (Act III, Scene I)

Love—or the memory of it—can be a trap for a ghost. A glimpse of its past can disrupt its journey. Ghosts have a single power, to make their presence known in unexpected and subtle ways, when people allow themselves to surrender to faith. When sorrow and hopelessness break through all disbelief, only then can the ghost address the interference and move on.

Don Genaro looked up at the bright disk suspended in the infinite darkness. He was spellbound, singing his song to that bright angel hanging in the sky. But there was something else that compelled him to leave the house.

"I'm coming." Don Genaro didn't need to know the way; he would follow the soft voice that called out to him. "I'm coming," he repeated without taking his eyes off the full moon peeking through the branches of the avocado tree. "Look at you! You are so beautiful!" He reached out as if he could caress its luminous face. Don Genaro was convinced it had talked to him. "If it wasn't true, how come she is smiling at me?"

The old man heard the cool moon command him, *follow me,* and so he did. He walked down the stairs and quietly counted every step, one by one, until there were no more steps to be counted. He walked past the potted plants, past the rose bushes sprinkled with the evening's moisture, past the pigeon tree, until he got to the chain link fence. "I have to be careful," he thought and removed the chain, "or else the kind woman in the house will be angry at me. No, we don't want that!"

His mind receded into a dark place where he could no longer find himself, let alone his memories. His past and present had become a series of truncated snapshots, bits and pieces of a life that had faded into oblivion.

He was deeply confused when she had yelled at him for opening the gate once before. "You're not supposed to do that!" she had castigated him like a four-year-old child. But Don Genaro was sincerely puzzled. *"What did I do? I just want to go for a walk, no danger in that!"* But soon he had forgotten about her angry outburst.

Tonight it was all right. "She's calling me!" He slid off the chain that kept the gate closed and smiled at the moon climbing from behind the trees.

Feeling lost, he stood in the middle of the field, wondering, *"Where did you go?"* and then looked up, searching for the light of the moon. A thick herd of rain clouds pushed along, covering the field in total darkness. Don Genaro hugged himself as the wind suddenly turned cold and a swift shower descended. The reflection of electrical discharge flashed in the sky, lighting up his way along the red clay path. Loud claps of thunder made him jump, but only one thing clung to his memory, "She's calling me!"

Like the thread of lightning fracturing the sky, Don Genaro had a moment of lucidity that unlocked the perfect symmetry of past and present with a single stroke.

"Minerva!" He called out the name that had lived in the shadows of his mind and on the fringes of his consciousness.

"Minerva!"

* * *

A life that began twenty six years ago flashes forward up to this day, as if it was only a single breath in time. Where does time go?

"Who calls my name?"

Thick rain clouds had darkened the sky. A thread of lightning broke through the somber spirit of the afternoon and the day became heavy as if carrying a deep sadness. Soon the rain managed to subdue all life in the forest. *The forest knows how to keep secrets.*

Minerva knew this, so it was fitting that when she received the devastating news, she returned to her safe haven. It was, after all, the tranquil sanctuary where she could gather her thoughts and pull herself together. Finally underneath the branches of *her*

❖ 200 ❖

orange tree, she rested her eyes on the umbrella of leaves above her head. Leaning against its bark, she let her tears out.

The bits of sky around the leaves seemed bluer, crisper. Her senses became sharper; she was surprised she could hear the buzz of honeybees hovering above the dandelions and morivivi. The crystalline flow of the river helped her purify her being before its final transition. The sound of running water soothed her, the unstoppable river that, unlike her life, would go on.

Minerva tried to be brave. She thought about her life. "It's been a good one," she lied to herself. But still she could not help but wonder, "Why me?" Resenting the inhumane, bitter dose of reality that brutally forced her to abandon her dreams, Minerva had given up her life in the city and sought refuge in the intimacy of Palo Verde's mountains. There is no sadder sight than a woman—just as fragile as a girl—sobbing helplessly. But if Minerva had to cry, she would rather do it under the tree that had reached out to her. The same tree that had welcomed her over the years, its limbs covered in blossoms. The fragile tree she had tended to for so long. Minerva looked beyond the mountains where the horizon blended with the sky. She watched as gathering black clouds created a shield over the tall trees. A sudden crack of lightning prompted a fine mist to fall. Rain, beautiful rain, the powerful, spiritual cleanser.

"Will I miss this place?" Minerva the warrior was not about to let go. "I'll fight until the end," she promised herself but wondered if her strength would fail her.

The soft rain first came down as a whisper, then in a deluge. She welcomed the falling drops, wading down the stream as the heavens cried with her. She thought about everything she had loved and mourned for the life she would never get to fulfill. Minerva bargained, pleaded, and prayed but she knew her only choice was acceptance. The end of natural life.

"Mateo! What will become of him?" The question cut deeper than anything else. But then she thought of Maria and regained her center. Maria was now her biggest hope. With her, Mateo would have continuity. She would be the strong compass to help him navigate the rough waters in his life; rough waters that were about to come all too soon. She lifted her face to the rain to forget for a moment and felt refreshed, renewed. Rain cleanses the spirit. "Is this all a dream?" she hoped fervently.

Since it could not weep, the orange tree watched the girl cry herself to a peaceful sleep in its lap. It cradled her with the same tenderness she had shown it so many years before. Love. The tree had much love for this woman-child who had saved it from the grip of wild vines and helped it see the sun. With her eyes finally empty of tears, Minerva wondered again, *"Is this a dream?"* But it was not and the tree heard the girl's cries again. Then, a call in the distance.

"Minerva!"

"No, it is not a dream." She was heartsick.

A grateful tree never forgets an act of kindness. So it never forgot Minerva. Minerva the troublemaker was also Minerva the fragile woman-child, the little barefoot girl that long ago had loved and nurtured it. How could it forget her? She, who with small hands folded broad leaves to bring it a drink of sweet water from the nearby river. Minerva, sweet child.

"Minerva!"

"Am I dreaming?" A voice in the distance pulled her out of her trance and her tears came back in torrents.

Let it rain! Let it rain! Virgin of the grotto
Little birds are singing, clouds are waking up!

"Minerva!" the voice in the distance called again.

* * *

"Minerva!"

Don Genaro's senses opened up to the familiar smells of the forest wafting in waves of wild jasmine and wet mulch. He heard the call, very soft at first and then stronger, calling him like a command he could not ignore. He adjusted his eyes to the darkness and peered into a clearing in the trees.

The soft glow of the moon lit up the raindrops over the dark greenery, and filtered through the fog that covered the field in a silky, moist cloud, setting up a natural stage. Don Genaro was speechless. He looked across the river but remained still as if his feet had suddenly sprouted roots into the ground. He took in the miraculous vision of an angel dancing under a waterfall of lights.

"*I've been waiting for you!*" He was not sure whether he had heard the angel talking and looked around, incredulous. "*Am I dreaming?*"

He walked tentatively with feeble steps over the wet mulch as if it was shallow waters that might suddenly open up into a void beneath the surface. He did not dare blink, afraid that what was in front of him was only a vision in the fog that might blow away into nothingness.

"Is it you?" Don Genaro called out, his heart beating excitedly.

"Cross the river," the angel instructed softly.

Without hesitation, Don Genaro waded into the cold water, gingerly stepping on the small, soft *chinos* rearranging themselves against the soles of his feet. He felt the prawns scurrying from their beds under the rocks. Looking down, he saw his own reflection broken into shards infused by the light.

Transfixed, he followed the light floating ahead in the clearing. The cold night wind hung from every tree branch. Don Genaro asked the ghost before him, "Is it you?" He asked again with a big smile made even bigger by the light of the moon.

In the night, the crickets were silent, as were the toads and roosting birds. No creature wanted to miss the conversation that was about to unfold. For days the forest had watched a lost ghost wander in their midst. They watched it move from shadow to shadow, searching for something but not knowing what. And now a man, who for so long had been wandering within his own darkness too, was suddenly overcome with joy.

"*Is it you?*" Joy so powerful that it made him shine like liquid silver in the light of the moon. "*It is her!*" Joy so deep that it made the ghost glow as if it was made of fireflies! Yes, the old trees knew something significant was about to happen as the old man walked further into the forest in a daze, calling out Minerva's name. He saw her but she did not look back.

"Cross the river," she called out to him...

PART SIX

Down the Rabbit Hole

B illy dreaded coming home. The thought of his father unsettled him. Walking on the shoulder of the road, he stuffed one hand in the pocket of his jeans, and with the other pushed down the blue nylon cap on his head, covering everything but his eyes. Billy averted his face when a speeding car left him in a toxic cloud of dust and black fumes. With every step he took, layers of dirt gathered on the frayed cuffs of his jeans. His high-tops unsettled pebbles and spat them ahead of his path. He walked with detachment, going through the motions as if he had no real destination. With his gaze firmly on the ground, Billy measured the stretch of road ahead. Such was his routine, day in and day out.

"This sucks. There's nothing to do," he grumbled. A misstep yanked his jeans further down his backside. Embarrassed, he adjusted his pants with a swift pull, checking around for any witnesses. He shot a glance across the road and caught a glimpse of Doña Sol sweeping her yard. He struggled to balance his backpack over his shoulder. The intense afternoon heat made him unbutton his shirt. The metallic logo on it seemed to catch fire as a ray of sunlight made contact.

Something brought Billy to a complete stop. "What the heck?" he wondered as he watched the small gray cat walk atop the chain link fence in an impressive balancing act. "How can it do that?" The cat made its way towards him with skillful and careful steps. Billy could not take his eyes away and was instantly amused by its gravity-defying feat. But there was something else. "*Where have I seen this cat before?... Could it be?*" There was something eerily familiar about the cat. Billy could not quite put his finger on it. *"Could it be?"* It certainly looked like the same cat his father had chased away days before. Still, there was something else. Billy searched inside his head for an answer.

"Hmmm," he frowned.

Keeping his eyes on the cat, Billy dropped his backpack on the ground. The loud thud made the cat jump, causing it to lose its balance and fall off the railing. Billy watched it clamber up the links to the top of the fence and resume walking towards him once more. "That cat is amazing!"

Suddenly, the realization struck him like a thunderbolt when the cat got closer. "Wait a minute! It is you, isn't it?" Up close, Billy recognized the crest of silver hair on top of the cat's head.

Billy had a risky idea. *"What the heck, she's not even paying attention."* He watched Doña Sol move around her yard with broom in hand, totally immersed in her sweeping. Billy walked towards the cat. This time, the thought of his father almost stopped him. *"That old man hates anything that has a tail."* But the friendly cat was now calling out to him, "Meeaaawww!" Billy looked around. He decided he had to do something and he had to do it now. He would figure out what to do with the cat later.

MEEEAAWWWWWWW!

"Is it you?" Don Genaro asked the radiant angel standing under the soft cascade of light. But it moved away from him, aloof, as if it could not sense the old man's presence. "Minerva, can you hear me?" he begged.

He watched the ghost sit by the boulder as if waiting for something or someone. He sensed the weight on the ghost's shoulders. "I need your forgiveness! I didn't know." His throat tightened and a steady stream of tears clouded his eyes. The ghost's gaze was lost in the distance, its presence in another dimension. Don Genaro looked at his daughter Minerva the same way he did on the day she was born and asked her one more time, "Will you forgive me? You'll always be my little girl!"

With those words, as if a key was turned and a door to a new dimension was opened, the ghost turned around and glowed brighter at the sight of the old man standing under the moon. "I've been waiting for you!"

The ghost remembered the rule now: *"You'll have to go back. You'll only have one single moment."* There was no more interference.

Don Genaro was afraid to look away and lose her again. He marveled at the translucent dream before him, sparkling in the light of the moon. The old man breathed a sigh of relief, *the heavens have a way of solving life's mysteries.*

"I've moved on, why haven't you?" the ghost asked the feeble man. And with those words the ghost made its forgiveness clear. There was no more interference. The bond to earthly life was finally broken. It was a complex and at times painful love that had bound them in life, but it was forgiveness that finally set them free.

The following morning, Don Genaro was discovered curled up like a child underneath the pigeon tree, right by the bed of begonias, fast asleep with a big smile on his face. Even the mist of an early shower failed to wake him up. It wasn't until the break of dawn when a neighbor, noticing an unusual bulky shape under the bushes, alerted Doña Sol. "Have you seen Don Genaro? He's sleeping in the dirt!"

Doña Sol hurriedly ushered him inside. "What do you think you're doing?"

"It was her! My baby," he repeated excitedly.

"Yes, I know," she agreed, without the slightest idea of what he was mumbling about. She would not have believed him anyway.

He recounted his night experience, how the moon had called out to him and guided his steps to the waiting forest. *"She was there!"* With tears in his eyes he told his wife how happy he was to unburden his soul to Minerva and how she had smiled at him before walking away under a veil of fireflies!

"What's wrong with him?" Doña Sol was mystified at finding him sleeping under the shrubs like an abandoned infant. *"What are the neighbors going to think?"* Still she could not ignore the childlike smile on his face.

As she swept the floor, she caught a glimpse of Billy across the road. *"Poor boy,"* she thought. It was not the first time she had seen him sitting alone on his front steps without friends or much of anything to do since his mother had disappeared. Her own maternal instincts told her that behind his carefully built wall of indifference and aggression were the marks of a fragile boy struggling to find himself. *"God help him! Growing up in this small town doesn't make it any easier,"* she concluded before resuming her sweeping. She was well aware of the unkind accusations the boy endured due to his unfortunate biological association with Severo.

Unexpectedly, the anguished yelp of an animal brought her sweeping to a stop. "My dear Lord, this cat is going to turn my hair white, I swear." She turned towards the fence but the cat had vanished into thin air. "Where did it go now?"

Doña Sol straightened up when she heard a meow. "Muddy?" She paused as her eyes searched the garden. "Muddy, where are you?" she called out again. The cat was not in his usual spot under the begonias, nor by the poinsettias or the potted ferns.

"He's at it again. Where can he be now?" She took another peek under the pigeon pea bush but the cat was nowhere to be found. As unnerving as its antics were, she

was convinced the cat could get out of whatever mess it got itself into. *"It always does!"* She had spotted it earlier on top of the chain link fence, wobbling along like a skillful tightrope walker. Then she noticed Billy walking away from the other side of the fence.

Doña Sol was not quite sure what she was seeing but it looked like Billy was hurrying home carrying a small animal. She felt the blood drain out of her face as she heard the bewildered cat hissing and spitting with fright.

"Is that Muddy? Hey, Billy, what are you doing with him?" she called out from her patio. She was taken aback when he defiantly exclaimed, "This cat belongs to me!"

Doña Sol could not find the words to defend her ownership of the animal either, but she gathered the nerve to confront him. "How could it be yours? That cat has been roaming the streets for days!"

To her frustration, Billy did not bother to answer as he hurried away. The sounds of Muddy's desperate meows alarmed her, but a darker thought made Doña Sol hold her hand to her heart. *"How in heaven am I going to tell Mateo?"*

She had waited anxiously for Mateo and Sergio's return from the beach, when finally the two boys crossed the threshold exhausted, sun-burned, limping, and covered with scratches.

"What happened to you two?" she asked alarmed. But Sergio and Mateo were in no mood to go into the details of the awful wave-banging they had received the night before. Sergio plopped his aching body onto a chair, unable to carry his own weight any longer. Doña Sol could see Mateo was exhausted too but she could not think of a gentle way to tell him the bad news. *"I better not interfere, I'm not sure I actually saw Billy take Muddy."*

Although conflicted, she was also cautious; after all, the boy did not need another reason to go off the deep end. But neither could she ignore her grandson's newfound determination to save the poor stray. Among all the turbulence he was going through, *"at least he has found some focus."* There were no two ways about it, she had to speak up or risk Muddy's life. *"The longer I wait, the worse the chances will be for that animal to be saved."*

Visibly upset, Doña Sol finally managed to stammer, "Mateo, there's something I have to tell you."

"What do you mean? What happened?"

"Muddy is gone!" Doña Sol watched Mateo jump out of his seat like a puppet coming alive with a yank from its master.

"I think I saw Billy…" She was unable to finish her sentence before Mateo ran out of the house. Fearing her words had unleashed something terrible, Doña Sol ran after him. Ready for a fight, Sergio was right behind.

"THE CAT IS MINE!" Billy challenged Mateo.

"Where is it?" Mateo asked menacingly.

"That's none of your business!" Billy shot back.

"WHERE IS HE? I'M ASKING YOU!" Mateo's fingers curled into tight fists.

"Who do you think you are?" Billy taunted.

"GIVE HIM BACK!" Mateo's voice became more menacing.

"Try and make me." With those words, a line was drawn.

Without wasting any time, Mateo sucker punched Billy right on the chin. Caught off guard, he stumbled backwards. Barely recovered from the blow, Billy went on the offensive and struck Mateo back, hitting him in the eye.

Blind with rage, Mateo went after Billy with all his might. "YOU SUNAVABEECH ABUSER! YOU'RE NOT GOING TO GET AWAY WITH THIS!" he yelled as he struggled with Billy on the ground.

"C'MON, MATEO, DON'T DO THIS!" Sergio jumped between Mateo and Billy. "It's not worth it!" But Mateo was unstoppable as he threw another punch at Billy. Sergio jumped between them as they entwined in battle once more, trying to break off the fight. "C'mon guys, stop this!" he pleaded.

"He's going to pay," Mateo screamed as Billy struggled to get off the ground.

"Is something bad happening?" Don Genaro watched in confusion as Doña Sol ran to catch up with the quarreling boys.

"ENOUGH! ENOUGH ALREADY!" Doña Sol shouted, rushing towards the boys. Getting between them, she managed to pull Mateo aside and send Billy on his way with stern words. Thankfully their injuries were not serious, only minor scrapes and wounded egos.

"What were you thinking?" Doña Sol could not hide her anger.

"I'LL GET HIM IF IT'S THE LAST THING I DO!!" Mateo threatened.

"That's enough," Doña Sol admonished, still shaken.

From across the street they heard Billy's warning, "THIS AIN'T OVER, YOU HEAR?"

Mateo was left roiling. As brutal as the conflict had been, it was also a defining moment. Frustrated, he realized the fight had not accomplished anything. He feared he had failed miserably at protecting an animal that could not defend itself. He had watched Billy retreat from the fight but there were no signs of the cat afterwards.

He wondered if Billy had been bluffing. *"How can he keep a cat in his house with that father of his watching over his shoulder?"* But he knew that in order to find the animal, he had to consider all angles. A frightening thought crossed his mind. "What if I never see him again?" The next few days would test his resolve; not only had he waited too long to make the decision to save the stray, now the animal had disappeared, perhaps for good.

Sergio could see his friend was shaken up, he knew he had to help. "Don't worry, Mateo, we'll get Muddy back."

Severo witnessed the scuffle from a distance. He could not mask his disgust when he realized the cause of his son's fight: the gray stray. Severo knew he had no time to waste. He knew what he had to do, once and for all. He decided not to let his son know he had discovered the cat hiding in the basement. If anything, his son had unwittingly brought the dirty animal home for him to dispose of.

"This is a good thing after all!" he thought. It would be advisable to remain quiet until he figured out a way to get rid of it. *"Good,"* he thought. "One down, one to go!" Stumpy was his next target. Severo had not forgotten Sergio's assault only days before. *Not by a long shot!*

Following the fight, Mateo paced the house like a caged animal looking to break free. He kept an eye on the house across the street for any signs of Billy or Severo. *"Where are they?"* He scanned the front yard that had seemingly swallowed them up along with the cat. Even the recent drama of his oceanside camping trip and his grandmother's account of Don Genaro's mysterious adventure seemed insignificant in comparison to Muddy's disappearance. But it was his grandmother's constant surveillance that was slowly pushing him over the edge. If she was afraid he would jump at Billy at the first opportunity, she had good reason.

His jaws tightened, "Where could Muddy be now?" Without the cat around, the room felt big and empty, *like an abandoned nest.* Mateo felt that ugly sensation again: sadness. He felt sadness for the cat's absence and sadness for its uncertain future. "I wasn't here when I should have been." Even the sight of the small green plastic dish in a corner of the kitchen pained him; still filled to the brim, it sat untouched.

"I think he's gone this time," Mateo heard his grandmother say. He was convinced Billy or Severo was responsible. *"God help them if something happens to Muddy."* He was about to make good on his threat.

Mateo's despair took a new turn as he watched his options disappear one by one. Now he was forced to take a bold step. "Waiting around is not going to cut it. And being nice is not going to bring him back!" He thought defiantly, trying to deny his own promise, his contract of restraint and passivity. Without another thought, Mateo set to work.

Doña Sol saw Mateo cut off a small branch. Intrigued, she watched as he eagerly whittled it down to a Y shape skinning and polishing it with the sharp blade of his grandfather's knife. Fearing the beginning of yet another situation, she wondered, "What is he up to now?" Still, she had to ask, "Mateo, what are you doing?"

"Nothing," he answered curtly, without lifting his gaze.

"I see you're carving something," she insisted, watching him wrap a thin rubber strip around the sling shot and secure it with thin wire.

"Don't concern yourself. It's nothing."

And with that, he hurriedly climbed up the ladder leaning against the trunk of the mango tree and disappeared into his tree house...

For the next few hours, nestled in his secure fort of branches and leaves, Mateo kept watch on Severo's house and waited patiently. "He can't stay indoors all day." Finally the moment arrived when the watched the man set foot outside of his balcony and into the front yard. Mateo's heart began to beat wildly. Picking up a stone out of the small pile he had accumulated, with one hand he nestled it securely in the middle of the sling, while with the other, he stretched the rubber strip as far back as he possibly could. Taking aim, he closed one eye. "I got you now!" he thought as he released the stretched rubber band and watched Severo jump and yelp in pain. He tried to conceal his laughter as Severo looked around, cursing and wondering where the attack had come from. Mateo waited for a moment, his sling shot already loaded. Severo turned when another missile hit him squarely in the middle of his head. Mateo could see the man's fury starting to build. "What the hell?" the man cried out as he was thoroughly pelted with a shower of small stones. Mateo could not contain his glee as he watched the alarmed and befuddled man jump around like a rag doll being yanked in every direction. From his tree house, he could hear Severo's frustrated blasphemies as he searched earth and sky for the mysterious perpetrator. Mateo could not think of a better way to get even, even if his antagonistic effort would not bear any fruit at all. "This one's for Muddy, you jackass!" he muttered.

A sharp call snapped him out of his secret diversion. "Mateo! I know what you're doing! You better come down from this tree NOW!"

"Busted! Damn!"

If Severo claimed to have any talent, it was playing one person against another. "It's so easy! It's just ego." Severo had a surprising insight into what makes a person tick. He had learned the common weaknesses of the human condition early on and had played them to his advantage ever since.

"You never go to the source to ask for anything! If you want results, good results, you approach the beast from its weakest side." This, among others, had been the theme of one of his many drunken pontifications at the local pub. And this was his strategy to get back at Mateo. The boy was definitely asking for it and Severo was in no mood for forgiveness.

His contempt for the boy was for more than just being a disrespectful punk, it was for daring to protect the filthy cat as if it was something of value. And to top it off, the little punk had the gall to attack his son over the beast. Fortunately for Severo, Billy had helped him a great deal in his pursuit of the cat. But Billy still had to be dealt with. He had to be taught a lesson. An unforgettable lesson.

There was a more pressing target this morning though: Severo watched attentively as Sergio appeared at the top of the hill riding his bike. A smile crossed his face as he walked into the middle of the road…

"MATEO!" Sergio's voice broke the monotony of the morning, "MATEO!" he called out again with urgency. Mateo rushed downstairs to find him waiting on his bike, his face dulled by sadness.

"What's up?" Mateo rubbed the sleep off his face, "What happened?"

"Stumpy is gone too!"

"What do you mean?" He was now fully awake.

"I haven't seen him since last night," Sergio answered.

"Maybe he's wandering around." He tried to cheer Sergio up but could see his friend was on the verge of tears. "Let's check out the neighborhood," he offered and jumped on his bike. "I'm sure he'll show up."

He wondered whether Billy had anything to do with the dog's disappearance but there was no time to waste. "We'll deal with him later, Serge." Mateo shot a glance across the street. There were no signs of life at Severo and Billy's house. The thought that Muddy was missing had kept him awake all night and now with Stumpy missing too he knew something terribly wrong was about to unfold. "Serge, we have to find them now!"

Under an unforgiving sun, they whooshed down the road, stopping to ask anyone in their path—man, woman, or child—if they had seen the missing animals. They scanned the fields relentlessly, unable to find any trace of the cat or the dog. They followed any and every lead in the hope that Stumpy would finally come out from the home of some considerate Samaritan, barking happily. Sergio would have given anything to hear Stumpy bark again. But the accounts of people claiming to have seen the dog were contradictory and, for the most part, inaccurate or, even worse, made up. It seemed impossible to trace the dog's whereabouts.

Sergio did not want to accept that Stumpy might not come back. "We have to find him!"

Mateo's mind was somewhere else. He feared both Stumpy and Muddy were gone for good. He could not help but consider the possibility of Severo's involvement. *"Did he do it himself or set Billy up?"* The odds were firmly stacked against the animals from the beginning.

Sergio jumped off his bike on the side of a shady dirt road. "Let's take a break."

Mateo could sense Sergio was about ready to give up. He shared his friend's sadness and vowed to do whatever it took to find the dog. "Don't worry, we'll find him, I promise you. Has he ever followed anybody home before?" Mateo asked. But Sergio refused to imagine such a scenario.

"No, but you've seen how trusting he can be. Even when Severo abused him, he never tried to defend himself. He's trusting but he also knows where his home is," Sergio insisted.

Mateo had to keep Sergio's spirits up. "We'll find him and he'll be okay, I promise you!" But he was not sure how he could keep that promise. After all, Muddy was missing too.

Anything that can go wrong will go wrong. During his days in Palo Verde, Mateo had detected an indomitable pattern of mishaps, *bad things come in threes.* When something goes wrong, another bad thing will follow, and then another. A downward spiral, an out of control chain reaction. Mateo forced himself to search his mind for the very first thing that had triggered this very unpleasant string of dreadful events. "What the hell is going on in this place?"

He walked out of the house and found a secluded place away from everyone and allowed himself to be lulled by the flapping of banana leaves. He stared at the nearby hills beyond the orange trees that shaded the back of the house. It was at that moment the weight of the previous day's events brought him down.

"Why did I stay in this place?" He had a hard time coming to grips with the seemingly endless chain of misfortune and madness that was leaving him feeling hopeless and powerless. *"Maybe if I hide here..."* But he was still left with a serious question, *"What am I going to do now?"*

Bad things come in threes. When the "curse of three" strikes, it won't stop until it knocks you down and leaves you out cold. Mateo thought about this as he began to take inventory and pinpoint the precise instant when everything had started to go wrong. *"Meva's death, the moment I set foot in this town, and now, Muddy missing."* He had successfully traced the dreaded path of his misfortune. Still the heaviest load to carry was the image of his grandmother, just after he had returned from the hellish night on the beach, standing still in the middle of the room as if stuck in cement, all the color drained from her face, announcing, "Muddy is missing!"

Don't get too attached to anyone or anything. He could not help but feel regret.

"It's payback time!" Severo smiled at the whimpering sounds of the hungry dog tied behind his house. He was feeling very satisfied with his accomplishment. The dirty creature that had been roaming around his yard was about to get what it deserved. What had pleased him even more was watching its owner fly by on his bike, looking for the filthy dog up and down the street. *"I promise, you'll get yours too!"*

So when the time came for Severo to carry out his vengeance, he hadn't wasted a single moment. Ever since Sergio had challenged his authority, Severo had kept a close eye out for the wandering dog. Many times before, it had managed to escape unscathed, but this time around Severo was prepared. Today was the day when Stumpy, along with the filthy cat, would disappear for good.

Severo's long memory served him well. He might not exactly remember, for instance, the contents of his supper the night before, but he certainly kept a mental log of the offenses thrown at him, filed away by day, month, occasion, and depending on his clarity of thought, time of day.

His thin skin was most apparent when his point of view was challenged. After his encounter with the scruffy boy and his dog, Severo focused his venom at Sergio. "That little punk!" The only way his dignity would be properly restored was when the boy had finally paid for his transgression. With that thought, Severo propped his legs up on the edge of the porch railing, cradled his machete on his lap, and lovingly began to sharpen its blade.

The opportunity had finally been served up to him on a silver platter when Stumpy had stepped onto his property that early morning.

Wharf!

The bark made Severo lift his head and notice the yellow dog with short legs sniffing around his front yard. He watched as it dug around the pile of rusty car parts. He felt a wave of disgust rise to the top of his throat. "That filthy animal!" Watching the dog made him think of his owner. *"Oh yeah! That little punk,"* he thought as the image of Sergio popped into his head. Still, Severo showed surprising restraint.

"I warned you before," he murmured as he began to summon the friendly dog.

Whaaarf! Whaaarf! Whaaarf!

"Come here, boy! Yes, that's it, come here… How you doing?" Severo did not move as the dog, wagging its tail, came closer. "Very good dog!" he said softly before grabbing it firmly by the collar.

Mateo could not wait for Sergio to show up. "What's going on in this town?" He struggled to understand Muddy and Stumpy's disappearance. *Don't get too attached to anyone or anything.* The thought flashed across his mind but he had to admit it was too late now. He fought back the impulse to run across the street and raid Billy's house; he knew his grandmother would not be as forgiving a second time around. *"I'll have to be careful!"* But in any case, since their fight Billy was nowhere to be seen, as if he too had vanished with the animals.

"What's the matter?" Sergio asked, jumping off his bike. Mateo hesitated before answering. "Muddy is still missing."

"Have you seen Billy with him?"

"No, he's gone, too. Muddy has disappeared before, but he never takes this long to return."

"Have you checked the empty lot? He likes to hide there." Sergio tried to think of every possibility.

"I knew that cat was trouble." Mateo's mixed feelings began to show.

Sergio sensed his friend's anxiety but was not about to let him off the hook, not just yet. "Have you thought that maybe you don't really want him? That cat is always getting away!" Sergio saw a flash of anger in Mateo's eyes and realized his blunt remarks had stung like angry bees.

"PISS OFF! Is that why Stumpy got away too? How dare you tell me I'm irresponsible! I mean, you're a fine one to talk!" Mateo shot back defensively, but he regretted his words the moment they came out of his mouth.

"Just saying, if you really want him, you have to make a decision," Sergio admonished half-jokingly. "You just can't say you really care for the cat and then keep letting it run away. Talking about it is different than doing something about it. You have to do better. Make a commitment."

Mateo resisted the urge to take a swipe at Sergio. He felt his anger swallowing him up. His eyes almost popped out of his head but instead he bit his lip. His initial impulse to get back at Sergio subsided. After all, coming to blows with his friend would be the very last straw. A part of him had to admit there was some truth to Sergio's words.

"I try to keep up with him but he's a stray!" Mateo managed to say, afraid he had offended his best friend. After all, Sergio had kept his own worries about Stumpy to himself and now here he was coming to his friend's aid. *"Hermano!"* he thought, feeling somewhat remorseful.

"We have to do it now. Let's go find them!" Sergio slapped Mateo's shoulder, hoping secretly that Stumpy would find his way home soon too. The image of

Severo burned inside his head.

"Mateo, let's find these animals!" Sergio said, energized.

The short, plump woman turned around from the clothesline with a stern frown as the two boys barnstormed into her front yard on their bikes, sending dense clouds of gray dust and bits of gravel flying everywhere. With the back of her hand she wiped the moisture off her round, reddish face. The colorful kerchief wrapped around her head barely contained the sweat dripping down her forehead.

"How can I help you?' she asked the two strangers in her front yard.

Mateo and Sergio climbed off their bikes at the sight of the woman with her fists firmly planted on her hips.

"Good morning, ma'am." Mateo hesitated before stating his purpose.

"Yes? How can I help you?" the woman insisted.

"I'm looking for a cat," he said plainly.

"And a dog!" added Sergio.

"A what?" The short woman doubted her hearing.

Mateo gazed at his feet, suddenly feeling embarrassed.

"What kind of a cat is it?" she asked again.

"A gray, skinny cat." His awkward answer made him self-conscious.

"There are hundreds of skinny cats roaming around every day, and dogs too, as a matter of fact!" The woman began to resent this waste of her time. "There are many hungry, skinny cats around here. Take your pick."

"It has a crest!" Mateo tried to keep her attention.

"A WHAT, you said?" the woman shot back with a snort. She looked at him as if he had suddenly fallen from the sky.

"A crest... like a mohawk," Mateo answered with restraint, as if to assure her of his total sanity.

"A MOHAWK!" The woman looked around as if searching for a witness. "A MOHAWK? What kind of cat has a mohawk?"

"Well, the mohawk begins on its head but it goes all the way down its back," Mateo added, in case there was any doubt.

The boys stared blankly at the woman's incredulous reaction and took a step back as if she was about to blow apart.

Sergio offered more details. "He's kind of silver..."

"SILVER?" The short woman was on the verge of hysterics. "Is this the end of the world? A silver cat with a mohawk?" She could no longer contain herself and began to laugh so hard Mateo thought a heart attack was within the realm of possibility.

"Are you sure it's not a hyena or a—?" The woman cracked up with laughter at her own joke. Her cackles drilled into Mateo's ears and soon he realized the futility of his search.

"Never mind… Thanks for your time." He looked around disheartened.

"Are you sure you're not looking for a mutant?" The woman was obviously now going overboard to make her point. He tried but was unable to look away from the spastic movements of her belly as she laughed, which only stopped when she took a brief moment to wipe the tears from her eyes. He could tell she was grateful for this unexpected moment of levity at his expense.

"It's no use," Sergio concluded as they climbed on their bikes and sped off down the gravel path.

"I'll never find him again." It was a hard realization.

"I already told you, man, it's too hard to find him in a place like this. You did your best." Sergio tried to soften his friend's disappointment.

"I can't give up now. That animal needs help."

Once again they glided down the dirt road. Mateo searched both sides of the rolling hills overgrown with grass and wild bramble. He could not help but wonder, "*Where is it hiding, maybe afraid or even hurt?*"

"Sergio, why do people in this town hate animals so much?" he asked, out of breath. Sergio pretended he did not hear the question. If he answered truthfully, he would have to tell Mateo about the strange exchange he had had with Severo a few days before Stumpy's disappearance. With a chill he recalled the morning Severo had intercepted him in the middle of the road…

Sergio and Mateo rode their bikes relentlessly, crisscrossing the neighborhood on their quest as if the constant physical motion could make them forget that their mission was probably hopeless. As the day went on, Sergio's nagging guilt grew more insistent.

The tires of the bicycles thrummed under the forceful push of pedals. Mateo leaned over the handle bars as if the weight of his body could double his speed. There was no time to waste. Something began to open up inside Mateo's head. "*Sergio was right. This is all my fault. I should have done something when I had the chance. Now it might be too late!*" Crouched against the handles, he pointed the bike straight ahead, spraying a hail of pebbles from underneath his tires onto the pavement. The boys lunged on at full speed down the road.

Now even more determined, Mateo and Sergio continued on their search, scanning the neighborhood for the missing cat and dog. They followed every lead no matter how fruitless. The sweltering humidity of the midafternoon was starting to take its toll, covering them in sweat. Still, they approached anyone who happened to cross their path. Mateo tried to ignore the look of detachment on their faces when they realized, "A cat! But why?"

After a while, Mateo was beginning to fear their search was useless. Time was running out. "Sergio, he's gone for good this time. Muddy's nowhere around here." He felt at a loss.

Taking a rest under a tree, the two boys considered heading back home.

"There's going to be a storm," Sergio warned as raindrops began to sizzle on the hot pavement. Suddenly the road was wrapped in a dense cloud of steamy humidity. Sergio jumped to his feet.

"Mateo, I have an idea!"

"What's the matter? Where are you going?" he asked, following Sergio.

"There's one place we haven't looked," he answered. By the time Mateo caught up with him, Sergio was already crawling under the barbed-wire fence.

"Sergio, come back," Mateo called out. "The rain's starting to get heavy!"

"Hurry up! We haven't got much time," Sergio urged.

And with that, Mateo followed Sergio under the wire and ran into the field, his feet getting tangled in the wet grass.

"Wait up, Sergio!" Mateo shouted, trying to keep up.

A herd of black and white cattle pricked up their ears at the sound of footsteps and turned to look at them with wide eyes. A dark brown mare with a white star on its forehead, scaring away flies with the whipping of its tail, stood unperturbed. Having decided the boys were harmless, the animals lowered their heads to the ground and resumed yanking chunks of crisp grass with their teeth, oblivious to the rain and lightning.

"Mateo, where are you?" Sergio called from the middle of the darkened field.

Suddenly Mateo felt lost. "Wait for me!"

"Up here!" Sergio called down from the fork of a guava branch.

"What in the hell are you doing up there?" Mateo looked around and discovered what looked like a black cow staring him down. "Is this what you're afraid of?"

Relieved, he walked towards the young animal. The animal lowered its head to the ground and snorted.

"Where are you?" He heard Sergio's voice again.

"I'm here! By the cow!" he answered.

"Get away now! That's not a cow, THAT'S A BULL!" Sergio knew his friend was in trouble when he saw the beast pounding the ground with its hoof.

Breathing heavily, the animal suddenly charged towards Mateo. In a panic, he turned and ran to the same tree where Sergio was safely ensconced.

From his high vantage point, Sergio could trace the straight line the charging bull was making towards Mateo like a heat-seeking missile.

"Run, Mateo, run! It's going to kill you!"

Mateo needed no encouragement and ran through the field as if his life was on the line, all the while making a mental note to do something to Sergio so terrible *"that multiple, painful stitches would be required."* For the moment though, his only concern was making it to the guava tree in one piece.

"III wiiilll kiiiilll yooouuu!" he shouted breathlessly at Sergio as he ran through the wet grass.

Mateo had a hard time distinguishing between the sound of the bull's hooves pummeling the ground and the thud of his heart in his throat. As the bull charged behind him, Mateo could feel its hot breath. As the beast's pointy horns got closer, he tried to think of a prayer for the occasion but he could barely concentrate. He imagined himself in a full-body cast or, even worse, being delivered to his grandmother in a body bag. *"He was gored to death. Such a shame, he was so young! But he was sooo stubborn too! He was not a very fast runner though, poor dear. Anybody want some more coffee?"*

Just as he got a hold of a lower branch, the young bull managed to head-butt him. With surprising strength and skill, Mateo pulled himself up into the tree with one sweeping jump. From under the tree, the young bull stared up at him, shaking its head and snorting in frustration, foam seeping out of the sides of its mouth.

Sergio felt he owed his friend an explanation. "I think you got too close to its girlfriend."

Panting heavily, Mateo felt dizzy from the rush of blood throbbing in his head. He tried to calm down and bring his breathing back to normal.

Sergio was staring at him. "It's a bull."

"REALLY SERGIO? YOU DON'T THINK I FIGURED THAT OUT? THAT

DAMNED BULL WAS ABOUT TO MAKE ME ITS WIFE! YOU... JACKASS!"
Mateo yelled back, still out of breath. To their dismay, the young black bull
stationed itself right under the tree as if hoping to get another chance at them.

"You're DEAD, Sergio, or you will be soon!" Mateo was fuming, even more so
when he realized Sergio was about to burst out laughing.

"Why are you complaining? You run fast, besides I warned you!"

"YOU WERE IN THE DAMN TREE ALREADY! I WAS THE ONE RUNNING
FOR MY LIFE!"

"I'm just saying!" Sergio muttered, avoiding looking into Mateo's eyes.

"THIS IS ALL YOUR FAULT!" he screamed without taking his eyes off the bull
below. Tired of waiting, the animal began to gore the trunk as if it could make
the boys fall down like ripe fruit from the guava tree. Mateo and Sergio hunkered
down in the branches, enduring the falling rain like two wet birds.

From his position in the tree, Sergio could see a familiar figure in the distance
walking up the street. He watched silently as the man took a detour off the road
and went down the grassy hill into the forest. *"Oh, dear God! What have I done?"*

The ghost looked up the narrow path on the hill. *"Goaway, where are you now?"*
It had investigated every bit of movement, every moving animal within the forest,
to no avail.

"Heeesss gooone," hissed the black cat, as if reading the ghost's thoughts.

"There's not much time left, I have to go!" it lamented as it moved within the
shadows of the ceiba tree that stretched to the riverbank. The ghost stood there
under the tree's branches waiting, hoping for another tower of wind that would
whisk it across the river and up the hill. But the forest stood still. The incandescent
heat of the midday sun had wrung every bit of moisture out of the wind and
grounded all living organisms.

The ghost felt lonely. It also knew that three days were a very long time for
Goaway to be far from the place it loved. *"Please, little one, find your way here!"*

Sadly, neither the ghost nor Mateo had any idea what was about to befall the
missing young stray.

A few days without food or water had started to leave a mark on the dog.
Chained behind the house by the back steps, it had little protection from the
frequent rain showers and hot afternoons. Stumpy's whimpers fell on deaf ears;

even so, he wagged his tail at the sight of Severo. But Severo regarded the animal with cold eyes. A frustrated kick to the dog's ribs that made it yelp in pain served its purpose; the dog tried to hide underneath the steps as far as the rope would allow. Ignoring the dog's cries, Severo tightened the noose around the dog's neck.

For once, he was pleased with Billy since he had inadvertently helped him with his mission. Billy had gotten hold of the gray cat from across the street, saving him the trouble. Severo had waited patiently for his son to hide the animal in the basement. Meanwhile, Billy thought the animal would be safe in his room until he could figure out a way to keep it hidden from his father.

"Fat chance!" Severo thought with a tight grin on his face. He enjoyed knowing that his two prisoners were going nowhere. Now all he needed was a well thought out plan of execution, but he was in no rush, no sir! *"This is something I plan to enjoy!"*

The cat woke up from its nap and looked around at the unfamiliar surroundings. It blinked lazily and yawned with sudden hunger. It jumped to its feet from the pile of clothing and shook the sleep off its body with a vigorous stretch. It sat in the middle of the room and yawned some more, stretching the ends of its mouth into a wide comical grin. *"Where is it?"* The cat looked around again, this time searching for the plate of food that had been laid out for him at the foot of the bed. Now fully awake, it shook its body once more for good measure and with tail erect, walked straight to the dish and licked the remains of milk from the night before. *"Good!"*

Unable to find a way out of the room, the cat took a moment to scratch its chin. It lifted its head up to the closed window where thin slivers of light filtered through. With careful steps, it poked its head under the bed, sniffing around the confined space. *"Where am I?"* it wondered.

The cat jumped over the bed and onto the night stand with such flair that it barely disturbed the objects crowding the narrow table. After making a quick assessment, it leapt up onto the curtain rod above the closed window and tried to scratch its way out as if its life depended on it.

In its desperate attempt to flee, the cat lost its balance and began to fall. With lightning-fast reflexes, it dug its claws into the fabric and hung there steadfast as a paper doll velcroed to a bulletin board.

The cat heard the turn of the door knob. Once again its instincts kicked in, its pupils dilated, and the beat of its heart accelerated to a dangerous rate. From the smell, the cat knew instantly who was on the other side of the door.

"*Stinkanimal!*" it hissed.

That night, Sergio lay sleepless on his bed. He cupped his hands around the back of his head, his eyes fixed on the ceiling. Stumpy was still missing. Sergio could not stop the flood of tears.

His guilt kept him wide awake as rain drops hammered the windows. "What am I going to do? How am I going to tell him?" A disturbance of some other kind was brewing, one that might make the whole sky come undone! He had tempted fate and Severo had come after him with a vengeance. "I've betrayed my best friend."

Sergio's mind had become feverish with remorse the moment he saw the man carrying a hoe on his back in the distance. He knew then it was too late to right his wrong, but inevitably he would have to deal with the consequences. Suddenly a huge knot in his throat foretold what would finally come down between him and Mateo.

"*Dear God, what have I done?*" He swallowed hard, watching as the small figure disappeared into the forest. His mind flashed back to a couple of days before—the morning of their trip to the beach in fact—when he had to stop his bike in the middle of the road; someone was blocking his way. Severo was firmly planted in the middle of the pavement, his arms bent and fists on his hips. Sergio trembled at the sight of the old man staring him down. He was unsure of Severo's intentions, so he decided to play it safe. "*What the hell? —*" he thought.

"I have to talk about your dog," Severo spat out matter-of-factly.

"What about my dog? If you so much as…"

But Severo was in no mood to negotiate.

"Listen to me! I've warned you over and over to keep that damn dog away from my property."

"He doesn't do any harm, he's just—"

Severo cut Sergio off. "You'll have to pay me for the property he destroyed…" Suddenly Severo had an idea. "Or if you prefer, you can help me rid this town of unwanted animals."

"Since when are you concerned about this town?" Sergio knit his brow; the man certainly had his full attention now.

Severo could not restrain himself. "That filthy cat across the street better not set foot in my yard ever again."

"That's Mateo's cat!"

"Is that so? Then how come that animal is constantly roaming about my property? Some kind of guardian he is!" Severo snickered.

Sergio hated to admit it but the old man had a point.

"If you want to help that animal, here's what I want you to tell me. Where does it hide?"

"Whatsit to ya?" Sergio spat back.

But Severo was prepared. "Let's say I have a deal for you. Tell me where I can find that cat and I'll spare your dog. Otherwise," Severo gloated, "not only will I have animal control take your dog away, you'll have to repay me for the damage he caused."

Sergio felt hopeless, trapped under Severo's stern stare. Right or wrong, this threat was not to be taken lightly.

"Don't you think if he really cared for that animal, he would be more attentive?"

"I suppose so." Severo had touched a nerve. Sergio felt confounded at having agreed with such an abuser.

"Truly, I just want to help the animal."

Sergio heard Severo's words but had to remind himself this was the same man who would split an animal in two with a swift stroke of his machete.

"If you really care for your friend, you'll help the cat." Severo lowered his voice disingenuously. "And your dog too!"

Sergio finally relented. "He's always hiding by the chain link fence. Now about Stumpy…"

"We'll talk about that later." Severo dismissed him with a wave. As he made his way back to his front yard, Sergio stood dumbfounded in the middle of the road as if a dark cloud had descended upon him…

"What's the matter, Sergio?" Mateo broke the silence.
"Nothing," Sergio answered, his eyes fiercely focused on the man carrying a hoe over his shoulder. *"Dear God!"*

Sergio jumped over the barbed wire fence in one leap. He looked around the pasture, searching for any trace of the young bull from the day before. He could not help but chuckle remembering Mateo's spirited sprint across the field. But Sergio was on a new mission today.

"Where is it?" He shielded his eyes from the bright sun with the back of his hand

and scanned the horizon until he finally found what he was looking for. "There's my girl!" Sergio began to make a loop with the rope he was carrying. *"Careful, careful…we don't want to scare her now!"*

Sergio began to walk slowly with careful steps so as not to spook the mare grazing by the water hole, still keeping an eye out for the frisky black bull just in case it should materialize out of the blue and give him a run for his life like it had Mateo.

As if having a premonition, the brown mare lifted her head and used her ears to capture any suspicious noises. Her eyes followed the flicking of her ears, landing on the figure that stood still nearby. Even as bothersome gnats hovered over her face, the mare ignored them, her eyes firmly focused on the figure slowly moving closer and closer.

"Don't be afraid, little girl," Sergio called out softly, careful not to startle the mare. He felt relieved when she accepted him without concern, lowering her nose into the wet grass. "You're a good girl!" Very tenderly, Sergio caressed the blaze on her forehead. "There you go, little girl," he cooed while carefully sliding the rope around her neck. "Good girl. You're a beautiful, sweet girl!"

Mateo watched Sergio enter the front gate astride a beautiful brown horse like some modern but ragged cowboy.

"What is he up to now?"

"Mateo, there's no more time to waste!" Sergio shouted.

"Where did you get that horse?" he asked, suspecting the worst.

"Never mind! Hurry up!" Sergio pulled the reins as the impatient mare cantered around the yard. "This is no time for questions!"

"Did you steal this horse?" Mateo pressed on.

"Are you going to question me or are you ready to go on an adventure?"

"Methinks I've had enough of your adventures!" Mateo shot back, only to hear a big laugh from Sergio.

"Come on Mateo, hurry up! We haven't got much time… I'm dead serious!"

Mateo had no choice but to jump up behind Sergio on the mare's bare back and hold on as the horse began to neigh and snort.

"You stole this horse, didn't you?" He was beginning to foresee the inevitable.

Sergio kicked the mare's ribs and pulled the reins, making her rear up on her hind legs. "You know, Mateo, you worry too much! Let's just say I borrowed it from a dear friend! Let's say it's kind of a payback," Sergio answered with a chuckle. He wondered how Severo would feel about his characterization.

Sergio had formed a clearer idea where Muddy might be. "We have to find Severo."

As Sergio guided the horse out into the street, the sound of hooves clicking on the pavement brought Doña Sol to the window. She managed to catch a glimpse of the two boys as they disappeared into the distance.

Severo walked through the pasture towards the water hole. He accounted for the three black and white cows and got a glimpse of the young black bull. He scanned the field looking for the brown mare. *"Where's Rosina?"* he wondered, rather alarmed. Severo continued his search, flattening the stalks of tall grass along the way with his steps. "Where is she?" He felt his pulse starting to rise, when suddenly he was assaulted by a suspicion, "THOSE DAMNED KIDS!"

"THERE HE GOES!" Mateo shouted at the back of Sergio's head. They both watched as the man made his way down the dirt path to the river.

"That must be him!" Sergio yelled back into the wind. He spurred the mare ahead through the tall grass, feeling the sharp blades cutting his skin, his pants covered in prickly cockleburs.

"Hurry up, Sergio, he's going down the path!" Mateo yelled as Sergio kicked the mare's ribs more forcefully until her galloping broke into an unbridled race. As they rushed wildly down the path, Mateo held tightly onto Sergio. "Can you see where we're going?"

"I know what I'm doing!" Sergio shot back. He leaned against the mare's neck and grabbed a fistful of her mane, barreling out of control across the field down to the forest.

Mateo began to panic. "DON'T PUSH HER!" he yelled at Sergio.

Out of the blue, the ominous blare of a siren broke the silence. The boys had been so determined in their search, they hadn't noticed the police car parked on the side of the road. When they shot by at breakneck speed, the officer sitting inside his car turned on the red light on top of his cruiser. Welcoming the respite from small town monotony, he thought, *"This is going to be fun!"* But when he turned the key in the ignition, the engine sputtered and stopped.

"DAMMIT, NOT AGAIN!!" Frustrated, the cop watched the boys leave the road and head down into the field.

The blast of the siren made Mateo look back. He suspected it probably had something to do with the mare they were riding. But his impulse to reprimand Sergio would have to wait; they were on the verge of finding Muddy. He prayed that the cruiser would not catch up with them. Mateo's worries were interrupted when suddenly the spirited mare stopped short and reared up, flaring her nostrils in terror.

Sergio tried to calm her down by squeezing his heels against her flanks and steering her away. "WHOA! WHOA! Easy, girl, easy!" He had not seen the mongoose that had crossed her path and sent her into a panic. "WHOA! WHOA! Easy, easy!" he cried, but he could not get the mare to stop its neighing and snorting.

Sergio whipped her with the rope, but the horse's front hooves caught on a fallen branch, sending them all into a nosedive. The mare fell on her knees, throwing the boys violently into the air. Sergio was the first to hit the ground with a loud thud. Mateo fluttered his arms to soften the impact but landed on the side of his head by a bed of rocks. Sergio grabbed his elbow in pain as the frightened mare galloped across the field.

Mateo opened his eyes and looked up at the sky. For a second he watched swollen white clouds roll by, forgetting how he ended up on the ground. He lay on his side afraid to move; his head throbbed with pain and he felt the taste of blood filling his mouth.

"Serge, are you okay?" Mateo jolted to his feet when he discovered Sergio wailing in pain, cradling his left arm.

"I think it's broken," Sergio whimpered.

"Where's the horse?" Mateo looked around but the mare was nowhere to be found. "Let's go back. You need to take care of your arm!" he said, helping Sergio to his feet.

"No. You go ahead. Severo is down there! I know what he's up to!" Sergio urged.

"What do you mean?"

"Never mind, hurry up. I think he has Muddy hidden down there!"

The moment of reckoning had arrived as Mateo stumbled into the forest, panting and out of breath. Still in a daze, he looked around for signs of Severo. He finally spotted him bending over what seemed to be an opening in the ground by the river bank. *"That's him alright! I'd recognize that ratty hat of his anywhere!"* Mateo pushed his aching body forward in a desperate attempt to stop fate.

As he watched from a safe distance, he felt his heart leap—the freshly dug hole could only mean something evil. Mateo feared he might be too late. He looked around and, careful not to give warning, stepped on the carpet of dry leaves and grabbed a fallen branch. It couldn't have been a more incongruent scene: in a place of solace and quiet beauty, there stood of all people, Severo! Mateo's eyes burned a target on the man immersed in a mission. He wrapped his hands tightly around the branch to strike but stopped in midair when the man turned around to face him.

"YOU?!" Startled, Mateo let the branch fall from his grip. His surprise was greater than his confusion. "What the hell?—"

Before Mateo could regain his bearings, Billy jumped at him. Mateo stumbled back and lost his balance on the slippery moss. He flapped his arms wildly before splashing into the river. His body sank into the current until the side of his face hit a boulder on the bottom. Overwhelmed with terror, he gasped for air as his lungs filled with water. Like walking into a dream, he fell into a trance as the distorted reflection of trees swayed wildly within the ripples, as if disentangling their limbs from the fractured light.

A moment of strange calm overcame his will and his terror subsided. He realized his struggle was futile and allowed the water to fill his lungs. The arms of the river were deceivingly gentle. Mateo accepted its powerful embrace as he began to drown. He looked up and the last thing he saw was his crystal floating up out of his pocket, tumbling gracefully, almost dancing in front of his eyes. *"My Magic Crystal"* he thought just before he lost consciousness.

"Perfect peace. Is this—?"

The perfect darkness and silence were at first frightening but then, a sudden, blinding light.

"Weightless as a feather? No, lighter!"

Mateo sensed ripples in the perfect atmosphere.

Not too far away, the ghost felt restless when it saw the sparkle in the water.

"The fire!"

Mateo felt a light beckon, warm and inviting. He did not have to struggle anymore nor even breathe. He let himself be carried away effortlessly toward the brilliant light. He sensed the warmth of the stars surrounding him and the silence: Pure, perfect silence. All earthly worries had lost their meaning. He opened his eyes from a haze and found he could look beyond the universe.

From its perch on a nearby branch, the garrapatero noticed the burst of intense light dancing in the water. It ruffled its shiny coat of feathers with curiosity as the sparkling object floated along with the current.

Ah-nee, Ah-nee, Ah-nee

Excited by the beautiful light, the garrapatero flew over the river and with a graceful swoop, grabbed the rough cord holding the light and carried it back up to its branch.

Silence. Bright stars. Peace.

The sting of pain dissolved, vanished, disappeared. *"Where am I?"* Mateo finally embraced the cold darkness without fear, as peaceful as if staring into a moonless night. His soul began to lift up. He could see his own lifeless body left behind like an empty shell but he felt no fear as his soul floated above the river's current, above the trees, over the forest.

He looked down and discovered the luminous silver thread that was keeping him connected to the earth. Caught up on the wind that shook the tree tops, he hovered over his grandmother's backyard. Watching the banana leaves flap softly, he saw someone down below. Doña Sol clasped her hands in prayer and looked up but did not see him.

"Here, Grandma! I'm here!" But the words did not seem to leave his mouth. "Please don't cry, the thread will break!" he called out to the woman. He could see her eyes filling with tears when a jolt made the thin luminescent silver thread snap. His soul, now free of any earthly bond, began to ascend faster into space. Mateo

could no longer see the tree tops as he rose beyond the clouds and closer to the stars. The perfect darkness of the universe enveloped him. From up here he could see the glowing circumference of Earth…

"Not yet."

He heard the living light's voice and could not move forward.

"Not yet!"

Mateo heard it repeat, *"Not yet. Not yet! You'll have to go back!"* He felt the white light closer now.

He was enveloped by the brightest cloud and realized a ghost was floating before him. *"An angel?"* Mateo reached out but the ghost rejected him. *"No! Go back—it is not your time!"*

"You were the one I trusted the most," he said but the ghost didn't answer. Its gaze wandered among the stars above.

"Go forward. You can't stay here. Not yet," the ghost repeated.

"Please!" he begged and felt a deep happiness as the ghost reached out to him before vanishing into the perfect darkness.

"Mateo, Mateo"

From his altered state, Mateo felt his soul slam against his body with such force that he began to convulse.

"Mateo, Mateo!"

Regaining consciousness, he opened his eyes and tried to focus on the shadow before him. Sergio shook him by the shoulders, breathing a sigh of relief as his friend turned on his side and coughed up a mouthful of water. Mateo lay on the ground motionless, his thoughts muddled. *"What happened? Where am I?"* And then he remembered. *"Was it her?"*

Sergio's voice broke the silence. "Are you all right? Everything will be okay. Breathe now."

Still shivering from his near-death experience, Mateo sat on the ground, his jaws chattering and his wet, mud-stained clothes clinging to his body like a second skin.

"Thanks, Serge," he managed to say but he felt hopeless, as if he was sliding out of control down a rabbit hole. He sobbed quietly with his face buried in his hands.

"Let's get you out of here!" Sergio said, helping Mateo to his feet.

Trudging across the field for home, the boys finally reached the edge of the road.

"How's your arm, Serge?" Mateo asked, still shivering from his wet clothes.

"I'll survive," Sergio answered, wiping the sweat off his brow with a trembling hand. Just as they reached the road, the sudden deafening sound of a police siren behind them stopped them in their tracks.

"Stop right there, you two!" They looked back at the police cruiser approaching them.

"We didn't do anything!" Sergio managed to say as the policeman stepped out of the car.

"Hold it there!" the officer threatened, placing his right hand on his holster and cupping his left one on the end of his baton. Mateo and Sergio stood frozen, as if a spell had rooted them to the ground. With a deliberate, cocky swagger, the cop approached the two boys, blocking their way with a menacing stance. The boys had to look up to face the law officer towering over them.

"I think you are mistaken," Sergio repeated, convinced it was some kind of mix up.

"I will not repeat myself," the man in uniform said, lowering his face to meet Sergio's.

"You two better start singing from the beginning," the man in uniform pressed on. Mateo saw the policeman grasp the butt of his baton as if to send a warning message. He opened his dry mouth to defend them but no sound came out. *"How are we going to get out of this? This is a mistake I'm sure."*

"We're looking for a cat and a dog," he finally managed to say.

"What did you say?'" the cop asked with intimidating authority.

Mateo opened his mouth once more, but it felt as if it was filled with cotton balls. He knew they had to get out of this situation but his head was empty of ideas. He considered the consequences: the feel of a sturdy billy club breaking through his bones or the scorching silent scolding from his grandmother. *Which would hurt the most?*

"I understand you two punks broke into private property and stole a horse!"

Mateo turned to Sergio in disbelief, "Excuse me?"

"Well, I'm still waiting young man! I haven't got all day!" It became clear to them the policeman's patience was beginning to wear thin.

Mateo watched nervously as the policeman reached for his walkie-talkie. The boys listened to the crackling reception of the radio. "I have two kids here in custody. I'm ready to take them to headquarters to be processed."

Sergio and Mateo began to panic when they heard the cop reciting the charges, "Property trespassing... Theft... A horse... Yep, two boys." The officer's intense stare nailed the boys in place; by now they were trembling like dry leaves in the wind. Under the intimidating pressure, Sergio ignored the throbbing pain in his broken arm and Mateo completely forgot about nearly drowning.

Through the static, Mateo and Sergio tried to decipher the respondent's unintelligible answer, but the inescapable outcome became clear when a second officer jumped out of the cruiser.

"Need reinforcements?" he asked rather eagerly. Mateo paled at the way the officer rhythmically hit the palm of his hand with the head of his baton. Suddenly Mateo had difficulty swallowing and his heart began to tumble inside his chest. He caught a glimpse of Sergio who was also visibly shaken but then saw a fine stream of yellow liquid begin running down Sergio's leg as his body began to convulse with fright. The policemen kept their hands wrapped tightly around the butts of their shiny black guns.

"This can't get any worse," he thought. Meanwhile, he was taken aback by the smell coming from Sergio's direction. *"Did he just crap his pants?"* The thought made him want to explode with laughter but the sight of the black guns convinced him to stay quiet and very still.

A situation like this could easily get out of hand. He had watched way too many episodes of *Adam-12* and *The Untouchables* and seen enough "breaking news" reports on TV to know that a half-twisted look at an officer would only invite a clubbing of epic proportions! Mateo was certain they were about to become the main subject of a similar episode starring as the clueless victims. But even the dire circumstances of his present situation did not pack as big a punch as his next terrifying thought, *"How is grandma gonna take this?"*

TOO LATE, NO WAY TO TURN AROUND

With my head turned inside out,
Here I go, so help me God,
Down the rabbit hole.
Too late, no way to turn around,
No end in sight, can't see the light,
So down and down I go.

Mateo and Sergio were unnerved by the intimidating red light flashing atop the cruiser, *twirling and twirling and twirling,* and even worse, the officers toying with their handcuffs. But their terror acquired a new shade of awful when, out of the blue, another car parked behind the patrol car.

"Is there a problem, officer?... OOOH! I see you caught up with these two!" Severo's voice cut through them like a hot sword.

No end in sight, can't see the light, so down and down I go. Mateo realized with a great deal of certitude, "*Things are about to get worse; way, way worse.*" Severo, of all the people in this blessed town, was about to take control of the situation and undoubtedly manipulate it to his advantage.

"*Shitballs, shitballs, shitballs!*" Mateo was overcome with uncontrollable chills but this time it was Severo's inauspicious presence—and not his own wet clothes—that was the cause. Worse yet, he was convinced that a whipping the likes of which he had never seen was in the cards for him. He braced himself for what was about to come. Just then, Mateo's worst nightmare began to materialize. Making her way through the small crowd that had gathered around the cruiser, was Doña Sol...

That morning, Billy had a bad feeling at the terrible, terrible sight of his father leaving the house carrying a hoe over his shoulder. To a stranger, seeing a man carrying a working tool seems as normal as a professional carrying a briefcase or a woman carrying her purse. But to Billy, who had known his father's crooked tendencies for years, there was something wrong with this picture. Something so terribly out of place that butterflies began to flutter in his stomach. Billy was convinced that something bad was about to take place. He could not predict his father's dark intentions with certainty, but he knew the only predictable aspect of Severo's actions was how much destruction they would unleash.

To the untrained eye, Severo looked as if he was heading to a farming patch on a regular work day, but Billy knew for a fact that his father never left his machete behind, ever. Severo's daily routine consisted of waking up early, before the sun had even cracked the horizon, and sitting on his balcony filing his machete, almost making love to it. Nothing ever diverted the man from caring for the weapon that was like an extension of his arm. The fact that he had left the house without it simply meant that Severo's mind was set on a much bigger, dirtier task. This way he would spare his beloved machete from making contact with the soil.

Billy had the most terrifying realization as he tried to piece together the puzzle of his father's nefarious intentions. First, he had to consider the facts: the mysterious disappearance of Muddy and Stumpy without a trace, his father's frequent disappearances into the nearby forest, and even more intriguing now, the unusual sight of him carrying a hoe into the woods. *"There has to be some kind of connection."* But Billy had no way of proving it. Given the sequence of events in the past, it seemed to be more than just a coincidence. *"I know what he's up to!"* Billy had a horrible feeling in his gut.

Billy gave his father a considerable head start before following after him. When he first saw Severo walking away, he suspected it had something to do with the cat in his bedroom. Billy had been very careful about hiding it, but if his father had been waiting for a window of opportunity before striking, he certainly wouldn't have made any moves to alert him. The thought made him feel even more unsettled. *"What if he saw the cat in my room?*

There was no time to waste. The most important task at hand was to follow his father and hopefully get to the bottom of things as soon as possible before another tragedy happened. Grabbing one of his father's hats to camouflage his face, he followed Severo across the field and down the path to the river. He ducked behind the tall grass every time Severo scanned around for any witnesses.

Once he entered the dark woods it became hard to see. The rotting smell of wet mulch overwhelmed his nose. Still he was able to follow Severo's steps from the rustling of dead leaves. He could tell Severo was crossing the river by the swooshing sounds of his boots in the current. For a long moment, he watched Severo strike the ground with the edge of his hoe, digging deeper and deeper. From his vantage point Billy wasn't able to clearly see what Severo was doing, but he watched as the mound of freshly dug soil grew bigger. He waited patiently for his father to finish and abandon the premises. Billy was determined to find out once and for all why his father was so invested in digging up holes by the side of the river in the middle of the forest. Suddenly everything made terrible sense. "Graves!!"

After Severo left the woods, Billy tried to gather the strength to approach the hole. He waited patiently until he was certain Severo was gone before rolling up his jeans and stepping into the water. He knelt by the opening in the ground, puzzled. *"Why a grave? What is he up to now?"* he wondered, filling his fists with clumps of the moist soil.

But before Billy had the chance to walk away, he heard menacing screams behind him.

"YOU!" The word penetrated the back of his head like a sword. His father must have come back and now all hell was about to break loose. He thought of running. As he got to his feet, he turned expecting a blow but the surprise was even bigger. Instead of his father, it was Mateo coming after him. Billy had no time to react before Mateo overtook him.

"IT WAS YOU AFTER ALL!" Mateo kept accusing. His surprise was now as great as his confusion. "BILLY! WHAT THE HELL?!"

"YOU'RE WRONG!" Billy defended himself but Mateo was relentless. Billy kept pushing Mateo away, not realizing they were venturing out onto the boulder jutting from the river's bank. "Let me explain!" Billy kept yelling in defense.

Mateo lost his glasses in a moment of struggle, so Billy took his chance and pushed Mateo, sending him splashing into the pool of water below. Overcome with terror, Billy watched as Mateo's body sank under the water's surface.

"MATEO!" Billy panicked at what he had done and escaped out of the forest and up the hill.

Sergio finally broke through the trees but only caught the last moments of the struggle. The pain in his arm was making him feel unfocused and sweaty. Without hesitating he jumped into the river, making his way towards Mateo. He could see him lying at the bottom, his face resting on the flat cobblestones…

Of all the things to do when in Palo Verde, getting arrested was probably last on Mateo's list. The image of Doña Sol's icy stare was burned inside his head. "What in heaven's name is wrong with you?" she had hissed under her breath, livid. It was never a good sign when she confronted him with crossed arms. Never!

He had seen pain in his grandmother's face before, deep heartbreaking pain. Even anger that had flickered in her eyes with the wordless scream, *"you've gone too far!"* Her disappointment, perhaps because it had become a constant in her life, made her look small, like a little girl lost at the end of the road. But what he never thought he'd live to see was her rage.

"If you are going to endanger your life so carelessly, I promise you, I'll finish the job!" Doña Sol raged at him, feeling she had reached the end of her rope. "You put me through any more of your shenanigans and I'll smack you so hard, you'll have to pick up your underwear from the other side of the room!"

If it weren't for Don Genaro's vacant stare, Mateo would have thought his grandfather was taunting him when he said, "Are we in trouble?"

But Doña Sol was far from done with Mateo. "Come with me to the kitchen. NOW!"

Mateo thought it was best to keep his mouth shut. "Sorry," he muttered.

"This time sorry is not enough," she replied coldly.

"Open the pantry," she ordered him. "I want you to organize all my cans and boxes in alphabetical order."

"WHAT!?" Mateo barked at the ridiculous assignment.

Doña Sol would have none of it. "If it's a lack of things for you to do, this will take care of it," she concluded.

"This is INSANE!" he protested again. "And they called *me* the crazy one!" Mateo shot back defiantly.

"Get. Going. Now." There was no sign of humor in her voice and, without another word, she walked outside to the gate and coiled the heavy metal chain one, two, three times around the post.

"Lockdown. This sucks!" Mateo grumbled to himself while watching his grandmother triumphantly dangle the key before depositing it in her pocket.

"If you dare cross this gate again, you'll have me to answer to!" Doña Sol seethed.

"I had nothing to do with the stolen horse, don't you understand?!" Mateo yelled back in his defense.

"All I'm telling you is, don't you dare disobey me!" She was shaking with anger.

But Mateo was defiant and more determined than ever. Finding himself in the eye of a new storm, a wave of anxiety washed over him. *"This ain't over yet!"*

The thought of Muddy still missing hit him hard. Even worse, Sergio, in his zeal to find the animals, had worsened their odds. But Mateo fought to stay true to his promise; nothing—not even a locked gate—would keep him from finding the cat. He would find Muddy even if it meant disobeying his grandmother. Mateo pressed his face against the chain link fence until it felt numb.

Mateo froze at the sight of the crooked man in front of him extending his arm in greeting as if taunting him.

"Hi, Mateo! I've been looking forward to meeting you," Severo said with a dry, forced smile. Mateo was repulsed at the bits of foam at the corners of Severo's mouth and the vulgar gold tooth peeking out between his cracked lips. "Doña Sol, I'm just happy he's okay," Severo offered disingenuously. "He's just a child. I do understand."

Hesitantly, under his grandmother's cold stare, Mateo extended his hand to Severo as if he had been asked to pet a viper. He cringed at Severo's contact. *"Cold as a dead man!"* He was afraid that once Severo had a hold of his hand, he might decide to cut it off. He could read between the lines. *"You're not fooling me, you asshole!"* He knew that Severo was up to something and was using this advantage to make a bigger point. *"He is not going to play games this time."*

"I want you to thank Severo for kindly intervening with the officer," Doña Sol said between pressed lips.

"WHAT!" Mateo lost his cool.

"I'm warning you." His grandmother's words came out through grinding teeth. "He's forgiven you for your lack of judgment."

Mateo stared at her in disbelief, as if she had been suddenly taken over by an alien life form. "YOU MUST BE—"

"That's enough." She crossed her arms, her eyes burning with impatience.

"Well, I'm going to get going now, Doña Sol." Severo shot a cold glance at Mateo who shuddered at the flash of pent-up hatred reflected in the man's eyes. A chilling realization hit him: Severo was never more terrifying than when he tried to feign sympathy.

Once Doña Sol was out of earshot, Severo took the opportunity to confront Mateo. "You know, cats, more than any other animal, carry diseases. I'm just helping you, you little ungrateful speck of dirt."

Mateo glared at him, his hatred boiling up. "Where are Muddy and Stumpy? What have you done to them?"

Severo gloated with a menacing glare that left Mateo bewildered and puzzled.

"Never you mind! Hey, by the way, your buddy Sergio?… With friends like that, you have no need for enemies! Tell him thank you from me, will ya?"

Back alone in his room, Mateo stared blankly at his reflection in the mirror, his hand coming to rest where his crystal used to hang.

"Where's my Magic Crystal?" He thought of the many times he had squeezed it until its rough edges created red valleys in his hand, sometimes so hard it made his palm bleed but he did not mind. His Magic Crystal was the one reminder of his happy times with Minerva, happy, magical times.

"Here you go. It will keep the good spirits close by!" He remembered the moment she had presented it to him. Unable to understand her meaning then, he began to comprehend it more clearly as the years went by.

But even back then, her gift made perfect sense to him, especially on the night he had woken up from a terrible dream. "I dreamt you were gone," he said feverishly.

"It was just a dream," he heard her say as she placed the crystal hanging from twine around his neck. He had felt like a king, a king with the most powerful jewel on Earth. Mateo sensed its purpose then: as long as he kept it close, his memories would never go away. A Magic Crystal indeed. But now its potency, along with its power of memory, had vanished, maybe for good.

Severo's words ran once again through his mind. *"Your buddy Sergio? With friends like that, you have no need for enemies."*

For Sergio, his sleeplessness had begun even before the harrowing night at the beach.

"I'll see you later," he remembered telling Mateo before jumping in the waiting Jeep. Although he was exhausted and anxious to put an end to the previous night's experience, a disturbing loop played inside his head: how to tell his friend about his deal with Severo? *How can I tell him the truth now?* No matter how he framed it, Sergio knew the outcome would not be good. He also knew this was not going to end without a war.

"It's my fault Muddy is missing," he had to admit. *"Did I make a mistake?"* It became clear that he had never considered what the consequences would be if his plan backfired. Sergio was about to find out, maybe in the worst way possible. He felt like he was about to step on a land mine. In his eagerness to have Stumpy returned safe and unharmed, he had endangered Muddy's life. But as he discovered

too late, Severo, in a typical act of betrayal, had hidden Stumpy too. Now he was unsure whether Muddy or Stumpy would ever be found. Worst of all, Sergio had to face the inevitable showdown with his friend. With his selfish act, Sergio not only managed to endanger the life of two innocent animals but he had also risked his friendship with Mateo, maybe ending it forever.

Sergio managed to squeeze his lithe body through the gap in the front gate and make his way across the yard where he found Mateo swinging in the hammock. "Hey, man!"

"Hey, you. How's your arm?" Mateo straightened up, still swinging in the hammock.

"Better. The break wasn't that bad," Sergio answered, stroking his cast absentmindedly.

"Have any horses to ride?" Mateo jabbed before breaking into a laugh.

"I can get them wholesale for you!" Sergio answered, breaking into laughter too, but then his expression turned dark, as if a black cloud had settled over him.

"Mateo, I have something to tell you," Sergio said, feeling the blood rush to his face.

Sergio could not deal with his guilt any longer. The lie had gone on far too long; he was convinced Mateo's near drowning had been a sign. He had to tell him the truth and, as much as he was certain Severo was responsible for Muddy and Stumpy's disappearance, he knew he shared a great deal of the blame.

"Mateo, I know why Muddy is missing." With those seven tortured words, Sergio came clean. But his confession only unleashed Mateo's wrath. He braced himself as all hell broke loose.

Mateo jumped out of the hammock, stiff with anger. His face turned white as the blood drained from his head, and his eyes gleamed with a cold, menacing stare.

"GET OUT! I don't want to see you again! GET THE HELL OUT! YOU ARE A BIGGER BASTARD THAN HE IS! GET OUT!"

"Can you think about anything else but yourself, just for once? Some people care for you and you just piss on them!"

"GET THE HELL OUT!" Mateo screamed enraged.

"Listen to me, man. I didn't mean to do it!" Sergio pleaded sheepishly.

"GET OUT! YOU'RE JUST LIKE THE REST OF PEOPLE IN THIS TOWN!"

Mateo screamed as Sergio jumped on his bike and disappeared down the road.

On the other side of the forest, the ghost paced within the shadows. The night was charged, vibrant, electric, and the hanging moon cut through the dense shadows beneath the trees.

"*Little one, he is in need now,*" the ghost lamented looking towards the horizon, hoping for a sign. "*Somebody, please!*" it begged but there was no one to hear. Separating the ghost and the cat was a river, the beautiful singing river. "*Only the forest can brew up a storm.*" The ghost thought about how to cross the current once more but it knew it couldn't on its own. "*Only a miracle, my little one, only a miracle!*" The ghost wished the cat could hear its voice.

So what's a hopeless ghost to do? A ghost can't fly, transform, or create spells and incantations. It relies on the secret powers of Nature. A ghost relies on something so magical and yet so simple, it might be taken for granted. Sadly, the ghost only had the moon to talk to. Unresolved earthly matters keep a ghost grounded: an old man lost in grief and regrets, a boy overwhelmed by his loss, a stray cat in danger. "*If only I could—*" The ghost despaired at the unfinished thought. Only then, could it complete its journey without interference.

Trapped in his thoughts, Mateo had no idea how or when to make his next move. Without Sergio's help, he felt this time around it was going to be nearly impossible to save the cat's life. He sank into the hammock with his chin resting on hands. His gaze wandered from one side of the garden to the other when the garrapatero flew overhead and perched on the telephone wires along with the noisy grackles. He watched as it fidgeted and cried with urgency.

Ah-nee, Ah-nee, Ah-nee… Ah-nee, Ah-nee, Ah-nee

It was not the same laid-back, soft singing it used when playing with the cat but a more forceful, determined, high-strung sound. Keeping his eyes on the bird, Mateo walked under the pole and watched it shuffle sideways along the high wires, calling incessantly. He turned to walk away when suddenly he felt the flap of a wing brush his ear. Looking up, he watched the black bird fly away and take its place back on the wire. "*Is it trying to tell me something?*" Even at a distance, he could tell the bird's alert eyes were staring at him. With every call, Mateo heard, "*Danger!*

"DANGER!"

With my head turned inside out,
Here I go, so help me God,
Down the rabbit hole...

Mateo woke up from a restless sleep, his mind still muddled by the tumultuous dreams he could not remember. Their heaviness broke him down and made him sob. *"Traitor!"* Curled up in his empty room, he mourned for the cat. A harmless cat that he had gone out of his way to ignore. A gentle, gray cat that raised its silver crest when it got excited or scared and when it felt playful.

Now Muddy was gone. Mateo's cheeks were flushed from the sobs he could no longer hold back. His tears formed puddles on his pillow. *"Where is he?"* There were no words to describe his heartbreak. *"Maybe, just once, I should have taken better care of him. I'm so stupid."* Mateo's thoughts were not only for the lost cat but for a lost friend too.

Doña Sol felt she had lost control over Mateo. *"Have I been unreasonable?"* Still, she decided to try talking to him one more time. The following morning she found him sitting in the hammock by the potted ferns.

"What are you doing?" she asked.

"I don't know what I'm doing in this place!" Mateo answered, lowering his gaze.

"Why do you say that?" Doña Sol asked gently.

He had to think for a moment. "Because it's the truth."

"Are you talking about Muddy?"

Without answering, Mateo turned his face away, feeling exposed. He hated himself for the embarrassing slip. "I feel like I don't know who I am anymore... Like I've lost myself."

Doña Sol finally got a glimpse into his state of mind. "Muddy will come back when he feels ready. You don't have to worry, you'll see..."

Doña Sol took pity on the boy. "You haven't lost yourself. In fact, I think it's the opposite; I think you've found the old Mateo, the one who is kind and who cares. Unfortunately, life doesn't give out answers, it just gives you hardships so you can decide what's really important. Have you stopped to think that maybe this is a test to push you and help you find your way? Never apologize for fighting for the life of somebody else... even if it's an animal! But be prepared to take everything in, good and bad. Do you understand?"

He lowered his head without answering her.

Doña Sol pressed on, "Even if it's hard, you have to find the good in people... And Sergio will always be a friend to you, regardless of how you feel now..." But she was not prepared for what was about to come.

"I don't need another lecture." Inadvertently, she had pushed a vulnerable button. "Not from you anyway," Mateo snapped.

Doña Sol was surprised by the burning spark in his eyes. Finally, from behind his seemingly impenetrable wall of resistance, Mateo's true feelings came out unfiltered. It was as if her grandson was suddenly possessed by some kind of strange force pushing him to unload the heavy burden of the past few weeks. She listened as Mateo's words came rushing out with perplexing intensity, as if his young life was beginning to unravel.

"What do you mean, *find the good in people?*" Mateo lowered his eyes to the ground in anger as his words spilled forth without pause. "I'm sure you are not talking about the goodness in this town ... You all took sides!"

Like an animal that has suddenly discovered the freedom lying beyond the open door of its cage, Mateo's blistering scorn flew out of his mouth with such conviction and hurt that Doña Sol was left speechless. His eyes, dulled by rage, never left the ground as he spoke without sentimentality. The lack of tears in his eyes marked his determination to hammer out the facts, just the facts as he saw them. So he spat out the thoughts that had been haunting him...

"Love is a weapon!"

"Where in heaven's name did you learn that?" Doña Sol asked, shaken.

Mateo lowered his eyes, teeming with anger. He took a deep breath before answering. "Maria. Maria told me. She says people use love to hurt each other. She said when someone says 'It's for your own good' what they really mean is, 'I'll love you as long as you do as I say!'"

Doña Sol struggled to keep her composure. *"Where is this coming from?"* Then it dawned on her; his outburst was nothing but the result of the deep void that Minerva's death had left behind. It became clear that his troubled ambivalence towards the cat—ignoring it while simultaneously obsessing about its safety—was a way to protect himself from being weakened by love.

"Yes, love!" She had found the answer. Even during all the tumultuous and uncertain times with Minerva, there had still been love and trust. It saddened her that her grandson could not understand. But she did understand the boy's feeling

of betrayal and abandonment; to him, Minerva's absence represented a broken promise. And now, the mysterious appearance of a stray cat the moment she was gone had become a fresh opportunity for him to rescue the love he had lost. But in order to do that, he had to let his guard down, open himself up, and trust again. Without saying another word, she placed a loving hand on Mateo's back.

Love is a weapon. The words were still ringing in Doña Sol's ears as she climbed the steps, feeling the weight of his indictment. She went into her room and sat still in the darkness. She had to admit there was some truth to the destructive power of love. Love could be a cure and remedy for the inconsistencies of life. Or it could be a malfunctioning tool that damaged in its misguided attempt to repair. She had witnessed it firsthand.

She thought about Genaro, now lost in a sea of darkness and confusion. A sad shell of the irrepressible man who would have gone to any lengths to prove the strength of his love. Love as a weapon...

* * *

Warily, Severo accepted Genaro's challenge to a game of dice. With increasing suspicion, he kept watch as Genaro lifted the dice with one swipe of his hand and blew into his fist before letting them hit the dirt.

But Severo had good reason to be vigilant, even more so than usual. Word had gotten around that Genaro had been looking for the right opportunity to settle an old score. Severo hardly ever felt fear; in fact, the bigger the affront he committed, the bigger the adrenaline rush inflated his ego. But this was different.

What happened next was the subject of legendary gossip. Brimming with the arrogance of youth and the artificial self-confidence only alcohol can create, Severo was deliberately confrontational as he took the opportunity to make his point.

"You are no man!" he challenged Genaro, pushing his chest forward, his arms spread like the tail of a sad rooster.

"You are the scum of the Earth, you filthy worm!" Genaro shot back, his bravado taking Severo by surprise. With those words, a line was crossed and improvised weapons were drawn. But before Severo could protect himself, Genaro, with incredible precision, traced a bloody path down his opponent's face with the broken neck of a beer bottle.

"That's for my daughter, you bastard! You'll live to regret this, you sonofabitch! Stay away from my family!"

And with that, Genaro branded Severo for the rest of his life. He had attempted to restore his daughter's tainted honor with a shard of glass. Genaro had drawn a line, a bloody line across Severo's face. Severo would never be able to hide the price he paid for his transgression. Love, the ultimate weapon.

* * *

Love is a weapon. After his meltdown, Mateo let his grandmother's words bounce off him. There was no time for sentimentalities. His priority now was to find a moment to break loose from her guard. From his seat on the balcony, he kept a watchful eye on the locked gate and his grandmother. He waited impatiently for the opportunity to escape the moment she resumed her chores. *"Sergio is no use to me anymore. I'll have to do this alone!"*

The instant Doña Sol disappeared into the kitchen, he carefully descended the stairs. He knew he was pushing past the limits of his grandmother's patience but he also knew without risk there could be no positive outcome.

Wailing, hissing, and spitting, Muddy sank his claws deep into the curtains. Grabbing the cat's back, Severo tried to disentangle it from the fabric and shove it into the burlap sack. He had carefully calculated Billy's absence to carry out his plan but the cat was not cooperating at all. Severo noticed the cat's fully dilated pupils as it thrashed its tail wildly in resistance. The more the cat hissed and complained, the more forceful Severo became. Losing his patience, he hit Muddy on the side of the head but the cat was not going down without a fight.

As Severo reached for the cat's belly, Muddy clawed Severo's forearms and bit one of his thumbs, sending him on a rampage. Severo finally managed to get Muddy inside the bag, but not before he was scratched and bleeding. Severo felt the deep red furrows burning along his arms as he coldly watched the brown bag tumble around the room. Just as Billy stepped inside the house, he dropped the burlap sack into the basement and closed the door behind him. Now Severo had to wait for the next opportunity.

Sergio struggled with his guilt. "This is all my fault." He had to find a way to save his friendship with Mateo. There were no two ways about it; he had to swallow his pride and face his friend again.

"I'm sorry but I did it for your own good, you ass!" Sergio found himself on the defensive.

Mateo was relentless. "Where on this Earth are we going to find him now? He might be dead because of you!"

"See, that's your problem. You don't want to admit you're responsible for this shit too!"

Sergio watched Mateo's eyes glaze over as he tried to apologize one last time. "I'm really sorry Mateo... But you know, you have to fight for it if that's what you want. Don't wait for things to come to you. It won't happen. Fight hard. If you want to save Muddy, do it now." Noticing the spark in his friend's eyes, Sergio added, "It's not doing him any good, you sitting here and waiting! Let's just go out there again. I promise you we'll find them this time!"

Mateo glanced at the cast on Sergio's arm and felt his anger subside. For a moment, the boys stood silently, staring at each other through the chain link fence.

"Let's go, Mateo. We have to take care of this now! I have the bikes right here."

Uncertain, Mateo looked back at the house. He saw his grandfather sitting on the balcony, humming to himself. Luckily his grandmother was busying herself in the kitchen.

"Hurry up, there's a storm coming!" Sergio looked up to the darkened sky.

Mateo decided he had to risk it. "Serge, hold on to the chain. Make sure it doesn't rattle!" Carefully he began to climb over the fence.

PART SEVEN

A Light at the End

"This cat belongs to me!" Billy had tried to justify his harsh decision to take the stray a few days before, even if it meant coming to blows with his neighbor. He was determined not to allow anyone to take it away, including his father. His fight with Mateo had been worth it; after all, he had the cat now. The thought of his father's reaction made him tremble, but all he had to do was to make sure he kept the stray hidden from Severo until he could come up with a plan.

Still, Billy struggled with his conscience.

"I can't do this, it's wrong." He suddenly remembered how it felt to be on the outs, pleading before deaf ears for what you feel is rightfully yours. He thought about Mateo. All his life Billy had felt like he was less than nothing. Now it was a revelation to discover that he had a conscience after all.

"I can't do this!" Billy headed for his room.

Discreetly carrying a small saucer full of milk, Billy walked to his room to check on the cat. When he heard the distressed howls of a dog, he stopped on his tracks. *"What was that?"* Then silence. He tried to go on his way but heard anxious barks coming from the basement again. Billy placed the saucer at the foot of the bed. He thought it strange the cat didn't come rushing up to the plate as it had done that morning...

Wharf, wharf, wharf!

Billy heard the barks again. This time he made his way down to the basement, following the dog's cries and yelps. Opening the basement door he was startled to walk in on his father. By the expression on his face he knew something was going on and something highly suspicious at that. "What are you doing?" he asked, only to take the befuddled look in his father's eyes as his answer. He knew that Severo was up to no good. Although he tried to prepare himself for the worst, Billy was shocked at the sight of the dog chained to the steps, whining with hunger and thirst. Even more so when he realized that it was no other than Stumpy, Sergio's missing dog.

Wharf, wharf, wharf!

Stumpy barked hopefully, wagging his tail at the welcome sight of Billy rushing towards him. "What the hell do you think you're doing with this dog?" Outraged by his father's latest transgression and finally out of patience, Billy lost all control.

"HOW DARE YOU! You're not getting away with it this time!"

"Oooh, really? Says the cat-snatcher himself! As soon as you explain to me what exactly you've done, then you'll have the right to question me," Severo defended himself, savoring the moment.

But Billy was not going to back down, not this time. He mustered all his courage to confront his father. "So it *was* you! Let that animal go!"

Severo was taken off guard. The intensity of his son's anger made him take a step back. "I don't have to tell you what you already know! No filthy animals on my property, let alone in my house! But it seems to me you'd rather learn your lesson the hard way." Severo began to unbuckle his belt.

"I will not let you hurt that dog!" Billy responded indignantly. Without thinking, he grabbed a broken curtain rod, ready to defend himself. "And where is the cat?"

Severo paused. For the first time, he saw Billy in a new light and he didn't like it.

"I will give you the opportunity to apologize to me once I'm through with you. Who do you think you are?! You disrespectful punk." Severo coiled the strap of the black leather belt around his hardened hand and took a bold step towards Billy. "You don't intimidate me!"

"ENOUGH!" Billy shouted at his father.

"You will not raise your voice to me, EVER!" Severo lifted the belt and, with a single stroke, cracked it directly on the side of Billy's face.

"ENOUGH!" Billy winced in pain but he was quick enough to dodge the second lash which landed on his shoulder. He could see Severo's empty expression. It was as if he was just trimming the lawn. Billy stumbled back clutching the curtain rod with both hands. He managed to strike Severo on the face with such force it sent him flying against the wall. Billy knew he was about to see trouble like he'd never seen before, but years of physical and verbal lashings from his father had taken a huge toll on his life. His only concern now was freeing the dog and ensuring the safety of the cat hiding in his room.

"ENOUGH!" Billy kept repeating, "ENOUGH FROM YOU!" He had reached his limit and finally felt liberated. With trembling hands, Billy quickly untied the knot around the dog's neck and pulled him along, running as fast as he could away from his father, away from the house.

Severo rubbed his bruised face, astounded not so much by the blow but by his son's unexpected rebellion. But all was not lost. In Billy's haste to get away, he had missed the jumping burlap sack in the corner of the room.

Pulling himself together, Severo tried to ignore the throbbing pain on the side of his face as he put on his straw hat and fastened his machete to his belt. "I have a job to do," he said, standing on his front steps. Severo looked around for signs of Billy and the dog, but saw they were nowhere to be found. He came to the realization that Billy had become a greater threat than he ever would have anticipated. He made a mental note: he had to address his son's outburst before a power shift took place and his authority destroyed beyond repair. *"No way!"* he spat on the ground. "Damn kid!" Picking up the burlap sack, he crossed the street and began descending the hill to the forest. "This is it!" Severo was more determined than ever. Billy had pulled the trigger and there was no backing down. *"Not on his life!"* he thought, trembling with indignation. The day Severo had been looking forward to had finally arrived. A wave of hot air made him lower his hat over his brow. *"There's going to be a downpour!"* Looking up at the heavy blackened sky, he knew there was no time to waste.

Holding his hat in place with one hand and tightly gripping the neck of his bundle with the other, Severo hurried along, ignoring the hissing, scratching lump tearing at the insides of the burlap sack. With renewed purpose, he headed for the forest, the perfect place to accomplish his mission *once and for all!* He did not notice when a revolving cone of wind pushed past him, parting a path through the tall grass down the hill.

The side of Severo's face still burned where Billy had struck him earlier. *"I'll deal with him later,"* he promised himself.

"LEAVE IT ALONE!! What has it done to you?" His son's anger still rang in his ears. He bristled at Billy's desperate attempts to reverse Stumpy and Muddy's fate. Severo shook with anger. "That damn kid never learn."

He was unmoved by the sudden darkening of the day as he continued heading downhill. He opened a path among the tall stems of grass, brandishing his sharp weapon from side to side with precision. In spite of the humid air, his brow became covered with sweat. Rain began to fall steadily but he concentrated on the chore ahead.

Absorbed in his vengeful thoughts, Severo didn't realize he had already arrived to his destination. He was taken out of his concentration by the sudden penetrating smell of wet mulch assaulting his nostrils as he tried to adjust his eyes to the darkness.

Severo was undeterred by the angry growls of the animal in the sack on his back. When he finally came into a clearing among the trees, he recognized the familiar site. Before putting an end to the miserable cat's life, Severo looked around for the grave he had dug by the river bank days before and began to uncover it. Now he would be able to complete his task without delay, so he prepared himself to strike the final, fatal blow. But not before he made a vow to teach a lesson to his son. "You will never question me. You will never cross me, ever again!"

Blind with rage, he threw the sack roughly to the ground just to make sure the creature inside felt the pain. "Should I kill it now?" Severo felt his ire flush down his arms and chest, making his whole body tremble. He used the handle of his machete to steady himself, paying no attention to the low rumbling of a sky that was about to come undone.

Still, he could not block out his son's angry words burning in his ears. "If you hurt that animal, I swear—!"

The more he fought to forget his son's threats, the angrier Severo became. "How dare he!" His rage bounced between the filthy animal that kept violating his boundaries to the son who had the audacity to humiliate him, questioning his authority. "Why can't anyone see it?" After all, he only wanted to rid the neighborhood of useless animals.

"I'm doing this town a favor!" His face stretched into a devilish smile. Severo watched the sack jump. He could hear the animal panting, meowing, hissing, spitting, desperately trying to tear through the tough fabric.

"Finally," was the only sentiment Severo was able to muster. A kick to the side of the sack sent it flying across the ground. The cat's cry of pain confirmed the accuracy of Severo's blow. The sweltering humidity made Severo undo the buttons of his shirt. He wiped off the sweat that came down like waterfalls from underneath his hat.

Heavy drops of rain began to hammer the forest canopy and poke the watercress bordering the river bank. The orange tree began to hum and the garrapatero, black as the eyes of night, hurriedly flew away. Like a mist at midnight, news of the impending death of the stray spread silently throughout the forest. In the distance, a small goat stopped mid-chew and lifted its head in alarm. The black cat awoke from its nap and jumped to its feet, hissing. An angry goose and gander straightened their necks and waded out of the water, honking in outrage. Eager for battle, the winged warrior signaled its alarm with a vigorous flapping of wings and waddled towards the man standing in the middle of the forest.

A-hooonk, A-hooonk, A-hooonk!

Billy felt the rain on his shoulders but could not stop running away from his house, away from his father. He ran until he was out of breath, as if by running he could forget the fight with his father. "What have I done?"

Stumpy's barking brought him back to reality. "C'mon, we have to get you home!" Somehow he felt relieved, proud of himself, for saving the dog from whatever fate his father had planned for it. Billy thought about Mateo too and knew he had to undo the damage he had caused.

Wharf, wharf, wharf!

"Cut it out, Stumpy!" Billy admonished the small dog that was rolling around in the wet grass overjoyed with pleasure. Billy suddenly felt his stomach turn, *"But where was the cat? I don't remember seeing—"* When he finally realized it, his eyes widened with horror as he suddenly pictured the burlap sack in a corner of the basement. The striking mental image made perfect sense! "SHIT! Muddy was there too! That sonavabitch got him out of my bedroom!" Billy jumped to his feet. The cat was in great danger now. Greater than before.

There was no way around it. He had to go back and face whatever awaited him. With his thoughts in turmoil now, Billy began to plot his next move. How could he rescue the animal while avoiding his father? How could he sneak into the basement without his father's knowledge? Billy swallowed hard, he could see it in his future, yet another catastrophic encounter with his father! Armed only with courage and Stumpy by his side, he took a detour across the grass field while the dog followed him, happy to be out and about once more.

Billy stopped in the middle of the field to gather his thoughts. Having bolted out of the house before his father could get him, he had not stopped to figure out how to return the dog to its home without letting Sergio know. He was convinced that his civil attempt would most certainly provoke yet another fight. "I'll get you home soon, Stumpy." Billy petted the dog's head, feeling pity at the sight of its rib cage.

Whaaarf! Whaaarf! Whaaarf!

As he crossed the backyard, Billy noticed the basement door was ajar. He moved cautiously, listening for the slightest noise from inside the house. Nothing. As he got to the door, he was afraid to call out for fear his father was waiting for him. He pushed the door open and tried to adjust his eyes to the darkness. Slowly, he walked down the wood steps where Stumpy had been tied up. As he took another step, the old slats creaked under his weight. Billy froze, hoping Severo had not heard him. Silence. Billy cracked a window and the diffused light brightened the shadows.

To his relief, his father was nowhere to be seen, but the cat was not there either. Billy's knees suddenly bent under the weight of his body. "Dammit, he took the cat!" Billy sat in a corner of the room, not knowing what to do next. His stupid prank to rattle Mateo had gotten out of hand and was about to end in the unnecessary death of a gentle cat.

"This is all my fault!" Billy could barely breathe. Even if he wanted to save the cat's life, there wasn't enough time to get to it before his father had his way. Now he couldn't even muster the strength to get up and walk out of the room. Instead, he sat on the floor crying, waiting for his father to return and give him the beating he deserved. From the corner of the room, Billy heard the happy barks of Stumpy rolling outside in the grass.

Whaaarf! Whaaarf! Whaaarf!

Severo's only regret was not getting an earlier start before the rain began to sizzle on the hot asphalt like bacon in a frying pan. He soaked up the sweat from his brow with the sleeve of his shirt and looked up at the sky darkened by rain clouds. He needed to finish digging the grave before the downpour got worse. He stared with pleasure at the jumping sack. From the cat's low growls, he could tell the animal's energy was waning. Severo pulled his machete from his belt. As the sprinkles of rain began to shake the treetops, lightning cracked the sky. The sudden precipitation stirred the musty smell of rotting leaves and the air became almost impossible to breathe.

From the soft cluster of shadows, the ghost watched in alarm as Severo thrashed and kicked the sack. *"Goaway! Little one!"* it cried, watching the cat's struggle from afar. But the ghost was helpless, without powers, so it paced among the shadows hoping for a miracle.

CCCRR-CCCRR...CCCRRAAACK!

Lightning brightened the sky again. Severo walked towards the sack, machete in hand, as the rain pelted his back with persistence. The stream of water pouring down the wings of his straw hat was beginning to affect his concentration. Eager to put an end to the creature's life, he stood over the struggling animal.

"Goaway! Little one, no!" the ghost cried.

The garrapatero flew so low, its long tail feathers brushed against the young goat's forehead. The goat looked up at the bird urgently flapping its wings. It had become clear to the goat that danger was brewing up in some part of the forest.

Ah-nee, Ah-nee, Ah-nee! *Danger! Danger!*

The garrapatero called out loudly and with determination, making the goat so nervous that it, in turn, loudly bleated its own warning.

Baaaah, Baaaah, Baaah! *Little one, beware!*

The goat's urgent message was as dark as the sky above. The small, white kid lifted its head and ran down the field, sounding its bleating alarm.

Baaaah, Baaaah, Baaah! *Little one, watch out!*

Climbing over the boulders along the river, the goat's bleating became even more distressed when it spotted the man kicking a sack.

In another corner of the forest, the black cat jumped up on a branch in the ceiba tree to get a clearer view of the man digging a hole in the ground. The sight of the jumping sack made it arch its back. With its tail puffed in anger, it hissed at the cruel, moving figure, just as another cry of alarm filled the heavy atmosphere…

A-hooonk, A-hooonk, A-hooonk! *Enough!*

Severo was not aware of the commotion his actions had awakened, or if he did, he chose to ignore it. Had Severo been more alert, he might have stopped what he was doing when he heard the intimidating sound of the gander honking. Approaching its target at incredible speed, the angry bird coiled its neck back in indignation, lowering its head to the ground as it came dangerously close. But Severo didn't even know it was there until he was knocked to the ground with such force that he almost fell into the very same grave he had been busying himself with only moments before.

"WHAT THE—!!"

Befuddled, Severo rose to his feet and wiped off the mud caked on his pants. The gander lowered its neck to the ground once more and charged, wings spread wide. Severo stepped back and tried to grab the handle of his machete as the gander flapped its wings in a loud and terrifying display of aggression. But there was no time to run for cover. The gander took flight long enough to draw level with Severo's face before striking him with the tip of its wing, sending him down on his back. Severo covered his eyes and managed to free his machete, but the break in eye contact with the crazed fowl only reignited its fury.

A-hooonk, A-hooonk, A-hooonk! *You will not harm him!*

Blindsided by the impact, Severo swung his blade wildly, managing to clip the tip of the bird's wing. But the moment he steadied himself, the furious goat raced down the boulder at full speed, charging him from behind and striking the man's lower back with such force that it nearly broke. Severo was sent flying in an impressive acrobatic back flip that even a circus clown could not have executed with such precision.

A-hooonk, A-hooonk, A-hooonk! *Enough!*

"*SHIT!*" Severo felt his stomach turn at the warning sounds. Unfortunately for him, the battle was far from over. From the branch of the tree, the one-eyed black cat had watched the fight unfolding, but when it saw Severo grab a round stone and take a swing at the gander…

MEEEAAAWWW! *Your time has come!*

Jumping from its branch, One-Eye landed spread-eagle on Severo's bald head. Claws bared, it clamped its body down over the screaming man's scalp like an angry furry hat with deadly teeth and fangs. Severo desperately fought back at whatever kind of creature had attached itself to his skull. Thoroughly blinded by the distressing pain, he pulled and yanked but that only deepened the red furrows the cat was leaving along his face and neck.

Kneeling on the ground, Severo panted heavily as if, instead of having just survived an attack by an angry cat, he had run to the edge of the forest and back. "DAMMIT!!" Bewildered, he tried to figure out what curse had befallen him. With shaking hands, he wiped the blood out of his bleary eyes and looked around for his hat. He heard groans of pain from the gander and was thankful he had somehow managed to injure his first attacker. Swallowing big gulps of air, he tried to recover his strength and gather his wits.

A new guttural warning honk in the distance sent a cold chill down his spine. The goose, sensing its partner's injury, had emerged from its bath to come to its defense. As the blood on Severo's face began to mix with the sweat of his brow, he realized the situation was about to escalate to new heights of injury and pain.

Still kneeling on the ground and breathing haltingly, Severo had no place to run when the goose materialized out of nowhere, stretching its neck towards him. Waddling with wings outspread, it gained impressive speed with every step. Like a warplane ready to be airborne, the goose headed towards Severo as if on a suicide mission.

A-hooonk, A-hooonk, A-hooonk!

"OOOH SHIT, NO!! OOOH SHIT, NO!! OOOH SHIIIT, NOOO!!" Sadly, those were Severo's last words before he was struck senseless and left lying on the soaked ground with a mouthful of goose feathers.

Mateo found himself at the end of his rope. Without any clues, he didn't know where to turn. "What am I doing? It's just too late." He felt lost. "Serge, I don't think Muddy or Stumpy are alive."

But Sergio refused to believe it. "We have to keep going. I know we'll find them!"

"It's been days and—" Mateo wondered if a prayer would help. His eyes searched the distance…"*Please, God.*" Over the forest… "*I promise.*" And across the field… "*Let him be safe.*"

He felt his heart beat with new hope. In times of great need, the positive forces of the universe come together to shine their powers upon the hopeless. Just when Mateo thought everything was lost, a small miracle revealed itself.

"MATEO, SERGIO… WAIT!"

"Where do we start, Serge?" Mateo asked, looking around the open field. Both boys stood in the middle of the grass-covered hill, not knowing exactly where to begin their search. Sergio looked up at the menacing rain clouds hanging low, "Whatever we do, we have to do it before—"

"MATEO, SERGIO… WAIT!"

Mateo and Sergio turned around to see Billy at the top of the hill. Neither expected what they saw next. "STUMPY!!" Sergio yelled as his short-legged friend ran to him, barking happily.

Baffled by Billy's unexpected appearance, Mateo's face hardened in anger when they locked eyes.

"You want another fight?" he shot at Billy. It was the only explanation for his presence. It was also the last thing on earth he needed, to have Billy sabotage their search that was already not going well. But Mateo's perception changed when he noticed Billy's body language. Standing still at the top of the hill with his arms hanging limply at his sides, Billy no longer resembled the angry spitfire from days before. The menace was gone from his eyes. Instead of a threatening beast that everyone feared, there stood a fragile child looking diminished under the gray light of the brewing storm. When Mateo looked at Billy, this time he saw himself.

"Mateo, wait!" Billy stammered. "I'm truly sorry, I don't know what to tell you." Billy seemed sincere. "I swear to you I didn't mean to—"

"That doesn't matter now. Muddy is dead." Mateo winced at the finality of his own words.

"I swear, I don't know what happened to him!"

"What are you saying?" Mateo was now confused. "Muddy's been gone for days."

"What did you do to him?" Sergio jumped in.

"There's no time left. We have to find my father! Please, come on guys!" Billy urged.

Mateo knew at that moment that he had to move past his confrontations with Billy if there was going to be any chance of finding Muddy. "We have to find him, no matter what! Let's go now."

"How did you find Stumpy? Where was he?" Sergio asked, holding the dog tightly in his arms.

"There's no time for that now, we have to find my father," Billy insisted, as he ran ahead down the hill.

Mateo's mind buzzed impatiently. Even with Billy's unexpected help, he knew it was a race against time, maybe even a waste of it. Stumpy's constant barking kept him hopeful but there were still no clear clues as to Muddy's whereabouts. As he wondered which way to turn, he could hear the melancholy call of a bird above the hiss of falling rain. The garrapatero's cries were languid and heavy, a hopeless moan rising up from an ancient pain, a presage of an unhappy ending. Mateo thought it sounded familiar but his focus was now elsewhere.

Ah-nee, Ah-nee, Ah-nee!

grrrumble, grrrumble ... CCCRR-CCCRR ... CCCRRAAACK!

"We have to find my father!" With those words, Billy led the hunt to find Muddy. He had good reason to suspect that the disappearance of his father was linked to the missing cat. With new energy and optimism, they followed Stumpy's eager lead down the hill through the tall bank of grass. The small dog searched and sniffed, following every possible clue. Mateo worried that the storm would put a damper on their mission, but now there was no time to waste.

"C'mon guys, let's keep going!" Even the rain did not slow the boys down. As they maneuvered their way through the wet field down to the forest, they heard

Stumpy's insistent barks ahead. They all looked at each other with hope.

"Hurry up, guys! I think Stumpy is on to something!" Sergio exclaimed. The dog raced down the hill sniffing the ground, searching under the lantana bushes, then headed for the forest on a heated quest. Mateo and Billy lagged behind, struggling to get through the tall grass.

"I can hardly keep up with him!" Mateo yelled to Sergio.

"That's my boy!" Sergio encouraged Stumpy.

Whaaarf! Whaaarf! Whaaarf!

"C'mon, boy! Take us to Muddy!"

"Mateo, I've seen Muddy around here before," Billy said, brushing aside the tall grass.

"Muddy, Muddy, come here, boy! Where are you?" Mateo heard Sergio calling across the grassy plot. "Stumpy. Let's find Muddy!"

Whaaarf! Whaaarf Whaaarf!

With loud barks, the dog bounced across the field.

"MUUUDDYYY!" Mateo called out into the wall of tall grass at the side of the road, scanning every tree, bush, and thicket.

"He could be afraid to come out," Sergio offered.

"MUUUDDYYY!" Mateo funneled his call through cupped hands.

Whaaarf! Whaaarf! Whaaarf!

Stumpy barked out excitedly, refusing to slow down.

"I've seen him coming out of the woods before!" Billy said. "Let's go down this path," he suggested, as if their fight over the cat had never happened. Mateo was surprised but he wanted Billy to know there were no hard feelings on his side.

"Hey, Billy… Thanks."

"Guys, let's go!" Billy called out, taking the lead down the dirt path to the forest.

Whaaarf! Whaaarf! Whaaarf!

They all followed as Stumpy rushed ahead. Everything seemed off to a good start until a heavier downpour brought the enthusiastic search to a halt.

Frustrated, Mateo felt like giving up. "This rain is not letting up. I think we should head back." Fearing for the cat's fate, he wondered if he would ever see it again. He was afraid to accept it but he knew the cat might be gone forever. *"Time has run out."* Mateo felt defeated.

"What's the matter, Stumpy?" Sergio looked down at the dog tugging at his pants. He shook his leg trying to loosen the dog's grip but he knew Stumpy was as determined as he was relentless. "Stumpy, stop it!" Sergio admonished, but instead the dog got angrier, grunting louder and digging his hind legs deeper into the ground. Sergio began to get the message. "I think he wants us to follow him!"

WHARF, WHARF, WHARF!

Stumpy knew where to find Muddy, the problem was neither Mateo nor Sergio were listening. *"Hey guys! Let's go now!"* Stumpy yelled with every "Wharf, wharf, wharf!" *"There is no time to waste, let's go! I know where to find Muddy!"*

Energized by the adventure of the chase, Stumpy charged ahead barking urgently. When they finally got close to fringes of the forest, the late afternoon light began to dissolve into shadows. With a resounding deafening clap of thunder the clouds opened up and let out a merciless storm.

"Guys! Guys! The rain is starting to get heavy now, maybe we should take a break!" Sergio called out, seeking shelter under the coffee trees.

"Sergio! We have no time!" Mateo answered but stopped as a loud clap of thunder made the ground tremble.

CCCRR-CCCRR... CCCRRAAACK!

"Mateo, Sergio is right! We can hardly see ahead!" Billy yelled, as the heavy rain pelted him. Another clap of thunder seemed to set the field on fire.

CCCRR-CCCRR ... CCCRRAAACK!

"We can't stop now!" Mateo snapped back. Billy and Sergio were out of breath but still they followed the unstoppable dog. Stumpy dashed from side to side, impervious to the falling rain, sniffing the boulders. Following some scent on the damp ground, he ran towards the river where the coffee trees and angel's trumpet stood. The three boys were amused by the dog's energy.

CCCRR-CCCRR ... CCCRRAAACK!

A bolt of lightning struck a nearby palm tree, webbing it with a filigree of deadly energy. Now Mateo was forced to heed Billy's warning.

"Where can we go?" Mateo called out.

"Hurry up, guys! The forest is up ahead!" Sergio answered.

"NO! That's dangerous in a storm!" Mateo yelled back.

"We have no other place to hide!" Billy shouted. So they ran into the woods seeking shelter, chased by a new round of loud claps that illuminated the darkened sky. The rain came down mercilessly, without any sign of ending.

CCCRR-CCCRR... CCCRRAAACK!
CCCRR-CCCRR... CCCRRAAACK!

"I'm done!" Billy said, plopping his body down on a tree root, dripping wet. Mateo and Sergio followed suit, shielding themselves from the deluge between the roots of the ceiba tree. Mateo looked around and wished he could stay there under the trees forever, sitting by the river and never having to think about anything. Sergio, who was sitting by his side, seemed to be sharing the same thought. The three boys were forced to wait for a respite from the rain before resuming their search for Muddy. Mateo took a deep breath and let his eyes follow the flow of the water.

"Do you think there are ghosts in these woods?" Sergio tried to lighten the mood.

"Dammit, Sergio, don't start!"

"I'm just saying. There's no harm in asking, man."

"I think there are! Once my grandma told me..." Billy jumped in.

"Is your story about a headless woman too?" Mateo interrupted.

"What?—" Billy was confused.

"Never mind." Mateo shot a warning glance at Sergio.

"I swear this story is true!" Sergio insisted. "My father said one night, when his

Grrrumble, gruuumble . . . CRRR . . . AAACK-
CRAAACK . . . CRRRAAACK!

father was very young, he wanted to go to a dance in town because that's where his girlfriend lived. But there were no cars and his father did not want to let him ride his horse, so they got into a fight. And his father said, 'You cannot disobey me. You'll be punished, and not by me, mind you!'

"But my father's father was stubborn and REALLY wanted to see his girlfriend, so he waited until his father went to sleep and stole the horse and went to the party anyways and danced all night long. Then he had to go back home because it was about to be morning, so he jumped on his horse, but when he cut through this very forest he said he felt a chill, like somebody was telling him, 'Don't do it!' He thought about what his father said, but he paid it no mind because he knew he only said it to scare him.

"So he rushed through the forest as fast as he could, but the horse stopped and did not want to move. And then the horse reared up on its hind legs. When he looked across the river, he saw a woman dressed in white with long, long hair dragging through the grass and she said, 'My friend, can you give me a ride? I'm stranded here and I need to get home.'

"So he said, 'How come you're here so late?' She said, 'Never mind that, can you please take me home?' So he helped her get on the horse but the horse started to snort and rear up again and trot backwards.

"And then he asked her, 'How come you are so cold?' And she said, 'Because I've been waiting all night.' And he asked, 'Who are you waiting for?' and she goes, 'I've been waiting FOR YOU! WHY DID YOU DISOBEY YOUR FATHER?!' and when he looked back at her, he saw the woman didn't have a head!

"He almost had a heart attack and started screaming shitballs and rode through the forest like his ass was on fire. And as soon as he got home, he jumped off the horse and went to bed for days with a fever and chills. His mother gave him chicken soup but it didn't help. Everybody thought he was crazy, and his father said, 'I warned you not to take my horse!'"

Mateo and Billy looked at each other in silence and then snorted with laughter.

"That's the craziest story I've ever heard!" Billy guffawed. But Sergio noticed that after his tall tale, they all jumped at the sound of a twig snapping. The three boys became aware of every movement and noise, and wondered how many other secrets were hiding in the shadows.

"Those are made-up stories. Ghosts don't really exist," Mateo blurted out. Still he could not help keeping watch out of the corner of his eye. Another sudden lightning strike bolted them from their seats.

CCCRR-CCCRR... CCCRRAAACK!

With their hearts still racing from the scare, Mateo was the only one who dared to ask, "Did you guys hear that? It sounded like somebody screaming!"

From the depth of nearby shadows, the ghost heard Mateo's words. *"Only faith will let you see,"* it thought, looking at the boy enveloped by sadness. The ghost feared for Muddy's safety. *"Goaway is in danger!"* it pleaded into the humid wind. The boys didn't notice the subtle rustling of dry leaves, but at the sight of the ghost, Stumpy's fur stood on end.

In the dim light of the forest, all the boys could see was Stumpy barking anxiously as he slowly stepped backwards. Sergio frowned.

"What does he see?" asked Billy, trying to adjust his eyes to the shadows under the trees. Mateo and Sergio stepped ahead, intrigued by the dog's discovery.

"Could it be—?" Mateo's heart beat like a wild drum. He didn't dare guess what they were about to find. "Please, Muddy, be okay! Please," he whispered to himself.

They watched the dog move cautiously to the orange tree ahead as if it had discovered a significant clue.

Sniff, sniff, sniff, sniff...

"What do you see, Stumpy?" Sergio asked, lowering his voice.

As the dog got closer to the tree, he lifted one of his front paws slightly, as if thinking before taking his next step. His short tail stood at attention. The dog pointed his nose and sniffed the air. With very slow steps, he continued walking to the tree.

"I think he's found something!" Sergio said, following the dog. But what Stumpy had found was far more gruesome than the boys could have imagined.

Running after the dog, Sergio suddenly came to a stop. Stumpy continued barking, as if trying to make a point. Rushing ahead, Mateo could not focus his gaze until he was face to face with the scene. He was speechless. He heard rustling dead leaves behind him and knew Billy was just steps away.

"What's going on?" Billy asked, looking at Sergio and Mateo, who were now quiet with fright. He followed their gaze to the river's bank. Nothing could have prepared him for what he saw there...

Just moments before the boys had come face-to-face with the gruesome scene, something else was taking a turn for the worse. Not too far from them, the cat was gasping for air, hopelessly trapped inside the burlap sack. It grew more agitated at the sound of approaching voices until a familiar one caught its ears. Among the anxious calls it heard *Animalfriend*. The cat clawed at the sides of the bag as this new glimmer of hope pierced the mesh fabric.

"*I'M HERE, ANIMALFRIEND!*" it meowed, breathing and panting but now with purposeful energy. "*I'M HERE!*" it repeated loudly, tearing at the insides of the bag with claws fully drawn.

"*Mmmuuuddyyy! Whheeerree r yooou?*"

The boy's calls agitated the cat even more. It listened attentively as *Animalfriend's* sad sounds moved around the forest.

"*Mmmuuuddyyy! Whheeerree r yooou?*"

The cat heard its name again and tore at the insides of the bag more forcefully, determined to join *Animalfriend*.

"*Leeet'ss gooo. Muuuddyy iisssnoot heeere!*" Muddy heard another voice in the group say.

The cat heard *Animalfriend's* cries, "*I caaannt go noww!*"

"*Heeel com bkkk! Heeel com bkkk!*" called another voice.

Muddy heard *Animalfriend* one more time.

"*Wheeer iiisss heee? Eye ggt too fnnd hmmm!*"

Animalfriend's cries made the cat's heart pound furiously and its tail twitch nervously. Its ears turned sideways, picking up every stressful sound, and its jaws chattered in despair. "*I'm here, I'm here!*" it repeated as the voices faded away.

Severo felt the water pelting his face mercilessly. He awoke from his unpleasant dream to a sky darkened by the trees. It took him a moment to situate himself, to

remember where the unbearable pain in his head and neck had come from. Why was he lying on the wet dirt with the taste of blood on his lips and his mouth filled with feathers? Severo moaned in pain as he discovered how difficult the simple act of getting up had become.

"*What in hell*—," he thought before the memory of the fierce bird's attack trickled into his memory bit by bit.

As Severo's rage flared one more time, he jumped to his feet and looked around. But there was no sign of the damned goose, the black cat, or the stupid goat. He had a bad feeling about the black bird that sat staring down at him from the tree branch but it did not stop him. He was now more determined than ever. In spite of his pain, Severo was not about to let the rain keep him from his mission. He did not so much as blink in the heavy downpour as he located his machete on the ground nearby.

Severo ignored how the trees, now swaying from side to side, commanded the heavy clouds above their dense canopy. Instead he kept his eyes on the burlap sack. It pleased him to think that the animal inside, exhausted and gasping for air, had finally accepted its fate.

"*Good!*" he thought, not minding the rain soaking his whole body.

CCCRR-CCCRR...CCCRRAAACK!

The crackling thunder did not stop Severo, not for a second. He held the machete in his hand with such intensity his knuckles became white, as if they had fused with the weapon, making it an extension of his arm. Determined, Severo lifted the blade.

The orange tree began to shiver and hum.

CCCRR-CCCRR...

As Severo listened to the weak whimpers of the animal inside the bag, he began to calculate his deadly strike.

The trees began to shake with urgency, each time more forcefully than before, as if they were horrified by the cruel scene unfolding in their midst.

Severo lifted his machete high above his shoulders, calculating the precise swing of his elbow before deciding to lower his weapon with great force...

CCCRR... CCCRR-CCCRR...

A blinding blast of light tore through the heavy atmosphere. The fiery bolt of live energy caught the tip of Severo's machete so swiftly he had no time to react before it had traveled down his arm, across his chest, and exploded inside his head. By the time he smelled the burnt clothing covering his body, he found himself flying across the ground. Leaving his rubber boots behind, he landed face down in the river.

Had it been just a matter of refreshment on a hot day, the cool, sweet water would have done him wonders. Instead, his head was submerged in the river's current, eyes wide open as if he had suddenly realized how cleverly death had managed to outsmart him.

Severo never understood that rage also lives in the forest, beneath fallen limbs, a necessary force to protect itself. *Nothing is off limits when it comes to protecting one of its own.* Severo had a destiny to fulfill and ultimately he earned his undignified death. On that fateful afternoon in that fertile ground for myths, the orange tree had been witness to his transition.

If Severo could have read the language of the forest, he would have recognized the warning signs in their swaying branches. Especially the orange tree, where generations of bees had sipped from its scented blossoms and industrious spiders had spun their silvery webs; the same tree whose life had been saved by the kind, fragile hands of a girl of seven, many years ago. Thanks to her, there had been a place for birds to perch and sing in its arms for many years. And now a new guest, a lonely stray looking for safety, had made its roots into a home. So it was that the guardian of the forest had angrily shaken its limbs in protest. *Do not harm him!* The tree remembered the fright in the young cat's eyes. But Severo had ignored the warning signs.

From a nearby tree branch, the black garrapatero sang slowly before it flew away.

"*Am I dreaming? Is this real?*" Billy could not believe his eyes. Right in front of him, his father lay lifeless, submerged halfway in the current of the river. Billy looked at Mateo and Sergio, trying to convince himself he was not the only one dreaming. His father was dead.

Billy felt lightheaded. Suddenly all the poison thoughts and anger he had held against his father subsided. He felt as if his body was free from a heavy burden and was about to lift up and disappear among the tree tops. For most of his life, he had viewed his father as a threatening giant but to see him laying there lifeless in the water, he could not help but feel pity.

Pity was in fact the kindest sentiment that Severo had ever inspired. Pity was indeed merciful, even for a man who seemed deflated without his rage. Billy felt numb. He swayed from side to side as if trying to find his footing again. He looked at Sergio and Mateo but found no answers in their stunned faces.

"I'm sorry, Billy," Mateo muttered, his own voice sounded foreign to him.

Wrapped up in their astonishment at the surreal scene, at first the three boys paid no attention to Stumpy's insistent barks. Something new had caught the dog's attention. The boys tried to head back to the road but Stumpy fought to keep them there, barking furiously.

"What is it, boy?" Sergio knew Stumpy would not give up until he had his way. The dog ran off through the gathering of trees, barking at them to follow.

"Come back, Stumpy!" Sergio called out to the dog, as Mateo ran up the hill after Billy. He could not erase the image of Severo lying in the river from his mind. Spooked, he bolted up the red dirt path.

A few months before, Billy had tried to save the life of a kitten but...

"I hate you!" Billy felt his mouth fill with venom at the thought of his father. His face was red from holding back, from swallowing his words. He felt his own rage filling his throat, choking him. "I won't cry. Not in front of him." He erased the tears rolling down his cheeks with a single, furious stroke of the back of his hand. Billy knew how to conceal emotion; he had learned early on. His father's harsh words kept him in check.

"Are you a man?" Billy felt humiliated, mocked by his own father. He lowered his gaze to the floor so Severo wouldn't see the hate in his eyes. Billy knew better; he knew an animal only invites attack if it stares directly into the eyes of its enemy. *"Keep low, Billy, keep low."* It was best to let his boiling rage cool down to a steady simmer. *"Bite the inside of your mouth before you speak, Billy,"* he reminded himself. *"His time will come."* Luckily his father took Billy's silence as a sign of respect. But there was no escaping Severo's cruelty.

"LEAVE IT ALONE!! What has it done to you?" Billy shouted after his father tried unsuccessfully to snatch the cat from his hands.

"You never learn, do you?"

Billy closed his eyes, trembling at the sound of his father's voice. He knew what

was coming next. Billy could endure the beatings; after all, his father's derisive words were more hurtful than any physical abuse. But this time was different. Billy would not let his father take the trembling creature from him. Without a second thought, he ran outside with the kitten and down the road, leaving his father's threats behind.

"What am I going to do now?" he asked himself, placing the tiny gray kitten in his back pack. He felt dizzy from the adrenaline rush. Billy kept walking along the road without any destination. In his haste, he failed to notice his frail neighbor holding on to her cane by the side of the road. Out of nowhere, Minerva's voice made him jump.

"What do you have there, Billy?" Minerva asked, intrigued by the soft, muffled cries coming from inside his back pack.

After the storm, clouds scurried away and the sky opened up to the faint sunlight. The forest looked shiny and rejuvenated. The blanket of low grass that overflowed into the river's stream shuddered under the weight of raindrops.

Meanwhile on the ground, the cat finally scratched and clawed its way out of the sack, putting an end to its terrifying ordeal.

"Little one! Everything is good." The ghost greeted the cat with relief after witnessing the chaotic scene.

"*Scary, scary. Stinkanimal. It grabs me. It hurt!*" The cat was still shaken up by the experience. The ghost watched as the cat swung its tail nervously.

"Do not be afraid. It's over. You are safe now," the ghost said reassuringly.

"*It hurt. It mean, it mean!*"

"You are safe now, little one!" the ghost repeated, taking its place beside the cat. "There is always a price to pay," it added as they both stared at the figure lying face down in the river.

* * *

Minerva looked out her bedroom window and listened to the low, soft calls of the garrapatero preening its feathers high on the wires. Out in the yard stood the old mamey tree, the only one of its kind in the whole neighborhood. Its big thick oblong leaves were the color of freshly polished jade, a kind of deep green that shone under the daylight as if the whole massive tree had been meticulously polished at night by industrious elves, leaf by leaf. Its branches were barely visible behind the density of its leaves. Even a strong wind could not sway it. Maybe that's why it still stood, firmly rooted in place for so many years. Its generous branches were the perfect sanctuary for a stranded bird or solitary owl to hoot its loneliness through the night. The only evidence of its ability to bear fruit was at the tree's base, where the excess ones lay rotting and the fresh ones lay wrapped in skin resembling raw silk. The heart of the fruit was bright orange, perhaps due to the many sunsets the tree had swallowed in its long life. At night, the tree dropped its fruit as if to get rid of the excess weight, like a bad mother overwhelmed by its progeny's neediness.

Looking around the compact room, Minerva admired her mother's touches: the oversized print of El Santo Niño de Atocha over the headboard, the pink glass rosary draped around the mirror, and the old fashioned clover-leaf fan. On the dresser, Doña Sol had placed a small white vase with silk flowers, an old prayer book, and an assortment of votive candles. Nestled in her bed, Minerva ran her fingers across the cover of the family photo album. The worn out, old picture diary had sat atop the tower of books under the night stand for years.

"Mateo called again." Minerva watched her mother nervously smoothing out her apron with trembling hands.

"There's no sense in worrying him," Minerva said, trying to protect him. Her eyes turned towards the window. "I want to see out into the garden."

The afternoon light filtered through the embroidered curtains into the small room. The same room she returned to after being away for so many years. It was still her home. *"Even at 27,"* she thought with a smile. Minerva's gaze traveled over the wall covered with rough sketches, photos, and yellowed newspaper clippings. "FIGHT FOR THOSE WHO CAN'T" screamed one of the dated headlines. She struggled to put it into context. *"Where did I find that?"* But she was unable to remember what made her pin it to the wall in the first place.

Beyond the wooden frame of the window, her gaze settled on the garden full of color and light, and she listened to the quiet humming of the mango tree and the cackle of the crows on the power lines. She looked up at the cloudless sky. *"What a beautiful day!"* She felt her mother's hand in hers.

"There's that white rose again, mother. Right there by the curtains. Can't you see it? The white rose—" and she closed her eyes. *"Mother, its perfume... So sweet!"* Minerva breathed in deeply and let the rose's fragrance fill her lungs.

She realized how real this moment was and knew she did not have to accept fear. Her transition should not be diminished or trivialized by earthly vulgarities, insignificant limitations of the mind and the self. *Show no fear.* She reached out to the rose that circled above her head.

Minerva then sensed the layers of her life shedding with the same awareness she had felt cutting off all the blossoms on her mother's gardenia bush just to defy her, to show her the depth of her despair. Her shoulders felt lighter as if the heavy burden of other past lives had suddenly lifted.

She watched in wonder as the walls of the room began to crumble around her. She closed her eyes once more and heard the sound of waves crashing, the taste of salty ocean water lingering on her tongue. Minerva did not open her eyes, even as the living sea roared around her. She felt happy, serene. She cupped her hands into the water and lifted it to her lips. At the taste of blood, she opened her eyes to discover the intense, carmine tinge of the water. *"Mother's roses!"* Closing her eyes again, she reached out for the sun that warmed her face, her eyelids, her lips, her neck.

Minerva sat upright in her bed. She wished she could smell the flowers one last time in her mother's garden and bury her face in the rose bushes bending back with the heaviness of rain.

Then she saw the saddest of things: the sun setting behind stubborn clouds until it collapsed, breaking into shards of warm and cold light. The ancient crumbles of past lives had turned into stars. And then it was night, thick, impenetrable, dark. A luminous halo wrapped itself around the circumference of the Earth.

"That beautiful, bright light!"

A loud fluttering of wings drew her eyes to the window where the garrapatero was standing guard.

Ah-nee, Ah-nee, Ah-nee

Minerva heard the garrapatero call out as a thick darkness enveloped them. Like a vacuum inside an endless tunnel, her sensory awareness of space, light, and gravity were suddenly cut off. She found herself floating in an alternate reality, a dual dimension, where she was a pure entity beyond matter, like the mist that rises between the trees in early morning.

Ah-nee, Ah-nee, Ah-nee

Minerva heard the soft call again and before her eyes the beautiful bird transformed into a radiant angel with a star on its forehead wearing a robe with ocean waves crashing in its folds. Holding a blazing sword in one hand, the angel extended its other arm and commanded, "It's time."

When Minerva heard those words, she stepped out of her physical shell, her spirit transforming into part of the cosmos. Liberated at last, Minerva left her body forever.

The tiny town of Palo Verde was buzzing. Severo, El Rajao, the broken one, had been found in the river, dead. 'Justice was served,' the people thought but no one said it aloud. They headed down to the river in throngs, claiming forgiveness and sympathy for Severo, hardly convincing with their thinly veiled morbid curiosity. Severo was found with his eyes wide open; a stare frozen upon discovering that the force tapping on his shoulder was none other than the Angel of Death.

At the moment of his demise, Severo took his last soaking in the river, the narrow river that divided the small forest where tall cannas and angel's trumpets grew near the coffee trees. In the place where he had taken his last earthly breath, his head now rested on a pillow of smooth, slimy stones that shimmered under the current. His machete, broken in two, was lost among the bank of watercress and Bird of Paradise. His black boots had flown off his feet, landing by the orange tree.

On that stormy afternoon, in this fertile ground for myths and legend, only an orange tree had tried to warn him. Only an orange tree had seen his arrogance. Only an orange tree had witnessed his gruesome transition. Severo had paid the price.

Still the river went on, cutting a path through the small forest. Severo's transition had taken place in a beautiful, pastoral scene which he had never appreciated in life. It was ironic that such an evil man had met the end of his life surrounded by such beauty.

Gorgeous trees hummed, birds chirped, and the river sang happily after the storm. Unfortunately for Severo, even the lapping of the cold, sweet water could not bring him back to life...

Days after the tiny town of Palo Verde adjusted to Severo's death, little by little they cautiously began to open their doors and windows. Soon, dogs that had been kept indoors for safety began to run around the neighborhood, barking happily and chasing noisily after children. Cats jumped up to sit leisurely on sunny windowsills, grooming themselves without a hint of fear.

"Goaway, come outside. Look at the beautiful day!" The ghost woke the cat up from its comfortable nap. The new day crackled with energy. Massive cumulus clouds marched slowly across the sky. Even the reclusive black cat came out of hiding and sunned itself on the warm boulders. The morning hummed along and waves of air filtered through the trees, making them jiggle animatedly. A herd of cows waded into the river for an early drink as a flock of egrets rode on their backs, squeaking and spreading their white wings for balance. The small pot-bellied goat pulled chunks of rain-washed grass from the ground, while the goose and gander leisurely waddled along the river's current without a care in the world. In the branch of a tree, the garrapatero sank its beak into its lush, black coat of feathers, fishing out gnats and bits of dust.

"I want us to remember this day. Tell me, what do you see?" asked the ghost.

The cat lifted its head up to the sky and answered, *"Morning. Bright. Wind... Sun high, beautiful."*

"What else?"

"'Baughterflie, baughterflie' Animalfriend calls it."

The ghost laughed, amused. "What else do you see?"

"Oooh! Little green one runs! 'Leeezard' I chase, it run, it hide."

"All is good, little one, all is good now!"

The ghost knelt down close to the cat. "Goaway, I have to leave soon."

"Why?" the cat asked intrigued.

"I did what I came back for." The ghost had regained its peace. No more interference.

"Where you go?" asked the cat.

"Up sky." The ghost pointed to the clouds.

"Sad," whimpered the cat.

"Don't be, little one."

Compassion is a thing of beauty. The most basic of human impulses, often mocked as a sure sign of weakness. But truly, compassion is a clear measure of the depth of a human soul. To be compassionate is to extend a connecting bridge to another being, human or animal, in a time of need. Compassion is the moment of

clarity when someone—even a ghost—acknowledges a greater need beyond the immediate self.

Studying the boy from a distance, the ghost wanted to tell him, "I know how you feel. This is how I'm going to help you!" But a ghost's voice cannot cross into the material world. "I am here for you!" might sound like the wind shaking the trees. At last the ghost came to realize what its purpose had been all along. "To help him heal!" Yes, that was it. And then it thought about the old man, *So he can have some peace too!*"

It had watched the boy run his fingers through the soft fur of the cat, caressing it with tenderness. Compassion, it was in the boy's demeanor. It was as if the cat's long, lonely journey was finally clear to him. Yes, compassion, it was in the boy's smiling eyes. "Go on, take a chance!"

The ghost remembered the boy's promise to the cat, "I am here for you!" and glowed with happiness.

To those who acknowledge their humanity and recognize the troubled soul behind the eyes of another being, compassion is humbling. When such heartfelt desire moves a person to promise "I'm here for you," compassion is a thing of beauty. A broken link is restored and a new journey begins.

It pleased the ghost that the boy's rage had receded. "Finally!" The bright light in his eyes, as bright as the spark in the crystal, had returned. The ghost had hoped a cat in need might help ease his hurt. Yes, the ghost could see the boy's compassion had allowed him to break through a wall of anger. His sadness was finally replaced by a renewed sense of wonder. "Everything is clear now," the ghost was certain. No interference.

The ghost understood this was a good sign. It was time to move on, time to say goodbye to the forest, goodbye to the young stray cat. It felt light again as the remnants of memory that held it earthbound began to fade. "Goodbye, Mateo, until we meet again!"

Whaaarf! Whaaarf! Whaaarf!

"MMUUUDDY … MMUUUDDY … MMUUUDDY!"

From a corner of the forest by the orange tree, the cat shivered at the sight of its abuser. "*Stinkanimal!*" Its eyes were locked on the remains lying by the river's edge, partially hidden behind the small island of spidery, green papyrus. The cat heard its name being called from beyond the forest but still it did not dare come out. Bewildered, it wondered what it had done wrong. Its instincts warned it to stay put. Carefully stretching its legs, the cat circled around before settling down on its bed of leaves, trying to ignore the insistent barking of the dog, the loud calls, and rustling steps in the distance.

"MMUUUDDY ... MMUUUDDY ... MMUUUDDY!"

The cat heard the familiar voice of *Animalfriend* calling its name again and again but did not like the anxiety in his voice.

"Whrr r euuu?"

So the cat remained still, whipping its tail from side to side as the sound of high voices increased its fear. It suspected then it had worn out its welcome. "*Not loved.*" This had happened before: one day, fed and comfortable; the next day, abandoned, lonely, and hungry. "*No good. Sad, sad.*"

Luckily it had learned the language of the forest, so it listened to the advice of the orange tree: "You must go on. There's nothing left for you here."

Still the cat resisted. "*Do not trust.*" How could it forget the constant perils of the outside world? Looking down at the creek, its whole body shivered at the memory of *Stinkanimal* and the hurtful experience. But the young cat would never forget how, in a moment of extreme danger, an alliance of friends and the powers of the forest had come to his defense and ultimately saved his life.

The tree loved the sound of the young girl's laugh but over the years her songs and laughter had faded away little by little and in their place other voices—agitated ones—shattered the forest's peaceful existence. As the evening's dense shadows finally began to settle, the ancient gathering of trees resumed their harmonious humming and came alive once more in the glow of the moonlight.

But tonight felt different. Even for the forest, change—once unthinkable—was now inevitable. Somehow Severo's evil actions had broken a delicate balance. The forest was not safe anymore.

"You must go on." In spite of its own loneliness, the tree urged the young cat to leave. "Go on, Little One, it is time for you to move on!"

Throughout its long life, the orange tree had witnessed many small miracles as well as acts of evil, but it knew there was still hope for the young cat.

"Thanks, friend!" the cat said to the tree.

"Goodbye, Little One!"

The shocking discovery had put an abrupt end to the search.

Understandably, Billy retreated behind his new family members who, at the news of Severo's misfortune, had come out of the woodwork. Unfortunately for Mateo and Sergio, they still had the pressing task of finding Muddy.

"Would you dare go back into the forest?" Sergio challenged.

"Of course I would. I'm not afraid," Mateo answered unconvincingly.

From the safe distance of Doña Sol's balcony, they watched the constant comings and goings of curious neighbors into the forest. Like an overgrown ant farm, people passed on bits of information based on conjecture to others, who in turn, felt free to repeat and adorn their own versions to new arrivals. Despite the ghoulish activity, Mateo's thoughts were still circling around the missing cat. As soon as Severo's body had been removed, the crowd of curious onlookers began to die down. Mateo saw the opportunity to resume the search.

"Sergio, we have to go back. I need to find Muddy!"

"Where are we going to find him?" After all the commotion, Sergio was not sure if the cat would even still be around.

"Billy remembered seeing him walking down the dirt footpath," Mateo answered.

"Yes, but that was a while ago. With all this craziness, he's probably moved on by now," Sergio pointed out.

"Maybe he's hiding, waiting for people to leave. Cats don't like noise." Mateo struggled to keep his hopes high.

"I'm not sure whether it matters. What if Severo's ghost is wandering around there now waiting for us?"

Mateo did not appreciate the joke. "You're full of it, you know!?" But he could not help shuddering. His hope of finding the missing cat still alive began to wane. *"Muddy is gone."*

The young cat stared at the pond of the singing frogs, but this time everything seemed different. Sitting quietly by the narrow stream, he watched the urgent flight of late hummingbirds as they zigzagged among the hibiscus. The buzzing traffic of beetles and dragonflies prickling the river's back began to quiet down. The cat surveyed the tree-covered mountains beyond the meadow that was always alive with sounds and smells, even when the stars could barely pierce the darkness. But this night, everything suddenly seemed shallow and melancholy. "*I won't go back.*"

The cat was not sure anymore whether it was wise to leave the comfort and safety of the forest, but the memory of suffocating inside a bag and being kicked by *Stinkanimal* made him anxious. And there was one other sad thought to overcome: the field seemed even more desolate since the ghost had vanished. It remembered the ghost's words: "You need to go away from this place." The cat had resisted. It did not understand what the ghost was trying to say.

"*Whhyy?*" it had asked, stretching its legs slowly.

"You don't belong here anymore. You have a new name!" The ghost tried to cheer the cat up, "Don't be afraid. It is your time. I need to move on too, my time here is over. I've done all I could for you. Goodbye, Little One." And with those words, the ghost was gone.

"*Fallingstar, gone. Sad.*" The cat mourned the parting of the ghost and lifted its nose up to the drizzle that began to tickle the tops of the coffee trees. That night, the rain had not been enough to drive the cat from its bed of leaves under the orange tree. "*Rain. Soft. Pretty.*"

A strike of lighting in the distance lit up the wall of heavy clouds. Beyond the obvious sign of a rainstorm, it was a disquieting premonition, a sign of change all around.

"*Change,*" the cat lamented. But then it remembered not all changes were bad. There were also good ones, changes that pleased it. Like when *Animalfriend* called softly and lifted it up in his arms, laughing, "*Leeet's go hhme liiittle caaat, leeet's go hmme.*"

"*Good, good!*" thought the cat.

But the cat knew it could not move on before saying goodbye to another forest creature. "*Friend!*" it said when it found the black cat napping by the ceiba. The black cat opened its bright, yellow eye and lifted its nose to identify the unexpected visitor. The young stray sat politely on its hind legs and allowed the black cat to approach and gently sniff the young stray's forehead. After bumping noses, the black cat walked back to its bed of leaves under the tree.

"*Friends!*" it said, resting its head on its paws.

The young stray balanced its steps gingerly as it crossed over the fallen tree. Sniffing the air for a clue, it discovered the goose and the gander bathing in the soft current of the river. The young cat sat and watched them honk happily. While the goose floated smoothly over the clear plate of the water, the gander dove underneath and pulled out a tangle of prawns and wet moss from the bottom. The cat jumped over the bank and made its way through the papyrus waving its tail as it gently called out, "*Goodbye!*"

The gander lifted its wings above the water and flapped noisily, while the goose honked in recognition. "Honk! Honk! Honk! *One day our paths will cross again!*

The stray walked along the river's edge, past the angel's trumpet and heliconias and through the coleus. Its gaze was focused on the side of the hill ahead. With a sense of relief, it ventured out from the protective umbrella of trees. It looked among the overgrown bushes and flowering lantana until it recognized the small white kid nipping at the grass. Without a second thought, the cat set out to meet him. The goat lifted its head in alarm, only to discover the young gray cat squatting in front of it.

"Baaaah, Baaaah, Baaah! *Hellloooo theeeree!*" the small goat greeted the cat, pleased to see it was well.

In answer, the cat batted its eyes softly, comfortable in the presence of a trusted friend. "*Thanks!*"

"Baaaah, Baaaah, Baaah! *Weee'll meeet agaaain!*" the goat answered, chewing a mouthful of fresh grass.

THE HARDEST GOODBYE

"Out of this wood do not desire to go"

—William Shakespeare, *A Midsummer Night's Dream* (Act III, Scene I)

T hat night, the stillness in the forest seemed thicker and heavier without the ghost, as if all the air had gone with it. *Fallingstar,* the kind spirit that was born from a star, had finally continued on its journey. It had vanished quietly, unlike on the night of its arrival, but it had left an empty space behind. The dark forest took a deep breath in mourning. Even the breeze became still and the trees wrapped themselves in a sheath of intimacy once more, remaining quiet as if there was nothing left to say. They had seen the beginning; they had borne silent witness to an ordinary miracle that had come full circle. The narrow riverbed went quietly rushing on, eventually losing itself in the wide open sea. The moonlight shimmered over the leaves like fireflies trembling in the darkest of valleys. All the voices were gone as night spread slowly over the little town of Palo Verde.

Meanwhile, in a corner of the forest, the orange tree mourned too. But it took comfort remembering the ghost's previous life as a little girl and then as a young woman, before her link to life was broken. *"But how could I not?"* It thought with fondness of how the little girl with her hands covered in mud had nurtured it as a young seedling. It had watched her sing silly, made-up songs, her hair covered with its white blossoms. And the tree had shaken its leafy branches with joy when she returned as a bright, burning star. *"Fallingstar!"* She had cleared a path across the Earth to let her love be known, so she could move forward and flourish in another paradise.

The young stray coiled its body and settled in for the cold night on its bed of dry leaves. With sad eyes, it searched the sky for clues. *"Fallingstar gone,"* it sighed. A faint glimmer of light touched the small round object hanging from its neck, making it sparkle. *"Time to go! This is home no more!"* The young cat finally gathered the confidence to move on.

Change. The cat could see it coming. It was time to heed the ghost's advice.

The time had come too to say goodbye to another friend: the gentle tree whose leaf covered limbs had guarded him from the merciless heat and the incessant rain.

Under its splendid umbrella, the cat had heard the wind tickling its canopy, making it sing. The wondrous place from where it had watched hundreds of beautiful butterflies invade and brighten the shadows among the trees. Yes! The orange tree. Encircled by its roots, the cat rose from its bed of dry leaves and wiggled its nose up to the wind. It lifted its front paws and gently rubbed the side of its face against the trunk, "*So you'll never forget me!*"

The remains of the day spread over the surrounding field and fused with the nearby mountains into a mass of impenetrable darkness. Don Genaro took his seat next to his grandson who was already on the balcony watching the world go by. With Muddy's disappearance still fresh on his mind, Mateo was unable to concentrate on his reading.

"How'ya doing, my boy?" Don Genaro asked, kissing the top of Mateo's head. "Let's plant something."

"What are those?" Mateo put down his unopened book and looked at the bulbs Don Genaro held in his hands.

"We are going to plant malangas," he announced.

"What do you want me to do?" He followed his grandfather to the backyard, appreciating the opportunity to get the stray off his mind.

"First, you put the root in the middle of that hole and press the dirt around it," his grandfather instructed.

"Like this?"

Don Genaro watched as Mateo took to it right away. "Yes, but press tightly. You don't want oxygen getting to the root."

"How long before it comes up?"

"A few weeks." Don Genaro noticed Mateo's hands covered with black soil.

"Grandpa, why are you always planting stuff?"

"Well, my grandparents used to work on a tobacco farm..."

"What did you do on the farm?"

Don Genaro's gaze met Mateo's. "I worked in a field cutting tobacco leaves and putting them into big burlap sacks. At the end of the day, I carried them to a ranch where they were hung up to dry. I remember my grandmother sewing the leaves together before hanging them."

"Then what happened after that?"

"Well, they took them to the market and got paid a few dollars."

"A few dollars?" Mateo was taken aback.

"Yessir! Picking tobacco was a low paying job. But if you had a family to feed, you did everything you had to," his grandfather concluded.

"Wow!"

Don Genaro watched as the boy immersed himself in the process, carefully pressing the dirt around the bed of the planted root. *"Just like his mother!"* he thought with a smile.

"What if it doesn't make it?" Mateo asked.

"Good things just don't happen overnight. You plant the seed and then trust for the best." Mateo saw the light in his grandfather's eyes.

"We're done here! Let's go back upstairs." Don Genaro rested his arm on Mateo's shoulder as they walked back to the house. Mateo heard his grandmother calling.

"Mateo, you have a visitor," she said softly, pointing to the gap in the chain-link fence by the gandules bush. Mateo looked over expecting Sergio but instead came eye-to-eye with the small gray cat sitting in the small flower bed as if waiting for permission to cross the garden. Mateo kept still, afraid he was just imagining the stray's appearance.

"Muddy!"

When the small cat heard its name, it ran happily into the arms of *Animalfriend.* Mateo's eyes were caught by the round shiny object hanging around the cat's neck. *"My Magic Crystal!"*

The horror of Severo's death left Palo Verde shaken. The chain of unfortunate events had also left Mateo dispirited; he was ready to return home. Turning the window handle, he cracked open the aluminum slats and let the sound of crickets fill the bedroom. A flood of quivering light rushed in through the openings and stenciled the walls with shadowy jittery patterns.

Outside he heard the familiar rattling. "Sergio!"

Sergio jumped off his bike, followed by Stumpy. "I wanted to say goodbye before you left," he said shyly.

Mateo smiled, relieved. "Hey, thanks. How's Stumpy doing?"

"He's great," answered Sergio. Stumpy looked up and wagged his tail happily at the familiar sound of his name.

"Is your arm better?" Mateo tapped on Sergio's cast.

"Much better. I can move my fingers now, see?" He wiggled the tips of his fingers. "You busy?" Sergio asked.

"No, come on up. I have something for you."

"Oh, no!" Mateo heard his grandmother yelp from his room.

Mateo and Sergio came in from the porch to see what was the matter.

Doña Sol pointed at the bed, revolted by the discovery of a dead bird. Nearby, Muddy napped placidly.

"You better take care of this now!" she said, exasperated.

"It's a gift, Buela," Mateo teased, trying to appease her.

"Well, he can keep it to himself. That's disgusting!"

Muddy lifted his sleepy eyes and with an audible sigh, went back to his nap.

"He's thanking you for your hospitality! You should be grateful."

"Mateo, don't be funny. Just take that thing out of the bed now!" Doña Sol was not amused.

"I'm just saying..."

"Mateo."

"I'll take care of it!" he promised as his grandmother left the room in a huff. Mateo began to fold his socks into balls, throwing them into his suitcase.

"Sergio, catch this!" He tossed the sock bundle to Sergio. Throwing it back, Sergio grabbed a brush from the dresser and egged Mateo on.

"Mateo is called off the bench as the clock ticks down in the fourth quarter! With only seconds to go, Mateo enters the game and THE CROWD GOES WILD! MAH-TEH-OH! MAH-TEH-OH! MAH-TEH-OH! Mateo dribbles the ball down the court and drives it to the basket. Shaquille goes for the block but Mateo drains a three at the buzzer for the win! With 30 points, seven rebounds, and five assists, MATEO SEALS THE HOME TEAM'S VICTORY! MAH-TEH-OH! MAH-TEH-OH! MAH-TEH-OH! Mateo kicks it on fire!"

"YEAH!" Mateo yelled.

"Mateo, what's going on in there?" his grandmother barked from the kitchen.

"Nothing," he answered, suppressing a laugh.

Stumpy barked at the cage where Muddy was trying to nap. Wharf, wharf, wharf!

He stared in frustration at the cat that only ignored him.

"Shut up, Stumpy!" Sergio tried to calm him down.

"It's okay, I think he's happy to see Muddy again," said Mateo.

Wharf, wharf, wharf! *"Are you going to be okay?,"* Stumpy asked.

"I'll be fine. I just need a nap," answered the cat, flexing his paws and blinking lazily.

Wharf, wharf! *"You take good care now,"* Stumpy added.

Meow, said Muddy to the dog wagging his short tail. *"Thanks, friend!"*

Sergio woke Muddy from his nap with a frisky rub of his coat. "Take good care of him, Mateo."

The cat turned sideways and let Sergio scratch his belly before jumping on the pillow to carve out a new sleeping nest.

"I will. You take good care of Stumpy too!"

"Goodbye, brother."

Sergio threw his arms around his friend in a big bear hug. Mateo smelled Sergio's tangled mass of hair, toasted and brightened by the island's sun. *"It smells like the beach!"* he thought with a smile. He couldn't help feeling sad as he watched his friend jump on his bike.

"Sergio, wait!" Mateo called out. "I want you to have this." He placed his beloved crystal around Sergio's neck.

"Are you sure?" Sergio held the shiny glass medallion in the palm of his hand.

"Yes, hermano. You know something, Sergio?... Never stop being preposterous!"

Sergio chuckled, his cheeks flushed with embarrassment.

Even after the surreal event that removed Severo from the town landscape, Mateo could not help trying to analyze the man's cruel streak. *"Why was he so angry with the world?"* While Severo's evil acts violated the bounds of decency, his personality was still a fascinating study. *"How does someone get to that degree of cruelty? Was he conscious of the hatred growing inside himself or did it just materialize out of the*

blue?" Mateo tried to identify the roots of the dreadful possibilities. *"In a way,"* he thought, *"it was as if he was trying to shake up the town and force them to face up to their own notions of propriety.*

"Were they any less cruel than him when they contributed to forcing an innocent girl out of town?" Mateo felt a pang of fear when he finally understood Severo's dark machinations. *"He thought they were a fraud, so he treated them like it,"* he reasoned. *"Even in his craziness, the man was clever enough to figure out that their pets were their weakness. He certainly did not waste the opportunity to hit them where it hurt the most! When did he begin to lose his humanity? Was it a slow progression or did it just flare up like a wild fire in the brambles?"*

A subtle knocking on his door pulled Mateo away from his thoughts.

"Yes, Buela, come in."

Doña Sol sat by his side as he took a break from filling up his suitcase.

"How's the packing going?" she asked, running her hand through his hair.

"I'm almost done," he answered.

"I'm sure your mother misses you very much."

"I know!" Mateo could hardly believe it was time to go. Only days before, he could not wait to return home, but now he was not so sure.

Doña Sol noticed the somber look on his face. "What's the matter?" she asked him with a frown.

"Nothing," he answered almost absentmindedly.

"You can tell me," she insisted, sitting on the edge of the bed.

His words came out in a burst. "Buela, what made him such a cruel man?"

Doña Sol chose her words carefully. "No one knows. It's human nature. Some people know instinctively how to get along with others, but some rebel and go their own way."

"Yes, but to go that far..."

The source of his anxiety finally became clear to her. "Mateo, you are sometimes as mischievous as they come but I assure you, you have nothing to worry about."

Mateo was not convinced. "How do you know when somebody's life begins to change?"

His grandmother could understand his conflict.

He went on. "Does is start with being cruel to the people who love you?" He regretted the words the moment they left his mouth.

Doña Sol detected remorse in his voice. "Come here, you silly boy." She encircled him with her arms. "You have a great heart. Think what you put yourself through to save Muddy."

"Anybody would have done the same," he answered matter-of-factly.

"I don't think so. It takes a special kind of soul to go out of its way to save the life of an animal in need. Now tell me, what will you miss the most when you leave?"

"The mountains and the clouds…" he answered, looking out the narrow window slats.

"You have clouds up there, don't you?" she teased.

"Yes, but nothing like here… This is a different world." The image of mounds of dense snow and cold, gray days flashed inside his head.

Doña Sol smiled at him. "Well, I'll let you get back to your packing. By the way, where's Muddy?" she asked, looking at the empty crate.

"I let him out for a while," Mateo said, wondering if that had been such a good idea.

"Don't worry, he's been through tougher situations. He'll be okay." She tried to ease his fears. "Here, let's put this inside there. He'll be more comfortable." She placed a small flannel blanket inside the carrier.

"Thanks, Buela… for everything." Mateo wrapped his arms tightly around her.

"Buela, about the tree house…"

"Don't worry dear, I might just rent it out!" She was pleased by Mateo's laugh. "Goodnight, my sweetness!" She kissed him gently.

"Buela, wait!" Mateo called out to her, as he rushed to the dresser.

"What is it?" Doña Sol turned around.

"I want you to have this." Mateo extended his arm towards her.

"Your sling shot? Why…" She smiled.

"I won't need it anymore… I hope!" Mateo laughed.

"I'll keep it in a very safe place!" Doña Sol answered with a knowing smile.

"Goodnight, Buela." Mateo kissed her cheek. The familiar sweet smell of her hair lingered in the room after she left. From his window, he looked around the garden. Outside, the night was getting thicker. For a long time he stared at the forest at the bottom of the hill. Such an impassive place! Standing solid and still, as if frozen in time. No one would have guessed how many memories and experiences hid beneath their limbs. He turned his eyes back to the blue carrier.

FROM MATEO'S JOURNAL

Last night I dreamt about her. I miss her. She is gone. But I finally saw her last night.

She was radiant, smiling. It felt so good to hold her again, to hug her and kiss her.

"You are really here!" I touched her again so I would know I was not dreaming.

I noticed her strangely aged but beautiful complexion, radiant, refreshed.

She looked happy to see me. "I've been waiting for this moment," I told her again with a kiss. She looked rejuvenated in a snappy white dress and with her hair done (a particularly incongruent-jarring even-vision given the fact that in life, she hated anything and everything that reminded her of order or propriety) but in my dream, I remember feeling, that it was the way I always wanted to remember her from then on. She showed me she was happy to see me too after what seemed like such a long time since her transition. She looked transformed, radiant, otherwordly even!

I breathed easier, relieved. I eagerly showed her some kind of medal around my neck held by a red ribbon. She seemed proud. It was just a brief moment, only as long as a sigh, but now I can breathe easier. I finally saw her, she was happy to see me again, we were happy to be together. I woke up sad, but relieved. Now I know she still watches over me…

HOME, FAR AWAY

Thy shadow, Earth, from Pole to Central Sea,
Now steals along upon the Moon's meek shine
in even monochrome and curving line
Of imperturbable serenity.

How shall I link such sun-cast symmetry
with the torn troubled form I know as thine,
that profile, placid as a brow divine,
with continents of moil and misery.

—Thomas Hardy, *At a Lunar Eclipse* (excerpt)

Yet another day had lost its strength and the house with the red tin roof and small garden became enveloped by darkness. The town of Palo Verde began to nest for the night as the silence descended. The evening began to penetrate the walls of the house as the feeble light of a single bulb escaped through the windows.

Doña Sol sat quietly in the small room, reading from her weathered book of prayers. Clutching a small framed photograph, she allowed herself to cry quietly. Whatever had happened over the past weeks was now gone and replaced by solitude. Sunsets would go on inundating the sky in cascades of warm and fluid light that she had begun to notice again as if it was for the first time. She had stopped looking to the sky for answers to her prayers. Instead, she began to listen to the crickets and frogs with their songs, the crows, birds, and dogs with their calls. As the pillows of humid wind bounced off the blue mountains, she allowed herself for the first time to look out at the canopy of the nearby forest. She wondered why she had never noticed the light before. Illuminated.

La Luna, moon goddess... Mateo sighed deeply and stared at the soft light peeking from behind thin clouds. Soon the calm beat of his heart matched the slow progress of the moon's illuminating journey across the sky. *La Luna* and her beautiful magic made him remember her haunting myth. Such a beautiful myth tinged with romance and violence. *Savage beauty!*

Savage beauty! Don Genaro watched the moon low on the horizon as she climbed through the paper cut silhouettes of the trees up to the center of the sky, dragging the night with her. Stars followed her like subjects to their queen and timidly began to shimmer to please her. Spellbound, Don Genaro wallowed in the pale luminosity of her fragile glow. *"Beautiful!"* he mouthed silently. His eyes followed the brightest, biggest star. *"I knew it was you!"* he smiled happily. Sitting on the balcony in the soft darkness, Don Genaro began to dream with the silvery glow of the moon over his shoulders. *"It was you!"* he murmured, closing his eyes. *"It was you!"*

"Mateo!"

Mateo jumped at the sound of the disembodied voice coming from the dark.

"Mateo, are you up there?" He heard the voice calling.

"What are you doing here?" Mateo asked, when he finally made out the silhouette of his grandfather in the shadows.

"May I come up?" Don Genaro asked from the bottom of the clumsy wooden ladder.

"Sure Buelo, just be careful," Mateo answered, extending a helping hand down to his grandfather.

"I want to show you something," Don Genaro said with an air of mystery.

"What is it?" Mateo was intrigued. His grandfather sat down by his side, crossing his legs under him.

"Can you see what's up there?" Don Genaro asked, pointing to the star-studded darkness above.

Mateo lifted his face up to the sky, searching through the leafy umbrella of the mango tree. "You mean the stars and the planets... The moon?"

"Do you know why the moon comes out only at night?" his grandfather asked, eyes fixed on the silver plate hanging in the sky.

Mateo could easily have explained its rotation around the Earth, the spellbinding illusion of its glow from the sun's reflected light, but instead he decided to indulge the fantastic tale that was obviously brewing in his grandfather's imagination. He could certainly do with the diversion.

"Well, do you?" Don Genaro insisted.

"No, please tell me," Mateo answered.

"Many millions of years ago, when the Earth was still young and savage and there was no light in the night, no moon to look at, or stars to brighten up the dark sky, it was a time when the ancient Aztec gods walked the earth in darkness, a darkness of the soul. A time too when righteousness was more powerful than love. They wanted the world to have a good beginning but they could not agree on the best way or control their thirst for power. You see, rage is always the downfall of the mighty. There was only one thing they could agree on: the world needed light, even at night.

"Among the gods and goddesses, there was one named Coatlicue, which means 'the one with the skirt of serpents.' She was the mother of all celestial things but Coatlicue had a deadlier, wrathful side too. One dark night, Coatlicue's daughter dared to confront her mother, only to have her own brother cut her head off in protest. He threw it against the sky where it became the moon... Since then, mischief shies away from the sun but it is at night when it thrives and roams the earth!" Don Genaro concluded.

Mateo had listened in wonder as his grandfather seamlessly followed his own narrative. *"No one,"* he thought, *"would suspect the deep pools of darkness revolving in this man's mind."* But Mateo was at once grateful for his grandfather's sudden spark of inspiration and saddened by the shadows that settled over his face as the fleeting moon left once more. He reached out and tenderly squeezed Don Genaro's hand. He could see his grandfather was still smiling.

Mateo turned his eyes away from the hazy moon now hovering over the trees. In the comfortable darkness, he could see Don Genaro's silhouette outlined in a diaphanous glow. Looking closer, he could see that the deep furrows on his grandfather's face were softened, almost replenished, like rain falling on thirsty ground...

"Minerva!... Is it you?"
"I hear you calling me."
"What is heaven like?"
"I still don't know."
"Has your journey been long?"
"It's full of stars."
"Is there forgiveness in heaven?"
"Heaven must be forgiveness."
"I love you."
"I know you do... You have to let me go."
"Darkness, that's what my days are full of now."
"Don't fear it. It's easier."
"Will you forgive me?"
"Don't cry anymore."
"Will I see you again?"
"Just look up at the moon."

Back in his bed, Mateo cradled his head with intertwined fingers. Sleepless, he watched the night swallow the room around him. He contemplated the fractured moonbeams lighting up the wall. In the silence, he heard Muddy stir and sigh in his sleep. The sound made him smile. He could breathe much easier now.

Doña Sol looked at the slivers of moonlight through her window and gently bookmarked her worn-out book of prayers with her rosary beads. She wrapped her sweater around her shoulders, crossed her arms, and rested her head against the back of the chair as if getting ready for a spectacular display. Instead, the moon continued to slowly rise, quietly glowing before disappearing completely from the window. Doña Sol closed her eyes and began a new prayer, but not before reliving the darkest day of her life...

"My dear Lord... It should have been me." She struggled as her faith quavered under the insurmountable weight of the impending loss of her youngest child.

"Why not me?" She had tried to negotiate, to find a clue within the randomness of life. She hardly noticed when Don Genaro, sitting by her side, entwined his hand with hers.

"How's she doing?" he asked softly, his voice breaking too. Watching her shake her head in despair like a disillusioned prize-fighter acknowledging the futility of the fight was more than he could bear.

She tried to find comfort even in the midst of their tragedy, reliving one of her daughter's many antics. After all, what made Minerva special was precisely the contradictory cluster of traits that was their daughter's life, like a mischievous faint ray of light that manages to cut through the impenetrable darkness…

* * *

The news had spread throughout the neighborhood faster than sunshine over the tamarinds. It did not take a wizard to predict that within moments of the unfortunate development at the local movie house, its proprietor would march up the road thinking of revenge, cursing Minerva's name like an incantation. The town's children, mostly the same motley crue who were thrown out of the theatre moments before, were now following an enraged Maruca, egging her on and setting her up for a fierce battle.

"MA-RUUU-CA, MA-RUUUCA, MA-RUUUCA!!"

It did not take long before Maruca materialized in Doña Sol's front yard looking like she was coming fresh out of a wind tunnel. Doña Sol watched helplessly as Maruca opened her mouth and launched into a hateful, unintelligible diatribe against Minerva. At the sound of Minerva's name, Doña Sol felt beyond mortified and wondered what in heaven's name her problematic offspring had gotten herself entangled with.

"What's the matter, Maruca?" Doña Sol tried to appease the woman raging in front of her.

"SOL! YOUR! DAUGHTER! WRETCHED! WRETCHED DEMON CHILD!!" *she spat, summarizing her indefinable rage and frustration while flapping her arms about for dramatic emphasis.*

Doña Sol arched her brow both in frustration and empathy for the woman, "I'm sorry, Maruca. Do not worry. I will take care of it and she will have to answer to me! I promise you." To her relief, the woman accepted her sincere apology.

Secretly Maruca felt sorry for the woman who, looking at the situation from another perspective, had a bigger burden than hers.

"MINERVA! I WANT YOU OUT HERE. NOW!" Doña Sol called for her daughter

as her head began to throb with a smashing headache.

But now the jagged edge of the memory was softened by Minerva's absence. Doña Sol would give anything to turn back time. This time there was a faint smile on her lips...

"Are you ready to come back home?" Mateo heard Maria ask from the other end of the line.

"Yes, I guess..." he answered distractedly.

"You don't sound so sure. What's going on, Mateo?"

"Don't know." Mateo fidgeted with his T-shirt.

Maria tried to ease his anxiety. "Are you worried about Muddy? Just keep him next to you. He'll be fine, you'll see."

"I hope so." But Mateo wondered what the real reason for his uneasiness was. The commotion in Palo Verde following Severo's death had unsettled him, but in spite of everything, he had forgiven the man.

His eyes rested on the photograph leaning against the dresser. For a long time he stared at the picture of the young woman with short, cropped hair, staring back as if she was smiling just for him.

"Mateo?"

Mateo turned at the sound of a familiar voice. "Hi, Billy."

"You busy?" Billy asked timidly.

"No. Just finished packing," Mateo answered, noticing Billy's shy demeanor.

There was an awkward moment of silence. He felt sudden pity for his neighbor.

"When are you leaving?" Billy finally asked.

"Tomorrow morning," Mateo answered self-consciously.

"How's Muddy doing?" Billy stared at the cat's carrier.

"I think he's better. Not so jumpy anymore," he chuckled.

Mateo watched Billy nervously wipe the palms of his hand against his T-shirt.

"Hey, I'm sorry to hear about your Aunt Minerva," he finally uttered.

"She wasn't my aunt... She was my mother," Mateo felt his mouth dry up.

Billy stared at him speechless, not knowing what to say.

After another moment of silence, Billy finally headed for the door. "Well, I just wanted to say... Goodbye."

Mateo lifted his head and slowly smiled. "Thank you, Billy. Thanks for your help..." He didn't quite know how to finish his sentence.

"Hey, Billy... Good luck, okay?"

"Thanks," Billy answered from the doorway. "Good luck to you too. Goodbye, Muddy!"

Mateo watched the cat lift its head and sniff Billy's fingers before going back to its nap.

He realized it was the first time he had seen Billy smile. It pleased him to see Billy's face soften, revealing his truer self. It would be many years before Mateo realized the inexplicable connection between Billy and himself that allowed him to understand Billy's aggressive front. After all, just like him, Billy was still a boy.

* * *

"Who's the father?" Genaro's voice boomed across the room and made Minerva tremble. He spat out his question as if the words had turned to bile on his lips. He could not hide his frustration at his daughter's stubbornness. "Who are you trying to protect? You're only hurting yourself and us!" With each new question, his head throbbed in its futile attempt to get to the bottom of the issue. "You've disgraced this family. Have you no shame?" Genaro pulled out the most explosive question from his arsenal in a final attempt to get a rise out of his daughter. "Is Francisco the father?"

Minerva was paralyzed with fear. She wished that he had just hit her as hard as he possibly could; it would certainly hurt less than his humiliating questions. She could only lower her gaze to the ground in response.

"You leave me no choice. You cannot stay under this roof."

Minerva gasped for air as if someone had suddenly punched her in her stomach. Her father's words stuck inside her mind, scrambling her thoughts.

"I thought you loved me!" she managed to say in defense. Looking into the watery pools of her father's eyes, she desperately sought a hint of reassurance, an affirmation, a reconciliation. "Where's your compassion?" she finally shot back, collapsing on her mother's sofa, sobbing into the palms of her hands.

Minerva felt alone, like she was standing in the middle of a landslide, the last inhabitant on Earth. Her words of self-defense had no resonance, no power of conviction. She felt utterly empty. It was now clear her fate was sealed. She began to place her scarce belongings in the tattered brown suitcase. That night, she didn't sleep. With reddened eyes, she watched the morning sun climb slowly up beyond her window as if it too was trying its best to delay the inevitable progression of this fateful day. Minerva jumped at the sound of a gentle knock on the other side of the door.

"The car to the airport is here," Minerva heard her mother say softly, unable to conceal her desolation.

Maria could not believe what she was hearing across the telephone line. "I don't want to do that! You are insane!" she protested to her father. She tried to convince herself this wasn't all a bad dream. Overcome with frustration she paced around the room, fidgeting with the phone cable. It was hard for her to understand the lack of common sense in her father's proposal.

"Maria, don't be selfish. If you don't do this, you too will be guilty of endangering the boy's life! People will talk and make it a living hell for both of them." Don Genaro's arguments were in line with his deeply religious community. "This will give her time to get herself together." Don Genaro was firm. "She'll have to go live with you, and soon."

Unable to listen anymore, Doña Sol fled to her room. Her eyes burning with tears, she could not read a word from her book of prayers.

"I'll take care of everything," she heard her husband say from the living room.

Meanwhile Minerva sat frozen with fear on a corner of the kitchen table, her sweaty hands fused in a tight grip as if trying to make herself invisible. It was an unnecessary feat though since her father talked about, around, and for her as if she was unable to have a say in her own life.

So it was decided: Maria, the mature, sensible, oldest one was to carry the burden. As a young widow living away from the island—thus thousands of miles beyond judgment—Maria was the perfect cover.

"The plan is simple," Don Genaro insisted. Maria was to look after Minerva. The child, born far away from vicious, prying minds, would later be presented as Maria's own. Don Genaro's heart was crumbling but he was convinced it was better to conceal his daughter's pregnancy and spare her a life of cruelty and derision. For Minerva to flaunt the fruit of her poor judgment would have invited Palo Verde's scorn. *"If I don't act fast,"* he thought, *"I will be a participant in the destruction of their lives too."* Genaro was not willing to risk it, not in a place where someone's personal tragedy was everyone else's entertainment, where neighbors gorged with pleasure on the misery of others under the guise of compassion and the conviction of their holy beliefs.

"What do you care? They are nothing but ignorant hypocrites!" Maria tried to fight back in her sister's defense, but she could not break through Don Genaro's stony silence across the ocean divide.

But once Minerva's absence from Palo Verde sank in, Genaro's mind began to stall. He hated himself for his weakness, for having chosen to preserve his family's standing in the town's fickle morality code at the expense of his daughter's love. "My own daughter! What have I done?" His resentment, anger, and remorse accumulated steadily, like raindrops filling up a pond. Though it was only a few short years until her return to the island, the damage had already taken root. But it wasn't until her untimely death that his guilt pushed him into disquieting lapses of oblivion where his memories fused into a mass of confusion.

All is fair in love. Maria had to take a step back to consider what was best for Minerva. Now she only wanted to ensure happiness and safety for her sister and the child. Maria had gone along with the big lie but only because she had no choice. She fought it, and fought it some more, but in the end she had to make sense of her parent's decision. "Minerva is not fit to be a mother, she's too irresponsible." Maria had resisted their argument but had agreed in the end to be part of the lie. It was done in the name of love, in the "best interest" of the child. But now everything had backfired in the worst possible way. The question running in circles inside Maria's head was how to undo the undoable? How could she ever tell the child the truth? "He will never forgive me," she feared.

Even the happiest of days paled in comparison to when they first heard the news—Minerva had become a mother.

"It's a boy!" Don Genaro heard the voice of his older daughter on the phone.

"What's his name?" Doña Sol asked bursting with joy.

"Mateo," was her answer.

"Mateo!" They liked the name right away.

"Mateo!" Her first grandson. Doña Sol's tears slipped slowly down the receiver.

"How is she doing?" She wanted to know about her daughter, her broken daughter.

"She's very happy," Maria said, setting her mother's mind at ease.

"When will we see him?" Doña Sol asked eagerly.

Maria felt a sudden rush of bile in the back of her throat. "You'll have to wait," she answered, her voice thinly veiled with recrimination. An almost inaudible gasp of hurt at the other end of the line made Maria regret her words.

"You are to keep him there with you! He will not be safe with her, Maria." Don Genaro was convinced.

"She's the child's mother! I will not take part in this."

"Listen to me, Maria. She can't handle the responsibility! What if she does something that endangers his life?"

Maria covered her ears, heartbroken. "I can't do this! She is his mother!"

"What do you think will happen when people start talking? What if the government takes him away for good, is that what you want? It was humiliating enough she was thrown out of school by getting herself pregnant at 14!" She heard Don Genaro pacing around the room.

"You are wrong! She deserves better." Maria choked back tears, covering her face with trembling hands.

"We only want what's best!" Doña Sol said, not sure even she believed the words leaving her mouth.

"You'll regret this! I don't want any part of it." Maria slammed down the phone leaving Don Genaro speechless. The hardest part was going to be telling Minerva about their plans.

"I will not be a part of this!" Maria repeated. "Where is your humanity?" But her cries had no effect and instead dissolved into the air, like a prayer falling on deaf ears. What hurt her the most was her father's claim to righteousness while gunning ahead without concern for the devastating consequences. Maria empathized even more with her sister's pleas. *"How could I do that to her and add to her burden?"*

It broke her heart to realize that, even in the best of times, Minerva's happiness was not meant to be. Maria remembered how her sister had mourned for the love of her life. It was also the single, most macabre coincidence she shared with her. A distant war that had bonded them for life…

Minerva had found love the very first moment she met Francisco but in a cruel twist of fate he had to leave the island, along with Maria's young husband, to fight on the fields of Vietnam. Francisco never understood the logic of being transplanted to a land so strange and far away he had never heard of it before.

Worst of all, he would have to face the inevitable prospect of killing people he didn't even know.

Francisco and Minerva had prayed for time, but his marching orders arrived much sooner than the answer to their prayers. So Minerva watched him leave Palo Verde, fighting to remain optimistic but sadly wondering what the purpose of it all was. Francisco made promises to Minerva he was not sure he could keep, but trusting the wisdom of his government, he grabbed his tattered suitcase and headed out to face his unknown future. Francisco never looked back; seeing Minerva cry would only make him crumble. That was the last time Minerva ever saw him. Minerva saw her chance for love come undone and slip through her fingers like water from the river.

A gentle turn inside her stomach kept her grounded to her gray reality. *"What am I going to do now?"* Minerva wondered if this was how the end of the world felt. Not only for her but also for the baby nestled inside her. Without thinking, she caressed her belly and softly began singing a lullaby to her unborn child...

Rock-a-bye, rock-a-bye,
Rock-a-bye matted in cobwebs,
I can see, there it goes
Early light over the mountains.

Go to sleep, go to dream
Let yourself fly over palm trees,
Sing a song, laugh out loud
Let the music heal your heartache.

Rock-a-bye, rock-a-bye
Rock-a-bye matted in cobwebs
Night is long, go to dream
Let the moon shine on
Your heartache.

Minerva fantasized about all the things she would teach her new baby boy. Mateo, "Gift of God." Maria had found meaning in the child's name too. Mateo was a precious gift, indeed. She watched Minerva become the lioness. No longer the trouble maker, Minerva was guardian and teacher. Minerva, Earth-Mother.

Maria had to admit how happy it made her sister to focus on the new baby. As the boy grew up, she witnessed with relief how Minerva nurtured his creative mind. The new baby was her pride and joy. But Minerva was not destined to sustain her happiness. Her body began to give her warnings. She felt betrayed by it. Soon, she began to sense her imminent return home, sworn to silence, bonded to a lie in the name of love, in the name of Mateo...

* * *

Mateo's suitcase stood by the door right beside Muddy's blue carrier. Lingering in the small room, he took a final look out at the nearby mountains as he tried to come to grips with his departure. His gaze traveled across the yard, down the grass-covered field, and to the woods below. *"The illuminated forest."* His memory lit up at the thought of the dazzling, magical shower of light on that special night. He scanned the backyard where only a short while ago a small gray stray had charmed its way into his heart. He remembered with pleasure the bright mornings when Muddy quietly amused himself in his grandmother's garden.

An impatient horn blast pulled him back to reality. Mateo looked at his watch.

He heard his grandmother's voice calling. "The car is here, Mateo." Teary-eyed, Doña Sol embraced her grandson as he kissed her goodbye. She handed him a small metal box. "I think you'll want to keep this."

There was still one thing Mateo had to do before leaving the island.

"Buela, will you give me a minute?" he begged, stepping out of the idling car. He had finally gathered the courage to enter Minerva's room. As much as he had avoided it, now was his last chance. He had finally run out of time. He slowly opened the door, startled by the creaking sound. Somehow he expected Minerva to walk in on him at any moment and say, "Mateo, what do you think you are doing?"

Afraid that the daylight would unsettle the quiet ghosts in the room, he resisted turning the lights on and allowed his eyes to slowly adjust to the darkness. He gasped at the musty smell of dust that had settled undisturbed over every surface like an old memory. Mateo gazed out the window at the pigeon pea bush, from the bed of begonias to the ferns in the garden, to the mango tree towering over the front of the house. *"This was the last place she saw,"* he thought.

The early morning made the garden sparkle with color. Beyond the chain link fence where he had first seen Muddy, the tall green grass was crowned with yellow, white, and pink wildflowers. Mateo watched them sway as waves of warm air rolled gently past. He could still see himself and Minerva running through the tall bank of grass as the relentless sun beat down on them.

He stared at the simple drawing hanging on the back of the door and recognized his own childish sloppy handwriting, a forgotten piece of his rustic art she had kept like a treasure.

"That funny looking mannequin." He was glad to see it again, the headless prop that had assisted her many sewing creations and endured the constant pricking of pins. The fabric that covered it like a skin hung tattered and beaten by the years. Minerva had found it in the trash and given it a second chance at life. She had honored its purpose by carrying it with her wherever she happened to live.

Over at her night table, he found her yellow tape measure coiled carefully in a corner of the drawer. The same one she had draped around her shoulders like a fancy stole. *"I can't believe I'll never see her again."*

"Mateo, are you in there?" His grandmother's voice pulled him out of his thoughts.

"I'll be out in a minute," he responded.

"She asked me to give you this." Mateo turned around and faced his grandmother who was holding a tattered notebook.

"Her drawing pad!" He rested the fragile book in the palm of his hand. Without another word, his grandmother left him alone.

Mateo's fingertips traced over every drawing, thought, and scribble on its pages. The well-worn drawing pad was filled with random thoughts that illuminated her happiest and darkest moments. Child-like drawings of butterflies, *"which she chased with my help,"* he remembered. Thoughts filled with rage, charged with the desire to make sense of the disease that was overtaking her. "We are like blades of grass, the act of life and death is indifferent!" read a line of an unfinished poem, a reflection of her state of mind when her mortality had become apparent.

Mateo finally came to the last page where she had dedicated a poem to him in her unmistakable handwriting. *"For Mateo, so you'll never forget."* Even though she was no longer around, he wrapped himself in the words of her gift, as if he could hear her voice once more.

You may think you can run.
And you might hide
Or fly off the deepest canyon.
You might retreat under the sea.
No matter what,
If, when, and how,
Under a rock,
It'll prick and prod.
Love still will seek until it finds you!

He looked around the room where so many memories still remained. Before he walked back out into the sun, he went over to the drawer where he had found the old yellow tape measure and, folding it carefully, placed it in his pocket.

"Goodbye, Mom." Mateo closed the door quietly behind him.

A boy of 12 can relate to another boy's rage because he has been there himself. Mateo understood Billy all too well. A meaningless fight was nothing more than a cry for help; he knew that now. Finally he could see Billy as he really was, not like the defensive, tough guy he was so desperately trying to be. Mateo felt deeply sorry for Billy and regretted their past encounters. Suddenly all the arguments between Billy and his father made sense. *"He was just looking for a friend! Maybe I should've tried harder."*

Still, he wished a new beginning for Billy. Although he could not explain it, he felt they had a bond. After all, they had both fought for the life of an animal. Billy's actions had not gone unnoticed. In fact, they had taken Mateo by surprise. Thanks to Billy, Stumpy was safe. Mateo knew there was hope for him.

Billy's mother, keeping her promise, had come for him the moment she heard the news about Severo. And Billy was eager to start fresh too, away from the place that had left him with such bad memories. Mateo watched Billy come out of his house carrying a small suitcase and get into the car next to his mother. Mateo felt happy for him.

Billy waved sheepishly when he saw Mateo. In solidarity, Mateo lifted his arm and waved back. "Goodbye, Mateo!" he heard Billy call out as the car began to make its way down the road.

* * *

Minerva rested the weight of her body against her cane. She waited for Billy to get closer before speaking. "What do you have there, Billy?" She could tell he was trying to hide something.

Billy ignored her and continued walking down the road. But Minerva was not ready to give up. She had a pretty good idea of what he was desperately trying to conceal.

"Billy, wait up!" When she caught up with him, she could tell the boy was jittery. "What you got in there?"

"Nothing."

She knew he was lying.

"Please, let me see," Minerva insisted as the boy became increasingly nervous.

Billy pleaded with her, "Please don't tell anyone!"

Minerva watched Billy unfasten the straps of his backpack. When he lifted the flap, she could not believe her eyes.

"Billy, he's beautiful!" Minerva cooed at the small round head that popped out of the bag. "He is simply adorable!" She ran her fingers through the soft fur of the gray kitten staring back at her with big round eyes.

"Look, it has a mohawk, Billy!" Minerva loved the crest of hair on the cat's head. "But will Severo let you keep it?"

Billy looked in the direction of his house. Minerva saw his eyes fill with tears. It was clear the boy had not thought about it. Minerva wished she could take back her comment. She felt sorry the boy had such a cruel father. She feared the beautiful kitten was doomed.

"Can you keep it for me?" Billy begged her.

"I'll find him a good home, I promise you." Then an idea flashed through her mind. The beautiful kitten with the shock of wild hair on its forehead was to have a future after all. *"My gift to him. I'll make sure of it!"*

"You're very lucky, little one!" Minerva whispered as she cradled the kitten in her arms.

* * *

The downturn of a life can be traced back to a specific
point in time with absolute certainty.
A single tragic event can send it on its downward journey,
spiraling out of control. Even a cat, a young one,
was not immune to this fact.

Palo Verde was shaken by Minerva's passing. Even Severo, who had had his share of arguments with her could not help but feel sorry for her family. In a rare moment of humility, Severo decided to pay his respects even though he knew his act of contrition might not be fully appreciated. With slow steps he crossed the short stretch of busy road. From the chain-link fence, he called out to Doña Sol.

Severo struggled with his words. "I'm sorry about Minerva, Sol."

"Thanks, Severo. There was not much we could have done," she answered, looking at him with empty eyes.

"I know we've had our disagreements—"

"Well, Minerva had a talent for rattling nerves," she admitted with a sad smile.

"If there's anything I can do, please…"

"Thanks again."

Once he had said his piece, Severo turned back to his house when he heard Doña Sol's voice again.

"Excuse me, Severo! There's one thing… I don't quite know what to do about it."

"What is it?" he asked rather intrigued.

"Well, you see Billy gave her this kitten a few weeks ago…"

At the mention of the animal, Severo felt his skin crawl.

"…'I'm afraid, now that Minerva is not around, it will need somebody to care for it, you see—"

Severo swallowed hard so his words would come out steady, without any hint of disgust. "Don't say another word, Sol. I'll take care of it. Billy will be very happy."

Within minutes, Severo was holding a small cardboard box containing the gray kitten with the silver crest on its head. He could tell the cat was missing its owner. Staring at the contents of the box, Severo began his trip up the road. He passed his own house where Billy was sitting by himself on the front steps.

"What do you have in there?" Billy asked when he saw his father holding the shoe box.

"Nothing that concerns you. I'll be back soon!" Severo yelled at his son. Walking for what seemed like hours, he finally arrived at a secluded stretch of road high up on a hill where bamboo shoots had created a canopy over the road. He could hear the cat's hungry cries but he was unmoved. Severo dropped the box by the side of the road and began to walk back home.

"Good luck to you, little one!" Severo said with a smirk. In the distance, he could hear the animal's cries fading away.

"Hello, Mateo, can you hear me?" Minerva strained to hear Mateo's voice.

"Meva, are you there? I can't hear you!"

Minerva could barely understand what he was saying. She could hear him raise his voice as he strained to hear her words.

"Yes, I can hear you. The reception here is not very good. I will have to climb a taller mountain, hee, hee!" She thought a little joke would lessen his anxiety. She was pleased to hear him laugh, too. "C'mon, Minerva, do it for him," she thought, masking her pain. Minerva was afraid he would sense her weakness.

"Do you feel okay?" Minerva heard at the other end.

"Better than ever!" Minerva lied for his benefit. "You know, I will beat this thing."

"I'll be seeing you soon," she heard him promise. Minerva appreciated his attempt to lift her spirits.

"Yes, I know. I can't wait to see you too! I have a gift for you!" She couldn't wait to tell him about the little gray kitten with a crest.

"I have this quite unusual and beautiful kitten for you..."

Their connection ended abruptly. Minerva suspected he did not hear her last words.

Maria picked up the receiver and felt her soul leave her body as she heard the words she knew were coming. She hung up the phone and her legs gave way underneath her body. She sat down sobbing, choking on her tears and gasping for air. Looking out her window, she was weighed down further by the depressing gray clouds covering the sun. The dreaded phone call made her head buzz, like static coming from a television that had lost its signal. Her eyes, now swollen, stared unfocused at the wall. Maria had a cruel realization. *"This is what the end of the world feels like."* She cried some more.

Maria began, "Mateo, there's something I have to tell you." There was hesitation in her voice. There was no possible way to soften the blow that was about to hit him. There was no way to protect him from the devastating truth. She would never forget the moment her account of events reached his ears. She watched his body diminish with every word, like a sculpture being chipped away by its clumsy creator. She watched in terror as his face, contorted by an unfamiliar pain, drained of blood, reducing him to a trembling, fragile mass.

"I'm sorry, I'm so sorry!" she repeated but Mateo did not hear a single word of her heartfelt apology. She had to accept that even though she had pointed out the flaws in her father's plan, she had committed a greater crime: she had lied to Mateo too.

"Someday you'll understand." She tried to ease his pain with meaningless words. It pained her that she too was the cause of such hurt.

* * *

*Fantasy and reality travel hand in hand
but time seems to travel in circles...*

What seems like yesterday was in fact three years ago. It was a time when a boy of 12 felt that rage was easier than love and hid his pain away in a numbing cocoon. Rage was the dark place where his true feelings dwelled before he could acknowledge and deal with them. Instinctively, Mateo discovered that wrath had its benefits: it created a barrier to keep the world at a distance. Anger was the empty shell where reason and logic bounced off the walls until they lost all meaning. When love is gone, it leaves an empty place like an abandoned nest. The place where fragile chicks grew up protected from the elements stays behind as proof that, though it used to be a warm and safe center, it will never be home again. Emptiness.

Emptiness. Yes, Mateo knew how an abandoned nest felt. Minerva, his dear Meva was gone. He couldn't bear it. Hopelessness, pain, and emptiness were powerful emotions for a boy of 12. He resisted Maria's embrace like a wild animal fights at the sight of a cage. But rage is also debilitating; he cried himself to sleep, his black mane of tousled hair stuck to his temples. Sweat and tears stained his white pillow. His body became feverish and vulnerable. His eyes, red and burning from crying, finally closed. Yes, rage is easier than love. For a boy of 12, it is the safest place to be.

The morning shower brightened the garden to a lustrous shine. To celebrate, the blue jays, catbirds, cardinals, and squirrels descended with eager, loud cackles until their hungry chatter reached a feverish pitch. Mateo, with the cat settled on his lap, watched a young robin hop along the rim of the birdbath before jumping into the fresh rain water, vigorously splashing around in its first spring bath.

To Mateo, it seemed like such a long time had passed since that bright August morning when, without warning, a small gray stray had become entwined in his destiny. The sad thought of having never said goodbye to his beloved mother stayed with him, but he took great comfort in her words, "I will always be here."

Mateo watched his newly adopted cat run around, happy and out of control, and his mind wandered back to Palo Verde. Still, three years later, he wondered at the curiously timed alignment of his mother's passing and the appearance of the stray. *"A silver cloud filled with rain,"* he remembered, *"Meva would have loved him!"* The thought comforted him, and for years to come he would ponder the meaning of the coincidence.

As the day began to take shape before his eyes on that early spring morning, the sun struggled to chase away the chilly remnants of winter. Gone was the snow-covered wonderland. The dogwoods and the lean plum tree in a corner of the garden had awakened from their winter sleep and were now covered in pink blossoms. Timid patches of crocuses and daffodils peeked from the damp ground while nearby, trees rejuvenated their limbs with the sprouting of new green buttons.

From his comfortable corner on the couch, Mateo watched the cat run all over the house like a rambunctious two-year-old, its jaws trembling and its teeth chattering, at the activity outside the door. A busy squirrel was oblivious to the cat's frantic attempt to get a closer look. Mateo could feel the cat's frustration as it impatiently snapped its tail from side to side. Suddenly, the cat turned its attention to a flock of doves grazing around the garden's fountain. A robin that had been perching on a branch of the plum tree dipped into the fountain and shook its feathers vigorously in a frenzied bath. The gathering was broken up by yet another family of squirrels zigzagging up and down the trellis swaddled in yellow rosebuds.

Mateo's lips curled into a smile as he observed the yellow cat's every move. "What do you see, Simon?" He was relieved to find the cat had adapted well to his new life watching birds from the sunny window sill and listening to the hungry cackles of the blue jays and the spirited chirps of the bright red cardinals.

"Are you ready, Mateo?"

Mateo felt Maria's soft touch on his shoulder. "Yes. It is a beautiful day for it," he answered. His eyes traveled out the door framed with green ivy.

"I agree. I think she would have loved it too!" Maria answered wistfully.

Out in the garden, they watched the busy bird feeder, host to chickadees, finches, sparrows, and titmice. A greedy squirrel jumped and interrupted their feast in its search for nuts; an event not tragic at all but greatly appreciated by the cardinals and doves grazing underneath that benefited from the spilt seeds.

"Lots of customers today!" Mateo chuckled.

His hands cradled a small metallic box. "This is the best place," he suggested. "What do you think?"

"I think it's perfect," Maria answered, very pleased.

Mateo bowed his head in a silent prayer. Maria helped him expand the small hole in the moist ground. Carefully, he poured the ashes into the opening. Maria handed him the pale green sapling. With a firm push, he secured the soil around the tiny tree, much like his mother Minerva had done 21 years before...

With careful, delicate hands she brushed away the mulch of
rotten leaves and broke the black, moist ground by the river bank
into clumps. The touch of her small hands clumsily patting the dirt
around its frail stem made the tree feel cozy and safe.
"So you can grow up to be beautiful!"

Neither Mateo nor Maria were ware of the radiantly beautiful black bird sitting atop the plum tree, keeping its shiny eyes on them and cawing softly. Only Simon the cat noticed, the fur on its body standing on end, its back arched, and its pupils fully dilated in excitement...

Mateo walked out of the room, closing the door of Minerva's shop behind him. Shading his eyes from the sudden glare of the sun, his gaze followed the row of birds perching on the power line against the sparkling blue of the sky.

The sound of Muddy whimpering inside his carrier made him come back to reality. Suddenly he became aware of the beating of his heart.

"Don't worry, Muddy, you'll be far from here soon." He felt strange at the sound of his own words. At that moment, a voice from across the street pulled him out of his thoughts.

"Goodbye, Mateo!" Billy called out, as the car carrying him and his mother started to make its way down the road. Mateo waved back but suddenly, as if he had just remembered something, he ran after them carrying the blue carrier.

"WAIT! BILLY, WAIT!"

The car came to a halt as Mateo ran up to Billy's window.

"I think you should keep him!" Mateo blurted out. "You will give him a good life, won't you?" He felt his throat tighten. Mateo carefully lifted the carrier up to the window. Billy's eyes lit up as he opened the cage and Muddy jumped on his lap.

"I promise I will, I really will!" Billy answered, wrapping his arms around the cat. Mateo looked into Billy's eyes and knew he was telling the truth.

Although Billy's words were reassuring, Mateo felt his heart breaking into pieces. "Goodbye, Muddy." Mateo's voice cracked.

"Goodbye, Mateo!" he heard Billy call out one last time.

Agripino held the car door open for him.

"Thank you, Mr. Agripino," Mateo said appreciatively. He sank in his seat. He could hardly bear another goodbye. He remembered that just weeks before he had had to fight his reluctance to return to this place. Now he felt half of his heart was being left behind. He watched in a daze from the car as it traveled along the tall rows of roble oaks, transforming the small town nestled among the mountains into a blur. Mateo let his mind wander, conjuring up the picturesque town's characters that had so vividly given life and heart to Minerva's tales. Images of faces and places that he was now leaving behind too.

A smile curved his lips when he recognized the plump woman doing her laundry in the very same spot, hanging the wet clothes along the line, the one who had laughed so hard at his description of an exceptional cat. Mateo ducked as they passed by the familiar police cruiser where two officers sat inside chatting animatedly over cups of coffee.

On the opposite side of the road, in the distance by the cow's watering hole, was the young black bull who had literally given him a run for his life. And there too was Rosina, Severo's mare, pulling chunks of fresh grass to munch on as her new owner scratched her nose lovingly. Just as they crossed the town's limits, Mateo stuck his head out of the window when he noticed a middle-aged woman struggling to place a poster in front of the town's run-down theatre. *"Maruca?"*

Mateo watched her intently, when he caught a glimpse of the coming attraction's title: *In The Realm of the Senses...*

The tiny island grew smaller as the plane drifted up into the sky and away from its shores, until it was just a green speck in the ocean. Mateo's memories became clearer and brighter as the plane flew further away from his grandparents' island and Palo Verde. He felt a new sadness at leaving them, Sergio, and even Billy.

Don't bring home anything I did not take with me in the first place.

Mateo stared at the rules he had scribbled in a moment of frustration. He felt a bit embarrassed by the silly "contract." In a moment of despair, he had tried to protect himself from feeling anything. But seeing his promise again reminded him of Muddy, and he could not deny his great loss. He rested his face against the plane's window, no longer able to contain the outpouring of tears.

"Goodbye, Muddy," he thought. As he watched the clouds rushing by, his grandmother's words rang in his mind, *"Don't turn love away, no matter where it comes from, because when life's burdens become too great, it is good to know that you can rely on its strength."*

Mateo felt a void, but the thought of Billy caring for Muddy was comforting. Knowing that the young cat would finally be safe made him breathe easier.

FROM MATEO'S JOURNAL

Last Entry

I remember to this day watching as the car drove away, coming in and out of view between the rows of roble trees that bordered the road. With my eyes cloudy and swollen with tears, I tried to console myself thinking, "Minerva would have done the same." Deep inside I knew that Billy would give Muddy a great life. I thought of Billy and I trusted the sincerity I saw in his eyes. In a way, we were alike. He reminded me of myself. I knew he was just trying to prove that he too could love. I hoped that by offering Muddy as my gift, a chain of cruelty would finally be broken. It was the hardest thing I have ever done and, I must confess, at the time I didn't understand my own impulse. I had to accept that there are no guarantees but I chose to have faith.

To this day I want to believe that maybe my mother's death and the cat's appearance—a coincidence too great and too mysterious to ignore—had been a sign. Was it her final lesson of love for me? To place a cat in need in my path to teach me that love is healing? That compassion towards others—even in this imperfect world— would help me measure the depth of my soul? Or most importantly, to learn to see beyond myself?

In hindsight, the lesson I learned—although I didn't appreciate it at the time— was that by leaving Muddy behind, I had learned to let go. No transition is ever smooth. Most of the time they are hurtful and inevitable. So I had to say goodbye to Muddy. With forgiveness comes wisdom and acceptance. Goodbye, Muddy. Goodbye, Minerva.

I will never forget how heartbroken I was watching Muddy being driven away but I also felt somebody else needed a chance to prove his good intentions. That maybe my return to the island had served a purpose after all. I remembered my fight with Billy over Muddy and I take comfort in knowing that he too would have gone after him, even if it took him to the ends of the Earth.

THE END

AUTHOR'S NOTE

An Acknowledgment

For every new book I write, there is always a supportive group of friends and colleagues eager to contribute their thoughts and comments. I deem all of them invaluable because their views are offered not from a distant and technical point of view but from a sincere curiosity in my creative intentions and their vested interest in my evolution as a writer. For every idea, there is always a welcome challenge. To all of you, my love and gratitude.

Writing *The Illuminated Forest* has been at once the most exhilarating and the most terrifying act of creativity I've taken on. The process of writing is by nature hard and at times debilitating. I term it debilitating in this specific case because this story pushed me to relive a dark passage in my life. Not realizing it at the time, back in 2006 I was desperately seeking a way to soothe a deep wound that was not completely healed. But it wasn't until the fall of 2007 that it became clear to me I could no longer put off what I knew I had to do. The first roadblock in this very personal project came when I found myself unable to separate myself from my subject and allow the story to breathe and find its own path. Instead I attempted to "protect" the story, so as not to destroy its core, only to discover through the process that I was creating a contrived narrative.

I am the first to admit that there is a long road ahead of me in my quest to become a better writer but I also feel I would never have dared to share this story unless I felt I had given it my best. So I consider myself lucky to have found along my long, creative road a series of individuals and friends whose words, comments, and points of view helped me find my way and keep me focused on my ultimate goal: to produce an enjoyable read. During the four years that it has taken me to finish writing *The Illuminated Forest,* a handful of close friends have patiently witnessed, and at times relived with me, the most poignant passages of my story as it progressed and developed. To them, I give my most enduring appreciation and love.

I want to dearly thank Andy Keech whose incredible knowledge and experience as a pilot came in very handy for my benefit. To my dear friend Jorge Cancio. Also thanks to Paquita Vivó, Carmen Estrella, Marlowe Moore, Linda Smolkin, Tina

Casanova, and Sally Lowenstein, whose wonderful comments on my early and very incomplete work served as incentive for continuing the long journey ahead. Their reactions and suggestions stimulated me to undertake this terrifying act of creativity that increasingly threatened to become bigger than me. Thankfully, at that point I had the great blessing to work with John Kenney, Sandra Jackson, and J. Elizabeth Mills, who literally pushed me to overcome my own limitations and smash open a flood of inspiration. I'm also very grateful to writer and illustrator Lulu Delacre, whose comments were invaluable to the betterment of the story. To my editor Maria Rosa Jacks, who has guided me throughout the years and whose suggestions I value and appreciate. To Dr. Matilde "Maty" García-Arroyo, a valued collaborator and friend. And most of all and very especially to Scott Bushnell, who—blessed with the patience of a saint—pored over the many incarnations and rewrites I came up with, an excruciating process that most certainly would have prompted a less seasoned editor to run for the hills!

—*Edwin Fontánez*

A DEDICATION

In the last days of November 2006, I received the devastating news of my Aunt Juanita's death. The painful irony was that I was already set to visit her after a two year absence from the island. I was looking forward to spending some time with her and I had promised to cook the steaming pot of "fluffy white rice" she was craving. I had not talked to her during the previous month just to save the best of our conversation for our reunion. By the time I received my sister Ana's teary message from the hospital, it was too late. She died the following morning. I went back home to say my goodbyes and pay my final respects to my beloved *Titi* Juana. Within hours of my arrival a young cat showed up in my mother's backyard as if he had been waiting for me all his life. Since that moment, he has never left my side. This is the story they both inspired.

Juanita Fontánez (Titi Juana) with "Negrita"
May 5, 1916–December 2, 2006

OTHER TITLES
BY EDWIN FONTÁNEZ

Camila quiere escribir

I Promise You

Yo te Prometo

Hadas, Sirenas y Sapos: Un ramito de poemas encantados

On This Beautiful Island

En esta hermosa isla

Taíno: The Activity Book

Taíno: Guanín's Story (video)

Taíno: La Historia de Guanín (video)

The Vejigante and the Folk Festivals of Puerto Rico

The Legend of the Vejigante (video)

Heart of the Imaginero: Little Wood Carver (video)

All titles available through Exit Studio.
For information on personal appearances by Edwin Fontánez, news on
upcoming projects, and book sales, please visit **www.exitstudio.com**.

THE ILLUMINATED FOREST
Copyright © 2014 by Edwin Fontánez / Exit Studio

EXIT STUDIO, 1466 North Quinn Street, Arlington, VA 22209
www.exitstudio.com

Manufactured in USA
Book production by Exit Studio
The text is set in Minion Pro
Book design and layout by Edwin Fontánez
Art Direction by Scott Bushnell
Cover photo by Babak A. Tafreshi

All black and white illustrations were done in pencil on drawing paper. Some illustrations were manipulated and color corrected in Photoshop.

April 2014
First Edition

Library of Congress Control Number: 2013957721
Fontánez, Edwin
The Illuminated Forest by Edwin Fontánez—1st ed.
p. cm.

Summary: Mateo, a boy of 12, returns to the island of his grandparents to say goodbye to Minerva, a beloved family member. Unhappy to be back in a place so full of memories, he struggles to make sense of the abrupt and irreparable loss. When the mysterious appearance of a stray cat complicates matters, a series of terrifying incidents turn his life upside down. At the end of his very personal journey, he wonders if Minerva had something to do with the valuable lessons he learns about growing up and discovering that love materializes in different forms and in unexpected places.

ISBN 978-0-9831891-6-9

[1. Love—Fiction. 2. Grief—Fiction. 3. Metaphysical—Fiction. 4. Friendship—Fiction
5. Human/Animal Bond—Fiction. 6. Puerto Rico Landscapes—Fiction.]

Credits

The Gift, by Edwin Fontánez
I Knew You Were the One, Lyrics by Edwin Fontánez, Music by Lizabeth Flood
Lullaby Among the Palm Trees, by Edwin Fontánez
At a Lunar Eclipse, excerpt, Thomas Hardy
Las gotas de lluvia, Anonymous
The Rabbit Hole, by Edwin Fontánez
Quotes from William Shakespeare's *Romeo and Juliet* and *A Midsummer Night's Dream*

Cover photo: *Starry Night in Brazil*, copyright by Babak Amin Tafreshi. Used with permission by author. To view more of Mr. Tafreshi's award-winning photography, please visit: www.twanight.org/tafreshi

To find out more about the inspiration for this remarkable story, please visit illuminatedforest.com and exitstudio.com.